ABOUT THE AUTHOR

Berthold Auerbach was a German poet and writer. He founded the German "tendency novel," which uses fiction to influence public opinion on social, political, moral, and religious issues. Moses (Moyses) Baruch Auerbach was born in Nordstetten (now Horb am Neckar), Kingdom of Württemberg. He attended the Eberhard-Ludwigs-Gymnasium. He was supposed to be a minister, but after studying philosophy in Tübingen, Munich, and Heidelberg, and growing distanced from Jewish orthodoxy through Spinoza's work, he turned to literature. Under the pseudonym "Theobald Chauber," he wrote a biography of Frederick the Great (1834-36) while a student at Heidelberg. Berthold Auerbach was a German poet and writer. He founded the German "tendency novel," which uses fiction to influence public opinion on social, political, moral, and religious issues. Moses (Moyses) Baruch Auerbach was born in Nordstetten (now Horb am Neckar), Kingdom of Württemberg. He attended the Eberhard-Ludwigs-Gymnasium. He was supposed to be a minister, but after studying philosophy in Tübingen, Munich, and Heidelberg, and growing distanced from Jewish orthodoxy through Spinoza's work, he turned to literature. Under the pseudonym "Theobald Chauber," he wrote a biography of Frederick the Great (1834-36) while a student at Heidelberg.

CONTENTS

EDELWEISS

On the sunny slope of a mountain stands a house that is a joy to every eye; for it tells of happy inmates who have won their happiness by long and painful struggle,--who have stood in the valley of the shadow of death, and risen to new life.

The housewife comes to the door. Her face is young and fair, and of a bright complexion, but her hair is white as snow. She smiles to an old woman who is working in the garden, and calls to the children not to be so noisy.

"Come in, Franzl; and you too, children. William is starting on his journey," says the young white-haired mother. The bent old woman, as she approaches, raises a corner of her apron to her eyes, to stop the gathering tears.

Presently the father comes from the house, accompanied by a young fellow with a knapsack on his back. "Bid your mother good by, William," he says. "Be careful so to conduct yourself that you need never fear the eyes of father or mother on your actions. Then, God willing, you shall one day cross this threshold again with a happy heart."

The young woman with the snow-white hair embraces the sturdy boy, and says through her sobs: "I have nothing to add. Your father has said all. Remember and bring home an Edelweiss, if you find any on the Swiss mountains." The traveller sets off amid the shouts of his brothers and sisters.

"Good by, William; good by, good by." They play with the word "good by," and will not let it go.

"Mother," the father calls back, "I am only going with William and Lorenz as far as the cross-roads. Pilgrim will keep on with them to their first sleeping-place. I shall soon be back."

"All right; only do not hurry yourself, and do not take the parting too much to heart. Tell Faller's wife she must come to us at noon, and bring Lizzie with her. It is a great comfort," she continues, turning to the old woman as father and son depart, "that Faller's Lorenz goes abroad with our William."

Our story will tell why the young, white-haired mother asks the little plant Edelweiss of her boy when he is starting for foreign lands. It is a sad, a cruel history, but the sun of love breaks through at last.

CHAPTER I
A GOOD NAME

"She was an excellent woman."

"Yes, there are few such left."

"She was one of the old school."

"Go to her when you would, her help and counsel were always ready."

"And how much she went through! She buried her husband and four children, yet was always brave and cheerful."

"Ah, Lenz will miss her sorely. He will find out now what a mother he had."

"Nay, he knew that in her lifetime. His devotion to her was unbounded."

"He must be thinking of marrying soon."

"He can choose whom he will. Any house would be glad to receive such a capable, excellent fellow."

"A pretty property he must have too."

"Besides being the only heir of his rich uncle Petrovitsch."

"How beautiful the singing of the Liederkranz was! It thrilled me through and through."

"And how it must have affected Lenz! He has always before sung with them, and his voice was one of the best."

"Did you notice he did not shed a tear while the minister was preaching; but when his friends began to sing, he cried and sobbed as if his heart would break."

"This is the first funeral that has not driven old Petrovitsch out of the town. It would have been shameful in him not to have paid the last honors to his own brother's wife."

So the people talked as they went their several ways through the valley and up the mountains. All were dressed in sober clothes, for they were coming from a funeral. Near the church in the valley, where stand a few thinly scattered houses, the Lion Inn conspicuous among them, the widow of the clock-maker Lenz of the Morgenhalde had been buried. All had a good word for her; and their sad faces showed that each had met with a personal loss in the good woman's death. As every fresh grief reopens the old wounds, the villagers had turned from the newly covered grave to visit those of their own loved ones, and there had prayed and mourned for the departed.

We are in the clock-making district, among those wooded hills that send their streams to the Rhine on one side and the Danube on the other. The inhabitants are by nature quiet and thoughtful. The women far outnumber the men, many of whom are scattered through all parts of the world, engaged in the clock trade. Those who remain at home are pale from their close confinement at work. The women, on the contrary, who labor in the field are bright and rosy, while a pretty air of demureness is imparted to their faces by the broad black ribbons they wear tied under the chin.

Agriculture is practised on a small scale. With the exception of a few large farms, it is limited to a scanty tillage of the meadows. In some places a narrow belt of trees runs down to the brook at the very bottom of the valley; in others, again, a tall, bare pine, on the edge of a meadow, shows that field and garden-patch have been wrested from the forest. The ash-trees, whose branches are stripped every year to furnish food for the goats, look like elongated willows. The village, or rather the parish, stretches out miles in length. The houses are built of whole trunks of trees, dovetailed together, and are sprinkled over mountain and valley. Their fronts present an uninterrupted row of windows, arranged without intermediate spaces, as the object is to admit all the light possible. The barn, when there is one, is approached from the hill behind the house by a passage entering directly under the roof. A heavy covering of thatch projects over the front, and serves as a protection from the weather. The color of the buildings harmonizes with the background of mountain and forest, while narrow footpaths of a lighter shade lead through the green meadows to the dwellings of the villagers.

The greater number of the mourners to-day pursued the same road up the valley. Here and there, as a woman reached the path leading to her own house, she turned aside from the main group, and waved her hymn-book to the children, watching at the row of windows, or running down the meadow lane to meet her. Each, as she laid aside her Sunday clothes, heaved a sigh of mingled grief for the departed and thankfulness that she and hers were still alive, and living together in love. But it was hard to settle down at once to the every-day work. The world had been left behind for a while, and its labors could not be easily resumed.

One of the group, whose way led him with the others as far as the next cross-road, was the weight-manufacturer from Knuslingen, the man who made the most exact lead and copper weights in the country. "A sorry thing, this dying," said he; "here is all the wisdom and experience that Mother Lenz had gathered together laid away in the ground, and the world none the better for it."

"Her son has, at least, inherited her goodness," replied a young woman.

"And experience and judgment every one must get for himself," said a little old man, with keen, inquiring eyes, who always went by the name of Pröbler, the experimenter, from having ruined himself in inventions and experiments, instead of keeping to the regular routine of clock-making.

"The old times were much wiser and better," said old David, the case-maker, who lived in the adjacent valley. "In those days a funeral feast was spread, at which we could refresh ourselves after our long journey and hard crying,--for crying is hungry and thirsty work,--and after that the minister preached his sermon. If we did rather overdo the matter sometimes, no one was the worse for it. But all that sort of thing is forbidden now, and I am so hungry and faint I feel ready to sink."

"So am I, and I," cried out several voices. "What are we to do when we get home?" continued old David; "the day is lost. We are very glad to give it to a good friend, to be sure; but the old way was better. Then we didn't get home till night, and had nothing more to think of."

"And could not have thought of it, if you had," interrupted the deep voice of young Faller, the clockmaker. He was second bass in the Liederkranz, and carried his music-book under his arm. His walk and bearing showed him to have been a soldier. "A funeral feast," he continued, "is a thing Mother Lenz would by no means have allowed. Everything in its time, she used to say; mourning and merry-making, each in its turn. I worked under old Lenz five years and three quarters; young Lenz and I were fellow-apprentices, and set up as journeymen together."

"You had better turn schoolmaster and preach the sermon," said old David angrily, muttering something further about those conceited Liederkranz fellows, who think the world didn't begin till they learned to sing their notes.

"That I can do too," said the young man, who either had not heard the last words, or pretended he had not. "I can make a eulogy; and a good thing it would be to talk of something besides our own appetites and pleasures after laying such a noble heart in the grave. What a man our old master was! Ah, if all the world were like him, we should need no more judges or soldiers or barracks or prisons! He was a right strict old fellow. No apprentice was allowed to give up the file for the lathe till he could cut by hand as perfect an octagon as any machinery could make, and no one of us was considered a finished workman till he could make the smallest clock; for, as the old master used to say, the man who can make small things will be most exact in great ones. No wheel nor weight that had the least flaw in it ever left his shop. 'My credit is at stake, and that of the whole district,' he would say. 'We must keep up our good name.' Let me tell you one little anecdote, to show what an influence he had over us young men. Young Lenz and I took up smoking when we became journeymen. 'Very well,' said the old man, 'if you will smoke, I cannot prevent it, and I don't want you to do it secretly. I am sorry to say I have the same bad habit myself,--I must smoke. But one thing let me tell you,--if you smoke, I shall give it up, hard as it will be for me. It will never do for us all to smoke.' Of course we did not contract the habit. Rather would we have lost the use of our mouths altogether than have required such a sacrifice of our master.

"And the mistress,--she stands this moment before God, and God will say to her, 'You have been upright above most women on the earth. You have had your faults, to be sure. You have spoiled your son; you might have made a man of him by letting him seek his fortune in the world, and you would not. But your thousands and thousands of good deeds known to none but me, your allowing none to be evil spoken of, your making the best of everything and everybody, even to speaking a good word for Petrovitsch,--not one shall be forgotten. Come, and receive your reward.' And do you know what she will say when God offers her a reward? 'Give it to my son,' she will say; 'and, if there is any over, there is such a one and such a one in bitter need, help him; I am content to look on.' You would hardly believe how little she ate. The old master often laughed at her for it, but really she was best satisfied by seeing others eat; and her son is just as good, heart and soul, as the mother was. I would lay down my life for him gladly."

Such was Faller's eulogy, and his deep voice often trembled with emotion as he delivered it. The others, however, did not let him monopolize young Lenz's praises.

Pröbler maintained that he was the only one in the whole country round who knew any more than the generation before him. "If people were not so obstinate and jealous, they would long ago have accepted that standard regulator we made together; I say we made, but must honestly confess he did the greater part of it."

Nobody paid much attention to what Pröbler said, especially as he spoke so unintelligibly--hardly above a mutter--that little could be made out except the words "standard regulator."

With more interest did they turn to old David, who next took up the word. "Lenz never passes a man without doing him a good turn. Every year he takes some of his leisure Sundays for tuning the organ of the blind old organist of Fuchsberg, and charges nothing for it. That is a labor of love that must please our Father in heaven. I too have profited by his help. He found me once in trouble over my barrel, that would not turn easily. So off he started to the mill, fitted me up a workshop in the loft, put my barrel in communication with the wheel, and now I can accomplish three times the work with half the labor."

Every one hastened to throw in a good word for young Lenz, as if it were a copper into the poor's box.

The weight-manufacturer had said nothing as yet, but contented himself with approving nods. He was the wisest of the party. The truth, and nothing but the truth, had been spoken, he very well knew, but not the whole truth. He could tell them there was no better man to work for than Lenz. The work must be thoroughly done, to be sure; but then you got not only full pay, but good words besides, which were worth more than the money.

Faller parted from the group here, and took the path towards his house among the hills. Soon afterwards the whole party dispersed in various directions,--each, as he went, accepting a farewell pinch from Pröbler's birch-bark snuff-box. Old David, with his stout staff, went on alone up the valley; he was the only one from his parish who had come to the funeral.

CHAPTER II
THE MOURNER AND HIS COMPANION

Narrow footpath leads from the village to a solitary thatched cottage, only a small part of whose roof, just about the chimney, is covered with tiles. The house does not come in sight till you have climbed a good half-mile up the mountain. The path leads behind the church,--between hedges at first, then across open fields, where you hear the murmur of the pine-woods that cover the steep mountain-side. Behind this mountain, the Spannreute, rise still other peaks; but even this front slope is so steep that the harvest gathered on the upland meadows has to be brought down to the valley on sledges.

Along the footpath between the hedges two men were now walking, one behind the other. The one in front was a little old man, whose dress showed him to be a person of property. He carried a cane in his hand, with the tasselled string twisted about his wrist by way of precaution. His step was still firm; his face, a perfect mass of wrinkles, moved up and down as he mumbled lumps of white sugar, which he produced from time to time from his pocket. His sandy eyebrows were brushed out till they stood almost at right angles with his face, and from under them peered a pair of shrewd, light blue eyes. The young man who walked behind was tall and slender, with crape on his hat and on the sleeve of his long blue coat. He kept his face turned to the ground, and shook his head sadly as he walked. At last he stopped, and straightened himself up, bringing to view a fresh face, with light beard and blue eyes, whose lids were red with weeping.

"Uncle," he said, hoarsely. The sugar-eater turned round. "Uncle, you have gone far enough. Thank you heartily; but the way is long, and I would rather go home alone."

"Why?"

"I don't know why; but I feel it were better so."

"No, no; turn back with me."

"I am sorry not to oblige you, uncle; but I cannot,--I really cannot go to the inn just now. I am neither hungry nor thirsty; I don't know when I shall ever eat and drink again. It is a pity you should take this long walk for me."

"No, no; I will go home with you. I am not so hard-hearted as your mother tried to make you believe."

"My mother tried to make me believe no evil of you. She spoke nothing but good of any one, and especially against her relations she would hear no tales. 'To speak evil of a brother is to slander yourself,' she used to say."

"Yes, yes; she had plenty of proverbs. 'Marie Lenz used to say so and so,' is in every one's mouth. Nothing but good should be spoken of the dead, and in fact there can no evil be said of her."

The young man cast a sad glance at his uncle. He always managed to put a sting even into his kindliest words.

"How often she has said to me lately," continued the young man, "and how it pained me to hear her, 'Lenz, I have lived six years too long for you. You ought to have married at five-and-twenty; it will come harder now. You have grown too much used to my ways, and they cannot last.' I could not persuade her out of the idea. It imbittered her death-bed."

"She was right," said the sugar-eater. "She was too good-natured; self-willed she was also, but that was no matter. Her good-nature spoiled you. I did not mean to tell you so now, though; another time would be better. Come, do as I bid you, and don't be such a baby. You act as if you did not know which way to turn. It is all in the course of nature that your mother should die before you, and you have nothing to reproach yourself with in your treatment of her."

"No, thank God!"

"Show yourself a man, then, and stop crying and bawling. I never saw anybody cry in all my life as you did in the churchyard."

"I cannot tell you how I felt, uncle. I wept for my mother, but also for myself. When the Liederkranz sang the songs that I had always sung with them, and I had to stand there dumb and dead, I felt as if I were really dead, and they were singing at my grave and I could not join in."

"You are--" said the old man. He was about to add something, but choked it down and walked on. The little dog that was running in front looked up wonderingly in his master's face, as if he hardly recognized the look he saw there.

Presently the old man stopped. "I am going back," he said. "Only one word more with you. Take into your house none of your mother's relations whom afterwards you will have to send away. They will forget all your kindness, and only be vexed that it cannot continue. Neither give anything away, no matter who asks. If you are tempted to, go off somewhere for a week or so, and, when you come home, keep the keys to yourself. Now good by, and be a man!"

"Good by, uncle," said the young man, and went on towards his home. He kept his eyes fixed on the ground, but knew at every step where he was. Every stone on the path was familiar to him. When at last he reached the house, he could hardly bring himself to cross the threshold.

How much had happened there! and what was to come next? He must learn to bear.

The old serving-woman sat in the kitchen with her apron over her head. "Is that you, Lenz?" she sobbed, as the young man passed her.

The room looked empty, yet everything was there. The work-bench with its five divisions for the five workmen stood before the unbroken row of windows; the tools hung on straps and nails round the wall; the clocks ticked; the doves cooed; yet all was so empty, so desolate and dead! The arm-chair stood with outspread arms, waiting. Lenz leaned on the back of it and wept bitterly. Then he got up and tried to go to her chamber. "It is impossible you are not there," he said, half aloud. The sound of his own voice startled him. He sank exhausted into the chair where his mother had so often rested.

At last he took courage and entered the deserted chamber.

"Have you not forgotten something that I ought to have sent after you?" he said again. With an inward shudder he opened his mother's chest, into which he had never looked. It seemed almost a sacrilege to look now, but he did. Perhaps she had left a word or a token for him. He found the christening presents of his dead brothers and sisters tied up in separate parcels and marked with their names; his own lay among them. There were some old coins, his mother's confirmation dress, her bridal wreath,-- dried, but carefully preserved,--her garnet ornaments, and in a little box by itself, wrapped in five thicknesses of fine paper, a little white, velvety plant, labelled in his mother's handwriting. The son read at first under his breath, then half aloud, as if wishing to hear his mother's words, "This is a little plant Edelweiss--"

"Here is something to eat," suddenly cried a voice through the open door.

It was only old Franzl calling, but it startled Lenz like the voice of a spirit.

"Coming," he answered, shut the door hastily, bolted it, and restored everything carefully to its former place before going into the sitting-room, where old Franzl was indulging in many a solemn shake of the head at this mystery which she was not permitted to share.

CHAPTER III
WORK AND BENEFACTION

The bailiff, Lenz's nearest neighbor, though not a very near one, had sent in food, as was the custom in that part of the country when a death occurred, in the supposition that the mourners might not have thought of preparing any. Moreover, during a funeral, and for three hours after, no fire was allowed to be kindled on the hearth.

The bailiff's daughter brought the food into the room herself.

"Thanks to you and your parents, Katharine. Take away the food; when I am hungry, I will eat; I cannot now," said Lenz.

"But you must try," said Franzl; "that is the custom; you must put something to your lips. Sit down, Katharine; you should always sit down when you visit a mourner, not keep standing. Young people nowadays don't know what the custom is. And you must say something, Katharine; you should talk to a mourner, not be dumb. Say something."

The sturdy, round-cheeked girl flushed crimson. "I can't," she stammered out, bursting into a passion of tears, and covering her face with her apron, as she became conscious that Lenz's eyes were fixed upon her.

"Don't cry," he said, soothingly. "Thank God every day that you still have your parents. There, I have tasted the soup."

"You must take something else," urged Franzl. He obeyed with an effort, and then rose from the table. The girl rose too. "Forgive me, Lenz," she said. "I ought to have comforted you, but I--I--"

"I know; thank you, Katharine. I can't talk much yet myself."

"Good by. Father says you must come and see us; he has a lame foot, and cannot come to you."

"I will see: I will come if I can."

When she was gone, Lenz walked up and down the room with outstretched hands, as seeking to grasp some form, but he found no one. His eye fell upon the tools, and was chiefly attracted by a file that hung on the wall by itself. A sudden idea seized him as he raised his hand to take it.

This file was his choicest heirloom. His father had used it constantly for forty-seven years, till his thumb had worn a groove in its maple-wood handle. "Who would believe," the old man was fond of saying, "that many years' work of a man's hand would wear a wooden handle like that?" The mother always exhibited this wonderful file to strangers as a curiosity.

The doctor down in the valley had a collection of old clocks and tools, and had often asked for this file to hang up in his cabinet; but the father never would give it. Since his death, the mother and son naturally set a great value on the heirloom. After the father's funeral, when mother and son were sitting quietly together at home, she said, "Now, Lenz, we have wept enough; we must bear our burden in silence. Take your father's file, and work. 'Work and pray while yet it is day,' runs the proverb. Be glad you have an honest trade, and do not need to brood over what is past. A thousand times has your father said, 'What a help it is to get up in the morning and find your work waiting. When I file, I file all the useless chips out of my brain; and when I hammer, I knock all heavy thoughts on the head, and away they go.'

"Those were my mother's words then, and they ring in my ears to-day. Would I could always be as sure of her counsel!"

Lenz set himself industriously to work. Without stood Franzl and Katharine. "I am glad you were the first to bring the food," said the old woman; "it is a good sign. Whoever brings the first morsel at such a time-- But I have said nothing: no one shall say I had a hand in it. Only come back this evening, and be the one to bid him good night. If you bid him good night three times, something is sure to come of it. Hark! what is that? Saints in heaven, he is working now, on such a day as this! What a man! I have known him ever since he was a baby, but there is no telling what queer thing he will do. Yet he is so good! Don't tell he was working, will you? it might make people talk. Come yourself for the dishes this evening, and be composed, so that you can talk properly. You can generally use your tongue well enough."

Franzl was interrupted by Lenz's voice, calling from the door, "If any visitors come, Franzl, I can see none but Pilgrim. Are you still there, Katharine?"

"I am going this minute," said she, and ran down the hill.

Lenz returned to his seat, and worked without intermission, while Franzl as busily racked her brain to make out this extraordinary man, who, a moment before, was crying himself sick, and now sat quietly at work. It could not be from want of feeling, nor from avarice, but what could it mean?

"My old head is not wise enough," said Franzl. Her first impulse was to go to her mistress and ask what she could make of it; but she checked herself, and covered her face with her hands as she remembered the mother was dead. To Franzl's consternation, visitors began now to arrive,--various members of the Liederkranz, besides some of the older townspeople. In great embarrassment she turned them away, talking all the time as loud as if they were deaf. She would gladly have stopped their ears, if she could, to keep them from hearing Lenz at work. "If Pilgrim would only come," she thought. "Pilgrim can do anything with him; he would not mind taking the tools out of his hand." But no Pilgrim came. At last a happy thought struck her. There was no need of her staying at home. She would go a little way down the hill, beyond the sound of hammer and saw, and prevent visitors from coming up.

Lenz meanwhile was recovering composure and firmness over his work. When he left off, towards evening, he descended the hill, and, taking the path behind the houses, proceeded in the direction of his friend Pilgrim's. Halfway down he turned about as suddenly as if some one had called him; but all was still. Only the blackbird's ceaseless twittering was heard in the bushes, and the yellowhammer's monotonous whistle from the fresh pine-tops. There are no larks down in the valley and meadows, but on the upland fields you hear them chattering in the wide stretches of corn. The mists were rising from the meadows, too light to be seen just about him, but plainly visible in the distance behind and before.

Lenz walked rapidly up the valley, till the sun set behind the Spannreute and turned the lowland mist into flaming clouds. "It is the first time it has set upon her grave," he murmured. He stood still a moment, took off his hat at the sound of the evening bells, and went on more slowly. At a turn in the valley, just below a solitary little house, from which a thick bush screened him, he paused again. Upon a bench before the house sat a man whom we have seen before, the clockmaker Fallen. He was dancing a child on his knee, while beside him his sister, whose husband was abroad, sat nursing her baby, and kissing its little hands.

"Good evening, Faller!" cried Lenz in his old, clear tenor voice.

"It is you,--is it?" called back Faller's bass. "We were just talking of you. Lisbeth thought you would forget us in your sorrow; but I said, on the contrary, you would not fail to remember our need."

"It is about that I am come. Henzel's house is to be sold to-morrow, as you know; and if you want to buy it, I will be your security. It will be pleasant to have you for neighbor."

"That would be fine, glorious! So you stay where you are?"

"Why not?"

"I was told you were going abroad for a year or two."

"Who told you?"

"Your uncle, I think, said so. I am not quite sure."

"Did he? maybe so. If I do go, you must move into my house."

"Better stay at home. It is too late to go abroad."

"And marry soon," added the young mother.

"Yes, that will tie you down, and put an end to your roving. But, Lenz, whatever you do must prosper. Your mother in heaven will bless you for remembering me in your time of grief. Not a moment goes by that I do not think of her. You come honestly by your goodness, for she was always thoughtful of others. God bless you!"

"He has already. The walk here and our plan together have lightened my heart. Have you anything to eat, Lisbeth? I feel hungry for the first time to-day."

"I will beat you up a couple of eggs."

"Thanks."

Lenz ate with an appetite that delighted his hosts.

Faller's mother, much against her son's will, asked Lenz for some of his mother's clothes, which he readily promised. Faller insisted on walking part way home with him; but hardly had they gone twenty steps before he gave a shrill whistle, and called back to his sister, who inquired what was wanted, that he should not be at home till morning.

"Where do you spend the night?" asked Lenz.

"With you."

The two friends walked on in silence. The moon shone bright, and the owls hooted in the forest, while from the village came the sound of music and merry voices.

"It were not well that all should mourn for one," said Lenz. "Thank God that each of us can bear his own sorrow and his own joy."

"There spoke your mother," returned Faller.

"Stop!" cried Lenz; "don't you want to let your betrothed know you can buy the cottage?"

"That I do. Come with me, and let me show you the happiest household in all the world."

"No, no; you run up alone. I am not fit for joy, and am wofully tired besides. I'll wait for you here. Run quick, and be quick back again."

Faller ran up the hill, while Lenz sat down on a pile of stones by the roadside. As the refreshing dew was shed upon tree and shrub and every blade of grass, so a pure influence as of dew from heaven sank into the heart of the lonely mourner; a light flashed from the little house on the mountain-side, which had been dark before, and light and joy shone in hearts that had long desponded.

Faller came back breathless to tell of the great rejoicing there had been. The old father had opened the window, and shouted down the valley: "A thousand blessings on you, kindest of friends," and the dear girl had laughed and wept by turns.

The friends walked on again, each silently busied with his own thoughts. Faller's step was firm, and his whole bearing so steady and erect that Lenz involuntarily straightened himself up as he kept pace with him. When the path began to ascend again, he cast another glance back at the churchyard, and sighed.

"My father lies there too," said Faller, "and was not spared as long as yours." They went on up the mountain, Lenz taking the lead. What does he see white moving above him? Who is it? Can it be-- His mother is not dead! She cannot keep away from him, she has come back!

The mourner gazed with an inward fear.

"Good evening, Lenz," cried Katharine's voice.

"What are you doing there?"

"I have been with Franzl. She sent for our maid to keep her company, for she is old and timid. I should not be afraid if your mother herself came back. Good night, Lenz! good night! good night!"

She said good night three times, as Franzl had bidden her. There must be some charm in the words. Who knows what may come of them?

CHAPTER IV
EACH BEFORE HIS OWN DOOR

The cool evening following the excessive heat of the day had tempted the villagers out of doors. Some families sat on the bench before their houses, but more were gathered about the stone railing of the bridge, always a favorite place of evening resort for rest or social chat after the day's work. Thence can be seen the passing on both sides, while the babbling of the brook provokes conversation. Various woods were lying seasoning in the water below. The clocks were less likely to warp or shrink when the wood of which they were made had been thoroughly drained of its juices. But the people on the bridge understood the process of seasoning in all its branches. The subject of their talk now, even as late in the day as this, was the morning's funeral, which naturally led to a discussion of young Lenz and the necessity of his making a speedy marriage. The women were lavish of their praises of him, not a few of their encomiums being meant as hints to the men that they might profitably follow his example, since virtue, when seen, was so readily appreciated. The men, however, pronounced him a good sort of fellow enough, only too soft-hearted. The young girls, with the exception of those who had declared lovers, said nothing; especially as the suggestion had been started that Lenz was to marry one of the doctor's daughters. Some even asserted that it was a settled thing, and would be publicly announced as soon as the proper time of mourning was over. Suddenly, no one knew how or where it originated, the report circulated from house to house, and among the persons on the bridge, that Lenz had spent that day, the very day of his mother's funeral, in uninterrupted work. The women lamented that avarice should mar a character in other respects so good. The men, on the other hand, tried to excuse him. But the conversation soon turned upon the weather and the course of events,--both fruitful subjects, as nothing can be foretold of either. They were none the less comfortably discussed, however, till it was time to bid good night, and leave the stars in heaven and the affairs of the world to go on their appointed courses.

But the pleasantest resting-place of all was the doctor's pretty garden, further down the valley, whence a wonderful fragrance arose on the evening air. And yet not wonderful either, for the garden was stocked with all manner of medicinal plants in full blossom, the doctor being a mixer of drugs as well as physician. He was a native of the village, the son of a clockmaker. His wife came from the capital, but had made herself so completely at home in her husband's native valley, that her mother-in-law, the old mayoress, as she was called, who lived with them, used to say she must have led a previous existence as a child of the Black Forest, so naturally did she adopt its customs. The doctor, like his father before him, was mayor of the village. He had four children. The only son, contrary to general expectation, did not learn a profession, but preferred to study the science of clock-making, and, at the time of our story, was absent in French Switzerland. The three daughters were the most aristocratic ladies in the place, at the same time that they were unsurpassed in industry by any of their humbler neighbors. Amanda, the eldest, acted as her father's assistant, besides having the charge of the garden. Bertha and Minna took an active part in the housekeeping, and occupied their leisure in plaiting those fine straw braids that are sent to Italy and come to us in the shape of Leghorn hats.

This evening, the family in the garden had a visitor,--a young machinist, called in the village, for convenience, the engineer. His two brothers married daughters of the landlord of the Lion. One of them was a rich wood-merchant in the next county town, the other the owner of one of the most frequented bathing establishments in the lower Black Forest, as well as of a considerable private estate. It was said that the engineer was to marry the landlord's only remaining daughter, Annele.

"You speak well, Mr. Storr," the doctor was saying, in a voice whose tones showed him to be hale and hearty. "We must not rejoice in the beauties of mountain and valley, and take no thought for the people who inhabit them. There is too much of the superficial, restless spirit of change in the world of to-day. For my part, I have no desire to rove; my own narrow sphere contents me, body and mind. I have even had to give up my old hobby of botanizing, or, rather, I have voluntarily given it up, in order to devote more time to the study of humanity. In the general division of labor, every one should take what best suits his capacities. That is a lesson my country-people will not learn, and our native industry suffers in consequence."

"May I ask you to explain yourself more particularly?"

"The thing is very simple. Our clock-making, like all our home pursuits, is the natural result of the unproductiveness of our soil, and the indivisibility of our large, entailed estates. Younger sons, and all whose whole capital consists in their industry, must make the most of that, if they would earn a living. Hence that natural aptitude for work, that strict, unresting carefulness, that are common among us. Our forests supply the best wood for machinery and cases, and as long as our wooden clocks found a good market, a manufacturer, with the help of his wife and children to paint the dial-plate, could make an entire clock in his own house. But now that metal clocks have been introduced, and have, in a measure, supplanted the wooden ones, a division of labor has become necessary. There is a strong competition in France, in America, and especially in Saxony. We must give up pendulums, and take to springs. These changes cannot be effected without the help of some general and binding association among the workmen. The stone-cutters, in old times, used to form themselves into a guild, presided over by a chosen head, and that is what is wanted here. The workmen, scattered about on the mountains, must enter into a league with one another, and work into each other's hands. The difficulty is to bring about such a league among our people. In Switzerland a watch passes through a hundred and twenty hands before it is finished. But the very perseverance of the good people here, which is undoubtedly a virtue, makes them unwilling to adopt new ways. Only by unexampled frugality and application could our home manufactures have been carried on as long as they have. You would hardly believe what a morbid sensitiveness our people have contracted by their constant and close confinement at their work. They have to be handled as tenderly as their own clocks, which an awkward touch will break."

"It seems to me," answered the young man, "that the first thing wanted now is a better case for your clocks, that they may become more of a parlor ornament."

"I quite agree with you," said Bertha, the second daughter. "I spent a year with my aunt in the capital, and, wherever I visited, I found one of my compatriots, a Black Forest clock, like Cinderella, in the kitchen. In the best room, resplendent with gold and alabaster, was sure to be a French mantel-clock, never wound up, or never right if it was, while my compatriot in the kitchen was always going, and always exact."

"Cinderella needs to be metamorphosed," said the young man; "but she must keep her virtues, and tell the truth, when she gets into the best parlor."

The doctor did not let the conversation follow the turn the young people had given it; but entered into further explanations of the peculiarities of his country-people. A tolerably long residence abroad enabled him to judge them impartially, while yet he had lived years enough at home to know and appreciate their good qualities. He spoke High German, but with a decided provincial accent.

"Good evening to you all," cried a passer-by.

"Ah, is it you, Pilgrim? Wait a minute," cried the doctor. "How is Lenz?" he asked, as the passer-by stopped at the garden gate.

"I have not seen him since the funeral. I am just from the Lion, where I was fool enough to get into a quarrel about him."

"How was that?"

"They were talking about his having been at work all day to-day, and finding fault with him for it, and calling him a miser. Lenz a miser! Nonsense!"

"You should not let it disturb you. You and I know, and so do many others, that Lenz is a good fellow, above all such reproaches. Was not Petrovitsch with him to-day?"

"No. I thought he would be, and therefore did not go myself. Doctor, I wanted to ask if you would have time to come to my house to-morrow for a moment. I should like to show you what I have been doing."

"Certainly I will come."

"Good night to you all."

"Good night, Pilgrim; pleasant dreams."

"Send me back my songs to-morrow," cried Bertha, as he was going.

"I will bring them," returned Pilgrim; and soon after they heard his clear musical whistle in the distance.

"That is a remarkable man," said the doctor. "He is a case-painter, and an intimate friend of Lenz, whose mother was buried this morning. He is quite a hidden genius, and has rather a remarkable history."

"Pray, let me hear it."

"Some other time, when we are by ourselves."

"No, we should like to hear it again," exclaimed his wife and daughters, and the doctor began as follows.

CHAPTER V
PILGRIM'S ADVENTURES

Pilgrim was the son of a case-painter. Left an orphan at an early age, he was brought up at the public expense by the old schoolmaster. But he spent by far the greater part of his time with Lenz the clockmaker on the Morgenhalde. In old Lenz's wife he found almost a second mother, while their only surviving child, the Lenz who has been working to-day, was like a brother to him. Pilgrim was always the more ready and skilful workman of the two; for Lenz, with all his undoubted ability, has a certain fanciful dreaminess of character. Perhaps there is a genius for music in Lenz and for painting in Pilgrim that has never been developed; who knows? You must hear Lenz sing some time. He is first tenor in the Liederkranz; and it is chiefly owing to him that our society won the prize at two musical festivals,--one at Constance and the other at Freiburg. As the boys grew up, Lenz was apprenticed to his father and Pilgrim to a case-painter, but they continued close friends. Through the long summer evenings they would wander singing and whistling over hill and valley, as sure to be together as the twin stars in heaven. Winter nights Pilgrim had to walk up to the Morgenhalde through snow and storm; for Lenz, being, as I have said, the last of five children, was somewhat spoiled by his mother, and kept at home in bad weather. There they would sit together half through the night, reading books of travel or whatever else they could lay hands on. Many a volume out of my library has their thirst for knowledge devoured. Together they devised a plan for travelling abroad; for, with all the domestic habits of our people, there is a general desire among them to see the world. As soon as it was sure that both were exempt from military service,--Pilgrim by lot, and Lenz as being an only son,--they were anxious to carry their plan into execution. Lenz showed on this subject for the first time a persistent obstinacy which had never been suspected in him. He would not be dissuaded from the journey. His father was for letting him go, but the very thought threw his mother into despair. When the minister's persuasions failed, I was called in, and enjoined to talk the boy into a whole catalogue of diseases, if other arguments failed. Of course I pursued a different treatment. The two friends had always admitted me into their confidence, and now freely imparted to me their entire plan. Pilgrim, as usual, was the instigator. Lenz, notwithstanding his sensitiveness, has a sound practical nature, though limited to a small circle of ideas. If not confused by arguments, his instincts generally lead him in the right direction; and whatever he undertakes he clings to with a perseverance amounting almost to devotion. I will show you to-morrow a standard regulator he has set up, whose adoption would be a benefit to the whole country. Lenz's mind was in fact not so firmly made up in favor of Pilgrim's plan as he had given his parents to understand. He thought his friend would do better to learn clock-making thoroughly before going into the trade, as a merchant should be able to repair any clock that may come in his way, as well as those he carries with him. Pilgrim finally decided to enter on an apprenticeship. As soon, however, as he had learned what was absolutely necessary, the plan of his journey was resumed more resolutely than ever. The objects he proposed to himself were numerous. At one time he wanted to make money enough to visit an academy; at another he meant to become a great artist on his travels; then again he only desired to discomfit the moneyed aristocracy by coming home with a bag full of gold. In reality he despised money, and for that very reason would gladly have had it to throw away. There was, besides, some youthful fancy in his head at that time, I imagine. Greece, Athens, was the goal of his desires. The very name of Athens would make his eyes sparkle and his color rise. "Athens!" he would say, "does not the word transport you to marble staircases and lofty halls?" He seemed to imagine that the mere breathing of classic air would make another man of him, change him into a great artist. I tried to disabuse his mind of these mistaken notions, and succeeded in making him promise he would confine himself to earning a living, and leave all else for some future time. Old Lenz and I gave security for the merchandise he was to take with him. He finally set out alone, Lenz yielding to our persuasions, and remaining at home. "I am like the wave," Pilgrim used to say, "that is drawn from the Black Forest to the Black Sea." He hoped to introduce our domestic clocks into Greece and the East, where they had never been so favorably received as in northern countries and the New World. It is pleasant to hear Pilgrim tell how he went through various foreign countries, through cities and villages, with his Black Forest clocks hung about him, making them strike as he went along, himself taking notice all the while of everything on the way. That was the trouble with him. His eyes were too busy with other things, with the landscape and beautiful buildings and the manners and customs of the country,--a great mistake for a merchant. As our clock-work never changes, go where it will, over sea and land, so our people remain the same in every latitude. To make and to save, to live frugally, and never be content till they can come home with a full money-bag, that is the one thing they care for, let the world wag as it may. A very good and necessary thing it is, too, in its place. One head must not have too many projects at one time. But the day of peddling and saving is past. We must be men of business now, and establish permanent markets in other lands for our merchandise.

"Did Pilgrim ever reach Athens?"

"Indeed he did, and he has often told me that the joy and devotion with which the Crusaders greeted Jerusalem could not have exceeded his on first seeing Athens. He rubbed his eyes to convince himself it was really Athens. He expected the marble statues to nod a greeting to him as he went jingling through the streets. But not a single clock did he sell. He was reduced to such extremity at last as to consider himself lucky to get a piece of work to do; and what work! For fourteen days, under the blue Grecian sky, in sight of the Acropolis, he had to paint the green lattice-work fence of a beer-garden."

"What is the Acropolis?" asked Bertha.

"You can tell her, Storr," suggested the doctor.

The engineer gave a hasty sketch of the former beauty of the citadel of Athens and its present scanty remains, promising to bring a picture of it the next time he came, and then begged the doctor to go on with his story.

"There is little more to tell," he resumed. "With the closest management, Pilgrim contrived to dispose of his clocks, so that we were no losers. It required no small courage to return poorer than he went, to be a general laughing-stock among his old neighbors. But as his enthusiasm led him to despise the moneyed aristocracy, as he was fond of calling it, he put on a bold front, and let who would laugh. Of course, he went first to the Morgenhalde. The parents were standing with folded hands about the dinner-table. Lenz gave such a cry, his mother used to say it would kill her to hear the like again. The two friends fell into each other's arms. Pilgrim soon recovered his good spirits, and laughed about his luck being better at home than anywhere else; for there he found at least a well-spread table. Certainly he could nowhere have found a warmer welcome than from the parents and son at the Morgenhalde. Old Lenz wanted to take him into his house; but Pilgrim resolutely declined. He was always jealous of his independence. He fitted up a nice workshop at Don Bastian's, very near us. At first he took pains to introduce new patterns of clock-cases; but he could not succeed in changing essentially the shape of our Black Forest clocks,-- the square with a pointed arch. Not disheartened by finding his novelties unacceptable, he cheerfully fell back on making the old-fashioned cases, for which he gets plenty of orders. He has some skill in coloring; but his drawing is faulty. You must know that different countries have different tastes in clock-cases. France likes the case well covered with bright colors; North Germany, Scandinavia, and England prefer simpler outlines, architectural ornamentation, like gables or columns,--at most, nothing more florid than a garland. Shepherds and shepherdesses are for the Vorarlberg. No clocks can be sent to the East with human figures on the dial-plate; lately Roman numerals have been allowed, but formerly none but Turkish. America likes no painting, but requires carving more or less elaborate. American clocks, as they are called, have the weights raised by pulleys on one side. Hungary and Russia fancy fruit-pieces and landscapes. Ornaments of the best taste are not always preferred; on the contrary, a finical style is often most popular. If you can improve the appearance of our clocks, you will be doing Pilgrim a service. Perhaps you can give him a fresh start in life; though he hardly needs it, for he possesses the rare art of being happy without being prosperous."

"I should like to make his acquaintance."

"You shall call upon him with me to-morrow. Only come bright and early, so that we can take a walk over the hills. I will show you some fine views, and nice people beside."

After bidding the engineer a hearty good night the doctor and his family re-entered the house.

The moon shone clear in the heavens; the flowers sent out their fragrance into the night, with none to enjoy it, and the stars looked down upon them. No sound was heard, save from a house here and there the striking of a clock.

CHAPTER VI
THE WORLD PRESENTS ITSELF

"Good morning, Lenz! You have had a good night's rest, just as children do who have cried themselves to sleep." Thus was Lenz greeted the next morning by Faller's deep bass voice. "O my friend," he answered; "it brings back all my misery to wake up and remember what happened yesterday. But I must be calm. I will proceed at once to write the security for you. Take it to the mayor before he starts on his round, and greet him from me. I remember I dreamed of him last night. Go to Pilgrim's too, if you can, and tell him I shall wait at home for him to-day. Good luck with your house! I am glad to think you will have a roof of your own."

Faller started off for the valley with the paper, leaving Lenz to his work. But before sitting down to it he wound up one of his musical clocks and made it play a choral. The piece goes well, he said to himself, nodding his head approvingly over the wheel on which he was filing. It was her-- my mother's--favorite tune. The great musical clock with the handsomely carved nut-wood case, as tall as a good-sized wardrobe, was called "The Magic Flute," from the overture of that opera, which was the longest of five pieces that it played. It was already sold to a large tea-dealer in Odessa. A smaller clock stood beside it, and near that a third, on which Lenz was working. At noon, after laboring uninterruptedly all the morning, he began to feel hungry; but no sooner had he sat down to his solitary meal than all hunger forsook him. He asked the old serving-maid to eat with him, as she used to do in his mother's lifetime. She consented, after a great show of maidenly delicacy at the idea of dining alone with so young a man; but by the time the soup was finished, she had so far recovered her self-possession as to bring up the question of his marriage and gave her advice against it.

"Who says I mean to marry?"

"I think, if you do, you ought to marry the bailiff's daughter Katharine. She comes of a respectable family, and has the greatest respect for you; she actually swears by you. That would be just the right sort of wife,--not one who would treat you like the very ground she walks on. Girls nowadays are so--so exacting, they care for nothing but dress and show."

"I am not thinking of marrying; certainly not now."

"You are quite right. It is not at all necessary you should. Take my word for it, you will never be better off than you are now. I am used to your ways, and I will keep everything so exactly as your mother did that you will think she is alive again. Don't your beans taste good now? Your mother taught me to cook them so. She understood everything from the greatest to the smallest. You will be as comfortable as can be when we are by ourselves. You see if you are not."

"I don't think we shall keep on as we are, Franzl," said Lenz.

"So you have some one already in your mind,--have you? People fancy Lenz thinks of nothing but his clocks and his mother. Much they know about it! If it is only some girl that comes of a good family. Katharine, now, would be a wife for every day in the week,--for working days and for holidays. She can look after the house and the field, and can spin--you'd think she would spin the very straw down from the roof. Then, too, she swears by you; all you say and all you do is perfect. She always says whatever comes from Lenz is right, however it may look,--like your working yesterday, for instance. Besides, she is well off; what she inherits from her mother alone would be a portion for one of your children."

"I have no thought of marrying, Franzl. Perhaps--I don't know, but perhaps--I shall sell or lease my house and go abroad."

Franzl stared at him in speechless amazement, forgetting even to carry her spoon to her mouth.

"I will provide for you, Franzl; you shall want for nothing. But I have never been out into the world, and should like once to see and learn something. Perhaps I may further my art in some way; who knows?"

"It is none of my business," said Franzl; "I am only an ignorant servant-woman, though we Knuslingers have the reputation of keeping pretty good eyes in our heads. I don't know much about the world; but one thing I do know, and that is, that I have not lived in service twenty-seven years for nothing. I came into this house when you were four years old. You were the youngest and dearest of all the children, and your brothers and sisters in their graves,--but no matter for that now. I have lived with your mother twenty-seven years. I cannot say I am as wise as she was; where is the woman, far or near, who can say that for herself? You'll never find her equal as long as the world lasts. But I learned a good deal from her. How often I have heard her say, 'Franzl, people rush out into the world as if somewhere, across the

Rhine or over the sea, fortune were running about the streets, and crying to Tom, Dick, and Harry, "Good morning, Tom, Dick, and Harry; I am glad to see you." Franzl,' your mother used to say, 'if a man can't succeed at home, he won't succeed abroad. There are people enough everywhere to pick up gold, if it does rain down, without waiting for strangers to come and help them. What sort of a fortune can a man make in the world? He can't do more than eat, drink, and sleep. Franzl,' she'd say, 'my Lenz,'--excuse me, it was she that said it, not I,--'my Lenz, like the rest of them, once got into his head that silly notion of travelling; but where can he be better off than here? He is not fitted for the wild world. One must be a robber, like Petrovitsch, a good-for-nothing, stingy, greedy, cruel wretch.' I don't mean she said that; she never said such a thing of anybody; but I say it and think it. 'If my Lenz were to go abroad,' she said, 'he would give the shirt off his body to the first beggar he met; any one could deceive him, he is so kindhearted. Franzl,' says she, 'if the wandering spirit comes over him when I am gone, Franzl,' says she, 'hang on to his coat, and don't let him stir.' But, good gracious! I can't do that; how can I? I can only speak; and I must speak, for she made me solemnly promise. Just think how well off you are. You have a comfortable house, a good living; you are loved and respected. If you go out into the world, who will care for you? who will know you are Lenz of the Morgenhalde? When you have no place to lay your head, and are obliged to spend the night in the woods, you will think of your house at home and the seven well-stuffed beds that are in it, and the plenty of furniture and dishes, and the wine on tap in the cellar. Sha'n't I fetch you a glass? I'll get you one in a minute. Always drink when you're out of spirits. A thousand times your mother has said, 'Wine cheers a man up, and makes him think of other things.'"

So saying, she hurried out of the room and into the cellar, soon returning with a flagon in her hand. Lenz insisted on her bringing a second glass, and filled it for her himself; but she was too modest to do more than touch her lips to it till she had cleared off the table and retreated with her wine into the kitchen.

Lenz worked on again industriously till evening. The wine or something else made him restless, so that he was several times on the point of throwing down his tools and going out for a walk. But upon second thoughts he concluded to stay at home, and receive the friends who would be sure to seek him out and relieve his loneliness. No one came, however, except Pröbler. He liked Lenz for being one of the few who did not make fun of him, nor laugh at his constantly refusing to sell any of his works of art. He would mortgage them till he lost all power to redeem them. It was said that the landlord of the Lion, who carried on a large business as commissioner and wholesale dealer, owed Pröbler quite a handsome sum on the works he had pawned to him.

Lenz used to listen with all attention and seriousness while Pröbler would talk of his great discovery of the *perpetuum mobile*, and how he wanted nothing further to bring his work to perfection than the twenty-four diamonds on which it needed to move. In return, the old man willingly gave his help in setting up the standard regulator which was to benefit the whole district; and he really contributed some valuable suggestions, which Lenz was very glad publicly to give him credit for.

To-day, however, Pröbler came neither about a new discovery nor the *perpetuum mobile*, but to offer himself as mediator in case Lenz was desirous of marrying. He proposed to him a whole list of marriageable girls, among them the doctor's daughters. "You are too modest," he added in conclusion; "all houses are open to you. Tell me honestly in what direction your preference leads you, and I will see that you are met half-way." Lenz hardly vouchsafed an answer to his proposition, and the old man finally departed. The idea that he could have one of the doctor's daughters lingered in Lenz's mind. They were three noble girls. There was a thoughtfulness--an almost motherly carefulness--about the eldest, while the second played and sang beautifully. How often Lenz had stood before the house and listened to her! Music was his one passion. He longed for it as a thirsty man for a spring of water. How would it seem to have a wife who could play the piano? She should play him all the pieces he wanted to put into his clocks; he could make them sound a great deal better after he had heard them. But no; such a wife would be too aristocratic for him. One who could play the piano would not look after the house and the garden and the stable, as a watchmaker's wife must. He would wait quietly.

When twilight came on, Lenz changed his clothes and went down into the valley.

All houses are open to him, Pröbler had said. All houses? that is as bad as none at all. Unless you can enter a house without interrupting the inmates in their occupation; unless no glance, no expression asks, What have you come for? what plan is on foot? unless you are made to feel at home,--you have no house open to you. Lenz went in imagination up and down the whole village, stopping at every door. Everywhere he would find hands stretched out to greet him, but nowhere a home. Yet he had one friend with whom he would be as much at ease as in his own room. Pilgrim, the case-painter, had wanted to go home with him yesterday after his mother's funeral, but fell back because he was joined by his uncle Petrovitsch. The two despised each other for different reasons; Petrovitsch Pilgrim, for being a poor devil; and Pilgrim, Petrovitsch for being a rich one. To Pilgrim's, therefore, he would go. His friend lived down in the valley with Don Bastian, as he called him, a man who had been a dealer in clocks and made a considerable fortune during a twelve years' residence in Spain. On his return home he had bought a farm, resumed his peasant's clothes, and retained no traces of his Spanish journey except the gold and a couple of Spanish words which he liked to air occasionally, especially in midsummer when the travellers from all quarters of the world returned to their native valley.

CHAPTER VII
THE LANDLORD'S DAUGHTER PLAYS HOSTESS

In the public room of the Lion, at a table comfortably laid before the balcony window, sat a young man alone, eating with that relish which is the privilege of a stout young fellow in his twenties, after a day's walk over the mountains. Sometimes, however, his eye wandered thoughtfully from the viands themselves to the heavy silver plate on which they were served. It was a remnant of the good old time, when interest-bearing investments were not the only ones allowed. At last the young man, who was no other than the engineer who had spent the evening before at the doctor's, lighted a cigar and, drawing a brush from his pocket, began smoothing his full, light beard. He had a marked countenance. A high, full forehead projected from under his brown hair, his cheeks were fresh, and there was an expression in his deep-set blue eyes that inspired instant confidence.

A cool evening breeze was blowing in at the open window, quickly dispersing the blue smoke from the cigar.

"Smoking already? then you will have nothing more to eat," said a girl, entering from an adjoining room. She wore a fresh white apron made with a stomacher, and was peculiarly neat and nice in her whole dress. Her figure was slender and supple; her face oval yet full, with bright, intelligent brown eyes; and three tiers of heavy brown braids were wound like a crown about her head.

With a ready flow of words she continued: "You must excuse us; we had done expecting you to dinner, it was so late."

"Everything was excellent. Come and sit down by me a little while, sister-in-law."

"In a minute; as soon as I have cleared up. I cannot sit down with the things all standing about so."

"You must have everything as neat and orderly as yourself."

"Thank you for the compliment. I am glad you have not spent them all at the doctor's."

"Come back as soon as you can; I've ever so much to tell you."

After leaving the guest alone again for a while, the landlord's daughter returned with a piece of knitting-work in her hand, and took a seat opposite him at the table. "Well, let me hear," she said.

The engineer told her how he had been accompanying the doctor on his daily round over the mountains, and could not sufficiently praise his wondrous insight into the life of the people. He found them as the doctor had described, industrious and pious, yet without bigotry.

"We have been into three or four inns to-day," he said. "Generally, when you enter a country tavern of a summer's noon, you find some miserable creature besotting himself on a bench behind the table, half asleep over his stale beer or schnapps, who will stare at every new-comer, and brag and rail in some unintelligible fashion. It is a very common sight in other places, but I saw nothing of the sort here."

"Our mayor, the doctor," said Annele, "shows no mercy to drunkards, and we are principled against giving to one."

The engineer entered with enthusiasm into a description of the doctor's character. Wherever he went, the day seemed to grow brighter. His honest sympathy brought something like contentment even into the huts of the poor, while the confidence which his character as well as his words inspired everywhere imparted fresh courage.

The girl listened in some embarrassment to this glowing description, and only answered as she pressed a knitting-needle to her lips, "O yes, the doctor is a true friend of the poor."

"He is your friend too; he said a great deal of good of you."

"Did he? That was because he was out in the open air; he does not dare speak well of me at home. His five womenkind would not let him. I must except the old mayoress, though; she is always kind."

"And are not the others? I should have thought--"

"I don't want to speak ill of them or any one else. I desire to be thankful I have no need to exalt myself at the expense of others, to help myself out of another's purse, as old Marie Lenz used to say. Thousands of persons are passing in and out here who can let the whole world know what we are. A hotel is not like a private house, where the family can appear most loving to one another, and keep everything in beautiful order for two or three days, while a visitor is present, and then, behind his back, be ready to scratch each other's eyes out, and let the housekeeping go at sixes and sevens; or, where a young lady can begin to sing when she sees a gentleman going by, or can take her work into the garden and make herself ornamental. But I don't want to speak ill of anybody, only--" here Annele slipped as by accident into the familiar German "thou." "Oh! I beg your pardon; I forgot I was not talking to my brother-in-law, or I should not have said 'thou.'"

"I have no objection to it. Let us say 'thou' to one another."

"Not for the world! I cannot stay, if we are to talk in that way. I wonder what keeps father so long?" said the landlord's daughter, blushing.

"Where is your father gone?"

"He had to see to his business, but he may be back any minute. I wish he would give up business. What is the use of his working so hard? He thinks he could not live without it. A man might as well die as give up business, he says; watching and working, thinking and planning, keep one's faculties awake. And I believe he is right. For my part, I cannot imagine how any one in youth and health can sit and play the piano all the morning, or dilly-dally about the house, singing. To turn your hand to this thing and that keeps you wide awake. To be sure, if you count what we women earn in money it is not much; but to keep a house in good order is worth something."

"Yes, indeed," said the engineer; "the devotion of people to their work here is wonderful. Many of the clockmakers work fourteen hours a day. They deserve great praise for it."

The girl cast a look of surprise at him. What have those stupid clockmakers to do with the matter? Couldn't he, or wouldn't he, understand what she meant?

There came a pause which the engineer broke by asking about the landlady.

"Mother is in the garden, picking beans. Let us go and find her, for she cannot leave her work."

"No, I'd rather stay as we are. Tell me, sister-in-law,--I may call you so without offence, I hope,--is not the doctor's oldest daughter, Amanda, a ladylike, amiable girl?"

"Amanda? why should she not be? she is old enough. She is high-shouldered, too, as you would see if her city dressmaker did not pad her so skilfully." The girl bit her lip. How silly to have said that! He was thinking of Bertha all the time he asked about Amanda. "Bertha, now," she added, recovering herself, "is a merry--"

"Yes, a noble girl," interrupted the young man, then suddenly stooped to pick up a needle the landlord's daughter had dropped under the table. He seemed vexed at having betrayed himself, and hastened to change the subject.

"The doctor told me a great deal about Pilgrim yesterday."

"What is there to tell? The doctor can make a story out of everything."

"Who is Petrovitsch? They say you know all about him."

"No more than every one knows. He dines here every day, and pays when he is done. He is an obstinate old curmudgeon, as rich as a jewel and as hard. He lived ever so many years abroad, and cares for nobody. Only one thing he takes delight in, and that is the avenue of cherry-trees leading to the town. A row of crab-apple trees used to stand there, and Petrovitsch--"

"Why is he called Petrovitsch?"

"His name is Peter, but he lived among the Servians so long that people got into the way of calling him Petrovitsch."

"Tell me more about the avenue."

"He was in the habit of walking about with a knife in his hand, and lopping off the superfluous branches by the roadside. One day, the superintendent of the roads arrested him for mutilating the trees, so he had a new row of cherry-trees planted at his own expense, and for six years has had the fruit picked before it ripened, that thieves might not injure the trees. They have grown beautifully, certainly. But he cares nothing for his fellow-men. See, there goes his only brother's child, Lenz of the Morgenhalde, who can boast of having received no more from his uncle than he could put on the point of a pin."

"That is Lenz,--is it? A fine-looking fellow he is, with a delicate face, just as I had imagined him. Does he always stoop like that when he walks?"

"No, only now, because he is feeling so badly at his mother's death. He is a good fellow, though a little too soft-hearted. I know two eyes that are looking out at him from a vine-covered house, wishing they might tempt him in; and the eyes belong to Bertha."

"Indeed? Is there any engagement between them?" asked the engineer, the color mounting to his forehead.

"I don't suppose they are engaged, but she would be glad enough to catch him; for he has a pretty property, while she has nothing but a pretty straw hat and a pair of ragged stockings."

The landlord's daughter--or Annele of the Lion, as she was commonly called--congratulated herself on having administered this bitter pill, and quite forgot her own vexation in delight at the pain she had caused.

"Where are you going?" she continued, as the young man took his hat, and prepared to depart.

"I want a farther walk, and think of going up the Spannreute."

"It is beautiful, but as steep as the side of a house."

Annele hurried into the back garden as soon as he left, and watched him. He did, in fact, go a little way up the mountain, but soon retraced his steps, and went down the valley towards the doctor's.

"Plague on you!" she said to herself; "not another kind word shall you get from me."

CHAPTER VIII
THE DEPARTED SAINT AND THE NEW MOTHER

"He is not at home," cried Don Bastian's wife, as Lenz came up the slope to the house. "He must have gone to see you. Did you not meet him?"

"No; is his room open?"

"Yes."

"I will go up awhile," he said, and approached the familiar room. But, on opening the door, all power to enter forsook him. There stood his mother smiling upon him. His first thought, on recovering his self-possession, was one of gratitude to the faithful friend who had fixed upon the canvas those dear features, so honest and kindly, before their memory had faded. "He is always my good angel," he said to himself. "He was doing me service when he could not be with me, and such a service!--the greatest in all the world."

Long and fixedly, through gathering tears, Lenz gazed at the beloved face. "While I have eyes left, they shall look upon her. O if I could only hear her speak! if the voice of the departed could only be brought back!" He could hardly tear himself away. It was so strange to have his mother there alone, looking and looking with no one to look back at her. Not till it grew too dark to see did he leave the room. "My tears must cease here," he said to himself, as he turned away. "Whatever I feel shall be shut in my own breast; no one shall call me unmanly." As he passed the doctor's house, a sound of music reached him through the open windows. He distinguished the words of a foreign song sung by a powerful baritone voice that belonged, he knew, to no one in the valley. Whose could it be? A beautiful voice, to whomever it belonged.

"Now, Miss Bertha," he heard the stranger say, "you must sing to me."

"Not now, Mr. Storr; we shall be going to tea soon. Later in the evening we will sing together. Meanwhile I want you to look over this piece of music."

Aroused to a consciousness of his long fasting by the mention of supper, Lenz suddenly formed a bold resolution, and with a firmer step and more erect carriage went straight towards the town, and into the Lion Inn.

"Good evening, Lenz. I am glad you remember your old friends in your grief. Not a minute has passed that I have not spoken your name, and everybody that has come in through the day has talked of you. Has not your right ear burned? You will surely be rewarded in this life, dear Lenz, for your devotion to your blessed mother. She and I were the best of friends, as you know, though we did not see each other as often as we should have liked; for she did not leave home much, nor I either. Will you have a glass of the new wine, or the old? Better take the new; it is right good, and will not fly into your head. You look so red and heated!--of course, after losing such a mother"--Here the landlady of the Lion--for she it was who thus condoled with Lenz--expressed by a wave of her hand that her feelings would not let her say more.

"But what can we expect?" she began again, while setting the bottle and glass on the table. "We are mortals, after all. Your mother lived to be seventy-one,--a whole year beyond, the allotted age. To-morrow I may have to follow her. With God's help I too will leave behind a good name for my children. Not that I pretend to compare myself with your mother,--who could? But now might I venture to give you a little bit of advice? I mean it for your good."

"Certainly; I am always glad of good advice."

"I only want to warn you against your too tender heart, against letting your grief take too entire possession of you. You won't be offended,--will you?"

"No, no; why should I be? On the contrary, you show me, as I never knew before, how many good friends my mother had, and how fortunate I am to inherit them."

"You deserve them all. You are--"

"Welcome, welcome, Lenz!" interrupted a clear, youthful voice, and a full, plump hand was held out to him, behind which appeared as full and fresh a face. It was Annele of the Lion, who came in with lights. "Why did you not let me know, mother, that Lenz was here?" she added, turning to the landlady.

"You are not the only one that is privileged to talk with a young man at twilight," replied the mother, with a meaning smile.

Annele saw that Lenz did not fancy the joke, and continued, without heeding her mother's words: "You must see by my looks, dear Lenz, how I have wept for your mother these last two days. I have hardly got over it yet. Such people ought not to die. To think of all the good she did being so suddenly swept away! I can imagine how your room seems to you; how you look into all the corners, fancying the door must open; that she cannot have gone away and left you; she must come back. All day I have found myself thinking, Poor Lenz, if I could only help him! I should be so glad to bear a little of his burden for him! We looked for you here to dinner to-day. Your uncle fully expected you. He always insists on having dinner served the instant the clock strikes; but to-day he said, 'Wait a little, Annele; keep back the dinner awhile. Lenz will surely come; he never will sit down all by himself up there.' And Pilgrim said you would not fail to come and dine with him at his table. Pilgrim takes his meals here, you know. He is like a brother to me, and so fond of you! Your uncle always has his dinner served at a little table by himself, and likes me to sit down and chat with him. He is an odd man, but as clever as the Evil One. Don't disappoint us at dinner to-morrow, will you? And now what will you have for supper?"

"I have no appetite for anything. I only wish I could sleep on and on for weeks, and forget myself and all that concerns me."

"You will feel differently by and by.--Yes, I am coming!" cried Annele to some teamsters who had just sat down at another table. She quickly supplied their wants, and then resumed her place behind Lenz's chair, keeping her hand on the back of it while answering the questions of the other guests. The touch thrilled like an electric shock through his whole frame. The sight of others at their supper presently reminded him of his own hunger. In an instant Annele was in the kitchen, and back again with fresh table linen. Her hands laid the cloth and set on the dishes so invitingly, and her voice pressed him so cordially to eat, that his supper relished as he had thought food never would relish again.

Who so neat and nimble as Annele, so ready and quick at repartee? Pity she lets her fondness for making fools of people spoil the charm of her wit.

Lenz had no sooner finished his first bottle than she was ready with a fresh one, and filling his glass herself.

"You don't smoke,--do you?"

"I ought not, but should like to."

"I will fetch you a cigar such as my father smokes. We don't let many of the guests have them." She brought the cigar, lighted a paper by the lamp, and handed it to him.

The landlord had entered meanwhile,--a tall, stout, imposing figure, of venerable aspect, with thin, snow-white hair, and a little black velvet cap like a priest's on his head. His silver-bowed spectacles, with their big round glasses, were only meant to be used for reading, and were therefore generally worn pushed up on his forehead, from which a serene and quiet intelligence appeared to be gazing. Very quiet mine host was, quiet even to solemnity, and accounted very wise. He spoke little, but must not great wisdom have been needed to attain the position of the landlord of the Lion? His face was rosy, and, as we have said, venerable, except in respect to his mouth, which he had a trick of drawing in as a person does who is smacking his lips over something savory. He was silent and serious, as if wishing to make amends by his lack of words for the fluency of his wife and daughter. When the landlady was particularly talkative and complaisant, he would shake his head, as much as to say, "That is not to the taste of a man of honor." A man of honor the landlord was known to be through all the country round, and a thorough business man. He had made a fortune as packer,--that is, by buying clocks of the manufacturers, and forwarding them to purchasers in different parts of the world.

"Good evening, Lenz," said the landlord, with a breadth of voice that spoke volumes. Lenz respectfully rose. "Keep your seat," he said, offering his hand; "don't stand upon ceremony; this is a public house." His concluding nod seemed to say, "I make my respects to you; the requisite sympathy is as safe with me as a triple mortgage." With that he walked to his own table and took up the papers.

"By your leave," said Annele, politely, as she came up with a stocking in her hand, on which she was knitting, and took a seat by Lenz. She talked much and well, so that Lenz knew not which most to admire, her kindness of heart or the readiness of her wit.

"I am sorry to have to take money from you," she said, when he was paying for his supper; "I would much rather you had been our guest. Good night. Don't grieve too much. I wish I could help you. By the way, I had nearly forgotten to ask when your great musical clock, I hear so much of, is going to Russia. It must be the finest ever made here."

"It may be sent for any day."

"May I come up with my mother, some time, to see it and hear it play?"

"I shall feel honored. Come whenever you will."

"Good night, and pleasant dreams. Remember me to Franzl. She must come to us if she wants anything."

"Thank you; I will deliver the message."

It was a long mile to Lenz's house, and a steep one too; but he was not conscious of the way. Not till he found himself again in his lonely room did the former feeling of sadness come over him. He gazed out into the summer night, thinking of he knew not what. No sight nor sound of human life reached him, except a solitary light that shone for a moment from the blacksmith's house on the opposite mountain, and then vanished. The happy can sleep.

A wind-mill stood near the smith's cottage, and in the perfect stillness of the night he could hear it working, as a gust of wind set it in sudden motion. The stars shone bright above the dark outline of the mountain ridge. The moon had sunk below the trees, but still tinged the fleecy clouds, and left a trail of pale blue light behind her.

Lenz pressed his hands to his burning brow. His temples throbbed. Everything swam before his eyes. It must be the new wine: he would drink no more at night. "How kind and affectionate Annele was! Don't be a fool; what is Annele to you? Good night; pleasant dreams!" he repeated, and found in fact that night deep and quiet sleep.

CHAPTER IX
FRIENDLY ADVICE

When Lenz awoke the next morning, the journeyman and apprentice whom he had sent home at the time of his mother's death were already at work in their old places. Never before had they been on hand before their master. He was surprised to find the sun high in the heavens when he threw open his window, and to hear the various clocks in his room striking seven. Had his wish that he might sleep for weeks been really granted? Weeks seemed to lie between yesterday and to-day. Yesterday, how long ago it was! how much had happened!

Franzl brought his breakfast and sat down with him unbidden. "What shall I cook for your dinner to day?"

"For mine? Nothing; I shall not be at home to dinner. Cook for yourself as usual. Only think, Franzl, that good Pilgrim--"

"Yes," interrupted Franzl; "he was here last evening, and waited a long while for you."

"Was he? and I had gone to see him. Only think, he has been secretly painting a picture of my mother. You would be amazed to see how lifelike it is. She seems on the point of speaking."

"I knew what he was about. He came to me privately for your mother's Sunday jacket, her red bodice, and fine-plaited ruff, her neckerchief and hood. Her garnet ornaments you had locked up with those other things that I know nothing about. It is none of my business; I don't need to know everything. But I can keep a secret as well as another; I would not tell if you tapped every vein in my body. Did a breath of what Pilgrim was about escape me? Did I drop a hint of why he did not come? You may trust me with anything."

As Lenz did not seem inclined to take her into his confidence, she began questioning him.

"Where are you going to-day? Where did you spend last evening?"

Lenz looked at her in surprise, and made no answer.

"Were you at your uncle Petrovitsch's?"

He still made no answer beyond a shake of the head, and Franzl helped both him and herself out of the difficulty by saying: "I have no more time now. I must go into the garden to pick the beans for dinner. I have engaged a woman to-day to help me dig potatoes; are you willing?"

"Certainly; only see that everything is done as it should be."

Lenz, too, went to his work, but could not fix his mind upon it. None of his tools suited him. Even his father's file, which he was generally so careful of, he threw roughly aside.

The Magic Flute began to play. "Who wound up the clock?" asked Lenz, surprised.

"I did," said the apprentice.

Lenz was silent. He must expect everything to go on in its old way. The world does not stand still because one heart has ceased to beat and another longs to be at rest forever. He worked on more quietly. The journeyman told of a young man in Triberg who had lately come home from foreign parts and wanted to set up a manufactory of musical clocks in the neighborhood.

I might sell out to him, thought Lenz, and be free to travel and see the world. But the thought awoke no enthusiasm in him now; it was only like the echo of what he had once desired. The very fact of his uncle's having spread a report of his going, wishing thereby to compel him to it, made him averse to the plan. He took his father's file once more in his hand. The man who used this file, he thought, spent his life on this spot, except for one short season of absence, and was happy. To be sure he married young; that makes a difference.

Lenz's habit was, when he had business at the foundry on the other side of the mountain, to send his apprentice. To-day he went himself, and sat but a little while at his work after his return. Before the morning hours were half over, he went down into the village and thence up the meadow to Pilgrim's. His old friend was sitting at his easel, painting. He got up, passed both hands through his long, lank, sandy hair, and offered the right to Lenz, who began at once to thank him for the joyful surprise his mother's picture had given him, as well as for his friend's kindness in thinking of it.

"Pooh, pooh!" said Pilgrim, thrusting both his hands into his wide leather breeches, "I did it for my own pleasure. It is desperately stupid work painting that blessed village from one year's end to the other; the same old church with the bishop's mitre for a steeple and a hole to put the dial-plate in; the mower with his scythe, who never budges a step; the mother and child always running towards each other and never meeting; the baby, stretching out its little hands, and never reaching its father; and that plaguy fellow with his back turned, who never lets us see what sort of a face he has. Yet hundreds and hundreds of times I am made to paint that staring grass-green thing because the world must have what it has been used to. I could paint it with my eyes shut, I do believe, and still am kept at it. For once in my life I have done myself a pleasure, and painted your mother. It is my first and last portrait; for I don't like the faces about here, and don't mean to bore future generations with the sight of them. Your uncle was right never to consent to have his picture taken. When a travelling artist some time ago asked him to sit: 'No,' said he, 'I have no idea of seeing myself one of these days hanging in a rag-shop side by side with Napoleon and old Fritz.' He has queer fancies, that old fellow. There is no telling where he will strike out next."

"Never mind my uncle now. You painted my mother's picture for me,--did you not?"

"Yes, if you want it. Come here a moment; stand just there. The eyes are the least satisfactory part of the picture to me, and the doctor said the same thing when he was here this morning. He meant to bring a friend with him who is something of an artist, but he did not get out of bed early enough. You have exactly your mother's eyes. Stand there a minute, just as you are. Now keep quiet, and think of something pleasant,--of some one you are going to do a kindness to. Remember Faller and his house, then you will have just your mother's hearty expression; not a smile, but such a kind, cordial look. So,--that is it exactly. Don't blink. Nay, I cannot paint you if you cry."

"The tears will come," apologized Lenz. "I could not help thinking how my mother's eyes--"

"Well, well; we will let it be. I know now what is needed. Let us take a recess; and high time we did too, for it is almost noon. You will eat your dinner with me, won't you?"

"Don't be offended; but I must dine with my Uncle Petrovitsch to-day."

"Nothing you could do would offend me. Tell me now about yourself."

Lenz laid before his friend the plan he had half formed of going abroad for a year or two, and urged him to carry out their boyish project of going together. Perhaps the luck they had hoped for in those days might be realized now.

"Don't do it; don't go," urged Pilgrim. "You and I, Lenz, were never meant to be rich men, and it is best so. My Don Bastian is the sort of man to make money. He has travelled over the whole world, and knows as little about it as the cow does of the creed. Wherever he went, whatever place he entered, his one thought was how to make money, how to save and to cheat. So he got on everywhere. The Spanish peasant is as cunning as the German, and likes nothing so well as to get the better of his neighbors. When my Don Bastian came home, he brought nothing with him but his money, and had nothing to do but to dispose of that to the best advantage. Such a man as that will get on in the world."

"And we?"

"He whose pleasure lies in things that cannot be had for gold needs no money. All the superfluous chink that I have is my guitar, and it is all I want. I heard Don Bastian's youngest boy saying the Ten Commandments one day, and a bright thought came into my head. What is the first commandment? 'I am the Lord thy God: thou shalt have no other gods beside me.' Every man, then, can have but one God. You and I take pleasure in our art. You are happy when you have accomplished a work that harmonizes in all its parts, and so am I, though I do complain sometimes of the everlasting village with the same old mower and the eternal mother and child. But I am glad when it is done; and even while I am doing it I am as gay as a bird,--as gay as the finch there on the church-roof. Now a man that delights in his work, and puts his whole heart and soul into it, cannot be always thinking how he can make money, how he can speculate and cheat. And if he has a joy that money cannot buy, what does he want of money? I am satisfied with the sight of a beautiful group of trees,--with watching the sunbeams flicker in and out among the branches, and play bo-peep with one another so happy and loving. What should I gain by having the forest my own? 'Thou shalt have no other gods beside me.' That is a good saying. A second god is pretty sure to be the devil, as you may see by your Uncle Petrovitsch. The apostle says the same thing: 'Ye cannot drink the cup of the Lord and the cup of devils.'"

"Come and live with me," was Lenz's only answer. "I will have our upper room fitted up for you, and give you a chamber besides."

"Thank you, but that would be a mistake for both of us. Lenz, you are one of a thousand. You were cut out for a husband and father; you must marry. I imagine already the pleasure I shall take in telling your children stories about my travels. When I am too old to work, you shall give me a home with you, and kill me with kindness, if you will. But now keep your eyes open. Don't seem too fond of me. I not only will not be offended, but I advise you to put me in the background, that you may have a chance of a place in your uncle's will. We should make capital heirs. I have a real talent for inheriting; but unhappily my relatives are all poor devils, rich in nothing but children. I am the only one in the family that will have anything to leave, and I shall play the rich uncle one of these days, like Petrovitsch."

As a passing shower, which began to fall while the friends were talking, put a fresh brightness on the face of nature, so did Lenz's heart grow lighter under Pilgrim's influence. They waited till the rain was over, and then set out together for the hotel; but did not enter at the same time, as Pilgrim was unwilling to be seen by Petrovitsch in Lenz's company. A wagon stood before the door, and a young man was taking leave of the landlord, who accompanied him a few steps, and offered him his two fingers, pushing his little cap on the back of his head as he did so. After a parting salutation to the landlady and her daughter, the stranger ordered the coachman to drive on, and wait for him at the doctor's.

He raised his cap in greeting to the two friends as he passed them.

"Do you know him?" asked Pilgrim.

"No."

"Nor I either," said Pilgrim. "That is odd! Who is the stranger?" he asked of the landlord.

"The brother of my son-in-law."

"Oho!" whispered Pilgrim in Lenz's ear; "now I remember; some one told me he was a suitor of Annele's."

He did not see the change these words wrought in his friend's countenance; for Lenz turned hastily away and ran up the steps before him.

CHAPTER X
LENZ DINES WITH PETROVITSCH, AND IS KEPT WAITING FOR THE SWEETS

Petrovitsch had not yet come. As Lenz sat at his table waiting for him, Pilgrim and he fell into conversation with the hosts. Annele was strangely reserved to-day. She would not even shake hands with Lenz when he entered, but pretended to be busy with some household work. Her hand is promised, he thought; she can give it to no one now, even in greeting. At last his uncle arrived, or rather his forerunner in the shape of a mongrel cur, half terrier and half rat-catcher.

"Good day, Lenz!" said the surly voice of Petrovitsch, who followed behind the dog. "I expected you yesterday. Did you forget I had invited you?"

"I confess I did entirely."

"I will excuse you under the circumstances; but generally a business man ought not to forget. I never forgot even a pocket-handkerchief in my whole life, and never lost so much as a pin. A man should always keep his seven senses about him. Now let us have dinner."

Annele brought the soup. The uncle helped himself, put some into another plate, and told Lenz he might have what was left. Then he drew from his pocket the paper, which he took daily from the post, cut it open while his soup was cooling, laid his tobacco-pouch and meerschaum upon it, and finally began his dinner.

"This is the way I like to live," said he, when the soup was removed and he was crumbing bread into the plate for the unknown guest,--"take my meals in a public house where I can have fresh table linen every day, throw down my score when I am done, and remain my own master."

When the meat was brought on, Petrovitsch, with his own hand, put a slice on Lenz's plate, took another himself, and cut again for the third plate. It must be meant for some very intimate friend, for the old man put his finger into it, after sprinkling some water over, and stirred up the food. At last the mystery was explained by his calling to his dog: "Come, Bubby, come; gently, gently, not so rough, Bubby; quiet, quiet!" He set the plate on the floor, and the dog attacked the dinner with a relish, licking his chops when it was over, and looking up gratefully and contentedly in his master's face. For the rest of the meal Bubby, as the dog was called, to the disgust of the villagers, got nothing thrown him but an occasional crumb. Petrovitsch said little during dinner. When he had finished, he lighted his pipe and took the paper, which Bubby understood as a sign that he might jump up into his master's lap. There he remained, half sitting and half standing, while Petrovitsch read the paper over the dog's head. Lenz found his position rather embarrassing. The old man's habits were too settled to be easily interrupted.

"Uncle," he said at last, "what made you spread the report that I was going abroad?"

Petrovitsch took three comfortable pulls at his cigar, blew out the smoke, stroked his dog, pushed him gently off his lap, folded the paper, restored it to his pocket, and finally answered: "Why, Lenz, what a queer fellow you are! You told me yourself you wanted to renew your youth by going out to see the world."

"I don't remember saying so."

"Very likely not; you hardly knew what you were talking about. But it would be a good plan if you did go away awhile; you would get out of many a rut. I have no desire and no right to force you."

Lenz was actually persuaded by his uncle's positive assertion that he had expressed such an intention, and apologized for having forgotten the circumstance.

"Draw your chair up closer, Lenz," whispered Petrovitsch, confidentially. "There's no need for the world to hear our conversation. Look here, if you take my advice, you won't marry."

"But, uncle, what makes you suppose I am thinking of marrying?"

"There is no telling what you young people won't do. Profit by my example, Lenz. I am one of the happiest men in the world. I have been enjoying myself for six weeks in Baden-Baden, and now everything seems pleasant to me here again. Wherever I go, I am my own master and command the best service. Besides, there are no girls nowadays who are good for anything. You would die of ennui with the simple and good-natured, while the bright and clever expect you three times a day, at every meal, to send off fireworks for their entertainment, besides boring you with continual complaints of 'this tiresome housekeeping that you men know nothing about.' Then there are the crying children, and the poor relations, and the school-bills, and the dowries."

"If every one thought as you do, the world would die out in a hundred years."

"Pooh! there is no danger of its dying out," laughed Petrovitsch, as he pressed his tobacco down into his pipe with a little porcelain instrument he always kept by him for the purpose. "Look at Annele now." A chill he could not account for struck to Lenz's heart. "She is a natty little woman, always in harness. I call her my court jester. Those old kings were wise in keeping a fool to make them laugh over their dinner: it helped digestion. Annele is my court fool; she entertains me here every day."

When Lenz looked round, Pilgrim had vanished. He seemed determined his friend should disown him before the rich uncle. But Lenz considered it his duty to tell Petrovitsch that he was a faithful friend to Pilgrim, and always should be.

The old man commended his nephew for his constancy, and further surprised him by praising Pilgrim, who, he said, was just like himself, and cared nothing for marrying and womenfolks.

The dog became uneasy, and began to whine.

"Quiet!" said Petrovitsch, threateningly. "Be patient; we are going home now to sleep. Come, Bubby! Are you coming too, Lenz?"

Lenz accompanied his uncle as far as his house,--a large, imposing building, where he lived entirely alone. The door opened at their approach as if by magic; for the servant was obliged to be on the lookout, and open for her master without his knocking. No stranger was admitted who could not explain his business satisfactorily. The villagers used to say that even a fly must have a pass to enter that house.

There the nephew bade his uncle good by, and was thanked with a yawn for his politeness.

Lenz was happy to be at his work again that afternoon. The house, which had seemed too desolate to live in, began to feel once more like home. There is no true comfort to be found in outside excitements, but only between one's own four walls. He chose a place for his mother's portrait directly above his father's file. She would look down on him from there as he sat at work, and he could often look up at her.

"Keep the room nice and neat," he said to Franzl. "It is always neat," she answered, with pardonable indignation. Lenz could not explain that he wanted it particularly nice because he was every moment expecting Annele and her mother to see and hear the musical clock before it was sent to Russia. When she came, he would ask her plainly what foundation there was for the stories about herself and the engineer. He must ask, though he felt he had no right. Then he should know on what terms he might stand with her.

Day after day went by, and still no Annele came. Lenz often passed the Lion without going up, finally without even looking up.

CHAPTER XI
THE GREAT MUSICAL CLOCK PLAYS ITS OLD PIECES, AND HAS NEW ONES ADDED

The report that the famous Magic Flute, the great musical clock of Lenz of the Morgenhalde, would start in a few days for its place of destination in Russia, set the whole valley in a ferment. A perfect pilgrimage began to Lenz's house. Every one was anxious to admire this noble work once more, before it disappeared forever. Franzl had as much as she could do to welcome the guests, shake hands with them,--wiping her hands first on her apron every time,--and usher them into the sitting-room. There were not chairs enough in the house to seat them all. Even Uncle Petrovitsch came, and with him not only Bubby, which was a matter of course, but Ibrahim, the old man's companion at cards, who was said to have turned Turk during his fifty years' absence from home. The two old men said little. Ibrahim sat smoking a long Turkish pipe, motionless except for an occasional contraction of his eyebrows; while Petrovitsch was as constant in his attendance upon him as Bubby in attendance upon his master. Ibrahim was the only human being who possessed any influence over Petrovitsch, and he preserved it only by never exercising it. He shook off all applicants who hoped through him to gain access to the rich man. They played cards together every evening, cash down. Petrovitsch was stirred to special activity and officiousness by Ibrahim's imperturbable tranquillity, and now seemed desirous of doing the honors of his old homestead. He stood by the work-bench during the playing of a long piece, and amused himself with observing the tools which lay upon it, as well as those hanging upon the wall. At last he took down the familiar file with the well-worn handle. "Was not this his file?" he said to Lenz, when the piece was ended.

"Yes, my poor father's."

"I will buy it of you."

"You are not in earnest, uncle. You know I could not sell it."

"Not to me?"

"Not even to you,--begging your pardon."

"Give it to me, then, and let me give you something in return."

"I hardly know how to answer you, uncle. Really, I cannot let it go out of the house."

"Stay there then," he said to the unconscious tool, as he returned it to its place; and shortly after he and Ibrahim went down the hill.

People came from a great distance, some from the next valley, to hear and admire the clock. Franzl was especially delighted with the praise bestowed upon it by the weight-maker, one of the chief men of her village. "Such a piece of workmanship has not left our part of the country for a hundred years," he declared. "What a pity it has got to be silent through the journey, and cannot play from here to Odessa, to tell every one it comes from the Black Forest, where science has been brought to such perfection!" Franzl's face glowed with pleasure. It takes the Knuslingers to talk like that. She told of the patience and zeal with which Lenz had labored on this work; how he had often got up in the night to carry out some idea that had come into his mind. There were secrets in that clock that no one could fathom. She, of course, was initiated into its mysteries. No maiden's heart ever beat more tumultuously at a first declaration of love than Franzl's when the first man of her village said, "And the house, Franzl, whence proceeds a work so delicate and exact, the house must have been well ordered too; you have contributed your share, Franzl."

"With all deference to others, I must say there is no one quite equal to us Knuslingers. This is the only man who has said just the right thing. The others stood there like cows before a new barn door. Moo! moo! Thank Heaven, I come from Knuslingen!"--so spoke Franzl's whole manner. You could read it in her hand, which she laid upon her beating heart, and in the frequent raising of her eyes to heaven.

Lenz could not help laughing at her seasoning every meal with congratulations that he was now so famous in Knuslingen.

Knuslingen was not such a small place either. It had two chapels of ease, at Fuchsberg and at Knebringen.

"To-morrow evening I shall close the case and send off The Magic Flute," said Lenz.

"So soon?" lamented Franzl, and cast imploring glances at the great case, as if entreating it to stay yet a little longer in the house to which it brought so much honor.

"I wonder," continued Lenz, "why the doctor's family has not been; and--and--the ladies from the Lion promised to come too."

Franzl rubbed her forehead and shrugged her shoulders, lamenting her ignorance. It was not for the like of her to know the secrets of great houses.

Annele of the Lion had long been urging her mother to make the visit, but the landlady would not without her husband. Majesty is wanting where he is not present. Majesty, however, does not seek; it requires to be sought.

But now Annele learned through certain trusty informers that on this last day the doctor's family was going to Lenz's house. Majesty, therefore, must consent. This was the day of all others,--the day when the aristocracy would be present. The mother and daughter determined not to start till they had seen the doctor's family go by. Nothing of this diplomacy was revealed to his Majesty, whose punctiliousness and dignity would have taken umbrage thereat.

"Here comes the thou-teacher," cried Franzl, early the next morning, as she was looking out of her kitchen window.

The elders of the village called the young schoolmaster the thou-teacher, because, to the great scandal of some good people, he addressed all who were unmarried with the familiar "thou." His companions called him the singing-master,--a title more to his taste. He was the founder and moving spirit of the Liederkranz, and with Lenz, Pilgrim, and Faller made the best quartette. Lenz gave him a hearty welcome, and Franzl begged him to stay a couple of hours to help her receive the numerous visitors who would be sure to come in the course of the morning.

"Yes, do stay," urged Lenz. "You cannot think how badly I feel at losing my clock; it is like bidding good by to a brother or a child."

"You carry your sentiment too far," objected the schoolmaster, "in thus putting a piece of your heart into everything you make. You will soon start some fresh work. For my part, I do not fancy these wound-up organs, as you know." Franzl made a wry face, but the teacher went on. "They are for children and for a people in its childhood. Even a piano I don't think much of, because the tones are ready-made. A piece of music played on the piano is not much better than the whistling of a song that should be sung. The works of your clocks have tongues and lungs, but no heart."

Franzl left the room in indignation. Thank Heaven, there are still Knuslingers in the world, to rate things at their proper value. She heard the two friends within singing the touching song, "Morgen muss ich fort von hier." Lenz's voice was a pure, though not very strong tenor, which the schoolmaster's powerful bass would have drowned had he let out the full force of his voice. They were interrupted by Franzl calling through the open door, "The doctor's family is coming."

The school-teacher, as master of ceremonies, advanced in front of the house to receive them.

The doctor entered with his wife and three daughters, and said at once, in his kindly way, which, without being in the least dictatorial, yet admitted of no refusal, that Lenz must not waste his valuable time in talking, but must set the clock going without delay.

It was done, and all were evidently delighted. When the first piece was finished, Lenz was fairly overwhelmed by the praises bestowed upon him,--such hearty praises, too, evidently not spoken merely from politeness.

"Grandmother sends you her congratulations," said the eldest daughter; while Bertha cried, "How many voices in one case!"

"Don't you wish you had as many?" replied her father, jokingly.

"You have a true talent for music," continued the eldest, her brown eyes shining with honest pleasure.

"If my father had only let me have a violin to play on when I was a boy, I really think I might have done something in the way of music," said Lenz.

"You have done something now," said the stout doctor, as he laid his hand kindly on the young man's shoulder.

The schoolmaster, whose chief delight was in the construction of the works, relieved Lenz of the trouble of explaining them to the ladies by describing, better than the manufacturer himself could have done, how the delicacies of crescendo and diminuendo were introduced, and what a nice ear was required to make the tones powerful without harshness, and to preserve the distinction between the long and the short notes. He dwelt repeatedly upon the accuracy of ear and mechanical skill necessary to produce such a work, called attention to the admirable expression of the pathetic passages, and reminded his listeners of the difficulty of bringing out the expression, and, at the same time, following the strokes of the metronome. This mechanism had not the advantage enjoyed by the performer of dispensing with the metronome and varying the time to suit the music. He was going on to explain how the various qualities of tone were rendered; the solidity of the barrel-work; the necessity of fitting the cylinders so firmly together that they could not give way; the reasons for having the soft alder outside and various woods of different fibres inside; when his explanations were interrupted by the voice of Franzl without, giving a peculiarly hearty welcome to some new-comers. Lenz went to the door, and found the landlord of the Lion, with his wife and daughter. The landlord shook hands with him, and gave a nod at the same time, as much as to say that no higher compliment could be paid than for a gentleman of well-known pride and honor to spend a quarter of an hour in examining a work to which a young man had devoted years of industry.

"So you have come at last!" was Lenz's greeting to Annele.

"Why at last?" she asked.

"Have you forgotten that you promised to come six weeks ago?"

"When? I cannot remember."

"On the day after my mother's death you said you would come soon."

"Yes, yes; so I did. I have had a feeling there was something on my mind, I could not tell what. Yes, yes; that is it. But, dear me, you have no idea how fast one thing crowds out another in our house." Lenz felt a pang through his heart at Annele's light words.

But he had no time to analyze his feelings of pleasure and pain, for the ladies now began to exchange greetings. Annele seemed inclined to follow the city fashion and kiss the doctor's daughters,--those friends whom, however, she hated most cordially for the reserve that always appeared in their manner towards her. Amanda, the botanist, had taken off her broad hat, quite as if she were at home, and Annele followed her example. Annele's hair was more abundant than that of all the other ladies put together, and long enough to sit on. She held up her head, with its triple crowns of braids, and looked about her with an air of satisfaction.

Lenz put in a new barrel, and made The Magic Flute, which was generally rather grave, play the merry song of the Moors, "Das klinget so herrlich, das klinget so schön."

"H'm, h'm!" growled the landlord, and a long speech he made out of his growl, nodding his head the while, and drawing in his under lip, as if tasting a delicate wine.

"Very well," he added, after a pause, and spreading out both hands as he said it, as if he would literally be openhanded in bestowing his commendations,--"very well indeed." Those were weighty words, coming from mine host.

The landlady folded her hands, and looked admiringly at Lenz. "To think that such a work should be made by human hands, and by so young a man too! and yet he acts as if he were nothing more than the rest of the world. Keep so always; nothing becomes a great artist so well as modesty. Go on as you have begun; make more such works. You have a great gift, my word for it."

That poverty-stricken individual, that may-pole, cannot use such language, said her triumphant glance at the doctor's wife, after this speech. And, if she did, what would her words signify? It is very different coming from me.

"Your mother's blessing rests on your noble work, Lenz," said Annele, "for she lived to see it finished. How hard for you to part with it! Bring me the music, won't you? and I will learn to play it on the piano."

"I can lend you the notes," said the doctor's eldest daughter, who had heard Annele's concluding words.

"But ours is arranged for four hands," said Bertha.

"And I have but two," said Annele, snappishly.

The girls would have gone on chatting longer, had not the doctor commanded silence. A new barrel had been put in, and the second piece was beginning.

When this was ended, and the guests had gone into the other room to partake of the bread and butter, cheese and wine that Franzl had prepared, the landlord began upon business.

"How much do you receive for your musical clock, Lenz? You need not hesitate to tell me; I won't take any unfair advantage of it."

"Twenty-two hundred florins. I don't gain much at that price, for the work has cost me a great outlay of time and money. If I make another, I shall drive a better bargain."

"Have you begun another?"

"No, I have had no order."

"I cannot give you an order, for musical clocks are out of my line of business. I cannot order one, therefore, as I say; but, if you make another, perhaps I will buy it. I think I could dispose of it."

"If that is so, I will begin a second work at once that shall be better than the first. The idea almost reconciles me to having this one go and carry away all the years I have spent on it."

"Not a word more or less have I to say about the matter. I am always accurate and precise. I give you no order, but--there is a possibility."

"That is quite enough; I am perfectly satisfied. Annele has said just what I was saying to Pilgrim yesterday, that I could not tell how badly I felt at having to part with the work my mother took such delight in."

Annele cast her eyes modestly to the ground.

"I shall take the same delight in it your mother did," said the landlady.

The doctor's wife and daughters looked at her in surprise as she spoke, the landlord frowned threateningly at his wife, and the pause that ensued gave additional weight to her words. Franzl relieved the general embarrassment by hospitably pressing refreshments upon every one, and was radiant with happiness when Annele commended her for keeping the house in such good order that no one would imagine it was without a mistress. The old woman put her newly washed apron to her eyes.

The landlady hit upon an excellent topic in asking Lenz if his uncle had been to see his work, and if he were not pleased with it.

"He came," answered Lenz, "but said nothing, except that I had sold it too cheap, and did not know how to look after my own interests."

There could not have been a happier inspiration than to turn the conversation upon an absent friend, especially one so open to criticism as Petrovitsch. The only question was what tone should be assumed in speaking of him. Annele and her mother had already opened their mouths when a warning look from the landlord silenced them. The doctor began to praise the absent uncle. He only put on a rough exterior, said his apologist, to hide his kind heart. "Petrovitsch," he continued, turning to Lenz and the schoolmaster, "is like the coals which once were trees; they have rich warmth within, and so has Petrovitsch." The schoolmaster smiled assent, Lenz looked embarrassed, and the landlord growled. "Petrovitsch likes music," said the doctor's eldest daughter, "and no one who likes music can be hard-hearted." Lenz nodded approvingly, and Annele gave a gracious smile. The landlady was not to be outdone. It was she who had turned the conversation upon this fertile subject, and she was not going to let it be appropriated by others. She praised Petrovitsch's cleverness, and hinted that she possessed his entire confidence, which naturally suggested her cleverness also in appreciating this sage as the rest of the world could not. Annele, too, must bring her offering of praise. Petrovitsch was so neat, she said; he wore such fine linen and made such good jokes. A crumb even fell to Bubby's share from this rich feast of compliments. Annele described Petrovitsch as the perfect model of a kind, true family friend,--almost a saint, in fact. He wanted nothing finally but a pair of wings to become an angel outright.

The visit came to an end at last. The schoolmaster escorted the doctor's daughters, and Lenz joined the doctor, who was walking behind.

"I have a question to ask you, doctor," said he, "but you must not seek to know my reason for asking."

"What may it be?"

"I want to know what kind of a plant Edelweiss is."

"Don't you know, Amanda?" asked the doctor.

"It is an alpine plant," answered Amanda, blushing, "that is said to grow on the line of perpetual snow,--in fact, under the snow. I never saw a living specimen of it."

"I believe you, child," replied the doctor, smiling; "only the boldest alpine goatherds and hunters venture to pick the hardy little plant from its native soil. The possession of one is a proof of unusual daring. It is a peculiar plant of delicate construction, and containing very little sap, so that it can be preserved a long while, like our everlasting. The blossom is surrounded by white velvety leaves, and even the stem has a down upon it. I can show you the plant if you will come to my house. The Latin name is *Leontopodium alpinum*, which means Alpine lion's-foot. I don't know where the German name comes from, but it is certainly prettier than the Latin."

Lenz expressed his thanks, and took leave of the doctor and his family, who continued down the mountain.

The landlady lingered in the kitchen with Franzl after the rest had gone. She could not find words to express her admiration of the old woman's neatness and orderliness. "You are like a mother in the house," she said with her magpie laugh, as Pilgrim called it; "Lenz ought to hold you in great honor, and confide everything to you. He should have no secret from you."

"He does not; that is--only one."

"So there is one! May I know what it is?"

"I don't know myself. When he came home from his mother's funeral, he rummaged in the chest that the mistress would never let any one have the key of; and when I called him, he pushed to the door and rummaged awhile longer, locking everything up again tight. Whenever he goes out now he always tries the lid, to see that it is fast locked. Yet he is not naturally suspicious."

The landlady cleared her throat and gave utterance to another little magpie laugh. The old mistress must have laid by a stocking full of gold, she thought; who knows how much? "Come and see me," she said, condescendingly; "come whenever you like. If you should want anything, do not fail to come to me for it. I should never forgive you if you were to apply to any one else. Your brother often comes to us with his wares; have you any message for him?"

"Yes; I should think he might come up and see me sometimes."

"Be sure I will tell him so, and if he has not time to come so far, I will send for you to come down. We have a great many Knuslingers at our house, and very sensible people they are; at least I like to talk with them better than with any one else. If the Knuslingers were only rich, they would be famous the country round. We often speak of you, and your townspeople like to hear of the esteem in which you are held."

When the landlady paused for breath, Franzl gazed at her with rapture, and would gladly have supplied her with her own, had she had any to spare; but hers too was exhausted. She could only lay her hand on her heart; to speak was quite out of her power. What a change had come over the kitchen! Merry Knuslingen faces seemed to be laughing from all the pots and pans; the shining copper kettles turned into drums and began to play; the tin funnels blew a blast, and the beautiful white coffee-pot stuck its arms akimbo and danced just like her godmother, the old burgomaster's wife: oh, it has danced itself off its feet! Franzl seized the excitable coffee-pot just in time to save it from falling.

"Good by, Franzl," concluded the landlady, rising. "It does one good to chat with an old friend. I enjoy myself far better with you than in the doctor's parlor, with his affected daughters, who can do nothing but play the piano and make up faces. Good by, Franzl."

The musical clock played no sweeter melodies than were sounding in Franzl's heart at this moment. She could have sung and danced for joy. She looked at the fire and smiled, and then turned again to the kitchen window to watch the landlady's retreating figure. What a fine woman she is, the first in the whole town, and yet she called herself your good old friend! While Franzl was laying the cloth, she stole a glance at herself in the glass, as a maiden might who is returning from her first ball. So looks Franzl, the best friend of the landlady of the Lion. She could not taste a morsel of the good things she had provided; she was satisfied,--more than satisfied.

CHAPTER XII
GOOD WISHES, AND A FAIR
START ON THE JOURNEY

Now it is ready, said Lenz to himself, casting a last look upon his work before taking it to pieces; God bless you! The various parts were carried down separately into the valley; the great carved case in a barrow, there being no carriage-road to Lenz's house.

The two enemies, Petrovitsch and Pilgrim, met at the wagon on which Lenz was standing, packing together the detached pieces, each of which, in its turn, was carefully wrapped in a stout covering.

On one side stood Petrovitsch. "I know the man and the house," he said, "that your work is going to. One of my best friends lives in Odessa. Your clock will be in capital hands. Why don't you go with it and set it up yourself in Odessa? You would get half a dozen more orders."

"I have a new order already," answered Lenz.

"Lenz," said Pilgrim on the other side of the wagon; "let us go a little way with The Magic Flute; we can be back in good season this evening."

"I am willing. I could not work to-day, at any rate."

As the wagon, followed by the two friends, was passing the Lion inn, Annele looked out of the window and cried, "Good luck to you!"

The young men thanked her.

A still pleasanter greeting awaited them at the doctor's. The servant-maid ran out and laid a wreath of flowers on the wagon.

"Who sends it?" asked Pilgrim, for Lenz was mute with astonishment.

"My young mistress," answered the girl, and disappeared into the house.

The two friends looked up at the window and saluted, but saw no one. A few minutes afterwards they heard The Magic Flute played from the doctor's parlor.

"It is a grand family, that of the doctor's," said Pilgrim. "I never know my own mind so little as when I ask myself which one of them all is the best. My favorite is the old mayoress. The neighborhood ought to sign a petition to God that she might live forever. Now that your mother is gone, she is the last one left of that generation of dignified, motherly old ladies. But the granddaughters are fine women too. Amanda will make just such a grandmother as the old mayoress, one of these days."

Lenz was silent, and remained so during the whole walk to the city. But there, when the wagon had gone on, and the friends were sitting over their wine, he recovered his spirits, and felt, as he said, that he was beginning life anew.

"Now you must marry," was again Pilgrim's verdict. "There are two choices open to you; one is to marry a woman of thorough education,--one of the doctor's daughters, for instance. You can have one, if you will, and I advise you to take Amanda. It is a pity she cannot sing, like Bertha, but she is good and true. She will honor you, if you honor her, and will appreciate your art." Lenz looked down into his glass, and Pilgrim continued: "Or you will make your home comfortable by marrying an honest peasant, the bailiff's daughter Katharine. As Franzl says, the girl would jump to get you, and she would make a good, economical housewife. You would have half a dozen stout children tearing down the landlord's pine-trees behind your house, and you would grow a rich man. But, in that case, you must expect no sympathy from your wife in your art or in any of your great plans. You can have which you like, but you must decide. If your mind is made up, send me to which you will. I rejoice already in my dignity as suitor. I will even put on a white neckcloth, if necessary. Can the power of friendship go further?"

Lenz still looked down into his glass. Pilgrim's alternative excluded Annele. After a long pause, he said: "I should like to be for once in a great city, that I might hear such a piece of music as The Magic Flute played by a full orchestra over and over again. I am sure my pieces could be made to sound much better than they do. I am haunted by the idea of a tone I cannot produce. People may praise me as much as they like, but I know my pieces have not the right sound. I am sure of it, and yet I cannot make them better. There is something squeaking, dry, harsh about them, like the sounds made by a deaf and dumb person, which are like words, but yet are not words. If I could only bring out the right tone! I know it, I hear it, but I cannot produce it."

"I understand; I feel just so myself. I am conscious of a color, a picture which I ought to be able to paint. I seem on the point of seizing and fixing it, but I shall die without succeeding. That is our fate, yours and mine. You will never produce your ideal. It cannot be otherwise. Bellows and wheels cannot take the place of human breath and human hands; they bring tones from a flute and a violin which your machinery never can. It must be so. Come, let us empty our glasses and be off."

They finished their wine, and went merrily homeward through the autumn night, singing all sorts of songs, and, when they were tired of singing, varying their music by whistling. At Pilgrim's house they parted. Lenz's way led him past the Lion inn; and, as he saw it was still lighted, and heard a sound of voices within, he entered.

"I am glad you are come," said Annele, giving him her hand; "I was thinking you must be as lonely at home, now that your clock is gone, as you were when your mother died."

"Not quite that, but something like it. Ah! Annele, people may praise my work as much as they like, I know it is not what it should be. But one thing I may say of myself without conceit,--I do know how to hear music, and to hear music aright is something."

Annele stared at him. Know how to hear music! Indeed, what art is there in that? Any one can hear music who has ears, and does not plug them up! Still, she fancied that Lenz must have some hidden meaning. Experience had taught her, that, when a man wants to bring out an idea of which his mind is full, his first utterances are apt to be rather disconnected; so she threw another wondering glance at Lenz, and said, "To be sure, that is something."

"You know what I mean," cried Lenz, delighted.

"Yes, but I cannot express it."

"That is just it; neither can I. When I come to that I am a wretched bungler. I never regularly learned music; I cannot play the violin or piano; but when I see the notes, I hear exactly what the composer meant to say. I cannot interpret music, but I can hear it."

"That is well said," chimed in Annele. "I shall remember that as long as I live. To interpret music and to hear it are two different things. You show me so clearly what I have always felt, and yet never could express."

Lenz drank in the good wine, the kind words, and the kind looks of Annele, and went on: "Especially with Mozart; I hear him, and I think I hear him right. If I could but once in my life have shaken hands with him! If he had lived in my day, it seems to me I should have died of grief at his death; but, now that he is in heaven, I should like to do him some service. At other times, I think it is fortunate I cannot play any instrument, for I never could have learned to render music as I hear it. The hearing is a natural gift, for which I have to thank God. My grandfather is said to have had a wonderful understanding of music. If my playing were necessarily below my hearing and my conception, I should want to tear my ears out."

"That is the way with me," said Annele. "I like to hear music, but am too unskilful a performer. When one has to be busy about the house, and cannot devote much time to practising, there is no use in trying to play. I have given up the piano altogether, much to my father's vexation, for he spared no pains to have all his children taught; but I think what cannot be done thoroughly had better not be done at all. Your musical clocks are meant for people like me, who like to hear music, but cannot make it. If I were master here, I should never allow your greatest work to go to Russia, but should buy it myself. It ought to stand in the public room to entertain the guests. It would bring you in ever so many orders there. Since I was up at your house, I have had constantly running in my head that beautiful melody, 'Das klinget so herrlich, das klinget so schön!'"

Beautiful and brave were the melodies playing in Lenz's heart. He tried to explain to Annele how the notes might be followed exactly, all the pins be put in the right places, and even the time in certain passages changed, and yet, unless the man himself felt the music, he would make nothing but a hurdy-gurdy, after all. The piano passages must be taken slower, the forte faster. A performer would naturally render them so; he could hardly help being more subdued at the piano passages and more animated at the forte. The same effect must be wrought by the pins; but the hurrying and slackening needs to be very slight. In the forte passages especial care is needed; for in them the works necessarily labor and are retarded, so that they have to be, in some way, favored. "I cannot tell you, Annele," he concluded, "how happy my art, my work, makes me. As Pilgrim says, I sit there in my room, and set up pieces lively or solemn, which play themselves, and make happy hundreds and hundreds of people that I never saw."

Annele listened intelligently to the end. "You deserve to be happy," she said, when he had finished. "Your beautiful words show me how beautiful your work is. Thank you very much for explaining it to me so thoroughly. Some people would be jealous if they knew you talked so to me."

Lenz passed his hand across his brow as she spoke, and said, "Annele, may I ask you a question?"

"Yes, I will tell you anything."

"Don't be angry with me, but is it true that you are as good as engaged to the engineer?"

Edelweiss A Story | 69

"Thank you for asking me so plainly. There is my hand upon it, there is no word of truth in the story; nothing has ever passed between us."

Lenz held her hand firmly, and said, "Permit me one question more."

"Ask what you will, you shall have an honest answer."

"Why is your manner towards me so different when Pilgrim is here? Has anything ever passed between you and him?"

"May this wine be poison to me, if I do not speak the truth," replied Annele, seizing Lenz's glass, and putting her lips to it, in spite of his assuring her there was no need to swear; that he could not bear oaths. "If all men were like you," she continued, "there would be no need of oaths. Pilgrim and I are always teasing and bantering each other, but he does not really understand me; and, when you are by, I cannot endure his jesting and nonsense. But now I must ask you a favor. If you want to know anything about me, no matter what, ask no one but myself. Promise me; give me your hand on it!"

They grasped each other's hand.

"I am a landlord's daughter," continued Annele, sadly. "I am not so fortunate as other girls, who do not have to receive every one that comes, and laugh and talk with him. I carry the thing through as well as I can, but am not always what I seem. I know I may say this to you. I might often be depressed; but the only way is to put on a bold face, and laugh sadness away."

"I should never have imagined you could have a sad thought pass through your mind. I fancied you as merry as a bird the whole day long."

"I like better to be merry," answered Annele, with a sudden change of tone and expression. "I like nothing sad, not even sad music. 'Das klinget so herrlich, das klinget so schön!' that is a merry tune to jump and dance to."

The conversation returned to the subject of music, and the clock that had been sent off that day. Lenz liked to tell of his having accompanied The Magic Flute through part of its long journey, and how he wanted to call out to every porter and driver and sailor on the way: "Take care! pity you cannot hear what you have got packed up there."

Lenz had never before been the last guest in the inn. He could not make up his mind to get up and go home. The great clock in the public room struck the hour noisily and admonishingly, the weights rattled angrily, but Lenz did not hear. The landlord was the only other person in the room, his wife having long since gone to bed. He left his seat at the adjoining table, where he had been reading the paper, and signed to Annele to put up her work. She could not have understood him, for she went on talking eagerly. He put out his light with a clatter, but even that failed to rouse the pair. He walked up and down the room in his creaking boots; Lenz paid no attention. Never before had the landlord's presence been thus ignored. He struck his repeater; Lenz gave no heed. At last--for mine host was not accustomed to put restraint upon himself for any man--he spoke: "Lenz, if you mean to spend the night here, I will show you a room."

Lenz roused himself, shook hands with Annele, and would have liked to do the same with the landlord; but that was too great a liberty to take unless invited. Revolving many thoughts in his mind, he left the house, and silently took his way homeward.

CHAPTER XIII
LION, FOX, AND MAGPIE

In the early winter, as in the early spring, the Morgenhalde was the pleasantest place in the whole country. Old Lenz was right in saying that the morning sun lay on his house and meadow all day long. But little fire was needed half the day. Flowers blossomed in the garden behind the house long after they had disappeared everywhere else, and put out their leaves again in the spring, when everything else was bare. This garden was as sheltered as a room, and in it grew, what was rare in those parts, a chestnut-tree, which attracted many an unwelcome squirrel and nutpecker from the neighboring forest. The house protected the garden on one side without keeping from it the sun after ten o'clock; and the mighty forest which covered the upper part of the steep mountain seemed to take special pleasure in both house and garden, and had stationed two of its tallest pines as sentinels at the gate.

Had there been many promenaders in the town, they certainly, in these first chilly winter months, would have often taken the path up the meadow, past Lenz's house into the wood, and returned along the mountain ridge. But there was only one promenader, or rather there were only two, in the town,--Petrovitsch and his dog Bubby. Every day before dinner Petrovitsch got up an appetite by walking through the meadow, past the house, and over the ridge of the mountain. Bubby doubled and trebled the distance by leaping back and forth across the gullies which to the right of Lenz's house the water had channelled down into the valley. The gullies were dry at this season, but served in spring and summer to carry off the rushing water. Petrovitsch was very loving towards his dog, and in moments of special affection would call him Sonny. The old man had come home rich from his foreign journeyings. His neighbors naturally estimated his property at three times its actual value, but it was really considerable. The longing for home which the inhabitants of the mountains and of Upper Germany never outgrow had brought him, in his old age, back to his native valley, where he lived, after his fashion, a contented life. His happiest time was in midsummer, when the merchants from all quarters of the world assembled at the Lion, and all the tongues of the earth were spoken there,--Spanish,

Italian, English, Russian, and Dutch,--while in the midst of them, from the very same men, would be heard good Black Forest German. Then was Petrovitsch a person of consequence, and great was his pride at being able to show off his knowledge of Spanish and Russian. Whereas in ordinary times he always left the Lion punctually at an appointed hour, then he would spend whole days there, staying sometimes even into the night. And when the market was over he stayed behind, and amused himself with calculating how far on their way such and such merchants were who had gone to the Lower Danube.

Petrovitsch kept the whole country in suspense. It was generally understood, though he had not said so, that he meant to found a great charitable institution for the neighborhood. Every room of the great house he had built for himself had a stove in it, signifying, according to the common report, which he neither denied nor confirmed, that he designed the building as a home for invalid workmen. Lenz, his only heir, was left in uncertainty also; for it was naturally taken for granted that a considerable part of the fortune would be left to him. Lenz himself, however, counted not much upon it. He paid his uncle all proper respect, but was man enough to take care of himself. He bade his apprentice keep always in good order the path where his uncle liked to walk, without any reference having been made to the attention on either side. The cackling of Lenz's hens and geese, and the barking of a dog, were the signal every noon of his uncle's approach. He nodded to him through the window where he sat at work. His uncle returned the greeting and passed on. Neither ever entered the house of the other.

One day the old man remained standing before the window. Bubby seemed to guess his thoughts; for whereas he was usually contented with driving Lenz's geese, cackling, behind the garden fence, and then returning in triumph to his master, to-day he pursued them through the garden and even into the house, where, however, they found a sufficient protector in Franzl. Petrovitsch administered a stern rebuke to his dog, and went on, thinking to himself, It is Lenz's place to come to me, there is no use in my troubling myself about him. As soon as a man begins to trouble himself about his neighbors there is an end of his comfort. He has to keep wondering whether they will do this or whether they will do that. I desire to be thankful I have nobody's business to mind but my own. But still he could not help questioning, What is this matter about the forest? Yesterday at dinner the landlady had taken a seat by him, and, after talking of a variety of subjects, had quite unexpectedly launched forth into praises of Petrovitsch's habit of taking a daily walk. It kept him in good health, she said; he might live to be a hundred, in fact had every appearance of it. She heartily wished he might; he had had a hard time in life and deserved some amends for it. Petrovitsch was wise enough to know that there was something behind this unwonted friendliness. He attributed it, perhaps not unjustly, to her having designs upon his nephew. She said nothing about that, however, but once more turned the conversation upon his daily walk, and said what a good thing it would be for him to buy of her husband the beautiful Spannreuter forest by the Morgenhalde. To be sure he would be sorry to sell it; indeed, she did not know whether he would consent to sell at all, but she should like to give Petrovitsch the gratification of walking every day in his own wood. Petrovitsch thanked her for her exceedingly delicate attention, but ended the matter by saying he liked quite as well to walk in another man's forest; in fact, rather better, because then it did not vex him to see persons stealing the wood, and to lose one's temper before dinner was bad for the digestion. The landlady smiled intelligently, and replied that no one could have a bright idea without Petrovitsch's having a brighter. Petrovitsch again made his acknowledgments, and the two were as sweet to each other as possible, much sweeter than the lump of sugar that Petrovitsch pocketed from dessert.

The thought passed through the old man's mind that the forest would be a good purchase for Lenz to make, he furnishing the means; for the landlord would ask him too high a price for it. That was what he wanted to tell his nephew, when he remembered his noble principle of not troubling himself about other men's concerns, and he desisted. He had done too much already in busying his head in the matter. He noticed that the ascent was more difficult to-day than usual; so much for thinking when you are going up a mountain; you should do nothing but breathe. "Here, you stupid fellow!" he called to Bubby, who was grubbing after a mole when a good cooked dinner was preparing for him; "what is a mole to you? let him dig!" The dog obeyed, and walked close at his master's side. "Back!" ordered Petrovitsch again, and with the dog put all unnecessary thoughts behind him. He would know nothing; his tranquillity must be undisturbed.

The old man found the family at the Lion out of temper. The landlord was in great wrath at hearing from his wife that she had offered the forest to Petrovitsch, who had refused it. "Now the report will get abroad that I am in want of money," he complained.

"Well, you said you wanted money," retorted his wife, pouting.

"I don't need you to do my business for me. I shall sell no paper at the exchange to-day!" he exclaimed in an unusually loud tone just as Petrovitsch was entering. The old man gave a knowing smile and thought to himself, You would not boast so loud if you were not in want of money.

Just as dinner was ready, the post-boy brought in a number of letters, some marked "Important." The landlord signed a receipt, but sat down to table without opening them, loudly repeating what he had often said before, "I read no letters before dinner. Whether they are good or bad they spoil one's appetite. I am not going to have my comfort disturbed by the railroads."

A wicked scoffer, sitting at another table, refused the due tribute of admiration to this piece of wisdom, and profanely thought, There is a locomotive running about in your body, put as good a face on the matter as you will. This scoffer, it is needless to say, was Petrovitsch.

After dinner Pilgrim walked several times past Petrovitsch's table with the evident desire of stopping at it. Four eyes looked at him wonderingly. Bubby, sitting in his master's lap, stared and growled as if he scented a beggar, while Petrovitsch's occasional glance up from his paper said plainly: What is he after? He has not a forest to sell too,--has he? None, certainly, but the one on his head, if he does not owe for that.

Pilgrim frequently passed his hand through his long lank hair, but found thereby no approach to Petrovitsch, who, so far from encouraging him, got up now, paid his score, and departed. Pilgrim hurried after him. "A couple of words with you, if you please, Mr. Lenz," he said, when he overtook him in the street.

"Good day; that is just a couple of words."

"I want nothing for myself, Mr. Lenz; but I consider it my duty--"

"Your duties are nothing to me."

"Imagine that some one else is speaking my words. So that you hear them, the rest is nothing."

"I am not curious."

"It concerns your nephew Lenz."

"I knew that."

"Yet more; you may make his happiness for life."

"Every man must make that for himself."

"It would only cost you a walk to the doctor's."

"Is Lenz ill?"

"No. The state of the case is this: he ought to marry and wants to marry. Now the best wife for him is the doctor's daughter Amanda, as I am convinced, after thinking the matter over on all sides. But he lacks the necessary courage. He thinks, too,-he has not told me so, but I am sure of it,--that he is not rich enough. Now, if the uncle makes the proposal, and thereby promises--"

"So? I knew it would come to that. If my brother's son wants a wife, let him get her himself. I am an old bachelor, and don't understand such things."

"If his friends do not exert themselves, Amanda will marry some one else. I know that an apothecary is paying his addresses to her."

"Good! she would be just the wife for him. I am not the disposer of the world."

"But if your nephew should foolishly get into trouble in some other quarter?"

"He must get out the best way he can."

"Mr. Lenz, you are not as hard-hearted as you set up for being."

"I am not setting at all, I am going. Good day, Mr. Pilgrim." And go he did. Pilgrim drew his breath hard as he looked after him, but presently turned homeward. In this gloomy weather, with no ray of sunshine, he could at least be grinding his colors for brighter days.

CHAPTER XIV
PRESSES AND EYES ARE OPENED

"Good day, Franzl! So you let us have a look at you at last! That is right; I am glad to see you." Thus was Franzl greeted by the landlady, as she entered the public room.

"I beg your pardon," stammered Franzl; "did you not send for me? My brother was said to be here."

The landlady knew nothing of any message having been sent. The brother had been there, indeed, but had left a long while ago. She had given the servant orders to notify Franzl when occasion offered, but knew nothing about today.

Franzl begged pardon for intruding, and was anxious to go back at once, feeling herself quite out of place. This mood suited the landlady exactly. The stupid servant-woman must suspect nothing, but esteem herself highly favored by having a few moments devoted to her. It was better to put her a thousand thanks in debt than owe her one. Franzl must stay, since she had come, and must wait a few minutes in the family sitting-room until the busy mistress was at leisure. The poor woman did not venture to sit down, but remained standing at the door, staring at the great clothes-presses that reached up to the ceiling.

"At last I have despatched everything," said the landlady, entering, and smoothing her gown; "and now I will have a good hour with an old friend,--the best possession in the world, after all."

Franzl felt highly flattered. She was made to sit down by the landlady, close to her on the sofa, while a servant-maid handed coffee and cakes. She put on all the airs of modesty that the occasion required, perhaps a few more; such as insisting upon turning into the landlady's cup the cream the latter had already poured into hers, until the hostess was obliged to tell her she should be angry if she stood so much upon ceremony.

At the second cup, Franzl began to tell how things looked on the Morgenhalde. Lenz worked as hard, she said, as if there was not a crumb of bread in the house, and yet there were abundant stores of all kinds. He scarcely ever went from home, except to see Faller, whose house he was helping to fit up. He had signed a security for the purchase of the house in the first place, and now he had contributed a bed, besides giving the old woman his mother's Sunday clothes. If some one did not come soon, and take his keys, he would give away everything he owned. But for himself he was as economical as could be. He neither smoked nor took snuff, nor drank, nor played; he spent nothing at all on himself, concluded Franzl, approvingly.

After the landlady had again bestowed fitting commendations on the Knuslingers, who knew everything, she added incidentally: "Only think, Franzl, of this report that your young master is to marry the doctor's botanical daughter! Is there any truth in it?"

"Yes, indeed."

"So?"

"That is, I mean, there is no truth at all in it. Pilgrim tried to persuade him to, but he would not; and I believe there has been a quarrel in consequence."

"So? That is a different matter. I always said that Lenz knew his own mind. He would do far better to follow your advice and marry the bailiff's Katharine."

"Do you hear that?" said Franzl, triumphantly, smiling and nodding her head as if Lenz were standing before her. "Do you hear that? The wise landlady of the Lion agrees with me. And here you thought she would be too rough for you; that nothing could be made of her. I will tell him you advise him to marry Katharine. That will be a help to me. I have been wishing to find some one on my side."

"No, Franzl; God forbid! You must not speak a word of me at home. Besides, he is quite right; Katharine would not be suitable for a man so refined as he. He should have a superior woman, one above the common run."

"Yes; but where is such a one to be found?"

"Good day, Franzl," said Annele, suddenly entering. "I am glad to see you once more in our house. Don't get up. You look, as you sit there, like the well-to-do mistress of some great farm, and you know as much as if you were. But finish your coffee; it is growing cold. Is it sweet enough?"

"Oh, too sweet!"

Annele's words acted like whole sugar-loaves upon it.

"I wish I could stay and hear you talk, but I must go back to the public room. One of us is needed there. Come again soon, won't you? and let me have something of you."

"Oh, what a dear, dear girl!" exclaimed Franzl in praise of the departing Annele. "She must make you a perfect heaven upon earth."

"We have our cares too. She is our last child; if she were only well provided for!"

Franzl opened her eyes wide, and gave a vacant smile, but did not venture to say a word. The landlady tapped her finger on her nose with her magpie laugh, at which Franzl considered it her duty to laugh too. She knew what were proper manners at a coffee lunch. Put a Knuslinger where you will, he will always do the right thing. The landlady now, with all her cleverness, did not seem to know what the right thing was.

"Do you like to see nice linen, Franzl?"

"O my heart! it is the one thing I delight in. If I were rich, I would have seven chests of the finest linen. The weight-maker's wife in Knuslingen has--"

"See there," said the landlady, opening the folding-doors of a great clothes-press and showing packages of linen in dozens, piled up to the ceiling, each tied with a bright-colored ribbon.

"Is that for the hotel?" asked Franzl, when her first exclamations of admiration were over.

"Heaven forbid! that is my Annele's dowry. As soon as my daughters were seven years old I began to put by their wedding outfit, for you never can tell how suddenly it may be needed. Then it is finished, and there is no further need of weaver or seamstress. I only wish the dowry of one of my daughters might remain in the town. It would be pleasant, too, to keep one child near us. Thank Heaven, all my children are well married,--more than well; but seeing their prosperity is better than hearing of it."

A sudden revelation broke upon Franzl's mind. The press with its wealth of linen danced before her eyes, and the blue, red, green, and yellow ribbons melted together into a rainbow. "O dear landlady, may I speak? I beg a thousand pardons if I am presuming, but--O dear Heaven, where such linen is how much else there must be! How would it do--might I say it?--if my Lenz--?"

"I have nothing to say. I am the mother, and my child is well known; you can easily inquire about her. You understand? I think--I don't know--"

"Oh, that is enough, quite enough! I fly home; I have borne him in my arms, I will bear him again hither. But there will be no need, he will leap over the house-tops. I am but a poor silly thing, dear landlady; don't be angry with me."

"You silly? You can draw one's inmost thoughts out of one. You are wiser than the seven wise men. But look you, Franzl, this is all between ourselves; between two trusty friends. I have said nothing; you have made your own discoveries. My husband naturally looks higher; but I should like to keep one child near me, God willing. I tell you honestly--for I know not how to speak falsely or to take back my word--that I do not reject your proposal."

"That is enough. I will show that we Knuslingers do not bear the name for nothing."

"What do you mean?"

"Ho, ho!" cried Franzl in a decided tone, and putting on a knowing look. "You will soon see. I shall take his tools away from him and drive him out of the house. He must be here this very day. You will help him out,--won't you? for he is shy with strangers."

The landlady soothed the excited Franzl, who in her enthusiasm alternately got up and sat down, raised her hands to heaven and folded them upon her breast. She advised her to show her wisdom by betraying to Lenz in no possible way that Annele's mother favored his cause; and further enjoined upon her, as the best means of success, to throw out warnings against every one else, while Annele's name should be scarcely mentioned. "Such matters should be delicately handled," concluded she. "'You must not point your finger at the lightning,' as the old proverb runs."

Franzl was always going, and never went. When at last she had the handle of the door in her hand, her lingering glance at the great linen-press said as plainly as words: We shall soon have you at our house. To every piece of household goods she nodded: You are ours now, and it is I who make you so. Then home she went in the keen autumn wind, as if every sheet and tablecloth had become a sail to waft her up the mountain.

"Mother," said Annele from behind the sideboard, "why do you tow that stupid old cow into the house? If anything comes of it, we shall have to pay court to her or else she will be crying out against our ingratitude. What is your great hurry?"

"Don't make believe you are ignorant of how matters stand. It is necessary and right that you should be soon provided for."

"I am not making believe, for I really know nothing. A little while ago you would not hear of Lenz; why have you changed your mind?"

The mother looked at her in amazement. Could the girl be really ignorant of their household affairs?

"Circumstances have changed," she answered, simply; "Lenz is alone now, and has a well-furnished house. I would never give you to a mother-in-law." Be false with me, she thought, as she left the room, and I will be false to you.

At the Morgenhalde Franzl went about with a smile on her face. Smilingly she abused all the girls of the village; the doctor's daughters, the bailiff's Katharine, every one but Annele. Her she did not mention, but threw out misterious hints about mountains of linen and persons who were of the right sort. Lenz thought the old woman's loneliness was beginning to affect her mind. She went quietly about her duties, however, and was merrier than ever. Lenz, too, grew daily more contented over his work, and a long time passed without his going into the town.

CHAPTER XV
YOUNG HEARTS AFTER A WEDDING

Lenz sat at home and worked untiringly. By great good fortune the weight-maker of Knuslingen had found a purchaser for the smaller work, which was nearly finished. He worked at its completion with real pleasure, and at the same time set things in train for beginning the new clock that the landlord had as good as ordered. He often thought, as he sat working so happily: What need have I of marrying? In fact, I ought not to marry. My head and heart are so full of my art, there is no room left in them for wife and children.

Pilgrim had resumed his former pet project of devising some new patterns of clock-cases, and devoted all his evenings to it, as he could not spare the time from his working-hours. Thus the friends met but seldom, especially as Lenz no longer went to the rehearsals of the Liederkranz.

Faller's marriage at length induced him to come down into the village. The good fellow gave the author of his happiness no peace until he consented, in spite of his mourning, to go to the church. The services at the house were very quiet, with neither guests nor music; for, as the bridegroom said, he would wait and invite his guests when he had some money, and music he could make for himself.

At the house Lenz had to submit to the warmest praises and thanks for all he had done. "If you are married soon," said the old dame,--"as God grant you may be,--I will wear your mother's clothes to church. I am not ashamed to wear them; on the contrary, it is an honor, as every one tells me."

"And I have a good bed," said Faller, his deep voice sounding almost ludicrous with emotion. "O Lenz, I hardly pray for myself to-day; I pray the Lord God for you. May he keep you from danger; but, if you ever do fall into great peril, may I be the one to rescue you! I long to turn round to the congregation in church and say, 'Behold, by God's help I stand here; but he helped me through my friend, on whom and on whose parents in heaven I pray the Lord's blessing.' You must be happy yourself, Lenz, for you have made a whole household happy."

The strong, resolute Faller fell to twirling his formidable mustache; he could say no more. Lenz was almost more an object of respect at the house than the young couple themselves, and was relieved when the party adjourned to the church.

The Liederkranz was there, and sang beautifully, though perceptibly weakened by the absence of the two best voices, Faller's and Lenz's. The whole village--certainly all the women, married and single--were present at the wedding. The married were glad to hear the solemn service read again, and the unmarried tried to imagine how it would seem when their turn came, as they hoped it soon would. The matrons wept, while the maidens cast curious glances about the church. If Lenz had looked up, he would have found himself the centre of many eyes. He separated from the bridal party after the ceremony and took his lonely way homeward. At the churchyard gate stood Katharine, the bailiff's daughter, with a nice-looking young man, dressed like one of the peasants from the neighboring valley. She greeted Lenz as he passed, and blushed under his earnest gaze. The next moment he raised his hat politely to the doctor's eldest daughters, who were picking their way through the wet streets, showing their pretty laced boots.

"We thought you had gone on a journey," said Bertha, the bolder of the two sisters.

"No, I have been all the time at home," answered Lenz.

"So have we," retorted Bertha. Lenz was silent.

"Are you engaged upon any new work?" asked Amanda.

"On a new and an old one too. Our work never ceases."

"Is not such constant labor a severe strain upon you?" Amanda asked again.

"Oh no; I don't know what I should do without it."

"You clockmakers," said Bertha, archly, "are like your clocks, always wound up."

"And you are a key to wind us up," replied Lenz, inconsiderately. It was not what he had meant to say; but the right words would not come.

"I am glad you pay her back in her own coin, Mr. Lenz," said Amanda. "Our ways part here; we must say good by."

"Perhaps Mr. Lenz is going in our direction," ventured Bertha. "Were you not going to Pilgrim's?"

Lenz felt his heart beat. He wanted to say yes; he wanted to say he was going to Pilgrim's; but involuntarily, almost in fear and trembling, he said, "No, I am going home. Good by!"

"Good by!"

Lenz breathed hard as he went up the hill. He would turn back; who knows what might come of it? He could still overtake them; they were at the Lion by this time; now they must be at the churchyard wall. But all the while he kept steadily on, and, reaching home with a beating heart, fled as for safety into the house. Fled? from what? He knew not what. He was not himself to-day; he was uneasy and dissatisfied as he had never been before.

In the evening he changed his dress and went into the village, meaning to call on Pilgrim or the doctor, who had long ago invited him. Pilgrim was not at home, and he stood long at the doctor's door without daring to pull the bell. He walked up and down before the house, hoping that perhaps the doctor would come out, recognize him, and invite him in; but neither he nor any of his family appeared. Don Bastian came down the road. Like a thief who hears the pursuer on his track, Lenz fled to the village. There he felt easier, and rejoiced to see a house door standing open. In the Lion he would find refuge. At least one quiet place was left in the world,--a place where there were chairs to sit down on, and tables to eat at, and persons who did not make his heart beat as if it would burst his bosom, but were calm and quiet; and here comes the calmest and quietest of them all and gives him a kindly welcome.

CHAPTER XVI
A HEART OPENS

The landlord's manner was truly fatherly, as he sat down by Lenz and entered into conversation with him. "Have you received the money for your musical clock?" he asked, incidentally.

"Yes," replied Lenz.

"You would do well to invest in the new railway; it will pay handsomely. Have you the money still idle?"

"No; I had eight hundred florins by me, and have lent three thousand to my neighbor, the bailiff, to pay his discharge."

"Have you good security? How much interest does he pay?"

"I have only his receipt. He pays five per cent."

"The bailiff is good, and five per cent is good; but, as I say, if you should want to make any investments, I shall be glad to help you with my counsel."

"I like to keep to what I understand; though, of course, I should be perfectly safe in following your advice blindfold. The new work you are to buy of me is progressing finely, and I think will be better than the first."

"Remember, Lenz, I made no promises. A man of honor goes no farther--"

"You have said quite enough. Your word I shall never--"

"As I say, plainness and accuracy should be observed among friends. I would have inscribed upon my gravestone, 'Here lies an accurate man.'"

Lenz was delighted with such solidity of character; here, at least, was pure gold.

"By your leave," said Annele, approaching, and taking a seat at the table with Lenz and her father. The landlord soon rose and left the young people to themselves. "You have reason to be proud of such a father, Annele," said Lenz; "what a man he is! it does one good to talk with him. He says but little, and for that very reason every word is--how shall I call it?--pure kernel, pure marrow."

"Nothing is pleasanter for a child than to hear such praise of a father," answered Annele. "Mine certainly deserves it. He is a grumbler, to be sure, and hard to please, as all men are."

"All men?" inquired Lenz.

"Yes, all. I may say so honestly to you; for you are one of the best of them, though you have your crotchets, too, no doubt. We need to be patient with all of you."

"That is right, Annele. Thank you for speaking so; I do not mean for your praises of me, which are quite undeserved. I cannot tell you how often I am angry with myself. I am always doing the wrong thing. I only half hear and half act because of the tunes that are running in my head. I seem clumsier than other men, and yet am not really so. I am hasty, too, and troubled by things that others make light of. I cannot help it, the devil knows. My mother often said to me, 'Lenz, in spite of all your goodness, you will not make a woman happy unless she thoroughly understands and loves you.' That is true patience and true love,--is it not?--to think, 'oh well, he is hot and hasty just this minute, but I know his heart is right.' Do not draw your hand away, Annele."

In the warmth of his speaking he had taken Annele's hand in his own, as he first perceived by the motion she made to release it. "We are not alone in the room," she said, blushing, and pressing her knitting-needle to her lips; "there are others present."

Lenz turned hot and cold in a moment. "Forgive me, Annele. I did not know what I was doing. I did not mean to be importunate. You are not angry with me,--are you?

"Angry? how can you ask me?"

"But friendly in your heart to me?"

"For Heaven's sake!" said, Annele, laying her hand on the back of Lenz's chair; "don't speak so. How did it all happen? what does it mean? I thought I might speak to you as to a brother; for, alas! I have no other."

"And I have no sister, no one."

"But every one is fond of you."

"Yet, if I need a friend, I have, none."

There was a long pause.

"Do you know," said Annele at length, "that the bailiff's daughter Katharine is engaged to a young fellow from the next valley? They have just, sent for the betrothal wine."

"So?" said Lenz. "I saw her standing with some one to-day, as I came from church. She is a good, honest girl. I wish her all happiness. Were you at the wedding in the church to-day, Annele?"

"Yes, and I saw you there. You deserve to go to heaven for your kindness to Faller?"

"Heaven is easily won then. How well the minister preached, did he not? There was some good lesson for every one, married or single. The word of God is like music. Every hearer, though there should be hundreds and hundreds of them, takes the whole without robbing his neighbor."

"I assure you, I would almost rather hear you than the minister. Every word you speak is so clear, so--I hardly know how to tell what I mean. I sometimes think it is a pity you are only a clockmaker."

"Only a clockmaker? I am glad I am a clockmaker; it is a noble calling. I could preach you a sermon upon it. The world is a clock, wound up by God from everlasting to everlasting. The stars circle in the heavens, one about another. There are no clocks in Paradise, Pilgrim says. That may be; but from the hour when men had to labor they had to divide the time. Just think, we should be like children and fools if we could not tell the hours!"

"You make all so clear to me! I never thought of that before."

Lenz grew more eloquent under this praise.

"I shall hold fast to my trade of clockmaker. If I can do no better, I will make the old-fashioned wooden clocks; they will at least secure me bread. Musical clocks bring in more money, to be sure, but they can only be made when ordered; and, as lovers of music do not turn up every day, I might find myself with nothing in my pocket. My pet project is to form a clockmaker's union, so that all could work together for the benefit of each. If I could but accomplish that, I would engage to make nothing but standard regulators for the next seven years,--for all the rest of my life, if need be."

"You are very good, I am sure," said Annele; "but your specialty is music."

"Ah, music! when I leave clocks and get back to that I am so happy, so--"

"Your heart dances for joy and keeps high holiday."

"Dear Annele, you are so--ah! if I only knew--"

"Well? what would you know?" There was a warmth, a tenderness, in the simple words that brought the hot blood to his face.

"I cannot tell," he stammered. "If you do not know, I cannot tell you. I am--Annele--"

"Children, what are you about? The whole room is looking at you," broke in the landlady. "I can perfectly trust you, Lenz; if you have anything so very special to say to Annele, I will have a lamp lighted in the private sitting-room, and you can have your talk out there."

"Oh no, mother," cried Annele, trembling; but the landlady was already gone. Annele flew after her. Lenz sat motionless, while the whole room swam before his eyes. He got up at length, stole out, saw the door of the sitting-room open, and was alone with Annele. She hid her face.

"Look at me," he entreated; "look at me while I speak to you. Annele, I am but a foolish, simple fellow; but--" he pressed his hand to his heart, hardly able to go on--"but if you think me worth it, you can make me happy."

"You are worth more than the whole world; you are too good; you do not know how bad the world is."

"The world is not bad, for you are in it. Answer me; answer me truly: Will you stand by me? will you help me to be industrious and good? will you be mother, wife, all to me? Say yes, and my whole life shall be yours."

"Yes, a thousand and a thousand times yes!" She fell upon his breast, and he held her fast.

"Mother, O my mother!" cried Lenz, as the landlady appeared. "Dear landlady, forgive me!" he added, apologetically.

"You have nothing to fear from me," returned the landlady. "But, children, I must beg one thing. Annele can tell you I have always been a good friend to you. 'Lenz must prosper,' I have always said, 'for his mother's blessing rests upon him.' But I pray you, children, to act with caution. You do not know my husband. He so worships his children that he is angry with every man that tries to take them from him. Thank God, we shall keep one near us, if it be his will. They will not all grow to be such strangers." Here the landlady wept bitterly, but after a vigorous wiping of her eyes and nose was able to continue. "For the present my husband must observe nothing. I will break the matter to him first, and let you know, Lenz, when you may regularly lay your suit before him. Till that time you must not enter the house. Bring your uncle with you to the betrothal. It will be showing him no more than proper respect to allow him to take your father's place. All my other daughters were received into large families with all the ceremony that is observed in the highest circles. God gave me no son, Lenz, and I rejoice that I am to find one in you. I am fond of my other sons-in-law, but they are too fine, too aristocratic for me. It is time now for you to go, Lenz. My husband may come any minute, and I would not answer for the consequences. Yet no; stop a moment. Take this. Give him this, Annele." She opened both doors of the great linen-press, and took out a gold coin. "Your godfather, our blessed minister, laid this in your cradle. It is an old medal, just the thing for you to give Lenz. But you must give her a present first."

"I have nothing to give. Oh yes, here is my watch, Annele. My dear father made it himself in Switzerland, and gave it to my mother. When we are married, please God, I will give you something else of my mother's that will please you. Here, take the watch. It has lain next my heart. Would I could take out my heart, and lay it in your faithful hand!"

They exchanged pledges. "Very good," explained the mother, who thought it her duty to say something. "A heart and a watch; they resemble one another, and love is the key that winds them up." She smiled at her own cleverness, since no one else did. "See," she continued, after rummaging in the chest, "this was the first little frock my Annele wore, and these were her shoes." Lenz looked with rapture at these mementos of her childhood, and begged permission to keep them, which was granted. "Now you must really go, Lenz," said the landlady, returning to her old theme. "I cannot let you stay. Go this way through the kitchen. There is my hand. Good night, Lenz!"

"May not Annele go a little way with me?"

"By no means. Don't be offended if I am somewhat strict. I have brought up three daughters, and take pride in the thought that no word of blame has ever rested on either of them. God willing, you can have enough of each other by and by, in all honor and with the parents' knowledge."

"Good night, Lenz!"

"Good night, Annele!"

"Once more, good night!"

"Good night, my heart's treasure!"

"Good night, dear Lenz! pleasant dreams!"

"The same to you a thousand-fold!"

"That will do, that will do!" admonished the landlady, laughing.

Lenz stood in the street. The whole world turned round with him. The stars in heaven danced. Annele--Annele of the Lion--was his! He hurried homewards; he must tell Franzl, who always praised Annele so warmly. How she will rejoice! If I could only shout it out from house to house! He checked himself, however, when he had almost reached his door. He must not tell Franzl; nothing was certain yet, and she could not keep a secret. But he must tell some one. He retraced his steps, and remained long standing before the Lion. To-night he must stand a stranger there; to-morrow he would be one of the family. He tore himself away at last, and went in search of Pilgrim.

CHAPTER XVII
A FRIEND'S WARNING

Thank God, he is at home! there is a light in his room. He is playing the guitar. O dear good Pilgrim!

May heaven keep me in my senses, and let me not die of joy! Oh, if my good mother had but lived to see this day!

Pilgrim was playing and singing so loud as not to hear him as he ascended the stairs. Lenz threw open the door, and, spreading out his arms, exclaimed, "Rejoice with me, brother; I am so happy!"

"What is the matter?"

"I am betrothed."

"You are? To whom?"

"How can you ask? to her, to the truest heart in all the world, and as wise and bright as the day. O Annele!"

"What! Annele? Annele of the Lion?"

"You wonder at her taking me, do you not? I know I am not worthy of her, but I will deserve her. God is my witness, I will deserve her. I will devote my life to her; she shall--"

His eyes fell upon his mother's picture. "Mother, dearest mother!" he cried, "in thy place in the seventh heaven rejoice, for thy son is happy!"

He fell upon his knees, and tears choked his voice. Pilgrim laid his hand on his shoulder. "Forgive me, dear Pilgrim,--forgive me," prayed Lenz, rising; "would I could beg the whole world's forgiveness! I have often resolved to be a stronger, firmer man. Now I shall have a wife who deserves a manly husband. But this once I must give way. I have been wishing, as I came here, that some hard task might be imposed upon me,--no matter what, only something, something so difficult it would take my whole heart and strength;--I would do it; I would prove myself worthy of the happiness God has granted me."

"Hush, hush! other men have got other women before now. There is no need to tear the world to pieces about it."

"If my mother had but lived to know this!"

"If your mother had lived, Annele would not have had you. It is only because you are without encumbrances, without a mother, that she cares for you."

"Say not that, Pilgrim! she so reveres my mother!"

"It is easy to revere her when she is no longer here. I tell you, you were nothing to Annele till your mother died."

"You have not even wished me happiness."

"I wish you happiness! I wish you all happiness!"

"Why do you say it twice? Tell me why twice?"

"Only because the words came out so."

"No, you had a meaning in them."

"True, I had. I will tell you to-morrow, not to-night."

"Why to-morrow? tell me now; you shall not hide anything from me."

"You are drunken now; how can I speak soberly with you?"

"I am not drunken; I am perfectly sober."

"Good; tell me, then, how this all happened so suddenly."

"I cannot tell. It came upon me like a flash from heaven, and now I see it had long been the one wish of my heart."

"I thought so; and yet I thought, too, you would do nothing without letting me know."

"Neither will I. You shall go with me to her father to-morrow. I have not yet laid my suit before him."

"Not yet? Thank Heaven! Then I hope it may come to nothing."

"What! would you drive me mad?"

"No need of that. Lenz, she is not yet your betrothed; she is not yet your wife; there is still time for me to speak openly. It would be wrong to draw back now, but it would be only one wrong. If you marry Annele, you will be doing a thousand wrongs your life long. Lenz, she is no wife for you,--she least of any."

"You do not know her, only joking with her as you do. But I have learned her through and through,--her goodness, her cleverness."

"You think I do not know her? Why, I have eaten a bushel of salt with those people. I can describe them every one to you. Annele and her mother are so much alike they cannot bear one another, though they do pretend to be so fond in public. They exchange sweet speeches, because the guests eat and drink better when pleasant sounds are going on. But none of their soft words come from the heart. They have no heart. I never believed, till I knew them, that there could be such persons. They talk of kindness, of love, of pity, of patriotism too, perhaps, and religion; but these things are empty words to them, meaning nothing, prompting them to nothing. The world, they firmly believe, has agreed to use the names for effect, without any one attaching the least significance to them. Annele has not a ray of heart; and without heart I maintain there can be no right understanding. She can never enter into another's feelings and opinions; can neither share them nor yield to them. She can, like her mother, catch another person's words, and make a fine show with them. They both have a peculiar faculty of blaming, even scolding, in such a way that you cannot make out to the end whether it is a declaration of love or of war. Father, mother, and daughter make nice music together for the public edification. Annele plays first fiddle, the old woman second, and mine host a growling bass. He, I must say, is the only honest one in the house. Here, as everywhere, the female bees are the ones that sting, and how they sting! The landlord speaks charitably of his neighbors, and cannot bear to hear his wife and daughter abuse them. Their special delight is to tear to pieces the good name of wife or maid. The mother does it with a certain hypocritical compassion, but Annele plays with the world like a cat with a mouse; and the burden of the song always must be, you are the fairest, the healthiest, the cleverest, and, if it is any compliment, the best. I have often studied to make out what constitutes the essence of ill-breeding, which may be highly polished to the eye. True coarseness is pleasure in the misfortunes of others. O Lenz, you have not the key-note of that household; all your knowledge of music will not help you find it. It is nothing but mocking and lies. These people will never understand you, your wants and your tastes. I tell you, only he that is of the truth can understand and love the truth. You will be always a stranger to them."

"I am ashamed of you, Pilgrim. You are saying these things of persons whose house you have entered daily for eight years, at whose table you eat, and with whom you are apparently on friendly terms. What must I think of you?"

"That I go to an inn, eat, drink, and pay my money. I pay daily, and am done with them daily."

"I cannot understand you."

"I believe you. I have had to pay dear for my knowledge, and would rather have remained ignorant, like you. It is not pleasant to know people as they are. Yet the world has some--"

"And you think yourself one of the good ones?"

"Not exactly that. I thought you would turn against me. I must bear it. Abuse me, do with me what you will, cut my hand off,--I will gladly beg, if I may know that thus I have saved a man like you. Give up Annele, I entreat you. You have not asked her yet of her father. You are not bound."

"Those are the tricks your knowledge of the world teaches you,--are they? I am not so clever as you; I never travelled abroad, as you have; but I know what is right. I have betrothed myself to Annele in the presence of her mother, and I will keep my word. God grant I may receive her from her father! I tell you, for the last time, I did not ask your advice. I am quite able to act for myself."

"I shall rejoice with all my heart if I have been mistaken. But no; Lenz, for Heaven's sake, be persuaded! There is still time. You cannot say I have ever dissuaded you from marrying."

"No."

"You were born to be a husband. I was a fool not to urge you more strongly to marry one of the doctor's daughters."

"Do you think I would have gone to them, and said, 'My guardian, Pilgrim, sends his compliments, and says I am to marry one of you,-- Amanda, if I can'? No: they are too fine ladies for me."

"They are, indeed, fine ladies, while Annele only acts the fine lady. Because the doctor's daughters are not on familiar terms with all the world, you thought it would be difficult to become intimate with them. It was easier with Annele. Oh, I see it all. Annele talked with you of your grief, as she knows how to talk of every thing, and that opened your heart. Annele has in every gown a pocketful of small coin. Her heart is such a pocket, from which she brings out change for every guest."

"Pilgrim, you are doing a wrong, a great wrong!" cried Lenz, his lips trembling with sorrow and anger. To convince his friend how sincere and true-hearted Annele was, he told him her words after the death of his mother and after the departure of his great work. Every one had been to him a revelation.

"My pennies! my coppers!" cried Pilgrim. "My poor coppers! She robbed a beggar-man to get her pennies! O fool, cursed fool that I was! All she said, every word, she stole from me. She is like a corkscrew for getting things out of one. I was fool enough to say those very words to her. It serves me right. Yet how could I think she would trap you with them? O my poor pennies!" The two friends sat long in silence. Pilgrim bit his lips till they bled. Lenz shook his head, doubtingly. "Do you know Annele's chief motive for taking you?" resumed Pilgrim at length. "It was not your tall figure, not your good heart, not even your money. Those were minor considerations. Her chief delight is that the doctor's daughter did not get you. He is not yours, but mine. You cannot understand a character like Annele's, to whom no pleasure, no happiness is complete that does not wound another; whose greatest triumph is to imagine another's vexation at seeing her so handsome, so rich, so happy. I did not believe there were such persons till I knew Annele. Brother, seek not to know her better; it would be your ruin. Why do you look so at me? why don't you speak? Break out at me, do what you will, do with me what you will, only give up Annele; she is poison! I pray you give up Annele! Think,--I have forgotten the crowning argument of all,--think, and God grant you may not think too late! I desire to be no prophet of evil--Annele cannot grow old."

"Ha, ha! now you would try to make her out sickly. She is sound to the core. Her complexion is of milk and roses."

"Not that; I do not mean that. Was there ever a woman whom it did one more good to be with than with your mother? And why? Because her heart shone in her face, her kindliness towards all men, her joy and care that they should be happy; that makes an old face beautiful, and all who look upon it blessed. But Annele! when she has no more hair to braid into a crown, and no more red cheeks, and no more white teeth to show when she laughs, what is left? She has nothing to grow old; no soul in her body, only pretty phrases; no true heart, no honest intelligence, only a spirit of mockery. When she grows old, she will be no better than the devil's grandmother."

Lenz pressed his lips hard between his teeth. "It is enough, more than enough," he said at last; "not another word. One thing, however, I have a right to demand,--that as you have spoken to me you speak to no one else, no one, and never to me after this day. Only these four walls have heard you. I love my Annele,--and--and--I love you, too, in spite of your jealousy. I no longer desire you to go with me when I ask for her hand. Good night, Pilgrim!"

"Good night, Lenz!"

CHAPTER XVIII
UNSPOKEN LOVE AND A BETROTHAL

Lenz was gone, Pilgrim sat long alone, gazing at the light and twirling his sandy beard. He was angry with himself. He had said everything,--too much, in fact,--and defeated his own ends. There was nothing to take back, all was true; but of what use had it been? He walked restlessly up and down his room, then sat down again and stared at the light. How strange life is! How few men work out the fate they were meant for! The young will not believe it. They scold their elders for grumbling, and then make botchery of their own lives. The world is all right; only we must not expect to have everything our own way.

There was a deep, hidden life in Pilgrim. Ten years ago he had gone abroad with a courage ready to conquer the world, and a silent happiness in his heart that needed the assurance of no pledge or spoken word. He loved Amanda, and the doctor's beautiful daughter had inclined to him like a princess; like a goddess she had stooped to him. During his holidays she let him help her in her garden work by copying the names of her foreign plants in his neatest hand from a book on the little wooden tallies which together they stuck into the ground to mark the different specimens. She was an angel of mercy to the poor forsaken boy, and even when he grew towards manhood he was frequently allowed to assist her. Always the same gentleness he found in her. Her every look was a blessing. When he passed the garden for the last time, on setting out upon his lonely journey, she shook hands with him over the garden fence, and said, "I have a whole album to remember you by in the little slips you wrote the foreign names on. If, where you are going, you find these foreign plants in their native soil, you must let them remind you of our garden and the household that is so fond of you. Good by, and come safe back!"

"Good by, and come safe back!" those words followed him over mountain and valley, over seas and through distant lands. The name of Amanda was shouted exultantly through many a foreign clime, and many an echo repeated "Amanda."

Pilgrim wanted to grow rich, to become a great artist, and win Amanda. He came home poor and in tatters. Many received him with cheap taunts, but she said,--she had grown taller and stronger, and her brown eyes beamed,--"Pilgrim, be thankful that you are at least strong and well, and never lose your cheerful courage." And he did keep his happy temper. He learned to love her as he loved the beautiful linden in his neighbor's garden or the stars in heaven. Not even to Amanda was his heart revealed by a word or a sign. Like those precious stones that are said to shine in the darkness like the sun did Pilgrim's secret love for Amanda illumine his life. Often he did not see her for weeks, and, when they met, his bearing was as calm as with a stranger. But he often wondered who would be her husband. For himself he would leave the world without her suspecting what she was to him, but she must be happy. Lenz was the only one whom he could have marry her. He would not grudge her to him, they were so worthy of each other. He would hold their children in his arms, and lavish all his store of songs and jests for their amusement. Now all that was changed, and Lenz stood, as he firmly believed, on the edge of an abyss.

Thus he sat long, gazing at the light. At last he extinguished it, saying, with a sigh and a sad shake of the head, "I could not help myself, neither can I help others."

Lenz, meanwhile, was on his way home. He walked slowly. He was so weary he had to sit awhile on a heap of stones by the roadside. All was dark when he came to the Lion inn. No star was to be seen. The heaven was overcast with clouds. He stood by the inn till the whole building seemed about to fall upon him.

When he reached home, Franzl was asleep. He waked her, that he might have some one to rejoice with him. Pilgrim had strewn all his joy with ashes.

Franzl was enchanted at the news he brought her, and made him smile by repeating for the hundredth time, in order to prove that she also knew but too well what love was, the story of her own "blighted love," as she called it. She always began with tears and ended with complaints, for both of which she had ample reason.

"How pleasant it was then at home, up there in the valley! He was our neighbor's son, good, and industrious, and handsome,--oh, far handsomer than any one nowadays, begging your pardon. But he--I hardly need mention his name, for every one knows it was Anton Striegler--he was bent upon going abroad, and he went abroad on business. There at the brook we said good by. 'Franzl,' he said, 'as long as that brook runs, my heart will be true to you. Keep yours true to me.' He had beautiful ways of talking, and he could write beautifully too. It is always so with those false men. I could not have believed it. I received seventeen letters from him during the first four years,--from France, from England, and from Spain. The letter from England cost in all a crown-piece; for Napoleon would allow no tea or coffee to come into our country, and so the letter, as our curate said, had to go by way of Constantinople through Austria, and, by the time it reached me, cost a whole crown-piece. Since that no letter has come. I waited fourteen years, and then learned that he had married a black woman in Spain. I would have nothing more to do with the base man,--the basest man that ever lived,--and I burned the beautiful letters, the lying letters that he had written me. My love went up the chimney in the smoke."

Franzl always concluded her story with the selfsame words. To-day she had had a good listener,--the best of listeners. He had but one fault, that of not hearing a word she said. His eyes were fixed on her and his thoughts on Annele. Out of gratitude Franzl came at last to speak of her. "I will tell Annele what you are. No one knows you as well as I do. In all your life you never harmed a child; and how good you have always been to me! Don't look so sorrowful. Be merry! I know,--ah, too well I know!--when so great happiness comes to us, we feel crushed under it. But, thank God! you are in earnest; you will stay quietly at home together and bid each other good morning and good night every day that God gives you. And now I must say good night, for it is late."

It was past midnight before Lenz went to bed, and then with a "Good night, Annele! good night, dear heart!" he fell asleep.

He awoke the next morning with a strange weight on his heart. He remembered he had dreamed, and in his dream he stood upon the high mountain ridge behind his house with one foot raised to step off into space.

"I never let a dream trouble me before," he said, and tried to forget it in admiration of his yesterday's gold coin, and of the still greater treasure he possessed in Annele's little shoes and first frock. They were holy relics, to be carefully preserved with those he had received from his mother.

A message came from the landlady that he was to be at the Lion at eleven o'clock. He put on his Sunday clothes and hastened to his uncle Petrovitsch's. After pulling the bell several times he was admitted and received by his uncle in no very amiable mood.

"What do you want so early?"

"Uncle, you are my father's brother--"

"To be sure I am, and when I went abroad I left everything to your father. All I now have I earned for myself."

"I have not come for money, but to ask you to fulfil the office of a father for me."

"How? What?"

"Uncle, Annele of the Lion and I love one another. Her mother knows it and sanctions it. Now I am to ask her of her father, according to the custom, and I want you to go with me as my father's brother."

"So?" said Petrovitsch, putting a lump of white sugar in his mouth and walking up and down the carpeted room.

"So?" he repeated as he faced about. "You will have an energetic wife, and I must say you have good courage. I should not have given you credit for having the courage to take such a wife."

"Courage! What do you mean by that?"

"No harm; but I would not have believed you had the presumption to take such a wife."

"Presumption? What presumption is there in it?"

Petrovitsch smiled, and made no answer.

"You know her, uncle. She is frugal and orderly and comes of an honest house."

"That is not my meaning. It is presumption in you to think that in your solitary house on the Mörgenhalde you can make up to a girl who has spent the twenty-two years of her life in an inn for a room full of flattering guests. It is presumption to want to keep to yourself a woman who can manage a whole hotel full. A wise man does not choose a wife who would consume half his life were he to live as she would have him. It is no trifle to govern such a wife. You had better try to manage four wild horses from the coach-box."

"I do not want to govern her."

"I believe you. But you must either govern or be governed. I will do her the justice to say she is good-natured,--only, however, to those who flatter her or submit to her. She is the sole good one in the house. As for the two old people, they are hypocrites, each in his own way; the woman with much talking, the husband with little. When he speaks he gives it to be understood that every one of his words weighs a pound. You can weigh it if you like. You will find it exact, no atom short. When he puts his foot down to the ground, every step says, 'Here comes a man of honor.' When he takes a fork in his hand, 'So eats a man of honor,' it says. When he looks out of the window, he expects God in heaven to call down to him, 'Good morning, thou man of honor!' And for all that I would bet my head he is in debt for the fork in his hand and the creaking boots on his feet."

"I did not come to hear that, uncle."

"I suppose not."

"I only came to ask you, in all respect, if you would act as my father's representative, and go with me to urge my suit."

"I don't know why I should. You are of age. You did not seek my advice beforehand."

"Excuse me for having asked you."

"Certainly. Stop," he cried, as Lenz turned to go, "a word more." For the first time in his life he laid his hand on his nephew's shoulder. The touch sent a strange thrill through the young man, and still more did the words which Petrovitsch spoke in a voice of deep emotion: "I would not have lived in vain for my own flesh and blood. I will give you that which many a man would have laid down his life to have had before it was too late. Lenz, a man must not drink when he is heated;--he might drink his death. Whoever should strike the glass from his hand at such a moment would be doing him good service. But a man may be heated in other ways, and then he should drink nothing--should do nothing, I mean--which will affect his whole life. He might contract a disease which would be a lingering death to him. You ought not to decide on any marriage yet, even if it were not with Annele. You are heated, excited. Let your present fever pass off, and six months from now think of this matter again. I will make your excuses to the landlord. He and all of them may abuse me as much as they please; it won't hurt me. Will you follow my advice, and give the thing up? You are drinking in a malady that no doctor can cure."

"I am betrothed. There is no use in further words," answered Lenz.

The cold sweat stood upon his brow as he left his uncle's house.

"That is the way with these old bachelors. Their hearts have turned to stone. Pilgrim and my uncle, they are just alike. Much they know about it! Here Pilgrim says no one of them is good for anything except the father, and my uncle says no one is good for anything but Annele. A third will come presently and say no one is good for anything but the landlady. They may say what they like. We need no witness. I am man enough to act for myself. It is time to put an end to this meddling of outsiders in my affairs. One hour more and I shall be firmly established in a good old family."

The hour was not over before he was so established. Neither the warnings of Pilgrim nor his uncle had moved him. One effect they did have.

As he so confidently, with so much pride and firmness, laid his suit before Annele's father, something within him said, "She will understand and thank me for giving way to no opposition." It was not a noble thought.

During the betrothal Annele held her apron to her eyes with one hand, and with the other kept tight hold of Lenz. The landlord walked up and down the room in his creaking new boots. The landlady wept, actually shed tears, as she cried: "O dear Heaven! to have to give up our last child! When I lie down and when I rise up what shall I do without my Annele? I insist, at least, that she shall not be married for a year. Need we tell you that we love you, Lenz, after giving you our last child? If your mother had but lived to see this day! But she will rejoice in heaven above, and will intercede for you at the throne of God."

Lenz could not keep back his tears. If the landlord's boots had creaked displeasure at his wife's words, they creaked still harder now. At length the sound of them ceased, and his voice began: "Enough of this. We are men. Lenz, control yourself and look up! so, that is well. What do you expect for a dowry with your wife?"

"I have never thought about the dowry. Annele is your child; you will not stint her."

"Quite right. We stand by the old proverb, 'So many mouths, so many pounds,'" replied the landlord, and said no more. He had no need to use many words.

Lenz continued: "I am not rich. My art is my chief possession. But, thanks to my parents, all wants are provided for. Nothing is lacking. We have our honest bread, and a little butter with it."

"That is well said, to the point. I like that. Now how about the marriage contract?"

"Nothing about it; the laws of the land provide for that."

"Yes, but a special contract can be made, if desired. You know a widow receives only half the property. She will need to have her portion helped out. If you should die before your wife, and leave no heirs--"

"Father," cried Annele, "if you are going to talk so, you must let me leave the room. I cannot stay and hear you."

Even Lenz changed color. But the landlord went on ruthlessly: "Don't be so silly. That is the way with you women; you can't hear anything said about money. O dear me!--no, not a word! You squirm as if a frog had hopped on your foot. But if there is no money forthcoming, you can clamor for it finely. You have never experienced the want of it, your life long, and I don't mean you ever shall; therefore, in case of life or death--"

"I will hear no more. Is this the joy of a betrothal that I have heard so much of?" remonstrated Annele.

"Your father is right," urged the mother; "be reasonable. It will soon be over, and then you will feel all the merrier."

"Annele is right," said Lenz, with unwonted decision. "We will be married according to the laws of the land, and there is no more to be said about it. Life and death, indeed! It is all life for us now. Your pardon, father and mother; we understand each other perfectly. Every moment now is worth a million? Do you remember the song, Annele?--

"Honor lies not in a golden store,
Shame lies not in poverty;
And so would I had a thousand dollars more,
And had my own true love by me."

Thus singing he was about to dance with Annele out of the room, when her father laid his hand on the young man's shoulder, and in a solemn voice said, "Stop; one word more."

Lenz stood in as much amazement as if a dagger had been put to his lips, instead of the expected kiss. "We have pledged our troth. There is no need of anything further!" cried Annele, remonstratingly.

"We men have still some matters to settle," replied the landlord, decisively. "Yes, let your father speak," said Lenz.

Mine host took off his velvet cap, looked into it, put it on his head again, and began: "Your intentions have been true and honest. If you are laughed at behind your back, you need not mind; and if you are ruined, you are responsible to none but yourself." Here he made a long pause. Lenz looked at him like a man in a dream, and finally asked what he had done, or what he meant to do, that was so dreadful.

"As I say, your intentions are honest and good; that I have always maintained," returned the oracle. "You and Pröbler have made a standard regulator together,--is that what you call it? I don't pay much attention to such things; some work for the common good. You understand, of course, that you can have no further partnership with Pröbler. The name of my son-in-law and that of Pröbler must not be coupled together; so that is settled and done with. Now we come to the main point. You are thinking about establishing an association,--is that what you call it? Whatever you call it, that too must be settled and done with." Here the landlady wanted to interpose, but her husband stamped his foot angrily, and went on: "Let me finish, wife! Lenz, I tell you, this thing must never enter your mind again. You will not think I speak thus from regard to my own interest. I fear no union or association whatever. Even if I did, my interest is now yours. But you will get neither praise nor thanks for it. I know mankind better than you do. If this plan were ever put into execution, your whole property would be sacrificed, and you reduced to beggary. Give me your hand upon it, that from this hour you lay aside all thoughts of this association."

Lenz stood hesitating, his eyes fixed on the ground. "Yes," cried the landlady, "give him your hand. He means well, he means right, by you; his intentions are those of a father towards you; he is your father"; and she nodded approvingly at her husband.

Lenz drew himself up. His face was crimson. "I will not give my hand," said he, with sharp decision. "Rather be it maimed, and unfit to hold a tool for the rest of my life!"

"Do not swear. You said we must not swear," interposed Annele. She seized his hand, and tried to put it into her father's, but he resisted. "Let be," he said, sharply, "let be! I will not abjure my faith; and it would be abjuring my faith to make such a promise. I will not do it, though you should drive me out of this house, where I had hoped to find a home. Landlord, I believe you mean well by me, but every man must follow his own reason. I have no partnership with Pröbler; but, if I had, I am Lenz; I have a right to associate with whom I please. You force me to say what I would rather not have said. I do not dishonor myself; on the contrary, I confer honor on others, and rejoice that it is so. As for this association,--it is called an association, you are quite right in the name,--I have thought it over night and day for years, and should understand it better than you do. You are right in saying there are plenty of fools and knaves who will laugh at me. I know that. But who, since the world began, tried to do it a service and was not laughed at? That does not disturb me. I thank you for your kind concern lest I should sacrifice my property. But I have carried on our entire business, had the whole house in my hands, for more than ten years. I will show you my books. You shall see for yourself if I have made any unlucky ventures. A man does not necessarily ruin himself by investing in a work for the common good. Once for all, the very morning of the day when I can bring about this union I shall put into it whatever portion of my property I judge best. I speak thus plainly to you, because you have spoken plainly to me. I will not give my hand. I am willing to take good advice, but must know best my own concerns. I will not give my hand in pledge of that which you desire, though my highest happiness upon earth depended on it."

Lenz felt a pressure and a shivering at his heart as he spoke, but he spoke sharply and firmly to the end.

"Unclench your fist. Will you not give me your hand? You are a brave man, my own proud, noble Lenz!" cried Annele, and threw herself on his neck, and wept and laughed convulsively.

"I felt it my duty to caution you. Now I wash my hands of the whole concern," said the landlord, somewhat dejectedly.

"Husband," returned his wife, "you have done a good thing, a very good thing. We never knew before what firmness our Lenz possessed. I confess I should never have suspected it in him, but am all the more rejoiced."

Lenz had as much as he could do to soothe Annele, who lay helpless in his arms. He was obliged to make her drink some wine before she would raise herself.

"Now go together into the garden, and I will set out the wine in the arbor," ordered the landlady. She preceded with a bottle and glasses, followed by the lovers in a close embrace.

"A strange being!" said the landlord to himself, as Lenz left the room. "These musicians have an engine constantly on hand. He bawls like a baby at the mention of his mother, the next minute he will sing like a lark, and wind up with a sermon, like an old Anabaptist. But he is a good fellow, after all; and when I win my Brazilian suit, or draw my prize in the lottery, I will pay him his marriage portion the first thing. He shall have it down in hard gold. No one shall get a copper till he has had his share."

With this comforting resolution mine host returned to the public room, where he refreshed himself after his unwonted exertions, and received with dignity the congratulations of friends and strangers. He spoke little, but gave it to be understood that a man in his position could afford to dispense with great riches in a son-in-law. If the man be but sound and honest,-- that was the burden of his remarks, to which all nodded assent. There lay wisdom in a nutshell.

Lenz and Annele meanwhile were sitting in the garden, full of delight, and bestowing on one another the fondest caresses. "I feel as if I had not been at home all this time," said Lenz, "but had been away in foreign countries, and had just returned from a long journey."

"You have been nowhere but at home," answered Annele, "only you have been strongly excited by talking with my father. I cannot tell you how I rejoiced to hear you speak as you did. I wish the whole world could have heard you and learned to honor you. But really you had no need to get into such a heat with my father."

"What do you mean?"

"He was not so much in earnest with his warnings and advice as he seemed. He likes to pretend he can see farther into a millstone than the rest of the world. If he had been in earnest, he would have brought up the matter before the betrothal instead of afterwards. He only wanted to make a show of wisdom before you; but I was glad you proved yourself to be the wiser."

Lenz looked about him at these words as if seeking something half forgotten. As a flock of pigeons in swift flight wheeled at that moment above the heads of the lovers, and threw their transient shadows on the ground; so did a swarm of thoughts that Pilgrim had conjured up pass in still swifter flight, throwing shadows that vanished more swiftly away.

"Others may be wiser, cleverer, and more respected than I, for aught I care," answered Lenz, "but no man in the world shall love his wife more tenderly and truly."

CHAPTER XIX
A VISIT TO GARRET AND CELLAR

The first congratulations Annele received were from Faller. She quite looked down on the poor fellow, but was gratified by his deference. He could not make too many apologies for coming so early. His fondness for Lenz would not let him rest till he had paid his respects to her. Lenz had grown to be a part of his very self. He would pour out every drop of blood in his veins to serve him.

"I am glad my bridegroom has such good friends. There is no one, however small, but may be of some service."

Faller did not or would not understand this last thrust, but began to describe in glowing colors Lenz's noble qualities. "Annele," he said in conclusion, with tears in his eyes, "his heart is as pure as an angel's, as a new-born child's. For Heaven's sake never be harsh with him, it would be sinning against the Highest. Remember that every quick word will wound him like the thrust of a dagger. His temper is not hasty, but he lays every little thing too much to heart. Don't be offended with me for speaking so to you; it is for your good. I would so gladly serve him in some way, if I only might. You are favored of Heaven in having such a husband. He is a man whose presence and word all respect. No one can reproach him with a single wrong action in his whole life. Be gentle with him,--kind and gentle."

"Have you done?" asked Annele, her eyes flashing, "or have you more to say?"

"No."

"Then I have something to say to you. You have been most insolent. You deserve to be turned out of the house this moment. What do you mean by taking such a liberty? Who asked you to be mediator between us? What business have you to suppose I shall be unkind? But I am glad to have found you out in season. I see now what a set of beggarly hangers-on my Lenz has. I shall make a clean sweep of them every one. You shall have no more chance to drain his substance with your pretty speeches. I make you a present of the wine you have drunk. Now you may go. But I shall let my Lenz know of your impertinence. It shall be recorded against you. Good by!"

Faller's protestations, asseverations, prayers, entreaties, were all in vain. Annele showed him the door, and he had to go; nor did she vouchsafe to cast a glance after him.

Soon after Faller came Franzl, radiant with happiness, and was taken at once by the mother into the private sitting-room. Franzl was full of self-congratulations at having brought about this happy result, and assured the landlady that now she could die content. But she injured her cause by claiming more credit than was her due, and so got none. She was soon made conscious of her mistake. "What are you talking of, Franzl? You had nothing at all to do with the matter, nor I either. The young people were too sharp for us. Only a few days ago we were discussing the possibility of the match, and they had settled it behind our backs long before. I might have suspected my Annele of such doings, but never Lenz. However, it is better so. It is the work of Heaven, and we will be thankful."

Franzl stood open-mouthed and open-eyed; but no more did she get to put into her mouth than she could have held in her eye. Empty she had to go home, and with scarcely a word from Annele, for, just as she was leaving, Pilgrim entered.

Annele did not venture to treat Pilgrim in the same way she had Faller. She knew he did not like her, and therefore, without giving him a chance to speak, at once began thanking him for his kindly interest. He treated the matter in his usual good-natured, joking way, at the same time protesting that no one was to be trusted, for Lenz had not confided a syllable to him beforehand. Thus he satisfied his conscience, and yet said nothing to disturb what he could not prevent.

There was one more tough knot to saw in Petrovitsch, which had to be left to the father to deal with. Petrovitsch took his place at table as if nothing had happened. The landlord officially announced the engagement to him, adding that Lenz would appear in a minute, as he was coming to dinner. Annele was extremely childlike and respectful to the old man. She almost went so far as to kneel, and ask his blessing. He shook hands with her kindly. The landlady, too, insisted on shaking hands with him, but received only his two left hand fingers. Most happy was Lenz, when he came, to find everything so amicably settled. The one drawback to his pleasure was having Pilgrim at table, after the language he had used the night before. But even that feeling passed off at last, under the influence of Pilgrim's perfect self-possession.

The skies frowned upon Lenz's betrothal. It rained incessantly for days. An ugly drizzle kept on all the time, like a monstrous talker, who never comes to a period. Lenz naturally spent much of his time at the Lion, which was so comfortably arranged that he could either be as retired as in a private house, or could sit in a "market-place with a fire in it," as he once called the large public room, with its sixteen tables. "That is capital," said Annele; "I must repeat that to my father. He enjoys a good joke."

"It is not worth while. If I say it to you, that is quite enough. Don't let it go further."

Lenz went up and down the long, and now almost impassable, footway between the Morgenhalde and the Lion as if he were only stepping from one room into another. All who met him, men and women, stopped and congratulated. "You look as if you had grown taller since your engagement," some would say. Lenz's bearing had, in fact, been more erect and proud of late than ever before. He smiled when persons said to him, "You stand high in the market, for the sort of wife a man gets is the test of his worth." "Without meaning to intrude upon others' concerns, I must say I never supposed Annele would remain in the village. It was always said she would marry a hotel-keeper in Baden-Baden, or the engineer. You may laugh, for you are a precious lucky fellow."

Lenz took no offence at being thought the lesser of the two; but, on the contrary, was proud of Annele's modesty in choosing him. He could not help saying sometimes, when he was sitting with her and her mother in their private room, the old man looking in occasionally, and growling out some of his pithy sentences: "Thank Heaven for once more giving me parents, and such parents! I have started life afresh. It seems incredible that I should be actually at home in the Lion inn. How grand it looked to my childish eyes when the upper story was added and plate-glass put in all the windows! We children used to think the castle at Karlsruhe could not be more magnificent. I remember seeing the golden lion hung out too. What should I have thought then to be told I should one day have a home in that castle? It is hard my mother could not have lived to see this day."

His sincerity really touched the two women, though Annele had all the while kept on counting the stitches of the embroidered slipper she was working for her lover. They said nothing for some time. At last the mother began: "What pleasant relatives you will find, too, in my other sons-in-law! I have told you how fond I am of them, though they are not the same to me that you are. I have known you since you were a baby. You are almost as near to me as if I had nursed you at my own bosom. But you know what refined, aristocratic gentlemen they are, and good business men into the bargain. Many men would be lucky if their whole property equalled what my sons-in-law make in a year."

"If this stupid rain would only stop!" said Annele, after a pause. "Do you know, Lenz, we will have the horses harnessed the moment it does, and take a drive together."

"I shall be glad to be with you once under God's broad heaven. The house is too narrow to contain my happiness."

"We will drive to the city,--won't we?"

"Wherever you like. I am glad my Magic Flute is so well protected. It would be a shame to have any harm come to it."

"You carry your feeling too far," remonstrated the mother. "The thing is sold. The risk now is with the purchaser."

"No, mother, you don't understand my Lenz. He is right. What he has made takes such deep hold of his heart that he would like always to keep a protecting hand upon it. We cannot bear to have a thing injured that we have cared for day and night for months."

"My own dear Annele!" cried Lenz, enchanted at this beautiful expression of her quick, intelligent sympathy.

"There is no use talking with you lovers," replied the mother, with pretended amiability; "unless one is in love himself, he can say nothing to please you." She went to and fro about the house, for Lenz had requested that Annele might be excused from attendance in the public room, at least for a few days. "Not that I am at all jealous," he assured her, "but I begrudge every look you bestow on any one but me. All are mine now."

One day towards noon the rain held up for about an hour, and Lenz teased Annele to go up to his house with him. "Everything is waiting for you there," he urged; "all the kettles and cupboards, and other things, too, that you will take pleasure in."

Annele resisted long, but at last consented to go if her mother would. Contrary to her expectation the mother was soon ready. Every person they met on their way through the village saluted. Hardly, however, had they gone a hundred steps before Annele began to complain: "O Lenz! what a horrid path! I sink in at every step. You must have it put in better order. And do you know you ought to have a road made up the mountain, so that carriages can drive to the door. Sister Babette's husband had a private road broken through the fields to his house."

"I could hardly do that," answered Lenz; "it would cost a great deal of money, besides my having to buy the field. See, my meadow does not begin till that hazel hedge, and our business requires no carriage-road. You know

I would do anything in my power to please you, Annele,--don't you?--but that is impossible."

Annele plodded on, without returning any answer. "Why need you have made such a talk about it?" whispered the mother in his ear. "If you had only said, 'Very well, dear Annele, we will think of it,' or something of that sort, you could have done as you pleased afterwards. She is a child, and children must be treated to pretty words. You can do what you will with her if you only set the right way to work. Don't weigh every word she says and make a great matter of it; let a subject rest over for a day or so, till you see the right moment is come for settling it. She will think it out for herself, or else forget it. She is only a child."

"Annele is not a child," contradicted Lenz, looking in displeased surprise at her mother; "I can talk over everything with her. There is nothing she does not understand."

The mother shrugged her shoulders. "As you please," she said, sulkily.

About half-way up the meadow Annele broke out again: "Good Heavens, what a journey! I had no idea it was so far. It will be a perfect eternity before we get up there."

"I cannot make the way any shorter," answered Lenz, sharply. Annele turned and looked at him searchingly. "I am sure," he added, in some confusion, "you will rejoice one day that the walk is so long, for it shows what a good large meadow we own. I could pasture three cows here, if it were worth while."

Annele gave a forced laugh. The house was reached at last, and she drew a long breath, complaining of being so hot and tired.

"In God's name, welcome home!" said Lenz, grasping her hand on the threshold. She stared at him as if he were speaking a foreign language, then suddenly exclaimed, "You are a dear good fellow. You manage to bring good out of everything."

Lenz was content, and Franzl's joy knew no bounds. First the mother shook hands with her and then Annele, while both praised the neatness of passage-way, kitchen, and sitting-room.

"I shall find it hard to get used to these low rooms," said Annele, stretching up her hand till it nearly touched the ceiling.

"I cannot make the rooms higher. Besides, they are more easily warmed than high ones."

"To be sure. You must remember, Lenz, what a big house I have always lived in. The ceiling seems to be pressing on my head at first; but I sha'n't mind it. Don't be afraid that will disturb me."

Lenz turned round the tool-receiver that hung like a chandelier from the ceiling, and began to explain to Annele the various implements with which it was covered,--the names of the different drills, and the special purpose each was used for. "But you will soon get acquainted with all these things that make up so much of my life. They are my silent work-fellows. Now I will show you our house."

The mother stayed with Franzl in the kitchen, while Lenz took Annele all over the house, showing her the seven beds already stuffed, besides two great bags of feathers from which others could be filled, and opening boxes and chests wherein were stored rich heaps of linen. "What do you say to that, Annele? Aren't you surprised? Did you ever see anything so splendid?"

"It is all very good and in nice order. But, dear me! I won't tell you of all my sister Theresa has, for of course, where there are often sixteen guests in a house, heaps of linen are necessary; they are part of the business. But if you could only see the chests that Babette's mother-in-law has! These are nothing to them."

Lenz turned as pale as death, and could hardly stammer out: "Annele, don't talk in that way, don't be making fun now."

"I am not making fun. I am in sober earnest. Really I am not in the least surprised, for I have seen finer and better linen, and more of it. Do be reasonable, and not expect me to stand on my head at a thing which is all very well, but no way remarkable. I have seen more of the world than you have."

"Very likely," said Lenz, with white lips.

Annele passed her hand over his face, and said jestingly, "What does it matter, dear Lenz, whether your stores astonish me or not? Your mother has done bravely, very bravely, for one in her position; no one can deny that. I do not marry you for your property, dear Lenz, but for yourself. You yourself are what I love."

The apology was both bitter and sweet. Lenz tasted only the bitter. It turned to gall in his mouth.

They returned to the sitting-room, where Franzl had laid out an abundant repast for them.

Annele protested she had no appetite, but upon Lenz remonstrating that it would never do not to eat something when she entered a house for the first time, she consented to take a piece of a crust of bread and ate it languidly.

Lenz had frequently to check Franzl in her lavish praises of himself.

"You must have done some good in the world to deserve such a husband," she said to Annele.

"He must have done some good too," said the mother. She cast a look at her daughter as she spoke, and was checked by an angry frown. He must have done some good, too, to deserve her, Annele thought her mother was going to say.

"Come, Annele, sit here by me," begged Lenz; "you have often said you should like to see how I set up a piece of music, so I have been keeping this till you should be by me. When I have put it all in order, it will play of itself. It is a beautiful piece of Spohr's. I can sing it to you, but not so well as this will play it." He sang the air from Faust, "Love, it is the tender blossom." Annele took a seat beside him, and he began to hammer the pins into the barrel where he had already marked their places from the printed notes. Every pin stood fast at the first blow. Annele was full of admiration, and Lenz worked on in high spirits. He was obliged to ask her not to speak, because the metronome which he had set going required his closest attention.

The mother very well knew that sitting still and idly looking on was hard work for Annele. She therefore rose presently, and said, with a gracious smile, "We all know your great skill; but we must go home now, for it is past noon, and we have visitors. It is quite enough that you have begun the piece while we were here."

Annele rose also, and Lenz stopped his work.

Franzl kept her eyes fixed on Annele and the landlady, and when either of them put her hand in her pocket, she started and hid hers behind her back, as much as to say she wanted nothing, they would have to urge her to accept any present. Now it is surely coming,--a gold chain, or a jewelled ring, or a hundred shining dollars; such people give handsomely.

But no present, great or small, did they give this time, hardly their hand at parting. Franzl went back into the kitchen, seized one of her biggest and oldest pots, and lifted it to throw after the mean, ungrateful women. But she had compassion on the pot. Was such a thing ever heard of? Not even to bring one an apron! Poor, poor Lenz! You have fallen into evil hands. Thank Heaven I had nothing to do with it! It is true I had not, they said so themselves. I want no pay from them, thank Heaven! Every penny would burn into my soul.

Lenz accompanied his bride and her mother to the end of his meadow, and then returned home. It was agreed, that, if the next day was fine, the young people should drive across the country to Sister Babette's. Lenz had many preparations to make, and directions to give his apprentice and journeyman.

It was strange to him to be once more alone. At the end of a couple of hours he wanted to go down to Annele again. There was a weight upon him he could not explain. She could and would relieve him of it. He resisted the temptation, however, and remained at home. Before going to bed he closed the boxes and linen-presses that had been opened in the morning, half expecting, as he did so, to hear some voice, though whose he could not have told. There lay the yarn his mother had wet with her lips and spun with her own hand. A spirit seemed following behind him, and uttering lamentations from every box and press.

Franzl in her chamber was sitting upright in bed, muttering imprecations against the landlady and Annele, and then praying God to give her back the words she should not have spoken, for every ill that befell Annele now fell on Lenz too.

CHAPTER XX
THE FIRST DRIVE

The next morning was the longed-for day. The sun shone joyfully upon the earth, and Lenz's heart grew light again. He sent his apprentice early to Annele to tell her she must be ready for him in an hour. At the end of that time he was dressed in his Sunday clothes, and on his way to the Lion. Annele was not ready. She yielded to his prayers and entreaties so far as to give him her hand through the chamber door, but would not let him see her. She handed him out some red ribbons and cockades, which he was to give to the boy to tie in the whip and about in the harness. After keeping him waiting a long, long time, she appeared, beautifully dressed.

"Is the wagon harnessed?" was her first question.

"No."

"Why did you not see to it? Tell Gregory to put on his postilion's uniform, and take his horn."

"O no! what is the use of that?"

"We have a perfect right to show ourselves before the whole world, without anybody's leave or license. I mean people shall look out when we drive by."

At last they took their places. As they passed the doctor's house, Annele called out: "Blow your horn now, Gregory; blow loud! The doctor's daughters shall look out, and see how we drive together. Look! there is not a soul to be seen. They have shut the window in the corner room. There they are, I know, dying of spite; they will have to tell about us, for I can hear the old mayoress asking, What is that horn-blowing? I should like to be behind the door, and hear it all."

"Annele, you put on strange airs to-day."

"And why not? you please me specially to-day. People are right in praising your eyes. How true and clear they are! I did not know they were so beautiful. You are really a handsome fellow!"

Lenz looked yet handsomer from the glow of pleasure which overspread his face. "I will have some new clothes made in the latest fashion,--shall I not?"

"No, stay as you are. You look much more comfortable and respectable so."

"Not only look so, but am so."

"Are so, to be sure. Don't treat every word as if it were a tooth in a clock-wheel."

"You are quite right."

They drove through the neighboring village.

"Blow, Gregory; blow loud!" commanded Annele. "See, there is where my cousin Ernestine lives. She was our maid a long while, and afterwards married a tailor, who now keeps shop here. She cannot bear me, nor I her. Her green face will turn blue with rage when she sees us drive by without stopping. There she comes to the window. Yes, stare your little pig's eyes out of your head, and open your mouth till you show your bunchy gums! It is I, Annele, and this is my Lenz. Do you see him? How is your appetite now? It is dinner-time. I wish you joy your last year's herring."

She snapped her tongue in triumph as they went by.

"Do you take pleasure in that, Annele?" asked Lenz.

"Why not? It is right that we should show evil to the evil and good to the good."

"I don't think I could."

"Then be thankful you have me. I will make them all crawl into a mouse-hole before us. They shall be grateful for every look we bestow on them."

As they approached the town, Annele gave her bridegroom directions as to his behavior. "If the engineer is here, my brother-in-law's brother, you must be on your dignity with him. He will want to have some fling at you, because he is frightfully cross at my not accepting him. But I don't like him. And if my sister begins her complaints, listen to her tranquilly. It is not worth while trying to comfort her, and does no good either. She lives in gold, and has nothing to do but cry. The truth is, she is not very strong. The rest of us are perfectly healthy, as you can see by me."

The lovers were not successful at their sister's. She was ill in bed, and neither her husband nor his brother was at home. They had both gone down the Rhine on a large raft. "Won't you stay with your sister? I have business to attend to in the town."

"Can't I go with you?"

"No; it is about something for you."

"Then I had certainly better go too. You men don't know how to choose."

"No, I cannot have you," insisted Lenz. He took from under the seat of the wagon a package of considerable size, and set off with it to the town. Babette's house was a little way out of the town, near a great lumber-yard by the brook. Unobserved by Annele, Lenz brought back the same package somewhat enlarged, and restored it to its place under the seat.

"What have you bought me?" asked Annele.

"I will give it to you when we get home."

Annele thought it hard she could not show her beautiful ornaments to her sister, but had already learned there were some things in which Lenz would have his own way in spite of entreaties and remonstrances.

They dined at the hotel. The landlord's son, Annele said, an excellent man, who now kept a great hotel at Baden-Baden, had also been one of her suitors; but she had refused him.

"Why need you have told me?" said Lenz. "I am almost jealous of the past, never of the future, that I promise. I know your truth, Annele, but it pains me to think that others have so much as raised their eyes to you. Let bygones be bygones. We begin our life anew."

Annele's face beamed with unwonted softness as he spoke. A portion of his own purity and candor fell upon her, and made her gentle and loving. She knew not how better to express this new sentiment in her than by saying: "Lenz, you need not have bought me any bridal present. You have no need to do as others do. I am sure of you. There is something better than all the gold chains in the world."

The tears stood in her eyes as she spoke, and Lenz was happier than ever.

The church clock was striking five when they took their places in the wagon and set out for home.

"My dear father made that clock," said Lenz, "and Faller helped him. By the way, that luckily reminds me. Faller says you took offence at some awkward speech of his; he will not tell me what it was. You must forgive him. He is a plain-spoken soldier, and often says awkward things, but he is a good fellow at heart."

"Maybe so. But see here, Lenz, you have too many burrs clinging to you. You must shake them off."

"I shall not give up my friends."

"Heaven forbid that I should ask you to! I only mean you must not let every one get hold of you, and persuade you into everything he likes."

"There you are quite right. That is a weakness of mine, I know. You must warn me whenever you see me in danger, till I am thoroughly cured of it."

At these words, so pleasantly and humbly spoken, Annele suddenly stood up straight in the carriage.

"What is the matter? what is it?" asked Lenz.

"Nothing, nothing. I don't know why I got up. I believe I don't sit quite right. That is better. Does not our carriage ride nicely?"

"Yes, indeed. We sit in an easy-chair, and yet are abroad in the world. It is right pleasant driving. I never before drove in my own carriage, for your father's is the same as mine."

"Certainly."

They passed Pröbler on the road. He stood still as the lovers passed, and saluted repeatedly.

"I should like to take the old man in with us," said Lenz.

"What an absurd idea!" laughed Annele. "Pröbler on a bridal drive!"

"You are right," answered Lenz. "We should not be so cosey all by ourselves here with a third person sitting opposite, seeing and hearing everything. It is not being unkind not to invite anybody to drive with us now. This is a time when we need to be happy all by ourselves. How beautiful it is! The whole world seems to laugh. Pröbler laughed too, and I am sure was not offended. He would understand that I could not give away a second of this hour."

Annele answered with a searching look, then cast her eyes down, and silently clasped her bridegroom's hand. Their first drive had not begun as merrily as they had expected, but both came home with a peculiar joy in their heart. Annele said little. A new experience was passing within her. It was still broad daylight when Lenz helped her out of the wagon at the door of the Lion, and left her to go up the steps alone, he following with the carefully covered parcel which he took from under the carriage-seat. He called her into the sitting-room, and there solved the mystery by saying: "Annele, I give you with this the best and dearest possession I have. My good Pilgrim painted it for me, and it shall be yours."

Annele stared at the picture for which Lenz had so mysteriously provided the gilt frame in the city.

"You cannot find words to describe the look my mother turns upon you,--can you?"

"So that is your mother? I see her gown and her neckerchief and her hood; but your mother! it might just as well be the carpenter's Annelise or Faller's old mother. In fact, it looks rather more like old Mrs. Faller. Why do you look so pale, as if you had not a drop of blood left in your cheeks? Dear Lenz, can I say what is untrue? You surely do not wish that. What fault is it of yours? Pilgrim is no artist. He can't paint anything but his church-towers."

"It is like losing my mother over again to hear you speak so," said Lenz.

"Don't be so sad," prayed Annele, tenderly. "I will honor the picture. I will hang it up at once over my bed. You are not sad now,--are you? You have been so kind and good to-day! I assure you, the picture will help me recall your mother whenever I look at it."

Lenz turned hot and cold by turns. Thus could Annele at her pleasure raise him to the highest happiness or wound him in his tenderest affections. Weeks and months passed in this way. Joy predominated, however, for a softness had come over Annele never known in her before. Even Pilgrim said one day to Lenz: "Most men are glad to be proved in the right, but I rejoice to see I was mistaken."

"So? In what?"

"There is no learning a woman. Annele has that in her which may make your life happy. Very likely it is all the better she should not be as dreamy and soft-hearted as you are."

"Thank you. Heaven be praised for bringing this to pass!" cried Lenz.

The two friends held each other long and closely by the hand.

CHAPTER XXI
A GREAT WEDDING WHICH LEAVES
A BITTER TASTE BEHIND

Lenz of the Morgenhalde is to be married! This is the wedding day of Annele of the Lion! Through the whole valley and far beyond its limits this was the one subject of conversation. The same household talked at one time of Annele only, and then only of Lenz. Their names had not yet been joined together. Not till the wedding was fairly over would Annele of the Lion be called Annele Lenz.

The day was clear after a heavy fall of snow, and the sleighing excellent. The jingling of bells and cracking of whips sounded from every hill and valley. At least a hundred sleighs stood before the Lion inn on the wedding morning. Strange horses were quartered in every stall. Many a solitary cow was startled by a visit from a span of noble horses. It is not for the like of a poor cow, shut up in her solitary winter quarters, to know what is going on in the world; that privilege is reserved for men. Such an event was indeed seldom witnessed in the village. Even the sick old grandmothers who lived on side streets, where they could see nothing and hear nothing but the whips and the sleigh-bells, insisted on being dressed and set up at the window.

Ernestine, the shopkeeper's wife, had been at the Lion for days beforehand helping on the preparations. This was no time to be sensitive at not having been visited or specially invited. The great house entertains, and the vassals must come of themselves.

Ernestine had left her children in charge of a neighbor and her husband to see to the house, tend the shop, and do his own cooking while she was away. When the Lion calls, no other duties must be regarded.

She knew all the arrangements of the house, and could put her hand on whatever was wanted. She presided over kitchen and cellar, enjoying her importance. The dressing of Annele, too, on the wedding morning, fell to her share, as there was no more intimate friend to claim the right.

The Lion showed that day what a wide circle of friends and patrons it had. The whole first-floor, running the entire width of the house, was turned into a single hall. The partition walls, which were nothing but boards, were taken down, so that the space was now really a great market-place with a fire in it.

Lenz would naturally have preferred a quiet wedding, but Annele was quite right in arranging otherwise. "I know what you would like," she said; "but we have no right to deprive our acquaintances of their good time. Besides, we are only married once in a lifetime. These people give us trouble enough the year through, we ought to let them have a chance to show their gratitude. Where is there a wedding anywhere about that we don't carry presents? Two thousand florins is the least we have spent in that way. Now let them give us a share. I ask no favors, only to be paid back a portion of what is owed us."

The wedding presents were, indeed, rich and abundant, both in money and in money's worth. Two days had to be given up to the marriage festivities,--one for neighbors and relations, the second for more distant acquaintances.

Pilgrim appeared at Lenz's house, on the wedding morning, with well-sleeked hair, and a bunch of rosemary in his button-hole. "I bring you no wedding present," he said.

"My mother's picture was present enough."

"That counts for nothing. I cannot do what I very well know custom requires of me on such an occasion. The truth is, Lenz, I have made myself a present on your wedding day. Do you see this paper? It makes me like the Siegfried we used to read about. I am proof against all the thrusts of fortune, with this hard shell about me."

"What is the paper?"

"It is an annuity. From my sixtieth year I begin to receive a hundred florins annually, till which time I shall manage to scratch through. When I am no longer able to live alone, you must fit up a little room for me in your house,--a warm corner behind the stove, where I can play with your grandchildren, and draw them pictures that to their eyes at least will seem beautiful. I had to work hard to pay the first instalment. My painting, stupidly enough, just gets me a living, with not a copper over. So for the last year I have done without my breakfast. The landlord noticed that I took my breakfast and dinner together. In that way I saved up enough. By and by I shall get used to doing without my dinner, and so on, by degrees, till I learn to do without anything. It would be fine to put up the shutters one after another, and with the last one, bid the world good night."

All the while he was talking, he had been helping Lenz on with his new clothes,--spic and span new from head to foot. He thanked his friend for making him, too, a family man; for, as he pleasantly explained, the annuitants were members of the same household, only they did not keep one another's birthdays. The omission proceeded from no ill will, but simply from their not being acquainted. Pilgrim had all the statistics of the matter at his tongue's end, and reeled them off for Lenz's entertainment, for the sake of warding off any unnecessary excitement or emotion on his friend's part.

When Lenz's toilet was made, came Petrovitsch, of his own free-will, to escort him to the wedding. "You get no wedding present from me, Lenz," he said, with an expression of mystery and cunning on his face; "you know the reason. You will have it in good time." By thus holding out the hope that Lenz should be his heir, though he made no actual promise, Petrovitsch secured for himself the place of chief importance at the wedding festivities. He liked to be the central figure, with all revolving about him, and enjoy the consciousness of having his keys in his pocket, and his fire-proof safe at home. That was a pleasure after his own heart. Two such merry days made a pleasant break, too, in the winter's monotony.

Mine host wore his apostle's cap somewhat higher than usual to-day, and was radiant with dignity as he walked to and fro, stroking his freshly shaven chin.

The clear cold winter air rang with music and firing and shouting as the bridal party walked to the church. The building could not hold the numbers that interest and curiosity had brought together. As many stood outside the church as in it. The minister preached a special sermon,--not one taken from a book, that would suit one case as well as another, but one adapted to this particular occasion. He laid great stress upon the sanctity of the home, the mutual dignity of man and wife. A child naturally inherits the virtues of its parents; but if he turns out badly, the parents are justified before God and man if they can say, We did our duty; the rest was not in our hands. A child of depraved parents may work his way up to honor and respect; his life is his own. The brother shares a brother's honorable name, but he may also cut himself adrift from it. Not so with the honor of man and wife. They are, in the truest sense, one flesh. Here should be perfect sympathy, a single end and aim. Where either seeks his own advancement at the expense of the other, there is discord, hell, eternal death. It is by a righteous ordinance that the wife retains her baptismal name, while receiving a new family name from her husband. She bears the husband's name, the husband's honor. The minister praised the good qualities of the two who now came before the altar. Lenz received the warmest commendation, but Annele came in for a goodly share. Yet he warned them not to think too highly of their peculiar merits. The quick and active must prize and honor the slow; the slow, in the same way, the more active. He reminded them that marriage was not merely a communion of worldly goods, according to the laws of the land, but a communion of spiritual gifts, according to the eternal laws of God; that all mine and thine should cease, and everything be ours,--and yet not ours, but the world's and God's.

In general observations, which were yet easy of personal application, he gave a certain degree of expression to the anxiety felt by many of those present with regard to the peaceful and perfect union of two persons so unlike in nature and habits.

Pilgrim, who sat in the gallery among the singers, exchanged winks of intelligence with the leader of the choir.

Faller kept his face hid in his hands, and did not look up. In the same strain did I speak to Annele, he thought. Who knows what words she would give the minister if she dared to speak! May God, who has worked so many miracles in the world, work but this one more,--plant good thoughts in her heart and put good words on her lips for Lenz, who is so good and true!

No voice sounded louder than Faller's in the hymn that followed the marriage service. The leader signed to him to moderate his bass, as the tenor was weak without Lenz's support. But Faller was not to be repressed. His deep, strong voice sounded above the organ and the voices of all the other singers.

After the ceremony the women who had been so fortunate as to see and hear had much to tell those outside. They described how the bridegroom had wept,--harder than any man they ever heard. The minister had been very touching, to be sure; especially when he called down a blessing from Lenz's parents Lenz sobbed as if his heart would break, and the whole congregation wept with him. At the recital the outsiders also began to weep. They had come to the wedding too, and had as good a right as the rest to all that went on, both the weeping and the rejoicing.

"Has any village a curate like ours?" said the men to the visitors from other parishes. "He speaks out so round and plain, and understands one as if every secret had been disclosed to him." Neither men nor women spoke of the personalities of the discourse.

As Lenz, with Petrovitsch on his right hand and the landlord on his left, was leaving the church, he was addressed by Faller's old mother: "I have kept my word, and worn your mother's clothes to the church. She herself could not have prayed for you more fervently than I did."

Lenz's answer was cut short by the landlord scolding the old woman for being the first to address the bridegroom. Though ridiculing the superstition that there was bad luck in having the first greeting come from an old woman, he called up a pretty boy, and made him be the first to shake hands with Lenz.

From this moment all was merry-making. It was hard to believe that any eye could have been dimmed by tears.

While Lenz in the little parlor shook hands with his new sisters, and kissed and embraced his brothers-in-law, and the doctor came with his daughters,--it was kind of them to come to the wedding,--and one person after another passed in and out and offered congratulations, Annele sat still in her chair, holding a fine white handkerchief pressed to her eyes. "I could not help crying as I did," said Lenz; "you know how happy I am. From this hour we will hold the one honor between us firm and true, and, please God, it shall grow with us. I never shall forget what a family you have brought me into. With God's blessing these shall be the last tears we are to shed together. But take your gloves off; I haven't any on."

Annele refused with a shake of her head, but gave no other answer.

Come to table! to table! to table! was called three times, and a threefold appetite seemed to respond to the summons. Only Franzl kept complaining that she could not eat, she could not swallow a morsel; it was a shame when there were so many good things, but she could not.

Dancing began in the upper hall while the lunch was going on below, and the bridal pair went to and fro between the tables and the dancers.

"It is abominable of the engineer to come to the wedding," said Annele, as they were going up stairs; "he was not invited. Don't speak a word to him."

"Never mind him," said Lenz, soothingly. "Let all be happy to-day. I am only sorry Faller is not here. I sent for him, but he has not come."

Pilgrim danced the first dance with Annele. "You are a capital dancer," she said.

"But not so good a painter, you think?"

"I did not say so."

"Then I won't paint your portrait, though I have been thinking of it to-day. After all, you have not a good face to paint. You are very pretty when you talk, but when you are still there is a look I cannot describe."

"Pity you can't use your brush as well as your tongue."

"Very good; you sha'n't have your picture painted by me. Paint--who is it?--on the wall, and he is sure--?"

"I would not have you paint me for all the world," retorted Annele. She had soon recovered her good spirits.

The bride and bridegroom were called down into the lower room, where the chief members of the family, both men and women, were assembled about Petrovitsch, trying to force him to some decided statement with regard to the amount of property he would leave Lenz. Don Bastian, Pilgrim's crafty landlord, was chief speaker. He was anxious to lard his meagre marriage gift with another man's fat, and had succeeded in driving Petrovitsch into a narrow corner from which escape seemed impossible. The smith, who felt himself of importance as being Lenz's only neighbor,--he lived really half an hour's walk off, but his house was the only one that could be seen from the Morgenhalde,--had been a playmate of Petrovitsch in his youth, and was warming his heart with reminiscences of old times. The landlady thought nothing was wanting but the presence of the bridal pair, and for that reason had sent for them. "Good! there is Lenz," cried the hard-pressed Petrovitsch as the young people entered the circle. "He knows what my intentions are. We are not accustomed in our family to proclaim such things from the town clock. You know how we stand towards each other, don't you, Lenz?"

"Certainly, uncle."

"Then I will waste no more words on the matter," he exclaimed, rising in great trepidation lest the smith or some one else should discover this was his sixty-fifth birthday, and overwhelm him with congratulations which he would have to pay for by a handsome note to Lenz. He pressed his way through the crowd of guests out into the street. A kick from some invisible foot brought a cry of pain from Bubby, who was following close behind his master.

Lenz looked after his uncle's retreating figure with some misgivings. Perhaps he ought not to have thus helped him out of his dilemma. He might have been brought to the point then, and now the chance was lost.

But Lenz dismissed all such thoughts speedily from his mind, and was merry and gay till late into the night. The relations who lived at a distance had already left. It was time for the bridal pair to be starting, for custom required them to be at home before midnight. "You were right, Annele," Lenz said when they were in the little parlor together. "I am sorry there is no carriage-way to our house. Wrap yourself up warm."

"You will find I am right in a great many things," answered Annele.

Pilgrim had arranged the procession with great skill. First went the musicians, then the bridal pair, preceded and followed by two torch-bearers, and, lastly, children carrying the beautiful presents,--bowls, plates, glasses, and salvers, interspersed with flaming pine-knots. On reaching the mountain the procession fell into disorder, as it had to move in single file. "You go in front," said Lenz to Annele; "I willingly yield precedence to you."

They reached the house at last, the presents were deposited, the musicians played one more merry dance, three cheers were given, and then the sound of music died away in the valley.

"We are in heaven, and know there is joy over us on earth," said Lenz.

"I had no idea you could talk so finely," returned Annele. "How still it is all of a sudden!"

"Wait; I have another musical clock here. Thank Heaven I can make my own music now, and for only our two selves." He set his instrument playing Beethoven's "Meerestille." Long it played on by itself, when all else in the house was still.

CHAPTER XXII
THE MORNING GIFT

"I am glad we celebrate our wedding again today,--aren't you, little wife?" asked Lenz, the next morning.

"No; why are you?"

"My crying spoiled my enjoyment yesterday; this morning, for the first time, I am perfectly happy. To-day will seem like going to a friend's wedding,--won't it?"

"What a strange man you are!" said Annele, smiling.

"Stop!" said Lenz, suddenly starting up. "I must give you something. Wait a minute."

He went into the chamber, and made a long search. What would he bring out? He must have remembered the gold chain and ear-rings that were the bridegroom's usual present. But he should have given them yesterday; why to-day? Annele had plenty of time to wonder before Lenz returned. "Here I have it," he exclaimed, coming back at last. "I had misplaced it. This is my blessed mother's garnet necklace. It is made of good old garnets, and will look beautifully on your dear neck. Come, try it on!"

"No, Lenz, it is too old-fashioned. I cannot wear it. It would scratch my neck too. I really cannot wear it. I will exchange it at the jeweler's.

"That you shall not."

"Just as you like. What else have you there?"

"This is something I can give to no one but yourself. My blessed mother so directed. It has no value in itself, but yet is very wonderful."

"Show me the wonder."

"See!"

"What is it?"

"It is Edelweiss, a little plant that grows under the snow. See what my mother has written there!"

"I cannot read it, it is so badly written; read it for me."

Lenz read aloud: "This is a little plant--Edelweiss--that grew on the highest mountain in Switzerland, under the snow. It was found by my husband, who thought of me as he picked it, brought it home with him, and gave it to me, on our wedding day. I wish it placed in my hand, when I am laid in the ground. Should it, however, be forgotten or overlooked, my son must give it to his wife the morning after their marriage, and, as long as she shall hold it in honor it will bring a blessing. There is no magic in it, however. This plant is called Edelweiss.--MARIE LENZ."

"Does it not go to your heart to hear one so speak to you from the dead? Let it not affect you too much. Be cheerful! She liked to have every one cheerful, and was always so herself, though she had seen much sorrow."

Annele smiled, wrapped the little plant in its paper again, and laid it aside with the garnet necklace.

The young people sat chatting together till a message came from the Lion that they must make haste down, for many visitors had already arrived.

Franzl was such an awkward lady's maid, that Lenz had to go down first, and send up some one from the hotel. He said he should go to Faller's, too, and invite him to the party; he must be there to-day, and Annele must treat him kindly, and forget whatever clumsy thing he might have said.

"Yes, yes," said Annele, "only go quick, and send me up Margaret, or, better still, Ernestine."

She made her appearance at length in her old home, and was warmly welcomed and embraced by her mother, and taken into the little parlor, where she at once began to complain of Lenz's having given her, that morning, an old string of garnets and a dried flower for her wedding present. She could not show herself before all the hotelkeepers' daughters, to say nothing of their wives and sons, without a gold chain. "He is an old skinflint," she exclaimed, "a stupid, petty clockmaker."

"Annele," her mother prudently answered, "he is no miser, for he did not ask a word about your dowry; and neither is he stupid,--rather too clever, if anything. Last night there came a silversmith from Pforzheim with a great box under his arm. Lenz ordered him, you may be sure; so now you can pick out the prettiest chain the jeweller has."

The landlady knew very well that Annele would not believe the falsehood, and Annele knew equally well that her mother did not think her so silly as to be taken in by it, but both acted as if perfectly sincere, and the event decided in their favor. Lenz had been missing for some time, during which interval he was standing with Ernestine on the dark cellar stairs. Presently, sure enough, he came, bringing Annele a gold chain from the silversmith, who was in the house. After all her hints he had not understood that he should have left the choice to her, and so got little thanks for his tardy gift.

Annele, however, soon recovered her good-humor, as became a landlord's daughter. What goes on in the family parlor does not belong in the public room.

If there was no end to the carriages yesterday, there was still less to-day. For now came all the hotel-keepers from far and wide, with their gay bells and handsome, well-fed horses. This was the time to show who one was and what he had. The landlords and their wives and daughters went about as if every back felt the weight of a whole hotel. Every look said: We live just so at home; and if we have not as much money as mine host of the Lion, we are quite satisfied with what we have.

Now began such greetings, such giving of presents, such admiration, such extravagant thanks for the rich gifts! Oh, that is too much! that is too superb! No one but the landlady of the Bear would have thought of that! I should know that was from the landlady of the Eagle! And the landlady of the Angel! I hope to show what we can do some day, but it will never equal this. It was wonderful how many pretty speeches Annele could make. Lenz stood by, and could not say a word. Those who did not know him thought he was dull or simple. But all this mutual giving and thanking did not please him.

Next came the poor clockmakers, whose works the landlord sent off to foreign markets, and who were kept very close under the great man's thumb. Annele paid them no attention, so they addressed themselves chiefly to Lenz expressing a certain pleased satisfaction at a clockmaker's becoming son-in-law of the landlord of the Lion. Many hoped for easier terms now with the landlord; others asked Lenz the plain question whether he meant to give up his profession, and turn merchant and hotel-keeper, and smiled when he assured them he should remain as he was. They also asked him sarcastically, whether, now that he had a rich dealer for his father-in-law, he should want to introduce his standard regulator, and establish the association which was to secure to every workman his full earnings. They made faces of astonishment when Lenz declared that the sooner the association was formed the better he should be pleased, and that he should be one of the first to join it. When these poor fellows, whose poverty you could read in their faces, who with fourteen hours' daily labor could only make out to live by practising an almost incredible economy and self-denial, pressed their half-florin or a sixpenny piece, sometimes only a threepence, into Lenz's hand, it burned him like live coals. He would gladly have returned the gifts, had he not feared to hurt their feelings. When a pause enabled him to get Annele's attention, he told her how he felt. She stared hopelessly at him, and said, shaking her head: "My father is right, you are no business man. You can work and earn your bread, but as for making others work and earn for you, you have no conception of it. You are always asking how this one or that one gets on. That is not the way. You must drive through the world as comfortably as you can, and not ask who has to go barefoot. But you would like to take old Pröbler and your whole swarm of beggars to drive with you. However, I will not read you a lesson now.--Ah, welcome, dear landlady of the Lamb! the later the hour the fairer the guest. I have long been thinking, and a minute ago was saying to my mother, Where can the good landlady of the Lamb at Edelshof be? Half my pleasure would be destroyed if she did not come to honor my wedding. And this is your daughter-in-law? Where is the husband?"

"He is below with the horses. It is hard to find shelter for them to-day."

"Yes; thank Heaven, we have many good friends. Such a day shows how full the world is of them. Lenz, show the landlady of the Lamb to the upper table. I have reserved a seat of honor there for her." And Annele turned away to welcome other guests.

That she should reproach him--reproach him on such a day as this-- with thinking too much of others was a cruel sting to Lenz, though he did not let it dwell on his mind. He was forced to own that she was right; that this very weakness of his made him less successful in the world than other men,--made him seem less capable than he really was. The recollection of a word or action would haunt him for days, destroying all his peace. Other men fare better. They live for themselves, and heap together what they get without asking about their fellows. He must learn to do so too, if he would have any position. Lenz stood for a while lost in these thoughts, as forgetful of all the noisy rejoicings about him as if they had no reference to him. But he soon roused himself again to take part in them,--and the chief part, as became the bridegroom.

The house was crowded, and pleasant it was to see so many persons collected together to share in a neighbor's joy. The merriment was so well kept up, that in the evening, when the guests began to think of leaving, the landlord played a trick upon them. He ordered Gregory to take all the poles from the sleighs and hide them. The distinguished guests consequently could not get away, and were obliged to stay till long after midnight. So much the better, they consoled themselves with saying, because now we shall have the moon.

No stratagem was used to detain the petty clockmakers, of whom many were anxious to be at home early, in order not to lose a second working-day. Others, however, wanted to get the full value of their wedding present, and sat and ate continuously, as if they had to lay in a supply for the next year. From morning till late at night fresh dishes were constantly served. The supply of meat and sausages and sour-krout seemed inexhaustible.

Faller moved about among the wedding guests quite stiff and embarrassed till Ernestine set him at ease by tying a great white apron on him and bidding him help her tend table. I only do it for Lenz's sake, he said to himself, and would like to have said to every one he handed refreshments to. For his own part, he ate and drank almost nothing. On getting hold of Lenz for a moment, he said to him: "I have given you no wedding present. Little I will not give, and much I cannot. How gladly would I give the heart out of my body!" Lenz only admonished his faithful comrade to help himself first, and be as merry as he could. Before it was yet too late, he remembered he had meant to invite old Pröbler, and sent Faller in search of him. The old man came, but could not be persuaded to enter the guest-room, having no Sunday clothes; so Lenz gave him a dish of eatables, enough to last three days, and a bottle of good wine into the bargain. Old Pröbler was so surprised he almost forgot to offer his usual pinch of snuff, and could only say, "I will bring back the bottle." "You may keep it," replied Lenz. In high glee the old fellow took himself off.

It was almost morning before Lenz and Annele set out for home. The moon had risen, but was obscured by clouds. They walked up the mountain this time, with neither escort nor torches. Annele complained that it was frightfully dark, and she was ready to drop with fatigue. "I ought to have stayed at home," she said.

"At home? up there is your home."

She made no answer, and the two went on side by side for a time in silence.

"Have you counted the money you received?" she asked, presently.

"No, I can do that at home. There is a good deal, for it is heavy in my hand. Luckily, your father lent me one of his empty money-bags."

"Empty? he has plenty of full ones!" said Annele, with temper.

"I did not ask for those, nor think of them."

As soon as they reached home she insisted on Lenz counting the money at once. But he was so slow she took it into her own hands, and showed that a landlord's daughter was much quicker at figures.

"I have been thinking the matter over," said Lenz, while she was counting. "It is well to accept presents even from the poor. It teaches them self-respect, and makes it easier for them to apply to us for help in their difficulties."

Annele stopped in her counting and stared at him. He had such strange reasons for the commonest things! He would adopt no custom until he could reconcile it with his ideas of right; then he embraced it heartily. Annele said nothing, but her lips kept repeating the number she had in her mind, lest she should forget it.

The money amounted to just one hundred and twenty florins, counting four counterfeit sixpences. Annele was terribly hard on the mean things who would cheat them with such money.

"Don't speak so," remonstrated Lenz; "perhaps they were poor people, who had nothing else."

Her eyes flashed. "You seem to understand everything better than I do. I should think I did not know anything."

"I did not mean so. Be kind, Annele!"

"I never was cross in all my life. You are the first person who ever called me cross. You may ask whom you like. You might have seen to-day what the world thinks of me."

"O, very well; it is not worth disputing about."

"I am not disputing. It makes no difference what it is, if it is only half a farthing. I will not be contradicted so whenever I speak."

"Certainly not; only do be quiet, or Franzl will think we are having a quarrel."

"Franzl may think what she chooses. I tell you now Franzl must go out of this house."

"But not to-day?"

"Not to-day, but to-morrow, or soon."

"Then we will talk about it to-morrow. I am tired, and so are you, you said."

"Yes, but when an injustice is done me it cures all my fatigue; there is no tiring me then."

"I have done you no injustice, and desire to do you none. Remember what the minister said: we have a common honor."

"You need not tell me what the minister said. He ought not to have said it. He preached as if he were trying to make peace."

"Please God, that shall never be necessary. We will be of one mind, and bear joy and sorrow in loving fidelity, as my mother used to say."

"We will show the world that we live honestly together."

"Shall I set the musical clock going?"

"No, we have had enough for to-day."

CHAPTER XXIII
THE FIRST NAIL IS DRIVEN.--PEACE ON THE HEIGHTS, AND THE FIRST SUNDAY GUEST

The next morning Annele was again on friendly terms with Franzl, and complimenting her good management. "I have never given you anything, Franzl," she said; "would you rather have a gown or some money?"

"Money would please me best."

"Then here are two crowns for you."

Lenz gladly added the same amount when Franzl showed him Annele's present. How thoughtful she is, he said to himself, and how careful always to do just the right thing! It never would have occurred to me to make Franzl a present; and yet only yesterday she was talking of sending her away. "She is a dear, foolish, hasty child," he added aloud. "Just like our young burgomaster's wife at home," interposed Franzl; "who, as the weight-manufacturer's wife once said, always planned for seven visitors when there were but six chairs, so that one had to go bobbing about while the others were seated." Lenz laughed. "We Knuslingers know a thing or two, I assure you. See now how quickly your wife has brought everything to order. Most women would have been three days about it, and have stumbled a dozen times and broken half the things to pieces. Your wife has no left hand. She is right hand all over,"--a compliment which much pleased Annele, when Lenz repeated it to her.

She showed now a new accomplishment. Lenz asked her to drive a nail above his father's file. She struck it firmly and squarely on the head at the first blow, and on the nail thus first driven in her new home he made her hang his mother's picture.

"That is good," he said. "If it is not just like her, it has her eyes, and, please God, they shall look down on a fair, good, happy life. We will make it such a life that she may always have pleasure in beholding it."

Only do not make a saint of her, Annele wanted to say, but checked herself.

This was Wednesday of their wedding week, the whole of which was to be kept as a time of holiday. Lenz worked a few hours daily, chiefly for the sake of reminding himself that he had an occupation; he was happier, too, after having worked a couple of hours. The wedding festivities were, of course, lived over again, and very funny it was to see Annele mimic the peculiarities of the different guests. She made you actually see and hear the landlady of the Bear and of the Lamb and of the Eagle, while her imitation of Faller's trick of rubbing his hand over his mustache was so perfect that you could almost fancy a growth of bushy hair above her roguish lip. There was no ill-nature, nothing but harmless fun, in it all. She was thoroughly happy. "O, how beautiful, how good and wholesome it is up here!" she cried, in the morning; "and how still! I never could have believed there was such quiet in the world. Sitting here, as I do, seeing and hearing nothing of what goes on below, and not having to give an answer to anybody, it seems to me I must be sleeping with my eyes open,--and such a pleasant sleep! Down in the village, life is like a mill-wheel; here I am in another world. I can almost hear my heart beat. For the next fourteen days I do not mean to go down into the town. I will wean myself from it altogether; I know I can. The people that live there have no idea how good it is to be out of the world,--out of the hurry and hubbub and stir. O Lenz, you do not know how well off you have been all your life!"

Thus in a hundred different ways did Annele express her delight as she sat in the morning by Lenz's side. "I knew you would like living here," he answered, his face beaming with joy; "and you may be sure I am thankful to God and my parents for having been allowed to pass my life in this place. But, dear little wife, we cannot stay up here a fortnight all by ourselves. Next Sunday, at the farthest, we must go to church, and I think we ought to pass even a little of to-day with our parents."

"As you like. Happily, we cannot take this blessed rest away with us, but shall find it waiting when we come home."

"And you, my mother," interrupted Lenz, looking up at his mother's picture, "you are our angel of rest; your pure eyes say, as they look down upon us, Thank God, children, that it is so with you, and so shall continue your life long."

"It seems impossible I have been here so little while," continued Annele; "I feel as if I had lived here forever. These quiet hours are better than years anywhere else."

"How prettily and cleverly you describe it! Only remember your words, if ever this place should seem too lonely for you. Those who did not believe you could be happy in such a solitude will be surprised."

"Who didn't believe I could be happy? I know,--your Pilgrim, your great artist. He is a pretty fellow. Whoever is not an angel he sets down as a devil. But one thing I tell you, he shall never cross this threshold."

"It was not Pilgrim. Why will you try to find any one now to hate? A hundred times I have heard my mother say, 'We can have no peace of mind if we do not feel kindly towards our fellow-men.' If she had but lived a year longer, that you might have learned of her! Was not that a good saying? You know how it is if you hate any one, or know you have an enemy. I experienced it once, and remember how hard it was. Wherever you go, or whatever you do, you feel an invisible pistol pointed at you. My greatest happiness is, that there is no one in the world whom I hate, and no one, so far as I know, who hates me."

Annele had but half heard him. "Who could have said so if it were not Pilgrim?"

"No one. I have only feared so sometimes myself."

"I don't believe that. Some one put it into your head. But you ought not to have repeated it to me. I might tell what persons have said to me about you,--persons you would never suspect of speaking so. You have your enemies, like the rest of us, but I know better than to make you uncomfortable by repeating their stupid talk."

"You only say that to pay me back. It is all fair; I have deserved it. But now we are quits, and let us be merry."

The two were, indeed, full of happiness again. Franzl in the kitchen often moved her lips, as she was wont to do when thinking to herself. That is natural and right; thank God they feel so. Such would have been my life with Anton, if he had not proved faithless, and married a black woman!

On Sunday morning Lenz said, "I had quite forgotten to tell you that I had invited a guest to dinner with us today. You have no objection?"

"No; who is it?"

"My good Pilgrim."

"You should have invited your uncle too; it would be no more than proper."

"I thought of it, but did not venture to, he is such a queer man."

For the first time they heard the bells in the valley ringing. "Is that not beautiful?" said Lenz. "I have heard my mother say, a thousand times, that we did not hear the bells themselves, but only their echo from the wood behind the house, so that it is like hearing bells from heaven."

"Yes; but we had better be starting now," returned Annele. On the way she began: "Lenz, I do not ask from curiosity; I am your wife, and have a right to know. I swear by those bells not to repeat it."

"You need never swear; I have a horror of oaths. Tell me what it is you want to know."

"You and your uncle seemed to understand each other perfectly on the day of the wedding; what has been settled about the inheritance?"

"Nothing; we have never exchanged a word on the subject."

"And yet you acted as if all were signed and sealed."

"I did nothing. I only said my uncle and I understood each other, and so we do. We never speak of such things. He is free to do as he will."

"He was pushed into a corner, that day, that he could not have got out of but for you. Such a chance will hardly occur again. He might have been made to leave us a handsome legacy."

"I cannot bear to have strangers meddling in our family matters. I am driven into no corner. If he leaves me nothing, I am quite able to take care of myself."

Annele was silent; in her heart was no ringing of bells such as were pealing clear over mountain and valley. They entered the church together, and after the service stopped to see their parents before going home. Not far from the open meadow Pilgrim called after them, "Admit a poor soul into your paradise." They turned round, laughing. Pilgrim was in excellent spirits on the way up, and still gayer at table, where he finished by drinking a full glass to the health of his future godson, and insisting on Annele's drinking with him. Her whole manner towards her guest was friendly in the extreme. At first she was disconcerted by occasionally meeting her husband's eye fixed upon her with an expression of wonder at her powers of dissimulation. Even when she refused to look his way, she fancied his glance of disapproval behind her back, and grew positively angry. On looking round at last, however, and seeing by his beaming face that he thought her perfectly sincere in her assumption of friendliness, she became so in earnest, and exclaimed heartily to Pilgrim: "How happy you and Lenz are in your friendship! from this day let me make one with you."

Pilgrim was loud in his praises of Annele, as Lenz accompanied him part of the way down the hill.

"Never has a dinner tasted so good as to-day's," exclaimed the husband, joyfully, as he re-entered the little room. "What greater happiness can there be in the world than to earn your meat and drink by honest toil, and have a darling wife and a faithful friend to enjoy it with you?"

"Yes, Pilgrim is an entertaining fellow," returned Annele.

"I am so glad you have converted him," added Lenz. "He was not quite inclined to like you; but you are a perfect witch; you can do what you like with everybody."

Annele was silent, and Lenz began to feel almost sorry he had told her that: there was no occasion for it. But honesty never can come amiss. He repeated that she ought to feel particularly happy at having turned an enemy into a friend. She still made no answer; and afterwards, when Pilgrim's name was mentioned, kept a resolute silence.

Annele despaired of doing anything with Lenz until she could make him give up his cheerful views of human nature. As time went on, she gained many a victory by showing him, on every possible occasion, how mean, how wicked and deceitful, men were.

"I never knew that such were the ways of the world. I have lived like a child," said Lenz.

"I have been abroad in the world for you, Lenz," Annele answered. "I have known thousands and thousands of persons in their business and other relations. I have heard how differently they talk behind a man's back from what they do to his face, and have seen them laughing at him for being taken in by fair professions. Hardly anybody says what he really believes. I can tell you more of the world than you would have learned in ten years of travel."

"But of what use is it?" asked Lenz. "I don't see that it does any good. If we keep on our own straightforward way, the world about us may be as bad as it will, it can do us no harm. Besides, there are plenty of honest persons in it. A child brought up in an inn is, as you say, at home among strangers. You told me that evening when we first talked together how keenly you felt your position. You must be glad to have at last a little home of your own, where every passer-by has not the right to come in, and defame himself and his neighbors over his mug of beer."

"Certainly," answered Annele, in no very cordial tone. Lenz had vexed her again by undervaluing her former life. He seemed to fancy she had not known what happiness was till he revealed it to her.

CHAPTER XXIV
OLD HEIRLOOMS ARE BANISHED, AND A NEW TONE IS HEARD ON THE MORGENHALDE

The wedding week and many other weeks and months passed, during which little occurred worthy to be recorded in our story. Almost every morning Annele laughed at Lenz for his astonishment over the loaf of fresh white bread which the landlady sent up daily from the town. It was not the delicacy that surprised him so much as the fact that persons should become dependent upon such things. Many luxuries that Lenz had considered only suitable for holidays were to Annele every-day necessities. She ridiculed his ignorance, which knew not how to double the comforts of life without increasing the expense; and a great improvement she certainly introduced into their way of living, baking better bread out of the same meal, and in all household matters bringing to pass much greater results with the same outlay. But, on the other hand, she was often discontented, and especially in the spring was apt to complain: "Dear me, how the wind blows up here! it is enough to take the roof off the house."

"I cannot help it, dear child. We get good fresh air to pay for it. Every breath we draw is like a draught of dew. Remember how you used to delight last autumn in our bright, cheerful sunshine, when the valley was shrouded in mist. And what good water we have too! People live to be old, ever so old, up here. As for the house, you need have no particle of concern for that. It is built of whole trunks of trees, and will stand for our grandchildren and great-grandchildren."

When the snow began to melt, and the usually empty gullies on the mountain-side were, to Lenz's great delight, filled with the rushing streams, Annele complained that she could not sleep for the noise of the water.

"You often complained in the winter of the deathly stillness up here,--that you could hear no wagon and see no passing; now you have noise enough." Annele gave her husband a sidelong glance, and, without answering, went into the kitchen, and had a good cry with Franzl. The old woman cautioned Lenz against contradicting his wife; it was not well for her or the child she bore.

Lenz was quiet and industrious, and took great pleasure in his work. Whenever he appealed to Annele to admire some tone that gave him peculiar satisfaction, she would answer: "O, it is nothing to me. I am really afraid your work will be the ruin of you; it will never repay you for the time you spend on it. The way to make a fortune is to turn off things quick, and not quiddle so over them."

"I know my own work best, Annele."

"If you know best, you have no need to talk to me. I can only speak according as I understand. If you want a post for a listener you had better go down to the doctor's and borrow one. There are plenty of painted red lips there that will speak never a word."

Days passed, and the spring that now broke in glory over the earth seemed to bring fresh life on the Morgenhalde. The landlady often came up and revelled in the good warm sun. The landlord, who had grown more of a growler than ever, seldom appeared. Annele openly withdrew herself more and more from her parents, and clung with increasing tenderness to Lenz. Of a Sunday morning or a holiday afternoon they often went together into the forest, where he had set up a bench among his father-in-law's trees. "Hark to that bird," said he, one day, as they were sitting there in a happy mood. "He is the true singer, caring nothing whether any hear him or not, but making music for himself and his mate, just as I do." And Lenz sent his voice blithely into the echoing wood.

"Yes," answered Annele, "and for that reason you ought to resign your place in the Liederkranz; it is no longer a fit society for you. As a bachelor you might keep company with Faller and the rest, if you chose, but for the head of a family it is not the thing. Besides, you are too old to sing."

"I old? Why, I am born new every spring. I was just fancying myself still a child, building a boat with my dead brother. How happy we were!"

"One would think your whole life had been a miracle. What do you mean by talking so?"

"You are right. I must learn to be old; I am almost as old as this forest. I remember, as a child, there were very few large trees here; most of the wood was of young saplings, and now it has grown high above our heads, and, thank Heaven, is our own."

"How our own? Has my father made it over to you?"

"No, it is still his,--that is, his with certain restrictions. He has no right to cut it wholly down, because it is all that keeps our house from being buried under the snow or the mountain itself."

"Don't talk so. What is it to me?"

"I don't understand you."

"Nor I you. You should not suggest such dreadful things to me now."

"Then I will sing to you, and let who will hear."

He took Annele's hand and, merrily singing, led her back to the house, where they arrived just in time to receive a visit from the landlord. He was evidently come upon business, for, taking his son-in-law into the inner room, he began at once. "Lenz, I can do you a good turn."

"That is well. A good turn never comes amiss."

"Is your money still with the bailiff?"

"He has paid me four hundred florins of it, but the greater part is still in his hands."

"Ready money is trumps now. You can make a good trade with it."

"I will give notice to the bailiff."

"That would take too long. Give me your note to sell, and I will guarantee you twenty-five per cent."

"Then we will go shares."

"It was foolish of you to say that. I had meant to give you the whole; but you are methodical in all your business matters, I see."

"Thank you, father-in-law, I like to be fair. I want no favors."

"Your best way would be to leave the money in my business, and let me hand you whatever interest it draws."

"I don't understand business. A regular percentage suits me better."

On returning to the sitting-room they found a nice lunch set out by Annele herself, but her father seemed in a great hurry to be gone, and would take nothing. "It is your own wine, father," Annele insisted. "Do sit a few minutes with us, we see so little of you."

There seemed no seat on the Morgenhalde broad enough to bear the whole weight of the landlord's dignity. He drank a glass standing, and then went down the hill, frequently pressing his hand on his breast-pocket as he went. "Father is particularly uncommunicative to-day," observed Annele.

"He has some pressing business on his mind. I have just given him my two thousand six hundred florins that the bailiff borrowed."

"And what did he give you in exchange?"

"I don't know what you mean; nothing. I will ask him for a written receipt some time, since that is the custom."

"If you had asked my advice, you would not have given him the money."

"Annele, what do you mean? I am sure I ought not to take amiss anything you say to me when you thus mistrust your own father. But, as Franzl says, we must be indulgent with you now, and let you have your own way."

"Indeed!" said Annele. "No one need be indulgent with me. What I said about my father meant nothing. I don't know how I came to say it. Franzl must go. It is she who sets you against me."

In vain Lenz defended poor Franzl, and protested she did nothing of the kind. Annele carried her point. In less than a fortnight the old woman had to leave the house. Lenz comforted her as well as he could, assuring her she should soon come back, and promising her a yearly sum as long as she lived. But she shook her head, and said, weeping, "The Lord God will soon put me beyond want. Never did I think to leave this house, where I have lived for eight and twenty years, till I was carried out. There are my pots, and my copper kettles, and my pans, and my tubs; how many thousand times I have taken them in my hand, and polished them up! They are my witnesses. No one can say I have not been neat and orderly. The nozzle of every pot, if it could speak, would tell who and what I have been. But God knows all. He sees what goes on in the great room, and in the kitchen, and in each of our hearts. That is my comfort and my *viaticum* and-- Enough; I am glad to get out of this place; rather would I spin thistles than stay here a day longer. I don't want to make you unhappy, Lenz. You might hunt me down like a rat before I would bring ill-will into the house. No, no, I will not do that. Have no anxiety about me; you have cares enough of your own. Gladly would I be crushed under the weight of them, if I could but take them from you, and bear them on my own shoulders. Have no fear for me. I shall go to my brother in Knuslingen. There was I born, and there will I wait till I die. If I join your mother in Paradise, I will tend upon her as she was used to being tended here. For her sake, our Lord God will admit me, and for her sake you shall still be blessed in this world. Good by; forgive me, if I have ever grieved you. Good by,--a thousand times good by!"

For some time after Franzl's departure Lenz continued silent and gloomy. All the higher did Annele's spirits rise in consequence. She was indeed a witch, who could do with him what she would. There was a magic in her tone, when she wished to please, that none could resist. Pilgrim used all his influence to reconcile Lenz to this new state of things. He tried to convince him that the old serving-woman had usurped a certain authority which prevented his wife from being mistress in her own house. Annele, in fact, had been brought up to take an active part in household work, and was much happier for having plenty to do. The care of such a little house, she said, was nothing to her, and she never meant to keep another maid. The apprentice must be called in to help. By the aid of his mother-in-law, however, Lenz finally succeeded in securing a new girl.

Matters how went on pleasantly and smoothly again till into the summer. Annele insisted upon her mother's obliging the landlord to pay Lenz back his money, and the father-in-law consequently appeared one day, and made Lenz an offer of the wood behind his house, in return for the money received, and for one thousand florins in addition. Lenz replied that he did not want the wood, but ready money, for which, however, he could very well afford to wait. No further steps were taken, except that the landlord, like the man of honor he was, gave a receipt, drawn up in due form, good in case of life or death.

Late in the summer, the usual quiet of the village was interrupted by two great events,--the marriage of the engineer with Bertha, the doctor's second daughter, the eldest choosing to remain single; and the return of the doctor's son, now a skilful clockmaker, from his studies abroad. It was said he meant to build a great clock-factory, not far from his father's house. A great outcry was raised among the native clockmakers, that they should be ruined if clocks were to be manufactured by machinery, as they were in America. Lenz took the matter quietly, and, with the schoolmaster, spared no pains to carry into operation his long-cherished plan of uniting the workmen in one common association. Perhaps necessity would compel them to a step of which they had not been able or willing before to see the advantages. The two spent whole days in going from house to house, explaining the standard regulator. They recommended the adoption of five different sizes, which would be quiet sufficient to show all the variety of works. Nothing but a division of labor could save the workpeople. The axles, wheels, and springs, and more especially the stoppers and screws, could be made cheaper and better by machinery, while the adjustments of the parts and the finishing touches must always be left to the hand of a master. Human understanding and thought are indispensable to the proper arranging and harmonizing of the whole. He urged the clockmakers either to contribute a share to the new manufactory or to set up one of their own. But he found idle complaints instead of active co-operation. Every one insisted on keeping to his old ways, thinking he understood best his own interests, and unwilling to risk them for the sake of the common good.

Lenz came home discouraged, only to be received by his wife with reproaches: "For Heaven's sake, stop setting up ninepins for other men to knock down. Let others alone; they don't trouble themselves about you. You would like to oil everybody's doors, that they should not creak, though no one's teeth are set on edge by them but your own."

Lenz smiled at his wife's sharp comparisons. No sooner had he relinquished his plan for the good of his fellow-workmen than she began urging him to set up a manufactory in company with her father. He could go abroad a year, if necessary, she said, and she would spend the time with her parents. Lenz maintained that he was not suited for such an undertaking, and, moreover, would certainly not travel now that he was a married man, after staying at home through his bachelor life. Annele took small satisfaction in his assurances that she might set her mind quite at rest as to the future, as he should never fail to make a comfortable living, in which assurances he was fully borne out by Pilgrim. Pilgrim, therefore, she regarded as the chief obstacle in Lenz's path to fortune,--a man who had never accomplished anything himself, and never would; and she used all the means in her power, though without success, to breed discord between the two friends.

Annele carried a perfect ledger in her head, so constantly was she revolving figures and plans. Knowing that Lenz had been Faller's security for the purchase of his house, she now teased him to withdraw his name. So strongly did she insist, that he was fairly obliged to consent, and had entered Faller's house for the purpose of announcing his determination, when he was met by his old comrade with a face half rueful and half laughing, and told of the arrival of a second pair of twins. "The little creatures know I am mad on the subject of children, and so come to me in couples." Of course Lenz could not increase the young father's anxieties by withdrawing his security at such a time, and was obliged to return an evasive answer to his wife's inquiries as to the result of his visit.

On the night before the marriage of the engineer with the doctor's daughter Annele gave birth to a son. As Lenz was standing by her bedside, full of his new happiness, she said: "Lenz, promise me one thing; promise me to break off all connection with Pilgrim, at least for three months."

"I can promise you nothing now," he answered, a bitter drop poisoning his cup of joy.

Annele was beside herself at hearing the music from the valley. So great was her excitement that her mother and husband trembled for her life. Towards noon, however, she fell into a quiet sleep. Lenz stopped up all the doors and windows, that every sound should be kept out. From this sleep she awoke more tranquil, and showed such patience and sweetness that Lenz was filled with twofold thankfulness for the happiness vouchsafed him as husband and father. It was wonderful how Annele's moods changed. In her present interval of tenderness she reminded her husband of their promise to Pilgrim that he should stand godfather, and expressed pleasure at the idea. Lenz was desirous that Petrovitsch should be second godfather; but the old man resolutely declined.

Pilgrim brought with him, and laid in the baby's cradle, a huge paper, containing a great number of signatures and illuminated by himself. It was a diploma of the Liederkranz, he said, making the new-comer, in virtue of his unquestionably good voice, an honorary member of that society.

"Do you know the sweetest tone in all the world?" asked Lenz,--"the first cry of one's child. Here is something else for you, my son. Take hold; see how he grasps it!" He put into the baby's little hand his father's file, as if for a special consecration; but Annele snatched it away.

"The child might kill itself with that sharp edge," she cried, and threw the instrument with such violence to the ground as to break off the point.

"There is my precious heirloom broken," said Lenz, sadly.

Pilgrim tried to console him, and declared, laughing, that there must ever be new men and new tools in the world. Annele said not a word.

CHAPTER XXV
THE PENDULUMS SWING EACH IN ITS OWN DIRECTION, AND THE CORD IS STRAINED ALMOST TO BREAKING

"Come here a minute, Annele, I have something to show you."

"I have no time."

"Just look; it will amuse you. See, I have set two pendulums on these two clocks swinging different ways; one from right to left, the other from left to right. In a few days they will both swing together, either from right to left or the other way. The force of attraction that they exercise upon each other gradually brings them to an exact correspondence."

"I don't believe it."

"You will see it with your own eyes, and the same will be the case with us. We began, like the pendulums, to swing in opposite directions; but we shall have, like them, to come into harmony. To be sure, two pendulums never tick precisely together, so as to give but one tone. A Spanish king once went mad, trying to make them."

"What do I care for all your mad stories? You, apparently, have time for such nonsense; I have not."

In a few days the two pendulums swung together, but the hearts of husband and wife held each its own accustomed motion. There were times when that miracle of the one stroke which no work of human hand could accomplish seemed about to come to pass. But it was only seeming, and made the reality all the harder.

Lenz meant to be yielding, but in reality held fast to his old ways. Annele had no intention of making concessions. She knew better than her husband from the start; for had she not had experience in all the ways of the world? Had not men from all countries, old and young, rich and poor, told her from her childhood that her mind was as bright and clear as the day?

Annele's character might be concisely, though not perhaps quite accurately, described as superficial. She took life easily, was capable and active, with great fluency of speech, which she abundantly exercised; but when her chat was over she never gave a second thought to what she had said or heard.

Lenz's character was deep and solid; but cautious even to timidity. He handled the world like a piece of delicate machinery, treating even the most indifferent concerns with the conscientious exactitude of his trade,--or his art, as he preferred to call it.

Annele, when nothing was going on about her, had nothing to say; while Lenz's communicativeness increased with the quiet of his life. Whenever Lenz talked, he stopped working; Annele, on the contrary, kept both tongue and hands busy at the same moment.

Annele liked to tell her dreams; and wonderful dreams she had,-- such as driving in a beautiful carriage, drawn by superb horses, through a magnificent country, with the merriest of companions; and every other minute she would exclaim, "Dear me, what a good time we had!" Or she had dreamed she was the landlady of a great hotel, and kings and princes had driven up to her door, to all of whom she had given a ready answer. Lenz cared nothing for dreams, and did not like to hear her relate them.

Annele, from the time of her getting up in the morning to her going to bed at night, was always neatly and prettily dressed, and liked to have Lenz often praise her for it; but he had a trick, which seemed to her foolish and tiresome, of repeating the same thing in the same words hundreds and hundreds of times, with the impression every time that it was an idea he had never thought of before. His habits of mind were somewhat like those of external nature, which gives an ever new freshness to the same garment; or, like those of his handiwork, which require what has been done a hundred times before to be labored over again with equal pleasure and exactness. Annele wanted Lenz to keep himself always nicely dressed as she did; but he bestowed too much attention on his work to have any thought left for his person.

Lenz, in the morning, could hardly speak a word. It took some time for his faculties to wake up. He would dream with his eyes open, even over his work, and never became fully aroused till quite into the day. Annele, on the contrary, the moment she opened her eyes, was like a soldier at his post, armed and equipped. She attacked the day's work with animation, and hated all half and half states of body and mind. Always neat and nimble, as became a landlord's daughter, she had everything, even to a dish of chat, in readiness for guests, come at what hour of the morning they would. At the bustle she made Lenz often raised his eyes to his mother's picture, as if to say, Don't let your calmness be ruffled; this snapping of whips is her delight.

If Annele watched him at his work, he became infected with her disquiet, turned over and over some piece he had just finished, or was finishing, feeling her impatient look upon him all the while, hearing her dissatisfied expressions at his slowness, and growing himself impatient and dissatisfied. It was an unwholesome companionship.

Little William throve excellently on the Morgenhalde, and when soon a little sister was running about with him, the house was as noisy as if the wild huntsman and his train were driving through it. If Lenz ventured to complain of the uproar, Annele answered sharply: "To have quiet a man needs to be rich, and live in a castle, where the princes can be quartered in a separate wing."

"I am not rich," answered Lenz, smiling at the rebuke, yet smarting under it.

Only in the same atmosphere or at an equal distance from the centre of the earth can two pendulums make the same number of vibrations in a given time.

Lenz became every day more quiet and reserved. Whenever he and his wife talked together, he was filled with amazement at the many words she used about every little thing. If he said in the morning, "The mist is heavy to-day," she would reply, in her animated manner, "Yes, remarkably so for the season. Still it may come out pleasant. There is no prophesying about the weather up here in the mountains. Every one judges according to his own desires. One hopes it will rain, another that it will be clear, as each has different projects on foot. If the Lord tried to arrange the weather to suit all tastes, he would have his hands full. Like that magician--" Here would come a story, and, on the end of that, another, and still others. This was her way of running on upon every conceivable subject, as if she were entertaining a teamster while his horse was eating in the stall, or beguiling the anxiety of a hurried guest, who had ordered dinner, and would have some time yet to wait, in spite of the quickly laid cloth and plates.

Lenz shrugged his shoulders, and relapsed into perfect silence, which lasted sometimes for days. "What a tiresome, unsocial companion you are!" his wife often said, at first good-naturedly, then sharply. He smiled at the rebuke, yet it wounded him.

The fears entertained of the manufactory were not realized; on the contrary, a fresh impetus was given to domestic industry. The manufactory confined itself at first to the casting of zinc dial-plates, which found a ready market. Lenz quite prided himself on having foretold that such would be the case, and received many compliments on his sagacity. His wife alone refused to see anything praiseworthy in it. Of course a man should be the best judge of matters connected with his own business. "Nevertheless," she added, "the engineer and the doctor's son will grow rich while the clockmakers think themselves lucky to be allowed to keep on in their former ruts. Old Pröbler is the best of you, after all; he does at least try to invent something new."

Whatever else went wrong, Lenz was happy in his work. "When I get up in the morning," he said to Annele, "and think of the day's honest work that lies before me, and the satisfaction of seeing it prosper in my hands, I feel a perpetual sunshine within me."

"You are a good hand at preaching; you ought to have been a parson," said Annele, thinking, as she left the room, There is a good home-thrust for you. We are all to listen to you; but as for what any of us may say, that is of no consequence whatever.

Not to be revenged on his wife, but from sheer forgetfulness, Lenz often at table, after she had been telling some long story, would suddenly say, as if just waking up: "I beg your pardon; I have not heard a word you have been saying, my head is so full of that beautiful melody! If I could only make it sound as I hear it! That change to the minor key is wonderful."

Annele smiled, but never forgave the slight he thus put upon her.

The pendulums swung more and more determinedly each in its own direction.

Formerly, when Lenz returned home from the foundry, or the locksmith's, or from any excursion, his mother always sat by him while he ate, and listened with delight to all he had to tell. The glass of beer he had drunk abroad she relished again at home; the kindly greetings he had received awoke fresh gratitude in her loving heart. Every incident he related was of importance, for it had happened to him. But now, when he came home, Annele had no time to sit by him; or if she did, and he began to relate his experiences, she would say: "What is all that to me? I don't care a pin about it. People may live as they like, for aught I care. They give me none of their happiness, and their unhappiness I don't want. You and they get on finely together; they have only to wind you up, and you play to everybody, like one of your musical clocks."

Lenz laughed, remembering that Pilgrim had once called him an eight-day clock, because he was always wound up fresh on Sundays. Through the week he gave himself no rest, and therefore welcomed all the more gladly the Sunday holiday. When the sun shone bright, he often exclaimed: "Thank God, thousands and thousands of human beings are rejoicing at this beautiful Sunday!"

"You act as if you were the Lord God himself, and had the whole world to look after," was Annele's response, which taught him to keep such thoughts henceforth to himself. If he wanted Annele to go with him of a Sunday to a meeting of the various musical societies in a neighboring village, or simply to join Faller and his wife in a walk up the valley, the answer always was: "You are at liberty, of course, to go where you will. It makes no difference to a man what company he keeps; but I shall not go with you. I rank myself too high for that. Faller and his wife are not fit society for me. You can go, of course; I have not the slightest objection."

Naturally, Lenz also gave up the excursion, and stayed at home, or went to the Lion,--in either place showing more ill-temper than the occasion at all warranted.

Lenz had never had in his hand a card or a ninepin ball,--those consumers of time and low spirits. "I wish I did take pleasure, as others do, in cards and ninepins," he said, innocently, quite unprepared for Annele's sharp retort: "it does a man good to play, if he only comes back the fresher to his business. Games are certainly better than playing with one's work."

The pendulums swung more and more determinedly each in its own direction.

Lenz sold the greater part of his stock on hand at good prices, but the work he had undertaken for his father-in-law did not advance satisfactorily. He could not help sometimes complaining to Annele that this or that part of it disappointed him; whereupon she tried to convince him that he did not give sufficient heed to his profits.

"Customers want the most work in the shortest time, but you make every little thing a part of your religion. You are a dreamer,--a dreamer in broad daylight. Do wake up! for pity's sake, wake up!"

"Good Heavens! I live in a perpetual turmoil. My sleep is no longer sleep; I might as well lie on a bed of nettles. If I could only have one good night's sleep again! I am so troubled that I start up every other minute. It seems to me my clothes are never off, day or night."

Instead of sympathizing with her husband, and inspiring him with fresh courage and self-reliance when he failed, Annele sought only to convince him of his utter unfitness to do anything for himself, and the necessity of his following her wiser counsels. When, on the other hand, he did a good thing, and could not help calling out to her, "Hark, what a beautiful tone!" she was very apt to answer: "I tell you honestly, I don't like such organ music. I heard that same piece in Baden-Baden a great deal better played."

Lenz had often said the same thing himself, had frankly acknowledged it to Pilgrim; but hearing it from Annele pained him, and spoiled the pleasure of his whole life's work.

Annele had a settled plan in her head, which, in her opinion, fully justified the course she was taking. She felt her best powers wasted in her present insignificant position. She longed to be earning something, and thought that keeping a hotel was the employment best suited for her capacities. In pursuance of this project, she changed her policy towards Pilgrim. Whereas she had formerly tried to breed dissension between him and her husband, she now determined to make him her confidant and ally. He had once told her it was a shame she was not a landlady; every one said she would give the Lion a fresh start. Pilgrim should now join her in urging Lenz to take charge of the Lion inn. He could, at the same time, pursue his art,--she called it art when she was good-natured, otherwise it was always trade,--either at the Lion or on the Morgenhalde,--perhaps better in the latter place, it being so much more quiet. A merchant often had his place of business even farther from his residence than the Morgenhalde was from the Lion.

When Pilgrim came, therefore, Annele received him most graciously. "Pray, light your pipe," she said, "I like the smell of it so much. It carries me back to my home."

You are indeed in a foreign atmosphere up here, thought Pilgrim; but he kept his thoughts to himself. When at length, after many circumlocutions, she disclosed her plan, Pilgrim declined all co-operation in it; and Lenz manifested an obstinacy and a disregard to both caresses and bursts of temper which she was quite unprepared for. "First you wanted to make me a dealer in clocks, and then a manufacturer," he said; "now it seems I am to be landlord of the Lion. What did you marry me for, if you want to make another man of me?"

Annele gave no direct answer, only saying, "Towards every one else you are as soft as butter, but to me hard as a flint."

Lenz looked upon himself as having a settled position in life; Annele was bent upon giving him one. She did not confess that she considered herself the more competent to support the family, but only wept and bemoaned her hard fate in never being allowed to make herself of use. She was not unreasonable; she wanted nothing but to be allowed to work, to earn something; and that little favor was denied her. Lenz told her that the garden used to be very profitable; she might work there. But she did not like gardening. The plants grew so slowly in the ground, making no sound, and never to be urged or hurried out of their appointed times; it was too tiresome waiting for them to come to anything. Three visits to the cellar, and three to the kitchen, would earn more than a garden could show in a whole summer. A woman could be hired by the day who would do quite well enough for that.

There was no end to the fretting and grieving and complaining at the stingy way in which they had to live. Lenz was often driven to the verge of despair, and flew into such fits of passion as to be hardly recognizable for the same man. Then he would bitterly repent of his violence, and assume a different tone towards his wife, telling her he was mortified to have the journeyman and apprentice see how they lived together; and that, if she did not leave him in peace, he should have to dismiss them both.

Annele laughed at the threats, which he was in no condition, as she thought, to put into execution. He proved his sincerity, however, by actually sending both apprentice and journeyman out of the house.

As long as Lenz's firm and quiet character had asserted itself, he maintained a certain influence over Annele; but when he came to fighting her on her own ground, which was, in itself, a confession of defeat, she gained a complete mastery, daily upbraiding him with being a do-little, who had turned his assistants out of the house from sheer laziness, and whose good-nature was nothing but incapacity.

Instead of laughing at such absurd charges, Lenz brooded over them for days together, as he sat at his work, and allowed them to assume colossal proportions, long after they had faded from Annele's recollection. Her isolated life began to seem to her like a rainy Sunday in summer, when she had put on her holiday clothes, in the reasonable expectation of enjoying herself, and having a merry time with her friends, and found, instead, the road impassable, and herself a prisoner at home. It shall not be so, I will not live in this way, was the constant cry in her heart. She grew suspicious and irritable, taking offence at every trifle, yet never confessed to her husband or herself the true cause of her discontent.

Lenz was driven to seek comfort out of his own home. The fact of his going abroad did not vex Annele so much as the manner of his doing it. He hung about so long before leaving the house, and, after having gone, would come back two and three times, as if he had forgotten something. He could not bear to go away with feelings in his heart which made him almost a stranger to himself. He hoped Annele would try to detain him, or would at least speak a kind word to restore him to himself. In his mother's lifetime, he never started on a long journey without her giving him a piece of bread from the cupboard to save him from temptation, as she said, while a better safeguard than any loaf was the kind word spoken from her heart. Now he had to go as if neither the house nor himself were his own. Therefore it was that he trifled away so much time without being able to tell what he wanted. There is no virtue in a thing asked for; the true blessing lies only in a free gift, voluntarily--almost unconsciously--offered and received.

Long before the working hours were over, Lenz would often be sitting at Pilgrim's, and Annele with her parents. The whole house seemed out of joint. Lenz said not a word to Pilgrim of the grief that was inwardly consuming him, while Annele poured her complaints into unsympathizing ears. Her parents appeared entirely absorbed in their own affairs.

Lenz spent much time, too, at Faller's, where he was almost happier than at Pilgrim's. The grateful couple greeted him with joy and respect, and honored him like the Lenz of former days. At home he had long ceased to be anybody.

Faller and his wife lived harmoniously together, each thoroughly convinced that the other was the most admirable being in the world. If they only could be once out of debt, and have a little money over, they would astonish the world. As it was, they toiled and scraped, and were always cheerful. Faller enlivened himself and his wife, as he sat at work over the machinery of his big clocks,--for he was not a sufficiently skilful workman to undertake the more delicate timepieces,--with tales of his barrack life, and the different plays he and his comrades enacted in varied and gorgeous costumes. Mrs. Faller proved a most gracious public. In her loving eyes her husband was actually clothed with the royal mantles, the crowns, and the diamonds he so vividly described. How dismal seemed Lenz's own life in comparison! Ever darker and darker grew the shadows in his soul. His every experience was changed into bitterness and sorrow.

When he was present, as he sometimes could not help being, at the meetings and rehearsals of the Liederkranz, and sang the songs of love, of longing, of blissful rapture, his heart within him cried: Is this true? is it possible? were any human beings ever so happy, so blessed? Yet you yourself were so once. He called for soberer, sadder songs, and startled his comrades by the pathos of his voice, which sounded like the wail of a breaking heart. Whereas in former days he could never get singing enough, now he soon tired of it, and wanted to stop, or took offence at a word, and the next moment was as hasty in begging his comrade's forgiveness, when there was nothing to forgive.

He recovered his self-possession at times, and, trying to believe that the sole cause of his discontent was want of industry, would labor diligently at his old tasks; but no blessing crowned his toil. The day often found him undoing what he had spent half the night in completing. His hand was unsteady. Even his father's file, which had been repointed, and whose touch had never failed to quiet him, lost its efficacy. The machinery which had required a whole day to make and put together he would pull to pieces in a fit of discontent, only to find that it had been good work, perfectly adjusted, but seeming discordant because of the discord within him.

He often put his hand to his head, as if trying to recall something which had escaped him. The consciousness--if we may so express it--had vanished out of his work,--that power by virtue of which many things had seemed to do themselves with no effort of his will. Indignant at his own inertness, he compelled himself to something like repose and interest in his work. If you lose that, he reasoned with himself, all is lost. You were once happy with only your art, you must learn again to find in that your sole happiness. You can listen to a piece of music when other noises are going on, you can distinguish the one sound from the others; so here you must be absorbed in your own work, and not heed the tumult about you. If you insist on not hearing it, you will not hear it. Let your will but be resolute.

Lenz really succeeded in settling down to his work again quietly and methodically. Only one thing he missed,--one little sentence that Annele might have spoken: "Thank Heaven you are once more content to be at home!" He had thought he could do without such encouragement, but he could not. It was often on Annele's lips, only her pride kept it back. Why should I praise him for doing his duty? it said. Now is the time for having our hotel. He works best when no one is about to watch him; with him at his work-bench and me in the public room all would be well.

Lenz worked twice as hard as he used to to accomplish the same amount. Never before had he known that work was wearisome, but now the evenings found him tired and spent. Yet he allowed himself no respite. All might be lost, all hope of having a home again, if he ventured to leave his house or his bench.

For weeks he did not enter the village, while Annele was much with her parents.

A fatality at length forced him from home. Pilgrim fell dangerously ill, and night after night Lenz sat by his bedside. A painful duty it was, for not even this act of friendship escaped the poison of Annele's tongue. "Your attentions to Pilgrim," she said, "are only a cloak for your lazy, slipshod ways. You flatter yourself you have been doing something in the world, while you have been doing nothing and are nothing. You are a regular do-little."

His breath came short as she spoke, and there fell a stone upon his heart, which nevermore departed, but lay there like a dead weight.

"You will tell me next that I ill-treated my mother; that is the only unjust taunt you have not cast at me."

"You did; I know you did. Your cousin Toni, who went to America, has told us a thousand times that you were the greatest hypocrite in the world, and that he often and often had to make peace between your mother and you."

"You only say that to drive me mad again, but I care nothing for your words. Why do you choose a man in America for your witness? Why not some one here? You only want to goad me. Good night."

He passed the night with Pilgrim, who was now recovering, and of course happy in the feeling of returning health. Not wishing to sadden him, Lenz listened patiently to his accounts of the experiences his illness had brought him. "I came to understand how a bird can keep forever twittering on two notes. There is a state between sleeping and waking in which one tone is all-sufficient. For four weeks only a couple of words have been running in my head. Man has no wings beside his two lungs, and with one lung I can eat potatoes for seventy-seven years. If I had been a bird, I should have kept piping: One lung, two lungs, two lungs, one lung, just like a hedge-sparrow."

Few were the tones ringing in Lenz's heart, but they were too sad for any human ear.

"The Bible," continued Pilgrim, cheerily, "has been my helper again, and has firmly decided me to live a single life. There it is plainly said that in the beginning man was alone upon the earth, woman was never alone; from which it follows that man is able to live by himself."

Lenz smiled, but the words smote him.

Sad, pale, and worn with watching, he went home the next morning to his work, and said, when the children met him at the door, "I hardly knew I had any children."

"Of course not; you forget them, like everything else," replied Annele. He once more felt the stab at his heart, but it scarcely pained him now.

"Mother, dear mother!" he cried, gazing at his mother's picture, "you too she has outraged. Can you not speak? Do not punish her,--pray God not to punish her! The penalty would fall on my head and on my poor children! Help me, dear mother; testify for me, that she may cease to wring my heart! Help me, dear mother! You know what I am."

"A great strong man like you begging! I won't listen to your nonsense," said Annele, going into the kitchen, and taking the two children with her.

The cord was strained almost to breaking.

CHAPTER XXVI
THE AXE IS LAID AT THE ROOT OF THE TREE, AND BREAD IS EATEN WITH TEARS

On the sultry evening of a sultry day, the landlord, in an open wagon, drawn by his two bay horses, was returning from a drive to the city. He looked about him to the right and left in a strange way as he entered the village, and saluted with great affability. The wagon drew up before the door of the Lion. Gregory, who, in his postilion's uniform, but without his horn, had been driving, dismounted, and began to unharness the horses. Still the landlord sat motionless in the wagon, looking thoughtfully from the inn to the horses, and again from the horses back to the inn. At last, with a deep sigh, he descended, and stood on the ground. It was the last time he should so drive. All was as it had been, and only one other beside himself knew what a change was coming.

Wearily he dragged himself up the steps, at the top of which his wife was waiting for him. "How do matters stand?" she asked, softly.

"All has been arranged," answered the landlord, pushing by her into the public room, without entering the parlor first, as was his custom on returning home. He handed his hat and cane to the maid, and, sitting down with the guests who were present, ordered supper to be brought him at the public table. When it came, however, he appeared to have no relish for it.

The company did not break up till late into the night, and he remained sitting with the last. He spoke little, but his mere presence was compliment and entertainment enough.

His wife had gone to bed, and was sound asleep long before he retired to rest. Rest, indeed, he did not find. An invisible power drew the pillows from under his head. This bed, this house, everything, would to-morrow be no longer his! His thoughts lingered most lovingly about the carriage and the two bay horses. Suddenly the bays seemed to have entered the chamber; he rubbed his eyes; there they were, stretching their heads over the bed, and glaring at him with their great eyes; he felt their hot breath on his face. Recovering his self-possession, he comforted himself with the thought that he had, at least, borne himself like a man. He had said nothing to his wife, but let her have a quiet night's sleep. To-morrow morning would be soon enough for her to learn the news, even to-morrow after breakfast. Trials are easier to bear in the broad sunlight, after a night's sleep and a-good breakfast.

When the daylight came, the landlord was tired, and begged his wife not to wait for him, but to take her breakfast alone. At last he appeared, seemed to be in excellent appetite, and, on his wife urging him to explain what arrangement had been made, finally confessed: "Wife, I have allowed you to have a quiet night and comfortable morning; now show yourself brave, and take whatever comes quietly and calmly. At this very hour my lawyer in the city is proclaiming me bankrupt."

The landlady sat for a time stiff and speechless. "Why did you not tell me last night?" she asked, at length.

"From kindness to you, that you might have a quiet night's rest."

"Kindness? You stupid blockhead! If you had told me last night, we might have sent off many an article that would stand us in stead for years to come. Now, in this broad daylight, it is too late. Here! here! help! help!" she cried, breaking from her quiet conversational tone into frightful screams, and sinking, half fainting, in her chair. The maids from the kitchen, and Gregory, the postilion, came rushing in. The landlady raised herself, and cried, in the most piteous tones: "You deceived me; you never told me you were near being bankrupt. On your head be all the sorrow and the shame. I am innocent! Unhappy woman that I am!"

It would now have been the landlord's turn to fall into a fainting fit, had not his strength of body and mind supported him. His spectacles fell of themselves from his forehead to his eyes, that he might plainly behold the farce that was acting before him. This woman, who had given him no peace till he, the successful baker and brewer, joined her brother in the clock business, and who, when his brother-in-law died, had almost compelled him to continue the business alone, although he had no proper understanding of it; this woman, who had been constantly goading him on to new enterprises, and knew his affairs almost better than he did himself,--this woman had now called in the common servants to bear witness that he alone was guilty, and that on him alone must fall the blame.

One moment revealed to the unhappy landlord the whole extent of his misery. Five and thirty years it stretched behind him, and forward--how far, none could tell. To save herself, to expose him, his wife had carried her hypocrisy to this extremity.

His glasses grew dim with moisture; he could see no more. Quietly he passed his handkerchief first over them and then over his eyes. From that moment a rancor that never softened struck its roots into his heart; but his pride presented the same quiet, unruffled front.

"You have your own reasons for acting thus," he said, when the postilion and maids had left the room. "They are beyond my finding out. I shall say no more upon the matter." And he kept his word. His wife might talk and lament as she would, she could not move him out of his silence. It almost entertained him to see what a fine face she could assume before the world. He grew to be almost the sage he had been taken for. It is wonderful what woman can do, he thought, as he watched his wife's manœuvres. Practice certainly makes perfect.

The unwise world, however, did not accept the landlord's fall so patiently. Like a thunder-clap the report spread over mountain and valley, The landlord is bankrupt! Incredible! impossible! What can stand if the landlord of the Lion falls?

Even the golden lion on the sign seemed to protest against it, and creaked angrily on its supporting hinges. But auctioneers subdue even lions, and make no account of a coat of gilding. The sign was taken down. Most pitiable the lion looked with one eye hidden by the wall, and the other seeming to blink wearily, as if it, too, would fain close for grief and shame.

There was a crash in the village below, and there was a crash above on the Morgenhalde.

Lenz hurried down into the town, and back again to the inn. The landlord kept walking solemnly up and down the great public room, saying, with dignity: "This, too, must I bear like a man,"--like a man of honor, he had almost said.

The landlady wrung her hands, and cried that she had known nothing of it all, that she was ready to kill herself.

"Father-in-law," said Lenz, "is my money lost too?"

"In the common pile, there is no distinguishing one man's money from another's," answered the landlord, oracularly. "But a compromise can be made. Give me three years, and I will pay fifty per cent. Take a seat. There is no use wringing your hands. Lisbeth!" he called out into the kitchen, "my dinner!" The cook brought in a regular dinner, such as was served on ordinary days. Mine host took off his cap, put it on his head again, settled himself comfortably in his arm-chair, poured out some water, and began to eat, with the composure of true wisdom. "Draw up a chair, wife," he said, looking up from his second plateful. "These are the best horses for pulling up a steep hill; a good piece of meat in your stomach is a great help on a hard journey. Has all the wine been sealed, or can you get me a draught?"

"It is all sealed."

"Then let me have a cup of strong coffee to wind up with; there is comfort in that."

Lenz pressed his hands to his head. Was he out of his senses? Can this man, in whose fall the fate of hundreds is involved, be actually sitting down, with a good appetite, to his dinner? The landlord was condescendingly talkative, and bestowed high commendations upon Annele for not rushing down too, and swelling the chorus of senseless lamentations. "You have a clever, capable wife,--the cleverest of all my children. It is a pity she is not a man, to turn her enterprise to account. The world would look up if she were at the head of affairs. My Annele ought to be the mistress of a great establishment, a great public-house; she would make it the first in the country."

Lenz was indignant at these ready compliments, and at the landlord's whole bearing in such an hour as this. But he fought down his anger, and the very struggle made his voice sound hesitating, almost submissive, as he said: "Father-in-law, take care, above all things, that the wood behind my house shall not be cut down. I have heard axes at work there the whole morning, which must not be."

"Why not?" cried the landlord, with all the more vehemence for Lenz's meekness. "Why not? Whoever owns the wood has the right to do with it what he will."

"Father-in-law, you promised me the wood."

"But you did not take it. The wood is sold to the lumber-merchant from Trenzlingen."

"You had no right to sell it; it is the roof of my house. A few trees can perhaps be cut down, but not the whole forest. That has been the agreement for a hundred years. My grandfather has often told me so."

"It is none of my business. I have other things to attend to now."

"Good Heavens!" cried Lenz, with tears, "what have you done? You have robbed me of the dearest possession I had in the world."

"Indeed! Is money everything? I did not know that your heart, too, was in your breeches pocket."

"No, no! not that. You have robbed me of my second parents."

"I should think you were big enough to stand alone. But you are that sort of fellow that when he is a grandfather will cry out for his mother, 'Mamma! mamma! your little boy is hurt!' You said once you were a man, but what a man! One that can establish a union in which all shall stand by each other like the trees in a forest,--a forest of miserable clockmakers! Ha, ha! Go on with your union, then, that shall take care of yourself and the rest of your set." This malice was a new feature of the landlord's character.

Lenz was the only one of his creditors that placed himself in the breach, and upon his head broke the full force of the ruined man's fury.

Lenz grew red and pale by turns; his lips trembled. "Father-in-law," he said, "you are the grandfather of my children. You know how much you have robbed them of. I would not have your conscience. But the wood must not be cut down. I shall go to law about it."

"Very well; do as you like," returned the landlord as he poured out his coffee. Lenz could stay in the room no longer.

On the stone bench before the inn sat Pröbler, a wretched object, forcing every passer-by to hear his story. He was waiting, he said, for the arrival of the officers, because his best work, containing all his inventions, had been pledged to the landlord, and was now in the house. It must not be sold, and sent out into the world for every one to copy and cheat him out of his profits. The officers must get him a patent from government which should make him a rich and famous man. Lenz used all his influence to pacify the poor old fellow, assuring him that he was the only one whom the landlord had treated honestly; that he had already received the full value of his works, all of which utterly unsalable and still on his patron's hands; that they had not been pawned at all, but sold outright. Pröbler, however, was neither to be reasoned out of his belief nor induced to stir from his place.

Lenz went on, having enough to do in looking after his own affairs. He hastened to his uncle Petrovitsch. "Did I not tell you so?" was the old man's triumphant greeting. "Did I not tell you here in this very room, when you asked me to further your suit for Annele, that the landlord was in debt for the velvet cap on his head and the boots on his feet? Here he has been all this while filling his big paunch with other men's goods."

"Yes, yes, uncle, you were quite right, you foretold it all; but now help me."

"There is no help possible."

Lenz told of the forest, and the circumstances connected with it.

"Perhaps something can be done in that direction," said Petrovitsch.

"Thank Heaven! If I could but get the forest!"

"That is out of the question; the wood is sold. But it can only be cleared, not destroyed. It is the safeguard of your house, and no one has a right to remove it. We will show the wood-flayer from Trenzlingen who is master."

"O God, my house!" cried Lenz. It seemed already falling in; he must be at home to save it.

"Your house? You don't seem to be much at home here certainly," said Petrovitsch, laughing at his own wit. "Go to the mayor and enter a protest. One thing more, Lenz; I never in my life again will believe in a human being. I told you then your wife was the only honest one in the house. You see I was not mistaken in the other two. But Annele knew of this all along. She has known for years, known to a certainty, the state of her father's affairs. You were the make-shift, because the doctor's son-in-law would not have her, luckily for him."

"Why do you tell me this now, uncle?"

"Why? because it is true. I can prove it by witnesses."

"But why now?"

"Is there any time when the truth should not be told? I thought you and your Pilgrim were such heroes of romance! But I tell you you were very nearly as poor as you could be before you lost your money; for a man so full of complaints and regrets has ever a hole in his pocket. You are always crying for what you did yesterday, and thinking, 'O poor me! and yet I meant so well!' A man who wants to be pitied is no man; only women beg for pity."

"You are hard upon me, uncle."

"Because you are so tender with yourself. Show yourself now a man. Do not visit this upon your wife. Deal gently with her; her sorrow is greater than yours."

"You think so?"

"Yes. It will be hard for proud Annele of the Lion to find that a greeting from her is no longer the honor it used to be."

"She is not Annele of the Lion now; she is my wife."

"She is, before God and man. It was your own choice; I warned you."

Lenz hurried to the doctor's, who, as we have said, also filled the office of mayor; he was not at home. Thorns beset him on every side. His friends were not to be found, and his enemies let out all their secret venom against him, choosing his moment of helplessness to mock and torture him. He hastened up the hill again, past his house and into the wood beyond, where he ordered the wood-cutters to stop their work.

"Will you pay us our day's wages?"

"Yes."

"All right." They shouldered their axes and went home.

In the house Lenz found Annele embracing the children, and crying: "O my poor children! You will have to beg your bread, poor little ones!"

"Not while I have life and health. I am the head; only be calm and pleasant!"

"I have never been otherwise. You are mistaken, if you think that, because my father has failed, I am going to crawl at your feet, and let you do what you will with me. Not a bit of it! I don't give way an inch. Now show your boasted good-nature! Now show how you can support your wife."

"I am most ready to; but how give to one with closed hands?"

"If you had taken my advice, and bought the Lion, we should have been provided for, and the house would not have passed into strange hands. Don't tell me a word about the money. Exactly where you are sitting now you were sitting that day, and I here, and there stood the glass close to the edge of the table,--so close that I pushed it further in. Do you remember? I said to you then plainly and honestly, a business man never gives his money in that careless way, even to his own father."

"Did you know as long ago as that how matters stood?"

"I knew nothing, nothing at all; I only know what is business-like. Now let me alone."

"Will you not go to your mother? She is grieving sorely."

"Why should I go to her? to have her set out crying again at sight of me? Do you suppose I am going down there to be stared at and commiserated by everybody? to hear the doctor's charming daughters sing and laugh as I go by? I am sufficient for myself here in my solitude: I need no one."

"Perhaps it is all for the best," said Lenz, consolingly; "perhaps from this day you will be happier and better alone here with me. Such days may, must come again as those when you said, 'Up here we are in heaven, and may leave the world to drive and bustle as it will.' Let us hold to that. We were happy once, and shall be again. If you will be but kind and loving, I will do the work of three. Have no fear; I did not marry you for your money."

"Neither did I marry you for your money; it would not have been worth the trouble. If riches had been my object, I might have chosen a very different husband."

"We have lived together too long to be talking of marrying," interposed Lenz. "Let us have dinner."

At table he related the affair of the wood. "Do you know what the result will be?" asked Annele.

"What?"

"Nothing but your having to pay the wood-cutters' wages."

"That remains to be proved," said Lenz, and immediately after dinner went again in search of the mayor, whom he had failed to find earlier in the day.

On the way he was joined by poor Faller, pale as death, and crying: "Oh, this is horrible, horrible! A thunder-bolt from a clear sky!"

Lenz tried to reassure him. Two and a half thousand florins was something of a loss, to be sure, but he hoped to stand under it. He thanked his faithful comrade for his sympathy.

"What!" cried Faller, stopping short on the road, "are you involved too? He owes me thirty-one florins. He had that amount of mine in good clocks, that I left with him as I should have left them in the bank, meaning to pay off an instalment upon my house. Now I am put back at least two years."

Lenz hurried on. He could not stop with his friend, but must be off to the mayor's.

Faller looked sadly after him, almost forgetting his own misfortune in that of his friend.

The doctor was shocked at the blow which had fallen on the landlord. His own loss was insignificant, but he felt the disastrous effect the failure would have on the whole district. The news of Lenz's loss filled him with consternation. "Has he involved you also in his ruin? Nothing now will surprise me. Is it possible? is it possible? How does your wife bear it?" he asked, after a pause.

"She lays it all at my door."

Lenz brought up the matter of the forest, and prayed for speedy help, that his house might not be exposed to the force of the storms, and perhaps be buried by the mountain itself. The doctor acknowledged he had right on his side. "To make a clean sweep of the forest would be an injury to the whole district; perhaps destroy utterly our best spring of water, that by the church, which is fed from the forest. Some of the trees, at least, should be left standing on the crest of the mountain, but I fear we are powerless to insist upon it. It is a great misfortune that the owners are at liberty to cut down the trees at their pleasure. To try to make a law against it now, however, would be the old story of locking the barn door when the cow has escaped."

"But, Mr. Mayor, I shall be the first victim. Is there no help for me?"

"Hardly, I fear. At the time that the restrictions on the tenure of land were removed, during the mayoralty of your father-in-law, the authorities neglected to protect your rights as well as those of the community. You may say, to be sure, that nobody would have built a house where yours stands, if the forest behind it could be cleared; but you have no legal document guaranteeing you its permanent shelter. Your only chance is to lay your case before the court. Perhaps something can yet be done. I will give you a paper that may be of service."

Lenz felt his strength forsaking him. He could hardly stir from the spot, but the case admitted of no delay. No cost must be spared. He hired a wagon, and drove to the city.

At the Morgenhalde, meanwhile, appeared in gorgeous attire an almost forgotten figure. The shopkeeper's wife from the next village, that cousin Ernestine whom Annele had so mercilessly ridiculed on the occasion of her first drive with Lenz, now came to call on her, resplendent in a new silk gown, and a gold watch hanging at her waist. She had been in the village to put some money in the bank, being, she was happy to say, very well off. Her husband was doing a good business in rags, besides being a real-estate broker and the agent of a fire and hail insurance company, whose beautifully printed advertisements were at all the shop windows, and which paid him a regular salary without exposing him to any risks. She had been collecting some back pay, and could not find it in her heart to be in Annele's neighborhood without coming up to see her.

Annele politely expressed her thanks, and regretted she had no entertainment to offer. Ernestine protested that it was not for that she had come.

"I believe you there," said Annele, meaningly. She was convinced that Ernestine had come to be revenged upon her, to witness the rage and jealousy of that Annele who had always asserted such superiority over her poorer cousin. But Annele was woman of the world enough to ward off the malice of her visitor with a few stereotyped phrases of politeness, and at the same time to maintain the proper distance between herself, the child of the Golden Lion, and a poor relation who had only lived in the house as her servant, by giving Ernestine to understand that certain employments which were perfectly respectable and profitable for some persons were for others entirely out of the question.

In truth it was not without a certain feeling of malicious exultation that Ernestine had ascended the Morgenhalde. Her fingers often closed with satisfaction on the bag she carried on her arm, in which were a pound of burnt coffee and a pound of sugar for Annele. But at the sight of her cousin her exultation melted into sincere compassion. All the humble deference of former days returned upon her at Annele's assumption of her old superiority. The silk gown and gold watch were utterly forgotten, and the coffee and sugar offered only as samples in the hope of gaining her cousin's custom. If the many whom the Lion had benefited would now only return the favors they had received, Annele's parents would have enough to live upon for a hundred years to come, she said, with heartfelt tears; and added cordially that, if Annele had but married and remained at the Lion, the house would still have been kept up in the good old way.

This praise was more than Annele could resist, and completely effaced from her mind the new clothes and all her old grudges against her despised cousin. They talked over the good old times,--bewailed the present and condemned the ingratitude of mankind, until such perfect sympathy was established between them that they parted as if they had always been the dearest of friends and had lived together like sisters.

Annele accompanied Ernestine a little way down the hill, and commissioned her to tell her husband he must be looking out for a suitable hotel for them, a post station if possible, which they could buy and improve, and sell their house on the Morgenhalde. Ernestine promised the commission should be faithfully executed, and begged Annele repeatedly to be sure and apply to her for whatever groceries and other household goods she might need.

Many thoughts chased one another through Annele's mind as she retraced her steps homeward. Shall our house have supported and raised to prosperity so many humble dependants, and shall we ourselves be nothing? Even that simple Ernestine has had her wits so sharpened by living among us as to be able to carry on a shop and make something of her miserable tailor of a husband. She used to wear my cast-off clothes, and now what a figure she cuts! for all the world like a magistrate's wife, with her pocket full of money. And am I to do nothing but wither away up here and be reduced to receiving favors from Ernestine? It was all a pretence her leaving the coffee and sugar as samples; she meant to make me a present of them if she had dared. No, Mr. Clockmaker, I will wind you up another way and to a different tune.

She rejoiced to think of the commission she had given. If anything should come of it, they would lead a different sort of life. Meanwhile she would keep quiet and say nothing.

Late at night Lenz returned from the city, weary and dejected. No paper had been found guaranteeing him the protection of the forest. When he awoke the next morning, and heard the axes at work on the hill behind his house, every stroke seemed to fall upon his heart. Would I could die! he thought, as he settled down to his work. Not a word did he speak the whole day; only when putting out the lamp at night he said aloud, "I wish I could put out my own life as easily!" His wife pretended not to hear.

Hitherto neither her parents' fate nor her own had drawn a tear from Annele. Except for the one exclamation of distress for her children, she had remained perfectly calm. But the next morning, when no fresh, white bread came up from the village, and she laid the usual coarse loaf on the table, the big tears rolled down her cheeks and fell upon the bread. She cut off the moistened slice before Lenz saw it, and ate it with her tears.

CHAPTER XXVII
EVERYTHING LAID LOW

The court of inquiry brought to light all the secrets of the Lion. The landlord was shown to be a perfect monster. In order to satisfy those who insisted upon fair dealing and their full rights, he had sacrificed the humble and dependent. His own postilions lost their little savings. Poor clockmakers walked up and down the village street in despair, complaining that the landlord had been stealing months and years of their life all the while they were upholding him as the most honorable man in the country. Even the landlady was not saved by her pretended innocence. She had always spread such a glamour about her house, and uttered such magnificent boasts, and so honored the world with her patronage! The landlord, at least, had only lied by his silence and his quiet acceptance of the titles of man of honor and such like that were showered on him from every side.

Many creditors were undeterred by the long walk from visiting Lenz on the Morgenhalde. They had come as far as the village, and had a right to see the whole extent of the disaster. There was a blending of compassion with comfort at the sight of misfortune greater than their own, in the condolences they expressed. Many tried to console him with hopes of inheriting from his uncle, and promised they would make no claims upon him when he should come into his fortune. Wherever Lenz appeared he was compassionated for the baseness of his father-in-law in thus robbing his own son. Only one man had a good word for the landlord, and that was Pilgrim, who quite won Annele's heart by asserting at Lenz's house, in all sincerity, that her father had not meant to be dishonest, but had only been out in his calculations, and unfortunately risked his all in that unlucky Brazilian suit. A report was circulated that the landlady was having everything that could be smuggled out of sight carried up to the Morgenhalde. One poor clockmaker came to Lenz and promised to betray nothing if he might but have restored to him what was rightfully his. Lenz called in his wife and declared he would never forgive her if she had received into the house a farthing's worth of goods that did not belong to her. Upon the head of her child she swore she never had and never would. Lenz took her hand from the child's head; he would have no oaths.

Annele had said truly that there were no forfeited goods at the Morgenhalde. The landlady was often at the house, but Lenz held little communication with her. Well it was for her that Franzl was no longer there; for the new maid, a near relation of Annele's, made frequent journeys in the night between the Lion and the neighboring village, carrying heavy baskets full of things to be exchanged by Ernestine for money. Her husband, the shopkeeper, was the only one of the landlord's dependants who had not suffered. The clockmakers, instead of receiving ready money, had had the privilege of taking various stores from his shop on the landlord's security. The poor fellows found themselves now with no clocks and deep in debt. The shopkeeper told them frankly that they were better able to pay than the man who had given them security.

To all expressions of condolence Lenz had made answer that he should be able to stand his ground; but fearful and unexpected demands poured in upon him. Every petty creditor clamored for the instant payment of his farthing debt. All confidence, even in him, was destroyed. He knew not which way to turn. The heaviest claim of all, and one which he could not tell Annele, because she had given him fair warning on that very score, was for the security on Faller's house. The poor fellow came to him, quite beside himself with grief, to say that the owner of the house no longer considered Lenz's security valid, and that with his large family he saw no refuge open to him. Lenz promised him certain help. His good name and that of his parents could not fail to be honored. The world surely had not become so depraved as to have lost all regard for long-tried honesty.

Annele, who knew only of the lesser debts, advised Lenz to go to his uncle for assistance.

To his uncle indeed! The same disinclination to encounter disagreeable sights which made Petrovitsch invariably leave the village when a funeral was to take place, prompted him now to start off on a journey. The day after the landlord's disgrace he had disappeared, leaving his roadside harvest of unripe cherries to be gathered by the boys in the street; nor did he show himself again till the winter was well on, a new landlord established at the Lion, and the two old people settled in a house near the city, adjoining that of their son-in-law, the lumber-merchant.

The landlord had borne his fate with an equanimity almost deserving of admiration. Only once, at sight of the engineer driving his two bays, did his composure forsake him; but it was outside the town, and no one saw how he stumbled and fell into the ditch and lay grovelling there without the power to rise.

Petrovitsch took his walks now in another direction, and was no longer seen on the path by Lenz's house, nor in the wood, little of which indeed was now standing.

Lenz often spent half the night looking over his accounts and trying to make both ends meet. A way was offered at last; but the money burned as if hot from the Devil's mint.

Ernestine's husband appeared on the Morgenhalde with a stranger whom he presented to Lenz as a would-be purchaser of his house.

"What!" exclaimed Lenz, in great surprise; "my house?"

"Yes: it is worth much less now, as you say yourself, than it was before the wood was cut down. It stands in a very precarious position, but that can be partially remedied by precautionary measures."

"Who told you I wanted to sell my house?"

"Your wife."

"My wife? Annele, come here! Did you ever say I wanted to sell my house?"

"Not exactly. I only told Ernestine that if her husband should hear of a good hotel, in a favorable situation, we should like to buy it, and then sell our house."

"It would be much wiser," suggested the shopkeeper, "to sell your house first. You would easily find a suitable hotel, if you had the ready money to pay for it."

Lenz turned pale as death, and with difficulty brought out the words, "I shall on no account sell my house."

The two men departed, complaining bitterly of those shiftless persons who did not know their own mind from one day to another, and put others to a vast amount of needless trouble.

Lenz with difficulty commanded his rising passion.

Annele paid no heed to the frequent glances he turned upon her when they were left by themselves, but preserved a sullen silence. At last he spoke.

"Why did you play me such a trick?"

"I have played you no trick. This is a thing that must be done. We shall have no peace till we leave this place. I will stay here no longer. I want to be mistress of a hotel. You will see that I can earn in a year three times as much as you with your barrel-organs."

"Do you think you can force me to it?"

"If I could, you would have reason to thank me. You seem quite unable to help yourself out of your old ruts."

"I am not; I am out of them already," he said in a hollow voice, as he hastily put on his coat and left the house.

Annele ran a few steps after him.

"Where are you going, Lenz?"

He made no answer, but kept steadily on up the mountain.

Arrived at the highest point he turned and looked behind him. There lay his old homestead, stripped of its shelter of trees, naked and bare as he felt his own life to be. He turned away and hurried on. Abroad, abroad into strange lands he would go, and never come back till all in himself and in the world was changed.

He ran on and on, an almost irresistible impulse all the while tempting him back. He sat down at last on the stump of a tree, and covered his face with his hands. It was a still, soft afternoon of late autumn, when the sun's beams still fell kindly on the earth, especially on the Morgenhalde, and spread lovingly over the fallen trees they had so long nourished. The voices of the magpies were heard busily chattering in the chestnut-tree below, mixed with the frequent chirp of the nutpecker. In Lenz's heart was the blackness of death. "Man, help me up with this!" suddenly cried a child's voice. He rose and helped Faller's eldest daughter lift upon her back the bundle of chips she had been gathering among the fallen trees. The child was terrified at his wild looks, so like a murderer or a ghost as she thought, and hurried down the hill. He stood long watching the retreating figure.

It was night before Lenz returned home. He spoke not a word, but sat for an hour staring blankly on the ground. When he looked up, it was only to turn a wondering gaze on the tools hanging about the walls and suspended from the ceiling, as if questioning in his mind what they all were, and what they were used for.

The child in the next room began to cry, and would not be pacified till Annele went in and sang to it.

The mother must sing for the sake of her child, though her heart be breaking. Lenz roused himself, and followed her into the chamber. "Annele." he said, "I have been out into the country; I wanted to be up and away from here. Yes, you may laugh; I knew you would."

"I am not laughing. I had already thought it would be a good plan for you to go abroad for a year. Perhaps you would come back a wiser man, and all might be well again."

It cut him to the heart to hear her urging him to leave her; but he only answered: "If I could not go abroad while I was happy, still less can I go with this miserable weight at my heart. I am nothing, and am good for nothing when my thoughts are not free and happy."

"Now you do indeed make me laugh," said Annele; "so you can neither go abroad when you are happy nor when you are unhappy."

"I do not understand you. I have never understood you, nor you me."

"That is the worst of all, that there should be misery within as well as without."

"Do away with it, then, and be kind and good."

"Don't speak so loud; you will wake the child," answered Annele.

As soon as the conversation took this turn, there was nothing more to be got from her. Lenz returned to the sitting-room, and when Annele followed him, and had gently closed the door, he said: "Now in our misfortune is the time to love and cherish each other. That comfort alone might still be left us; why will you refuse it?"

"Love cannot be forced."

"Then I must go away again."

"And I shall stay at home," said Annele, indifferently; "I shall stay with my children."

"They are as much mine as yours."

"Of course," said Annele, in the same hard voice.

"There is the clock beginning to play!" cried Lenz, in distress, "and that merry waltz too! I wish I might never hear another note. Oh, if one would but dash out these miserable brains that have lost all power to think! Can you not speak one kind word, Annele?"

"I know of none."

"Then I will. Let there be peace between us, and all will be well."

"I am willing."

"Can you not throw your arms about my neck and say you are glad to have me back again?"

"No; but to-morrow perhaps."

"And if I should die to-night?"

"Then I should be a widow."

"And marry some one else?"

"If any one would have me."

"You will drive me mad!"

"It would not take much to do that."

"Annele!!"

"That is my name."

"What is to be the end of this?"

"God knows."

"Annele! Is it true that we were once so happy together?"

"I suppose it must be."

"And can we never be again?"

"I do not know."

"Why do you answer me so?"

"Because you ask me such questions."

Lenz buried his face in his hands, and remained in that attitude through almost the entire night.

He tried to make out how and why things had come to this extremity; why to his other misfortunes this so horrible one was added. He could not explain it. He lived over every moment from the first day to this night, and still could not explain it. "I cannot make it out! I cannot make it out!" he cried. "If a voice would but come down from heaven and tell me!" But there came no voice from heaven. All was still save the monotonous ticking of the clocks.

He stood at the window, gazing out. The night was still; no living thing stirred. Only snow-clouds were chasing each other across the sky. All night long, a lamp burned at the blacksmith's on the neighboring mountain. The smith had died that day. "Why was he allowed to die and not I? I would so gladly be dead." Life and death drove in wild confusion through his brain; the living were not alive; the dead were not dead; life is but one great horror; no bird ever sang; no human being ever made melody. The whole world is waste and void as it was before the creation. All is chaos....

His forehead dropped upon the window-sill; the blow scared him from his horrible waking dreams; he tried to find rest and forgetfulness in sleep.

Annele had long been asleep. If he could but read her dreams! he thought, as he watched her. If he could but find some help for her and for himself!

CHAPTER XXVIII
A BEGGAR'S HAT, AND AN
OLD MAN'S EARNINGS

In this part of the country the frost, when it has once set in, holds on unrelentingly for many months. The Morgenhalde alone makes a happy exception to the rule. There the sun has sufficient power to make a dripping from the roof, when all elsewhere is hung with heavy icicles. But this winter even the sun in heaven failed to treat the Morgenhalde with its wonted friendliness. There was no thawing outside the house nor in.

Not only was the cold greater than it used to be,--that was easily accounted for by the cutting down of the forest, whose tall trunks lay scattered about, waiting for the spring floods to carry them down into the valley,--but a weight as of frost lay heavy on the hearts of the dwellers upon the Morgenhalde. Annele seemed to have lost the power of rousing herself to life. Something had frozen up within her, which no warm breath could have melted, had any such breath reached her.

Annele, the only child who had remained near her parents, felt herself now the most cruelly deserted by their removal. The secret mortification of being the only poor one of the whole family of sisters seemed more than she could bear. She could do nothing to help her father and mother; nay, might even be reduced to asking charity of her sisters, to begging their children's cast-off clothes for her own little ones.

She moved silently about her work, her love of talking all gone, answering whatever question might be put to her, but nothing beyond. She scarce ever left the house. Her former restlessness seemed to have passed into Lenz. He so wholly despaired of accomplishing anything by his old quiet industry that the chair on which he sat and the tools he held in his hand seemed coals of fire to him. Petty creditors whom he was unable to pay, and was obliged to put off with fair words, were constantly annoying him. He, the Lenz who had only needed to say, "Thus and thus it is," to command instant confidence, now had to make solemn promises to this man and that, that his money should be paid him. The greater was his anxiety lest he should be unable to redeem his word, and the more did he exaggerate the danger that threatened his honor. The thought of the various persons here and there who were waiting for the receipt of their money haunted his sleeping and waking hours and increased his restlessness. He had always been considered a man who could be perfectly depended upon; now he frequently disappointed hopes that he had raised, and even failed to keep his engagements. He had trusted that the mere knowledge of his distress would be a sufficient protection against outside annoyances; he soon learned that men accept no excuses in lieu of their ready money. The ring of that is better than the echo of any good name; the best have too often proved a poor dependence.

Annele saw that Lenz was tormenting himself unreasonably. She was often tempted to turn his importunate creditors out of doors, and bid him not yield so meekly to their cruel exactions. It was the way of the world, as she knew, to trample upon those who cringed to it. But she kept her thoughts to herself. His distress should drive him to adopt her cherished plan of buying a hotel. Then, and not till then, would matters assume a different aspect.

In his anxiety and despair Lenz felt keenly the desolation at his heart, and his sidelong glance at Annele often said, as plainly as words could have done: You are right. You have often reproved me for being shiftless and good-for-nothing. Your words are coming true; I am good-for-nothing. My heart is consumed with anxieties, and this unloving life is wearing me away. I am like a candle that is kept burning at both ends. May it soon be burned out!

Many persons brought him articles to be repaired, and obliged him to work off part of his debt in that way. Now, now when bread was needed for to-day, and there was no provision for the future, it was hard to have to work for the past.

Some sat by him while he did their little jobs, keeping him thus a prisoner in his own house; others with complaints and revilings took away again the commissions he had failed to execute.

Such an existence was not to be endured. He must find some remedy, some lasting remedy. His present state was neither living nor dying. "It is intolerable to hang thus suspended by the hair of my head. I am resolved once more to have solid ground under my feet," he said to Annele. She vouchsafed a scarce perceptible nod of assent, but the mere exercise of his will gave him new strength.

Early the next morning he set off across the mountain to visit his mother's relations in the next valley. He had always been a favorite with them, and felt sure they would not look on and see him perish.

The stars were just fading in the light of approaching day, when he reached the top of the mountain-ridge. He looked abroad over the snow-covered world. Nowhere a sign of life; why must he be living?

A phrase that had haunted him in one of his sleepless nights came now into his mind: "The white sleep," this was it.

An icy wind from the mountains blew against his fevered checks, and rudely recalled him to his senses by tearing the hat from his head and whirling it down the abyss on whose brink he stood. His first impulse was to rush after it; but a look showed him that it would be rushing to certain death. One instant the thought flashed through his brain that a happy accident might thus end his life forever; the next he had put the cowardly suggestion behind him.

The blinding snow drifted ceaselessly across the ridge. The very raven scarce was able to guide his flight, but, with fluttering wings, was driven now high aloft, now deep into the abyss.

Lenz plodded painfully through snow and wind, till at last his eyes were greeted by the sight of human habitations. The smoke, beaten down by the wind, was spread in light clouds above the roofs of the houses. Chimneys were almost unknown in this part of the country.

Lenz sought shelter at the first farm-house. "Welcome, welcome, Lenz! I am glad you have not forgotten me," exclaimed a tall, handsome woman standing by the hearth, with the pieces of a stout bough she had just broken still in her hand.

"What have you done with your hat?"

"I did not recognize you at first. You are Katharine, are you not? How strong you have grown. Katharine, I am come begging."

"Not so bad as that, I hope, Lenz."

"Yes, but it is though," said Lenz, with a bitter smile. He felt this was no subject for joking. "You must lend or give me an old hat; mine has been blown away by the wind."

"Come into the sitting-room. My husband will be sorry not to have been at home to see you. He is carting wood in the forest."

The bailiff's daughter opened the sitting-room door, and politely invited Lenz to precede her into the warm, cosey parlor.

He told her frankly when they were seated together that he had had no intention of coming to see her; that in fact he did not even know where she lived; but was glad that chance had led him to her door. She took the confession in good part, saying, "You always were a true, honest fellow, and I am glad you keep so." She brought out an old gray hat and a soldier's cap of her husband's for him to take his choice between, recommending the cap, as the hat was really too shabby to wear. It was very much crushed and wanted a ribbon besides. He chose the hat, however, and Katharine, finding he could not be induced to change his mind, cut off one of the broad black ribbons from her Sunday hood, and made it serve as a hatband, talking all the while of the people and things in her old home,--everything connected with which she held in fond remembrance.

"Do you remember throwing your hat up into the air one night as we were coming home from the musical festival at Constance, and my running down to the meadow to pick it up for you?"

"To be sure I do. I don't throw my hat up into the air nowadays; the wind blows it up."

"The summer is sure to follow the winter," said Katharine, comfortingly.

Lenz looked in wonder at the handsome woman so ready to help with hand and tongue. She soon had a cup of coffee ready which she insisted upon his drinking, sitting by him while he did so and talking over old days and old acquaintances. "Franzl often comes to see us," she said; "we are still the best of friends."

"I can see that life has prospered with you," said Lenz.

"Thank God, I have nothing to complain of. I have good health, money enough for myself, and something to spare for others. My husband is honest and industrious. It is not quite so merry here as it used to be at home, for we have no singing. I would not mind that, if only I had a child. My husband and I have agreed that, if we still have none of our own on the fifth anniversary of our marriage, we will adopt one. Faller must let us have one of his. You will try to persuade him, will you not?"

"Gladly."

"How old you have grown, Lenz! You look all fallen away. Is it true that Annele has turned out such a bad wife?"

Lenz's face flushed crimson. "Good Heavens!" cried Katharine; "how stupid I am! I beg your pardon, Lenz, a thousand times. I did not mean to wound you. I know it is not true. People will talk as long as the day lasts, and when the days are short they take the night for it. I pray you again and again to forget I ever said such a thing. I have been so happy at having you see me in my own home, and now all my pleasure is gone; I shall be miserable for weeks. You and the landlady said I was too stupid, and I really am. Please give me back my heedless words, Lenz."

She held out her hand as if expecting him to lay the words in it.

Lenz grasped her hand, assuring her that he was not offended, but, on the contrary, grateful to her from his very heart. The hands of both trembled. Lenz said it was time he was on his way again, but she held him fast, and seemed anxious, by talking of all manner of other topics, to efface the remembrance of her heedless speech. When he left at last, she cried out after him: "Remember me to your Annele, and bring her soon to see me."

Lenz went on his way with the borrowed hat; a beggar's hat, as he called it, sadly.

Katharine's words pursued him. The same pity that was expressed for him in that house was doubtless felt in many others. The thought almost unmanned him, but he would not give way. He told himself that it was his own fault; he ought to have showed more firmness.

Again and again his stick fell from his hands, and every time he stooped to pick it up, he almost lacked the power to rise.

So much for a man's brooding over his sorrows instead of giving heed to his way! You would lose your hands if they were not fastened to your body. Mind what you are about!

He straightened himself up and walked on more briskly. The sun shone bright and warm; the icicles on the rocks glittered and dripped; joyous mountain songs, that he used to sing with the Liederkranz, began to ring in his ears. Away with them! It could not have been he who once sang such songs out of the gladness of his heart.

The relations he visited gave him a friendly welcome. At first he related everywhere the adventure of the hat as an excuse for appearing in such a dilapidated condition; but, finding that no one seemed to think it required an explanation, he finally ceased to mention it. Of course, in those very houses where he said nothing of the hat, it excited great speculation; and was taken as a proof of the abject poverty into which he had fallen.

His request for money was everywhere refused with more or less civility. Some wondered at his applying to them when he had rich brothers-in-law and an uncle rolling in money; others more politely excused themselves on the plea of having just bought some land and needing all their money for building; or regretted he had not applied a few days ago, before they made their last investment.

Sorely dispirited, Lenz pursued his way. He could not bear to think of home. His one wish was that he might never see the Morgenhalde again, but could lie down in some ditch, or in the wood, or in any one of the many quiet places he passed; lie down and die. Still, an irresistible force drove him ever onward.

Before him lay Knuslingen, where Franzl lived with her brother. There was at least one person in the world who would be glad to see him.

Who indeed could be so happy as Franzl when Lenz entered her room? She was sitting at the window, spinning coarse yarn, and a great bound her distaff gave at the sight of him. Twice she wiped the chair on which he was to sit, uttering all the while many apologies at the untidiness of the room. She had never noticed before how damp and smoky it was. Lenz must tell all about himself, and yet she could not keep still long enough to listen. She began running on in her old way. "At first the cold here was more than I could bear, after being used to our good sun on the Morgenhalde. Whenever there is a ray of sunlight anywhere, we were sure to get it there. Whatever else may go wrong, Lenz, be thankful for so much good sunlight; that no one can rob you of. It is very different here. For seven weeks and five days not a glimmer reached this valley. On the second day after the festival of the Three Kings, at eleven o'clock, the first ray of sun fell on that pear-tree at the edge of the hill, and from that time the sun kept climbing up so that in summer it is warm and pleasant. By this time I have grown to feel quite at home here again. But, Lenz, what makes you look so? There is a something in your face that I never saw before,--something that does not belong there. Ah! that is better; when you smile you have your old look again,--your pleasant look. You must have felt how I have prayed for you and yours every morning and every evening. I bear no grudge against Annele, not the least. She was quite right. I am a poor, worn-out tool. Whom do your children look like? What are their names? When the spring comes again, I must get to see them if I have to creep on my hands and knees." Then Franzl went on to tell how she had three hens and three geese and a potato-patch, all her own. "We are poor," she said, folding her hands on her bosom, "but, thank Heaven, we have never been reduced to looking on and seeing others eat. We have always had something to put in our mouths. Please Heaven, next year I mean to buy myself a goat." She bestowed great praise upon her geese, and greater still upon her hens. The hens, whose winter-quarters were in a coop by the stove, politely clucked their thanks and took as good a view as their space permitted of the man to whom their good qualities were thus set forth. The gold-colored hen, called Yellow-hammer, flapped her wings with delight, and then gave herself a good, comfortable shake.

Lenz had no time to speak, before Franzl, thinking to comfort him, broke out into fierce abuse of the landlady, mixed with commendations of Katharine and her kindness to her, as well as to all the poor in the neighborhood. "She feeds my hens, and they in return feed me," said the old woman, laughing at her own wit.

Lenz at last made out to say that it was time for him to be going. He heard Annele's sharp words as plainly as if she were standing at his elbow, reproaching him for his foolish waste of time, in sitting listening to any old woman's tale that was poured into his ears. He cast a hurried look behind him to see if she were not actually in the room, and hastily seized his hat and cane. Franzl begged him before he went to mount with her into her little chamber under the roof where she had something to say to him. He trembled inwardly lest Franzl too was about to speak of his unhappiness at home. She did not refer to that, however, but brought out from the straw of her bed a heavy, well-filled shoe, tied with many fastenings, saying: "You must do me a favor; I cannot sleep in peace with this thing here; and I pray you to take it away and do what you please with it. Here are a hundred florins and three crown-pieces. You will take them, won't you? and give me back my quiet sleep." Lenz declined the proffered money, and again prepared to depart; but Franzl wept and held him fast. "If you have any message for your mother, let me know. Please God, I shall soon be with her, and will deliver it faithfully. And if your mother is too timid to tell our Lord God the whole truth, I will do it myself. You can rely upon me."

Still the old woman would not let go of Lenz's hand, and kept saying: "There was something else I wanted to say to you; it has been on my tongue, but now I cannot think what it was. As soon as you are gone I shall certainly remember it. I was to remind you of something; don't you know what it was?"

Lenz did not know what it was, and at last almost reluctantly took his departure.

He entered a wayside inn, where a noisy welcome awaited him. "Hurrah, hurrah! that is jolly to have you here too," cried a voice in greeting; and there at a table, on which stood a great flagon of beer, sat Pröbler with two of his associates. One of his pot companions was the blind musician from Fuchsberg, whose instrument Lenz was in the habit of putting in order every year. An expression of embarrassment and mortification overspread the blind man's face at the sound of Lenz's voice, but he assumed a braggadocio air, and, flourishing his glass above his head, cried out, "Come, Lenz, pledge me out of my glass!" Lenz courteously declined. Old Pröbler tried to get up and advance to meet him, but his legs soon admonished him that he was safer sitting, and he contented himself with calling out: "Take a seat with us, Lenz, and let the bankrupt world without snow itself away as it will. There is no good left in it. Here we will sit till the day of judgment. I want nothing more; when I have spent my last farthing I shall sell my coat for drink, and then lay me down in the snow and save you the cost of burying me. Here you have a proof, comrades, of what a worthless world it is, that can thus bring its best and noblest to ruin. Have a drink, Lenz! That is well. Look at him, the best and bravest fellow in all the world; and how has the world used him? When his mother died, and the whole town was talking of nothing but Lenz's marriage,--why, the sparrows could not be madder after a sack of corn than the girls were for Lenz."

"Enough of that," interposed Lenz.

"No, no; you need not be ashamed to hear the truth. The doctor's daughters, and the paper-miller's only daughter, who was so rich and handsome and married Baron Thingummy,--every one of them would have jumped at him. The paper-miller said to me the day after the betrothal: 'Lenz of the Morgenhalde might have had my daughter and welcome.' And now--Peace, Lenz; I have done--only the Lord or the Devil knows who will get the upperhand. Look at that man! His own father-in-law has robbed him, has sold the very hair off his head, and left his house bare in the middle of winter. I was honest too once, Lenz; but I have had enough of it, and you will see the folly of it presently. Go about the world, if you are in want, and ask of the good and charitable. Take a pinch; take a pinch! their snuff-boxes are open to you, and that is all. Take a pinch!" Pröbler pressed his snuff-box upon him and laughed immoderately.

Lenz shuddered at hearing himself thus held up to view as the most striking example of failure and ruin. Such a notoriety he had never thought to attain. He tried to convince Pröbler that a man had no right to ruin himself, and then cry out against the world for having ruined him. His arguments in favor of every man's helping himself instead of expecting the world to help him greatly strengthened his own confidence, but failed to affect his hearer, who drew a knife from his pocket, and forcing it into Lenz's hand, together with the knife that lay on the table, cried out: "There, you have all the knives; I can do you no hurt. Now tell me honestly, am I a good-for-nothing fellow, or might I have been the foremost man in the world, if the world had helped me? Your father-in-law, whose soul the Devil must weigh out like so much lead, smeared his creaking boots with the marrow of my bones; and capital blacking he found it. Tell me honestly, am I a good-for-nothing fellow, or what am I?"

Of course Lenz had to acknowledge that Pröbler would have been a master in his art, if he had remained in the right road; at which the old man shouted and beat upon the table, and was with difficulty prevented from throwing his arms about Lenz's neck and kissing him.

"I want no other funeral oration. Lenz has pronounced my eulogy. Drink, drink! empty your glasses!"

Lenz had to drink with the rest, and Pröbler, filling the glasses again, cried out exultingly: "The doctor wants to take me into his hospital, his manufactory. It is too late. The time for doctoring and manufacturing is past. There is Lenz of the Morgenhalde, whom all respect to-day and to-morrow, and how much longer? I was once like him, and now when I go through the town men point their fingers at me and shrug their shoulders and cry, 'Pah, there is that scamp of a Pröbler!' Follow my advice, Lenz. Don't wait till you are as old as I, but make your bow in good season. Hark to me, brother, I have something to tell you. Do you remember our setting up those standard regulators? Do you know what we were then? A couple of pattern fools. Did you want to unite the clockmakers in an association? You might as well try to make them join hands with the Devil. Hark to me, brother! Don't tear yourself away; stay here, stay here! I have something to tell you. I make you my heir. There is a way to buy jollity in the world, and forgetfulness, and good cheer. I know your heart is heavy; I know where the shoe pinches. Old Pröbler knows more than other men; he knows everything. Pour wine on the worm in your heart; wine or brandy. Whatever drowns it is good. Then we shall have no more clocks, no more hours, no day and no night, no more time, but all eternity."

The old man fell into the most frenzied ravings. At times a spark of intelligence shone through his wild utterances, and then again all was delirium. It was impossible to tell whether it was a fact, or only his fancy, that the landlord's failure had robbed him of all provision for his old age, or whether it was the sale of his mysterious work that had reduced him to this state of despair. The burden of his cry was ever "Lenz, drink your life out while you are young, and don't be so long killing yourself as I have been." Lenz turned sick with horror at this living proof of what a man may come to who has lost his self-respect, and whose only refuge is self-forgetfulness.

"Your mother had a good saying," began Pröbler again; "did I tell you that was Lenz of the Morgenhalde? Yes, your mother. 'Better go barefoot than in ragged boots,' she used to say. Do you know what she meant? I have a better proverb: 'Tear off the nag's shoes before you take her to market.' Landlord! here is another horseshoe for you. Wine, wine!" He threw down a dollar.

The mention of his mother's name, though in such an unworthy connection, acted as a warning to Lenz as effectually as if her eye were suddenly and sternly fixed upon him. He rose from his seat, in spite of all Pröbler's efforts to detain him. Gladly would he have taken the old man with him, but it was impossible to stir him from the spot. All he could do was to charge the landlord to keep him where he was till morning, and on no account to give him anything more to drink. "There is my last pinch gone," cried Pröbler, throwing his snuff-box after him as he closed the door.

Drawing his breath hard, as if escaping from a close and burning hell, Lenz staggered out into the free air of heaven.

The night was coming on. The ice-bird twittered by the frozen brook, and the ravens sought the cover of the forest. A buck came out to the edge of the wood, stood with his great eyes fixed on Lenz till he came close up to him, then with a bound vanished again into the thicket, marking his course by the fresh snow he shook from the tender firs as he passed.

Lenz often stopped, thinking he heard himself called. Perhaps Pröbler was following him. He shouted in reply till the echoes rang; he went back a space; but no one did he see or hear. Again he pushed on. The trees, the mountains, seemed dancing to meet him. A woman who looked like his mother came towards him. If his mother should see him thus! The old woman gave him a friendly greeting as she passed, and warned him not to linger in the valley after dark, for there were black gullies in the snow, and avalanches were falling which might bury a man and no one be the wiser.

A wonderful tone there was in the old woman's voice, just like his mother's. Thanks for the friendly warning!

A sacred vow Lenz registered in his heart.--

He also resolved, however, not to go home empty-handed, and, turning his steps to the city, sought the house of his brother-in-law, the lumber-merchant. The rich man was happily at home, but gave him such an ungracious reception that he found it difficult to state his errand. Sister Babette's husband laid all the family misfortunes at Lenz's door; he alone was to blame for not having taken affairs from the beginning into his own hands. Whether the accusation was made in good faith or not, it furnished an excellent excuse for refusing help. In vain did Lenz pray, with clasped hands, to be saved from absolute ruin. The lumber-merchant only shrugged his shoulders and advised him to apply to his rich uncle, Petrovitsch.

CHAPTER XXIX
ANOTHER WORLD

"Good evening, Mr. Lenz," a voice cried to the dispirited wayfarer, as he was turning sadly away. Lenz started. Who could be calling him "Mr. Lenz?"

A sleigh drew up by his side, and the engineer, throwing back his fur wrappings, pressed him to jump in and occupy his empty seat. There was no resisting his cordial manner. He made Lenz, who was warm from walking, take the fur robe, while he covered himself over with the horse-blanket. The horses set off at a brisk pace; the bells jingled merrily; they seemed to be flying through the strangely soft air.

Annele is right; I ought to have managed to keep a carriage and horses, was Lenz's bitter thought in his poverty and debasement. A tormenting spirit seemed ready to turn every occurrence of this day into a reminder of his life's failure, and a temptation to unholy desires.

The engineer was very communicative. He spoke with peculiar satisfaction of the friendly relations that existed between himself and Pilgrim. With his knowledge of drawing,--for he had studied a year at the academy before entering upon his present profession,--and Pilgrim's eye for coloring; they could not only teach one another a great deal, but hoped to invent some new designs for furniture and wooden ornaments. They had already made some sketches of clock-cases, which they hoped would be of benefit to the trade. Pilgrim was as happy as possible in the exercise of his inventive genius, and in the prospect of seeing his pet plan carried into execution.

Lenz listened as in a dream. What was the man talking about? Were there still persons in the world who took an interest in such things, and rejoiced to further another's plans? Lenz spoke little, but felt the better for his drive. To be borne along so was much pleasanter than to have to walk wearily over the mountain and valley. For the first time in his life he felt something like envy.

At the doctor's door he was most hospitably obliged to descend and enter the house.

How delicious it was within! He had almost forgotten there were such peaceful, happy homes in the world, where all was so genial and warm, and fragrant hyacinths bloomed at the double windows; where all things showed that no angry word was ever spoken, but that the kind, true hearts that lived together gave out a pleasanter warmth than the best of fires.

"I am glad to see you once in our house," said Amanda, handing him a cup of tea. "How is Annele? If I thought your wife would like to see me, I should be glad to call on her some time."

"I have not been at home since four o'clock this morning, or was it longer ago? it seems to me a week. I believe she is well. I will send you word when she is ready to receive visitors." His voice was firm, but his eyes turned searchingly from one to the other as he spoke. Strange thoughts were sweeping through his brain.

How different his life might have been had he tried to win this woman for his wife! Pilgrim had seemed sure she would not refuse him. Then he would be sitting here at home; would have a position in the world, a wife to honor and uphold him, and all these kind friends for his own family. His first swallow of tea almost choked him.

The old mayoress, the doctor's mother, who sat at the tea-table eating her oatmeal porridge, had a great fancy for Lenz. He was made to sit close beside her and raise his voice very loud in order that she might hear. She had been a playmate of his mother when a girl, and liked to tell of the gay times they used to have together, especially on their Shrove-tide sleighing parties, which now were given up with many other of the old sports. Marie was always the merriest of the company. The old mayoress inquired about Franzl, listened with interest to Lenz's account of his visit to her,--he omitting, of course, all mention of the money she had offered him,--rejoiced at hearing of Katharine's prosperity and beneficence, and sympathized with her desire to adopt a child.

The whole company listened with polite attention. Poor Lenz, so long accustomed to being contradicted in all he said, or interrupted by exclamations of "O, what is that to me!" looked from one to another in amazement.

The old mayoress urged him to come often and bring his wife, adding: "I hear a great deal said of her goodness and cleverness. Give my greetings to her and your children." Lenz hardly knew how to respond to such unwonted words. He would have thought she was mocking at him, had her manner been less sincerely cordial. It must be that nothing but good was spoken of others in this house, and therefore she had heard only the good of Annele.

"Just as you arrived," said the old lady, "we were speaking of your father and my dear husband. A clock-dealer from Prussia had been saying that our clocks were not so good as they used to be when your father and my husband were alive; that they did not keep so good time. I told him I did not agree with him; that, with all respect to the dead, I was sure the clocks were just as exact now as in old times, but that the men who used them were more particular. Was I not right, Lenz? You are an honest man; tell me if I was not right."

Lenz assured her she was perfectly right, and thanked her for not extolling the old times at the expense of the new.

The engineer cited railways and telegraphs as proofs of the superior exactness of the present day.

When the conversation became general, the doctor drew Lenz aside and said to him, "Lenz, you will not be offended at what I have to say to you?" Lenz's heart sank within him. So the doctor, too, was going to speak of the ruin in his house.

"What is it?" he said, with difficulty.

"I wanted to propose, if it were not distasteful to you, and I really do not see why you should object--but what need of so much preparation? I want you to be director in the clock manufactory which my son and son-in-law have set up here. Your knowledge will be of service to them, and you shall receive in time a share of the profits besides your regular salary."

Here was a hand stretched out from heaven to save him. "I should be very glad to undertake it, certainly," returned Lenz, turning red and hot; "but you know, doctor, it has always been my endeavor to form an association of all the clockmakers of our district. Various circumstances have thus far prevented my accomplishing this plan, but I still cherish it, and therefore can only join this enterprise on condition that your two sons promise to connect the manufactory with the association, perhaps in time even to make it a part of the property of the association."

"That is precisely our intention; I am glad to see you still so thoughtful of others."

"Agreed then; yet I must make one other condition; please say nothing of our plan till--" Lenz hesitated.

"Well, till when?"

"Till I have spoken with my wife. She has her own ideas on such matters."

"I know her well. She is always rightly disposed when her pride does not stand in the way. An honest pride is greatly to be respected."

Lenz cast down his eyes, accepting the doctor's lesson, so kindly and courteously given.

His thoughts quickly reverted to the manufactory, however, and he begged leave to ask the doctor yet another question.

"Certainly; don't be so modest."

"Who among our best workmen are to be admitted?"

"We have as yet spoken with no one. Pröbler we shall offer some subordinate position to,--not so high a place as yours, of course. He is ingenious, and his ingenuity may, perhaps, be turned to practical account. The poor devil ought to be put in the way of laying up something for his old age. He has been almost out of his senses since his grand secret was sold at auction."

After some hesitation Lenz told of the condition in which he had found Pröbler, and said, in conclusion: "I have one more favor to ask, doctor. I cannot myself speak with my uncle; will you intercede with him for me? You are the foremost man in our district, and one to whom nobody, with a heart in his body, can refuse a request. I do not think, the more I consider the matter, that my wife will consent to my entering the factory, and, as you yourself say, her pride is to be respected."

"I will go at once. Shall I leave you here, or will you go with me to the town?"

"I will go with you."

He shook hands all round, each one wishing him a cordial good-night, and the old mayoress taking his hand in both of hers with peculiar tenderness.

They heard Pilgrim playing on his guitar and singing, as they passed his house. The faithful fellow felt a hearty sympathy for his friend, but sympathizing with another's grief is a different thing from bearing it. One's own life asserts the first claim.

Where the path began to ascend the hill, Lenz and the doctor parted. "Wait at home till I come," the latter said. "What a singular softness there is in the air this evening! We shall certainly have a thaw."

Here have I been seeking help abroad, while it was waiting for me at my own door. There are good people still in the world; better than I ever was, Lenz said to himself, as he went homewards up the hill.

CHAPTER XXX
PETROVITSCH THAWS AND FREEZES AGAIN

"I know what you have come for," said Petrovitsch to the doctor as he entered. "Take a seat." He drew a chair up to the well-heated stove, in front of which a bright open fire was burning.

"Well, what have I come for, Sir Prophet?" asked the doctor, summoning all his good-humor to his aid.

"Money; money for my nephew."

"You are but half a prophet; I want a kind heart too."

"But money, money is the main point. Let me tell you at the start that I am not one of those who spend their tenderness over a drunkard by the roadside. On the contrary, if the fellow has a broken leg, he has no one but himself to thank for it. I speak thus freely to you because you are one of the few men whom I respect."

"Thank you for the compliment. An honest physician, however, must heal the diseases that are of a man's own making as well as those he could not prevent."

"You are a physician, and you are sick too, like our whole district,--like our whole race in these days."

The doctor expressed surprise at the new light Petrovitsch thus threw upon his character, revealing principle and not a love of ease as the groundwork of his misanthropy.

"Can you sit an hour with me? To-day is my seventieth birthday."

"I congratulate you."

"Thanks."

Petrovitsch sent the maid to Ibrahim to say that he should be an hour later than usual at his game that evening, and then, resuming his seat by the doctor, continued: "I am inclined to be communicative to-day and talk about myself. Let me tell you that, as for the opinion of the world at large, I care as little about it as this stick of wood which I am laying on the fire cares who burns it."

"I should be greatly interested in hearing by what process you have thus reduced yourself to the hardness of a log of wood."

The doctor was anxious to avail himself of the unusual mood in which he found the crabbed old fellow, to gain a better insight into his character, even at the expense of prolonging Lenz's painful uncertainty. He was not without hope of inducing Petrovitsch to advance a sum of money which would enable Lenz at once to become a shareholder in the new factory.

"You were eight years old when I went abroad," began Petrovitsch, "and therefore know nothing about me."

"Begging your pardon, we heard a deal about the wild pranks of the--"

"Of the goatherd, I suppose. Thereby hangs a tale. For the forty-two years that I was travelling by land and by sea, in all degrees of heat and cold that man or beast can endure, that name pursued me like a dog, without my having the sense to give it a kick that should silence it forever.

"Our family consisted of only three brothers. Our father was proud, in his way, of having us all boys; but children then were not thought so much of as they are in these days. They had to learn to take care of themselves. Fewer words, good or bad, were thrown them, and every one, therefore, was made to go farther than a hundred do now. My brother Lorenz, generally called by the family name, Lenz, the father of the present Lenz, was the oldest; I was the youngest, and between us came Mathes, a handsome fellow, who was carried away by that great butcher Napoleon, and lost his life in Spain. I once visited the battlefield where he fell, and saw a great hill under which all the dead bodies had been huddled together. There was no telling any man's brother. But why dwell upon that? Not long after our Mathes turned soldier, my brother Lorenz went to Switzerland for three months, and took me with him. Who so happy as I? My brother was a quiet, thoughtful man, regular and exact as clock-work, and fearfully strict. I was a wild, ungovernable child, inclined to no good, and with a special distaste to sitting behind a work-bench. What does my brother do but take me, soon after Candlemas, to a boy-sale at St. Gall? There were boy-sales held there then every year, where the Swiss farmers came to buy farm-hands from Suabia.

"As we were standing together on the market-place, a square-built Appenzeller came along, and planting himself in front of us asked my brother, 'What is the price of the boy?'

"'A cord of Swiss impudence,' I answered, pertly; 'six feet wide and six feet high.'

"The stout Appenzeller laughed, and said to my brother, 'The boy is smart, I like him.' He asked me various questions, all of which I answered as well as I knew how.

"My brother and the Appenzeller agreed upon the terms. The only farewell I received was, 'You will get thrashed if you come home before winter.'

"The whole summer I served us goatherd, and a merry life I had; but those words, 'What is the price of the boy?' often rang in my ears. I felt like another Joseph, sold into Egypt by my own brother, but with no likelihood of becoming king. In the winter I was at home again, where I was not well treated, nor, I confess, very well-behaved. In the spring I said to my brother, 'Give me a hundred florins' worth of clocks, and let me join you in the clock trade.' 'A hundred cuffs, more likely,' was all the answer my brother Lorenz gave me. At that time he had the whole charge of the business and the household, my father being sick and my mother not daring to interfere. Women were not of as much account in those days as they are now,-- fortunately for them and their husbands, too, in my opinion. I induced a travelling merchant to let me go with him and carry his clocks. He almost broke my back with the burdens he imposed upon me, and nearly starved me into the bargain; yet I could not get away from him. I was worse off than the poor horse in harness, for he is at least of value enough to be cared for. Many times I was tempted to run away with the wares intrusted to me; but always atoned for my evil thoughts by compelling myself to remain awhile longer with my tormentor. No harm came to me from this experience, however, hard as it was. I kept healthy and honest.

"One occurrence, which exerted a great influence on my future movements, I must relate here, because I shall have occasion to refer to it later. Anton Striegler and I were sitting chatting together one beautiful summer morning, before the posada--as they call the inns in Spain--of a large town about six leagues from Valencia, when a handsome boy, who happened to be passing, stopped, listened to our talk for a while, and then began wringing his hands like one possessed. Just as I was about to call my companion's attention to the boy, he suddenly sprang towards us, and seizing Striegler, cried out in Spanish, 'What is that you were saying?'

"'None of your business,' returned Striegler, also in Spanish.

"'What language was it?' asked the Spaniard again.

"'German,' answered Striegler. The boy seized the image of the saint that hung from his neck, and fell to kissing it as if he would eat it up. Finally he begged us to go with him to his house, where his father was talking in that language and no one could understand him. On the way he explained that his father was a blacksmith from Germany, who had lived in the town for forty years, and had married here; that for weeks he had been lying dangerously ill, and during the last few days had talked in an unknown language, so that he could neither make himself understood nor understand those about him. The whole family were in the greatest distress. On entering the house we found an old man with snow-white hair and long white beard, sitting upright in bed, and calling out, 'Give me a bunch of rosemary!' then he would begin to sing,--'And plant it on my grave.' The sight and the sounds chilled every drop of blood in my veins; but Striegler is not easily daunted, and, approaching the bed, said in German, 'How are you, countryman!' If I live to be a hundred, I shall never forget the old man's face when he heard those words. He stretched out his arms and then folded them on his breast, as if to gather the sounds to his heart. Striegler talked further with him. The old man was able to give sensible answers; a little confused at times, but in the main intelligible. He was a Hessian by birth, named Reuter, but had changed his name to Caballero. For fifty years he had spoken nothing but Spanish, and now at the point of death every Spanish word had forsaken him. I believe that, for the rest of his life, he never understood another word of that language. The whole family was made happy by having us as interpreters of the old man's wants. Striegler took advantage of this incident to gain for himself something of a position in the town and turn it to profitable account, while I sat by the sick-bed. The best part of my life abroad was that I spent with Striegler. I had plenty to eat and drink, and for the sake of the old man was abundantly well treated. At the end of three days we left him; but hardly had we gone a couple of leagues before the son came riding after us to say we must go back, for his father was crying for us. We went to him again. He was talking German; but too incoherently for us to make out his meaning. At last, with the cry, 'Now I will go; now I will go home!' he fell back and died."

Here Petrovitsch paused in his story. "The whole thing made a deeper impression on me than I knew at the time. Striegler, after a while, returned to Spain and, I hear, married a daughter of Caballero. I continued my travels through France. At Marseilles I met your father, who saw I was not such a good-for-nothing fellow as the world supposed, and gave me the means of starting business on my own account. The saving and starving I had long practised for others I now tried for myself. I met with considerable success, paid back your father's money, and received from him more wares.

My business led me over half the world. I could speak five languages; but a word of German, especially of Black Forest German, always made my heart leap in my bosom. One great weakness of mine was that I could never conquer my homesickness. It haunted my steps like a ghost, and spoiled the relish of many a jolly drinking-bout."

Petrovitsch paused again, poked the fire till it crackled merrily, and then, rubbing his hand over his old, wrinkled face, resumed: "I pass over ten years. I am in Odessa, and a made man. A fine city Odessa is, where all nations are at home. One friend I have there whom I never shall forget. There are villages in the neighborhood, Lustdorf, Kleinliebenthal, and others, occupied wholly by Germans; not from our part of the country, however, but chiefly from Wurtemberg. Many commissions were intrusted to me by persons at home; but I kept faithfully by your father until his death. Although my property was handsome, quite sufficient to enable me to drive, I travelled over all Russia on foot, not knowing what fatigue meant. Look at the muscles of that arm; they are of steel. What must they have been thirty years ago? They were something to be proud of then, I can tell you. I settled in Moscow, and remained there four years. Yet I can hardly call it settling, for I never rested an hour; never made myself at home, as the phrase is. In that way I could better earn and save. I never, in all my life, was called in the morning, nor turned over for another nap when I once waked.

"Many of our country-people came to me, and always found me ready to help. Not a few out in the world owe their fortune to me. I asked about home, and was told my father was dead, my mother was dead, and my brother was married. I asked if he never inquired about me. That was a hard question to answer. All he had ever been heard to say of me was that I should one day come home a beggar. But the cruelest thing of all was my countrymen's calling me the goatherd. My brother was to blame for my having to bear that nickname through life. I always meant to send him a couple of thousand florins, with a letter saying: 'The goatherd sends you this for the hundred cuffs you owe him, for all the good you have done him, and for your faithful care of him.' I kept thinking I would do it, but, the devil knows why, I never did, I got tired living in Moscow, and wanted to go home; instead of which I went to Tiflis, and stayed there eleven years.

"As I began to grow old my feelings changed, I resolved to go home with a bag of gold, that all men should see but my brother; with him I would have nothing to do. The more I thought of it, the more I was convinced that he had dealt cruelly with me, and would be glad to know I was dead. He should suffer for it. I hated him and often reviled him in my thoughts; yet my thoughts kept returning to him. An indescribable homesickness consumed me. No water tasted as good as that of the old well at home by the church, and no air was as fragrant as ours of a summer evening. Thousands and thousands of times I have thought how gladly I would give a hundred florins for a roomful of the air of my native valley. Then I imagined the delight of getting home and having all the dwellers above the town and below it gathering together to see Peter, or Petrovitsch, as they call me now. There should be long tables spread on the meadow before our house, where all should come who would, and eat and drink for three days,--all but my brother. Yet all the time I felt in my heart, though I would not confess it, that he was the only person I loved. Every year I said, next year I shall go; but I kept staying on. It is hard to leave a business in which everything you touch turns to gold. I wondered how I came to be so gray and old. At last I fell sick,--for the first time in my life dangerously sick. For weeks I was out of my head, and talked, as I afterwards learned, in a language that no one about me understood. The doctor was able to make out a few words, which he said were German. I frequently cried out, 'Cain!' and, 'What is the price of the boy?' Then I remembered Caballero in the village near Valencia. Suppose you should one day be lying so on your death-bed, and should cry out for water, and there should be no one to understand you!-- Now the time was come. Home, home, home! Thanks to a good constitution, I quickly recovered and proceeded to carry out my fixed resolution. Perhaps my brother would humble himself and acknowledge his injustice to me; then I would stay by him till I died. How much time might still remain to us? What was the whole world away from those of our own blood? On the way,--for I actually set out at last,--I was like a child who has been lost in the wood and runs crying home. I often had to remind myself how old I was. Hatred of my brother revived in my heart and tormented me. It was like a severed artery that will not heal: a touch, a thought, brings the bad, black blood again.

"I reached home.

"The mountains seemed to be rising and running to meet me, as I entered the valley.

"I drove through the different villages. There was where such and such a one lived; I could not think of the names till I had passed. The road was broader and more convenient than it used to be, and followed the valley instead of going over the Woltending mountain. I was in a strange land and yet at home. Mountains that used to be thickly wooded were now as bare as a Turk's head. There had been a terrible sacrifice of trees. I entered the village on a beautiful summer evening at haying-time, just as the bells were ringing. They seemed voices not of this world. I had heard many bells in the forty-two years I was abroad, but none like these. Involuntarily I took off my hat; it was so good, so heavenly to feel my native air blowing about my head! I know not what echo it woke within me. The gray hairs on my head seemed growing young again. Most of the persons I met on the way were strangers to me. You, doctor, I recognized from your resemblance to your father. No one knew me. I drew up at the 'Golden Lion' and inquired if Lorenz Lenz of the Morgenhalde was at home. At home? He had been dead these seven years. A thunderbolt falling at my feet could not have more confounded me. Fortunately I recovered myself before my agitation was observed.

"I went up to my room, and late at night walked through the village, meeting many familiar objects that convinced me I was once more at home. All was still about my parents' house. The pine trees at the back of it, that were hardly twice as tall as I when I left home, were now giants, ready to be cut down. I half resolved to depart before day. What should I do here? It would be easy to go, for no one had recognized me.

"But I did not depart.

"Persons came to me from all quarters, and offered me their hands--to be filled. But, doctor, I once to kill time fed the sparrows on my window-sill, and from that day the importunate beggars are possessed to come here every morning, and distract me with their noise; there is no frightening them away. It is easy to acquire habits, but hard to break them up. I stopped asking about anybody, for I heard of nothing but death and disaster, and a hundred times a day got a stab at my heart. Whoever came in my way was very well; who did not, was gone. All came to see me except my sister-in-law and her prince. 'My brother-in-law knows where his parents' house is,' she said. 'It is not for us to run after him.' The very first time I saw young Lenz, I conceived a dislike to him. He looked like none of us, but took after his mother's family. When I look round upon the village now, and the whole district, in fact, I am ready to tear my old hair out for having come home. Everything is stunted and lazy and spoiled. Where is the old light-heartedness, the old high spirit? Gone. The youths are good for nothing. Don't I have to pick the cherries before they are ripe to prevent the young trees from being broken? My musical nephew there cossets himself up in his room, while I, at his age, was out making my way in the world. I mind nothing; but he turns pale and sick at every rough wind and every rough word. There was a time when I hoped something from him, and thought he might still make my life happy. If he had married your daughter Amanda, the young people should have come to me, or I would have gone to them. My property would have come into your family, as it is right it should; for I am indebted to your father for the beginning of my good fortune, if good fortune it is. That cursed Pilgrim guessed my thoughts, and tried to make me a go-between. I would have nothing to do with it. I never give advice nor take it. Every man must work out his life in his own way. And this is the point I want to come at: that I won't give a red cent; rather would I throw my money into the fire. Now I have talked enough. I have made myself quite hot."

"How did the water of the spring by the church taste, that you had longed for so much?" asked the doctor.

"Bad; very bad. It is too cold and too hard. I cannot bear it."

With this for a text, the doctor undertook to reason Petrovitsch into a better way of thinking. He tried to convince him that the world had not changed for the worse any more than the spring of water; only his eyes and thoughts, as well as his palate, had lost their youth. He explained to him, that while he was perfectly right in strengthening his mental and bodily powers by contact with the outside world, yet domestic industry and economy required that many should stay at home, and be screwed, like their own vice, to the work-bench. He laid special stress on the delicacy, amounting almost to morbid sensitiveness, that accompanies a talent for music; at the same time pointing out to the old man the same soft-heartedness in himself that he censured in his nephew. He strongly urged upon him the necessity of extending a helping hand. But Petrovitsch had relapsed into his old obstinacy, and silenced the doctor by saying: "I keep to what I said before. I neither give advice nor take it. I shall take no steps in the matter. If you say another word, doctor, I will not answer for the consequences."

It was clear there was nothing further to be hoped for, and, as a message arrived at this moment from Ibrahim, Petrovitsch and the doctor left the house together. The doctor was obliged to draw his cloak close about him as he went up the Morgenhalde. It was blowing fiercely, though the wind was strangely warm.

CHAPTER XXXI
ANNELE THAWS AND FREEZES AGAIN

While Lenz, in his great distress, was wandering about the world, Annele was visited at home. She was alone, wholly alone; for her husband had left no parting word behind. He had gone away moody and silent, without opening his lips. Pooh! Two words would have brought him back, she thought, and yet a strange fear oppressed her heart, and flushed her cheeks. She had never been used to the company of her own thoughts. In the constant bustle and stir in which her life had been spent, she had never sat down quietly to think. Now it was forced upon her. No matter what she turned her hand to, or how persistently she went about her household work, something was always following her, pulling at her gown, and whispering, "Hearken to me!"

Little William was sitting by the servant-maid, winding the yarn as fast as it was spun. The baby had been put to sleep, and as Annele sat by the child's bed an invisible power held her in her chair, and forced her to listen to the voice of her own thoughts: Annele, what change has come over you? The gay, handsome Annele, whom all loved and flattered, sitting here in a darkened chamber of a lonely house, having to delve and to save!--I would not mind that; I would do it gladly, if I were but honored in the household. But nothing I do or say suits him. What do I do that is wrong? Am I not frugal and industrious, willing to work even more than I do? But this place is like a grave.--

She started, trembling, from her seat. A dream she had had in the night came vividly to mind,--not a dream, this time, of merry parties or flattering guests, but of her own open grave. She had stood beside it, and distinctly seen the little clods of earth rolling down into the pit that had been dug for her. She screamed aloud and stood as one paralyzed.

With an effort she recovered herself; all the life within her cried: "I will not die, not yet; for I have not yet lived, either at home or here."

She wept in deep compassion with herself as her thoughts travelled back over the years that were gone. She had imagined life would be so happy alone with the man she loved, far away from the world; from the publicity that had grown irksome to her, and the undefined feeling of insecurity that had begun to poison her enjoyment of the profusion about her. It was her husband's fault that she longed now for a wider field in which to use her wasted powers. He was like his own clocks, that play their little tunes, but hear nothing beyond. The comparison made her laugh in the midst of her wretchedness.

She would gladly have yielded obedience to one who showed himself a master among men, but not to a miserable sticker of pins.

Yet you knew who and what he was, whispered something in her heart.

Yes, but not like this, not like this, she answered.

Has he not a good heart?

Towards every one but me. No one who has not lived with him knows his many whims, his frightful bursts of passion. This clock-making is fatal; we must try another mode of life.

This was the point to which Annele's thoughts always reverted. If she could only be a landlady at the head of the first establishment in the country; could only be earning some money and have some communication with the world, happy days would come again.

She went to the glass and rearranged her dress. She could never go about in any slatternly fashion; no slippers for her, though Lenz often did not draw on his boots from one Sunday to another. For the first time for many months she dressed her hair in its triple crown of braids, and her proud glance as she stood before her glass said plainly: I am Annele of the Lion; I have no idea of pining away for any man. I have harnessed afresh, and he must drive with me. Our two strongest horses are put to the carriage. She snapped with her tongue, and raised her right hand as if brandishing a whip over the horses' heads.

"Is your mistress at home?" asked a voice without.

"Yes."

There was a knock, and, to Annele's great surprise, the minister entered.

"Welcome, sir," said Annele, courtesying; "did you wish to see me or my husband?"

"I came to see you, knowing your husband was absent. I have not seen you in the village since your parents' misfortune, and thought I might perhaps be of some service to you in your trial."

Annele breathed more freely. She had feared her visitor might have been sent by Lenz, or had come to speak with her about Lenz.

She spoke with sorrow of the fate of her parents; her mother, she feared, would not long survive the shock.

The minister talked with her kindly and seriously, urging her to be resigned to what had happened, whether merited or unmerited, and not to let distress and anger tempt her to shut herself from the world. He reminded her of the one honor that he had spoken of at her marriage; he spoke pleasantly of her father, whose misfortune was due to a miscalculation on his part, not to any intentional dishonesty.

"I have not forgotten your wedding day," pursued the minister, giving a slight turn to the conversation, "and wished to bid you good morning on this fifth anniversary of it."

Annele smiled and thanked him; but the thought struck to her heart that Lenz had gone away without bidding her good morning. With a return of her old fluency she expressed her pleasure at the honor her minister paid her; spoke of his great goodness, and of the daily prayers the whole village ought to offer up to Heaven for his life and health. She evidently was bent upon keeping the conversation away from her own affairs. She would allow no approach, on the minister's part, to the subject of her domestic difficulties. Under the influence of that determination she drew in her breath and moistened her lips, as the postilion Gregory might when he was about to blow one of his elaborate pieces on the horn.

The minister understood it all. He began by praising Annele for her many good qualities,--for her neatness and careful management in her parents' house, and her keeping her purity unharmed by the temptations which assailed her there.

"I have long been unaccustomed to praise," answered Annele. "I had almost forgotten I was ever of account in the world."

The minister saw his bait was taking. As a physician wins the confidence of his patient by describing to him all his aches and pains, till the sick man looks up joyfully and says, "the doctor knows my whole case; he will surely help me," so the minister described to Annele all her mental sufferings, and wound up with saying: "You have often seen blood flow from a wound, from a blow or a bruise, and know how the black blood gradually takes on all the seven colors. So it is with the soul's wounds. An injury, an offence, like that black blood gradually takes on all the colors,--hate, contempt, anger, self-pity, pain at the wrong, a desire to return evil for evil, and again to let all go to wreck and ruin."

It seemed to Annele that she was holding her heart in her hand, and showing how it had been bruised and lacerated and beaten to pieces. The good-for-nothing barrelmaker, he would have his full deserts now! "O, help me, sir!" she cried.

"I will; but you must help yourself. You do not need to change your nature. Alas for you, if you did! I am old enough to know how easy that is to say, and how hard to do. You only need to shake off something foreign to yourself that has taken possession of you. There is goodness in you, only you have forgotten it, wilfully forgotten and ridiculed it, and prided yourself on your sharpness of tongue. Have done with all pride and ambition. Where is no oneness of heart is a continual wearing upon each other."

The little man's figure dilated, and his voice gathered strength as he laid bare before Annele her false pride and her hard-heartedness towards Franzl. Annele's eyes flashed at the mention of Franzl.

So the secret was out. It was she, the thievish, hypocritical old woman, who had brought this upon her, and turned all against her. No cat ever mangled a mouse with greater pleasure than Annele now pulled to pieces old Franzl.

"If I could but have her once in my clutches!" she snarled.

The minister waited till her fury had spent itself. "You make yourself out to be wicked and vindictive," he said; "but I still maintain you are not so at heart."

Then Annele cried to think she should be so sadly changed; it was not like her to be so angry. It was all because she had nothing to do; was not allowed to be earning anything. She was not made to keep house for a petty clockmaker; she was made to be a landlady. If the minister would only help her to be landlady, she promised he should never see another spark of anger or cruelty in her.

The minister admitted that she had all the requisite qualities for a landlady, and promised to do everything in his power to make her one; but implored her, as she kissed his hands in gratitude, not to trust for her improvement to any external circumstances.

"You are not yet subdued by your grief and humiliation. Your pride is your sin, the cause of unhappiness to you and yours. God forbid you should need the loss of husband or children to bring you to your better self!"

Annele's seat was opposite the mirror, and as she caught the reflection of her face in the glass there seemed to be a cobweb floating before it. She passed her hand several times across her face.

The minister got up to go, but Annele begged him to sit with her a little longer; she could think better when he was by.

The two sat in silence. No sound was heard except the ticking of the clocks. Annele's lips moved, but no voice came from them. She kissed his hand devoutly when he at last departed, and he said: "If you feel yourself worthy, if your heart is softened, really softened, come to the communion to-morrow. God bless you!"

She wished to accompany him part of the way. "No courtesies now," he said; "be first pure and humble in heart. Judge not, that ye be not judged, says the Saviour. Judge yourself; look into your own heart. Accustom yourself to sit quiet and think."

Annele remained sitting where the minister had left her. She found it hard, for sitting with her hands before her and thinking was not her habit. She forced herself to it now. One sentence of the minister's kept ringing in her ears: "You have often good and pure thoughts,--thoughts of penitence; but they visit you as guests, drink their glass, and are gone. You put the chairs in place again, wipe off the table, and all is as if they had not been."

Annele reflected upon it and acknowledged it was true.

She could be hard upon herself as well as upon others. Why have you thus misused your life? she asked herself.

The child woke up and cried. "The minister has no children; it is very well for him to tell me to sit and think, but I must quiet my child."

She took the little girl out of bed and fondled her more tenderly than usual. The child helped to drive away her solitary thoughts.

She suddenly remembered the tune that Lenz had played the first time she was at the house, and she sang her baby to sleep by it now: "Love it is the tender blossom." She still sang on after the child was asleep and lying quiet in her arms, and as she sang the words she thought: Whom have I ever loved? whom?--I wanted to marry the landlord's son and the engineer in order to have a good position; but as for loving any man with my whole heart, I never did. And my husband? I married him because one of the doctor's daughters would have taken him, and because I wanted to get away from home, and because he was good-tempered and everybody spoke well of him.

Annele started as the child turned in her sleep. She quieted her again, but felt uneasy at being thus alone with her thoughts. There seemed ghosts lurking in all the corners, even in broad daylight. If only some one were here to cheer me up! Come, Lenz; come home! Be kind, and all will go well. We need no priest to help us; we can help ourselves. We are helped; I love you.

It was noon, and the sun was shining warm out of doors. Annele wrapped the child carefully up and carried it out in front of the house. Perhaps Lenz was on his way home; she would give him a cordial greeting, bid him the good morning he had forgotten to say, and tell him all should henceforth be peace between them. At this hour, five years ago, they had been married, and now they would be married again.

The figure of a man, still too far off to be recognized, was seen coming up the hill. "Call father!" she said to the child.

"Father! father!" the little thing cried.

The man came nearer. It was not Lenz, but Faller, hurrying up with an extra hat in his hand. "Is Lenz at home yet?"

"No."

"Good Heavens! this is his hat. My brother-in-law picked it up in the gully where he was cutting wood. If Lenz should have done himself any violence!"

Annele's knees shook; she pressed the child to her till it cried. "You are mad, and want to make me mad!" she exclaimed. "What do you mean?"

"Is that not his hat?"

"Good Heavens, it is!" she shrieked, and fell to the ground with the child.

Faller raised them both.

"Has he been found? dead?" asked Annele.

"No, thank Heaven! Come into the house. Let me take the child. Be calm, he has only lost his hat."

Annele staggered into the house, waving her hands before her face to brush away the mist that dimmed her sight. Was it possible? Lenz dead now,--now, when her heart had opened to him? It cannot be, it is not so. "Why should my Lenz kill himself?" she asked as she sank upon a seat. "What do you mean by it?"

Faller made no answer.

"Can you only talk when you are not wanted to?" she asked angrily. "Sit down, sit down, and tell me what has happened."

As if he could punish Annele by not doing her bidding, Faller remained standing, though his knees shook under him. The look he turned upon her was so full of sorrow and bitter upbraidings, that her eyes fell beneath it.

"How can I sit in your house?" he said at last. "You have taken the comfort out of every chair."

"I do not need your admonitions. I told you that long ago. If you know anything of my husband, tell it. Has he been found dead? where? Speak, you--"

"No, thank Heaven. God forbid! The shingle-maker from Knuslingen, Franzl's brother, reported him as having been with Franzl, and she lives almost two leagues beyond the place where his hat was picked up."

Annele breathed more freely. "Why did you frighten me so?" she asked again.

"Frighten you? Can you still be frightened?"

Faller told how Lenz had been everywhere, trying to borrow money to pay the security on his house, and added that that need burden him no longer, as Don Bastian had just advanced the required amount.

Annele drew herself up as he spoke. The old spirit of wrath and bitterness rose again within her, mightier, more vengeful than ever. He has deceived you, he has lied to you, her every feature said. He lives, he must live to atone for it. He told you he had withdrawn his security. Come home, you liar, you hypocrite! Annele went into her chamber, and Faller was obliged to depart without seeing her again. Gone was all sorrow, all contrition, all love. Lenz had deceived her, had told her a lie, and he should pay for it. Just like these good-natured milksops who, because they cannot stand up like men for their own rights, must be handled like a soft-shelled egg! Let me alone, and I will let you alone; refuse me nothing, and I will refuse you nothing, though you make me a beggar. Come home, you pitiful milksop!

Annele put no food on the fire, to be ready for her husband's return. A very different kind of cooking was going on.

CHAPTER XXXII
A NIGHT OF STORMS

Lenz went up the hill, after parting from the doctor, with a light and happy heart. From one of two sources help must certainly come,--from his uncle or the factory.

He saw the glimmer of a lamp as he approached his house. Thank Heaven, all is waiting for the good news, he said to himself. Poor Annele! you are more to be pitied than I, for you see the bad side of human nature, while I have only to go abroad to find the world full of kindness. I will help to lighten your burden.

Suddenly, like a burning arrow, came the thought: You have been a traitor to-day in your heart,--twice and thrice a traitor. At Katharine's, and again at the doctor's, you entertained the sinful thought that your life might have been different. Where is the honor you pride yourself upon? You have been five years married, and are the father of two children. Good Heavens! this is our wedding day.

He stood still listening to the voice within him: "Annele, dear Annele! This one day has seen my first and last unfaithfulness. May my parents in heaven refuse to pardon me if I ever give way to such thoughts again! From this time forth we will keep a new wedding day."

In this feeling of self-accusation, and of joy that all things would henceforth be well, Lenz entered his house.

"Where is my wife?" he asked as he saw the two children in the sitting-room with the servant.

"She has just lain down."

"Is she ill?"

"She complained of nothing."

"Annele," he said, going into the sleeping-room; "I am come to wish you good evening and good morning; I forgot it early to-day. I have good news, too, for you and for me. Please God, all things shall go well with us from this day forward."

"Thank you."

"Is anything the matter? Are you ill?"

"No; I am only tired, tired almost to death. I will be up in a minute."

"No; keep in bed if it does you good. I have news for you."

"I don't want to keep in bed. Go into the sitting-room; I will be out in a minute."

"Let me tell my news first."

"There is time enough for that; it won't spoil in a couple of minutes."

A shadow fell on Lenz's happiness. Without a word he returned to the sitting-room and fondled the children till Annele came out. "Will you have anything to eat?" she asked.

"No. How came my hat here?"

"Faller brought it. I suppose you gave it to Faller to bring to me, did you not?"

"Why should I have done that?" he answered. "The wind blew it off my head."

He told in few words his chance visit to Katharine. Annele was silent. She kept her charge of falsehood ready to launch at him when occasion offered. She could bide her time.

Lenz sent the maid into the kitchen, and, holding the boy in his lap, gave a full account of his day's experiences, all but of those thoughts of infidelity which had risen in his heart.

"Do you know the only one point of consequence in the whole story?"

"What?"

"The hundred florins and three crown-pieces that Franzl offered you. The rest is nothing."

"Why nothing?"

"Because your uncle will not help you. Do you see now the mistake you made in letting him off five years ago?"

"And the factory?"

"Who is to be admitted besides yourself?"

"I know of no one yet but Pröbler, whose ingenious inventions have certainly earned him a place."

"Ha, ha! that is too good; you and Pröbler! You are capital yokefellows. Did I not always tell you you would come down to his level? But you are more pitiful than he, for he at least has not dragged down a wife and children. Out of my sight, you poor, miserable milksop! Let yourself be yoked to the same team with Pröbler!" She snatched the child from its father's knee and, turning the torrent of her words upon the terrified boy, continued, passionately: "Your father is a pitiful milksop, who needs to have the bottle always held to his lips. Pity his mother is not alive to make his pap for him! Oh, how low have I fallen! But one thing I insist upon, you shall not enter the factory; I will drown myself and my children first. When I am dead you can go and ask the doctor's crooked daughter to leave her weeds and marry you."

Lenz sat motionless, chilled with horror.

"Mention not my mother's name," he cried at last. "Leave her to her eternal rest."

"I have no objection to leaving her. I neither want nor have anything of hers."

"What? Have you no longer that sprig of edelweiss? Tell me, have you not kept it?"

"Stuff and nonsense! of course I have kept it."

"Where? Give it to me!"

Annele opened a drawer and showed it.

"Thank God! you have it still; it will still bring us its blessing."

"The man has actually lost his senses with his superstition. The idea of pinning his faith to a wretched bit of dried grass instead of trying to help himself! Just like these beggars to go tearing about the world distracted."

Annele poured forth all this venom with her back upon her husband, as if calling the world to witness his degradation. Her utter ignoring of his presence, and thus speaking of him in the third person, was a keener stab than even her cruel epithets.

With great self-control he said: "Do not speak so, Annele; it is not yourself, but a devil speaking in you. And do not crush the little flower; keep it sacred."

"Ha, ha!" laughed Annele. "That is too much. I won't give way to such miserable superstition. Out of the window, Edelweiss, and take this precious bit of writing with you."

A tempest of wind was raging without.

"Come, Wind," she cried, as she threw open the window; "come, take all this sacred trumpery." She let go flower and letter. The wind whistled and howled, and whirled them high in the air over the bald mountain-top.

"What have you done, Annele?" groaned Lenz.

"I am not superstitious like you, nor am I yet fallen so low as to make an idol of such trash."

"It is no superstition. My mother only meant that so long as my wife honored the memory of my parents, a blessing would rest upon the house. But nothing is sacred to you."

"I do not hold you sacred, nor your mother either."

"That is too much, too much!" cried Lenz, his voice choked with the passion he in vain endeavored to repress. "Leave the room and take the boy with you. I have heard enough. Go, or you will drive me mad!--Hush! There is some one at the door."

Annele withdrew with the child into the inner chamber, just as the doctor entered the room.

"It is as I feared," he said. "Your uncle will not lift a hand to help you. He says you married against his will, and not another word can I get from him. I have used every argument in my power; all was vain. He at last almost turned me out of the house."

"And all because of me! I must bring evil on all who love me and try to serve me. Forgive me, doctor. I cannot help it."

"Why, how you talk; of course you cannot help it. I have known plenty of strange men in my life, but never one like your uncle. He opened his whole heart to me, and a tender heart it is; he is not a jot behind the rest of your family in that. I thought I surely had him and could guide him like a child; but when it came to money, off he was again." Here the doctor gave an expressive snap of his fingers. "Nothing more was to be got out of him. In fact, I don't believe he has anything besides a trifling annuity from some insurance office. Let us put him out of the question altogether. I shall talk the matter over with my sons, and if you prefer not to enter the factory, we can make some arrangement by which you shall employ five or six workmen here, or more, if you can accommodate them, to be paid by our establishment."

"Not so loud, please. My wife can hear us from the next room. I was prepared for the result of your interview with my uncle; there was little else to be looked for. As for the factory, the mere mention of the word has thrown my wife into such a state as I never saw her in before. She will not hear of it."

"Take time to consider it. Will you not come a little way down the hill with me?"

"Pray excuse me; I am so tired! My knees bend under me. Since four o'clock this morning I have scarcely sat down, and I am not used to such long tramps. I almost fancy I am going to have a fit of illness."

"Your pulse is feverish, as is natural after so much fatigue and excitement. A good night's sleep will set you right again. But you must be careful of yourself for some little time to come. You may really work yourself into a serious fit of illness if you don't rest more and husband your strength. Tell your wife from me," he continued, raising his voice so that his words could not fail to be heard in the adjoining room, "that she must take very good care of the father of her children during this season of thaw, and make him keep housed. A clockmaker, used to such constant sitting, gets to be delicate. Good night, Lenz; pleasant dreams to you!"

The doctor had a hard walk down the hill, often sinking deep into the melting snow, on whose surface lay a treacherous covering of stones and gravel. He was obliged to divest his mind of its anxiety for Lenz, and concentrate all his thoughts on the path he was treading. A remark of Pilgrim's constantly recurred to his memory, that Lenz could make as much of life as any man, but he craved joy and love; the dry companionship his home afforded was killing him.

Lenz meanwhile sat alone in his room. He was tired out, yet could find no rest. He paced the room like a wild beast in its cage. Racked with pains, and sick in body and mind, his heart cried out: Alas, to be sick and at the mercy of a cruel wife! to have no escape, to lie under the scourge of her tongue, to hear your fevered fancies blamed as evil passions, to be cut off from your friends; sick and dependent upon an unloving woman!--rather death by my own hand!

The wind put out the fire, filling the room with smoke. Lenz opened the window and gazed out. No light now in the blacksmith's house; he is buried in the dark ground. Would I too were at rest from my many sorrows!

The air was warm, unnaturally warm. The water dripped from the roof; from the bare mountain-top to the valley below, the wind was rushing and roaring as if one gust were driving hard upon another. There was a rattling and rumbling on the heights behind the house. The tempest, in rage at the loss of its playground in the forest, seemed to be wreaking its vengeance on the chestnut and pines in the garden, twisting them till they creaked and groaned. It was well that his house was firm in its stout oaken beams, else the wind might sweep it away with all in it. "That would be gay travelling," laughed Lenz, bitterly, starting at the same time and casting a frightened look behind him, as the old timbers cracked in ghostly sympathy with the misery within the dwelling. Such words were never heard within these walls before, nor did ever dweller here live through such a night in such a mood; neither father, nor grandfather, nor great-grandfather.

He turned to get his writing materials, and, as he passed the mirror, stopped involuntarily and gazed at the figure whose swollen and bloodshot eyes were reflected there. At last he sat down and began to Write, pausing often and pressing his hand to his eyes, then dashing his pen along the paper again. He rubbed his eyes, but no tears fell from them. "You have lost the power to weep," he said, hoarsely; "best so; you have wept too much already for a man."

He wrote:--

"Dearest Friend and Brother: My heart is breaking as I write, but I must talk with you once more. I think of the days and the many summer nights I have spent in happy walk's with you, my one ever-loving friend. It could not have been I; it was some one else. God is my witness, and so is my mother in heaven, that I never wilfully wronged a fellow-being. If I ever wronged or grieved you, dear brother, forgive me. I did it not intentionally, and humbly beg your forgiveness. I am not fit to live.

"Here is my confession; I see no escape but death. I know that to kill myself is a sin, but to live is a greater. Every day I am a murderer. I can bear it no longer. I spend my nights in weeping, and all the time despise myself for it. I might have been a quiet, honest, upright man, had I been allowed to remain in the beaten track; but I was not made for contest. I weep to think of what I have become; I who was once so different! If I live, my life will be a greater shame upon my children than my death. That will be soon forgotten; the next season the grass will be growing on my grave. By your faithful heart, and by all the acts of kindness you have ever done me, I conjure you to be a father to my forsaken children. My poor children,--I dare not think of them. I was foolish enough once to fancy I could make a good father; but I cannot; I can be nothing. If love is not freely given me, I cannot win it; that is my misery, that is my ruin. A wall of glass is about me that I try in vain to surmount. My mother was right in saying we can sow and plant and force a harvest by our industry, but one thing must grow of itself, and that is love. It will not grow for me where I had a right to look for it.

"Take my children out of the village when I am buried. I would not have them see me. Pray the mayor and the minister to have me laid beside my parents and my brethren. They were happier than I. Why was I alone left to live for such an end as this?

"You are my little William's godfather,--take him now for your own child. You always said he had a taste for drawing; take him to your own home and teach him. If it be possible, be reconciled with my uncle Petrovitsch. Perhaps he will do something for my children when I am gone, for I am sure he likes you; I would not tell you now what I did not know to be true. You may still be good friends together. His heart is kinder than he will acknowledge, as my mother always said. My wife--but I will say nothing of her. If my children are happy, let her be forgiven for my sake.

"I have been driven to hearing and saying such words as I had never imagined tongue could utter.

"I am in prison and must escape. I have lived through days and watched through nights that were as years. I can endure no more; I am tired, tired even to death. For months I have not closed my eyes and tried to sleep, without being assailed by visions of horror that pursue me through the day. I can bear this black and haunted sleep no longer; I must have the quiet sleep of death.

"In return for the money I owe you, take the watch which you will find on my body. It will tick on against your faithful heart when my heart shall have ceased to beat. When my effects are sold, buy my father's file and keep it for my son. I have no legacy to bequeath to him. Teach him that his father was not a bad man. He has my unhappy sensitiveness; drive it out of him, make him strong and self-reliant. And the baby-.

"It is hard--hard that I must die; I am still so young; but better now. The doctor must see that my body is not carried to Freiburg for the students to dissect. Give to him and all his household my cordial greeting. He has long known how things were with me; but they were past any doctor's help. Bid our comrades good by for me, especially Faller and the schoolmaster. My dearest, dearest brother, I have still much to say to you, but my head swims. Good night. Farewell.

"In eternity,
"Your loving

He folded the letter and wrote the address: "To be delivered to my friend and brother Pilgrim."

The day began to dawn. He extinguished the lamp, and, holding the letter in his hand, approached the window to take his last look of the world of nature. The sun was just rising above the mountain; first a pale streak of yellow, soon obscured by a long stretch of dark cloud; above the cloud, the deep blue of the open heavens, and beneath the broad expanse of snow shimmering in the ghostly light. A rosy flush floats on the black bosom of the cloud, and lo! in an instant the mass is rent with golden fissures; the whole heaven is spread with gold, that gradually turns to crimson, till of a sudden all is aglow with purple flame. That is the world of light, of bright existence. Take your last look of it before leaving it forever.

Lenz put the letter in his pocket, and went out to take a turn about the house. At every step he sank to his knees in melting snow. He returned to the sitting-room, and, finding that Annele was not inclined to get up, dressed the children himself and gave them their breakfast. When the village bells began to ring he ordered the maid to take William by the hand and the baby in her arms and go with them to Pilgrim's. He gave the letter into the girl's hand, but finally changed his mind about it, and taking it from her, concealed it in the little girl's pocket. When the child's clothes were taken off at night, the letter would be found. All would be over then.

"Go to Pilgrim's," he repeated to the girl, "and wait there till I come; if I do not come, wait till night."

He kissed the children, and, turning away, laid his head upon the table. Long he lay in the same position. Nothing stirred in the house. He waited till the last sound of the church-bells had died away, then rose and bolted the house door. "God forgive me, it must be done," was his bitter cry. He sank upon his knees; he tried to pray, but could not. "She often said her prayers, and before the last word had fairly passed her lips, her anger and abuse and mockery broke out afresh. She has sinned against everything in heaven and on the earth. She, too, shall--no; let her live. But in her presence I will do the deed; she shall see the work of her hands."

He covered his face with both hands, then clenched his fists and burst into the chamber, meaning to kill himself before his wife's very eyes. He drew back the bed-curtains. "Cuckoo! cuckoo!" cried the little girl from the bed. Lenz sank half fainting to the floor.

Suddenly there was a rushing sound;--the earth seemed opening to swallow them,--there was a rolling as of thunder over the earth and under it,--a mighty crash above their heads,--and it was night, deep, dark night.

"What is the matter? For Heaven's sake, what is it?" screamed Annele. Lenz rose to his feet. "I do not know; I cannot tell what has happened." Annele and the child were beside themselves; they wept and screamed with terror. Lenz tried to open a window; he could not stir it. Tumbling over the chairs, he groped his way into the outer room, where, too, all was in total darkness. "Annele," he cried, "we are buried under the snow!" A silence fell upon them both; only the child sobbed and shrieked, and the poultry in the wood-shed cackled as if a hawk were among them. An instant more and all was still as death.

CHAPTER XXXIII
A FRIEND IN NEED

At that very hour Pilgrim was on his way to church. When nearly there, however, he changed his purpose, took several turns in front of old Petrovitsch's house, and finally mustered courage to pull the bell. Petrovitsch had been watching him from his window, and muttered to himself, as he heard the ring: "You are going to make me a visit, are you? I will give you a reception you won't forget in a hurry."

Petrovitsch was as much out of sorts as if he were suffering from the effects of a night's debauch; and indeed it was pretty much so. He had committed an excess in calling up old associations, and admitting a guest to share them. The idea of having given way to the wretched weakness of desiring to appear well before a fellow-man angered him. How could he meet the doctor again in the full light of day? There was an end to his proud boast of caring nothing for the opinion of the world. Pilgrim was an excellent object on which to wreak his ill-humor; he would put a stop to the fellow's playing and singing for one day at least.

"Good morning, Mr. Lenz!" said Pilgrim, entering.

"The same to you, Mr. Pilgrim."

"Mr. Lenz, I have come to see you instead of going to church."

"I did not know I was considered such a saint."

"I do not come hoping for any great results from my visit, but only that I may feel I have done my duty."

"If every one did his duty it would be a fine world to live in."

"Your Lenz, as you know--"

"I have no Lenz but that one," interrupted Petrovitsch, pointing to the reflection of his carefully shaven face in the glass.

"You know that your brother's son is in great trouble."

"No; the trouble is in him. It all comes from a man's priding himself on his kind heart, and having friends who pet him till he thinks all other views than his are the whimsies of a crabbed old croaker."

"You may be right; but talking won't mend the matter. Your Lenz's difficulties are greater than you think."

"I never measured them."

"He is even in danger of taking his own life."

"He did that long ago, when he married as he did."

"I can say no more. I thought I was prepared for everything, but this I had not expected. You are much more,--you are a different man from what I took you for."

"Thanks for the compliment. I only regret I cannot wear it as a medal about my neck, as you singers wear your badges."

The gay, open-hearted Pilgrim stood before the old man as disconcerted as a fencer who at every sally finds his weapon struck from his hand.

Petrovitsch hugged himself on his success, and putting an unusually large lump of sugar into his mouth, said, as he smacked his lips: "The son of my deceased brother has done according to his own will and pleasure. It would be unjust in me to try to defraud him of the fruits of his own choosing. He has squandered his life and money,--I cannot restore them."

"Good Heavens, Mr. Lenz, you can. His life and that of his whole family may yet be saved. The discord in his house will cease when plenty returns and this wear of anxiety is removed. 'Horses quarrel over the empty crib,' says the proverb. Wealth is not happiness, but it can command happiness."

"Young people nowadays are very generous with others' money, but have no taste for earning their own. I will do nothing for the husband of Annele of the Lion, whose fair words have to be bought with gold."

"What if your nephew should die?"

"He will probably be buried."

"And what will become of the children?"

"We can never tell what will become of children."

"Has your nephew ever offended you in any way?"

"I know not how he could offend me."

"Then what can you do better with your money than now--"

"If I ever need a guardian, I will ask to have you appointed, Mr. Pilgrim."

"I see I am not clever enough for you."

"You do me too much honor," said Petrovitsch, putting one foot over the other and playing with the lappet of his slipper.

"I have done my duty," said Pilgrim again.

"And cheaply, too, at the expense of a couple of fair words. A bushel of them would not cost much. I would buy at that rate."

"This is my first and last request to you."

"And this is my first and last refusal to you."

"Good morning, Mr. Lenz!"

"The same to you, Mr. Pilgrim."

At the door Pilgrim turned, his face crimson and his eyes flashing. "Mr. Lenz, do you know what you are doing?"

"I generally know pretty well what I am doing."

"You are absolutely turning me out of your house."

"Indeed!" said Petrovitsch with an ugly smile; but his eyes fell before the look of mingled pain and defiance in Pilgrim's face. "Mr. Lenz," continued the young man, "from you I bear everything. There lives not a man within sight of a hedge or a tree that can yield a stick, who can boast of having insulted Pilgrim with impunity. You can: and do you know the reason? Because I am willing to bear insults in my friend's cause. Unhappily it is all I can do for him. No angry word shall you hear from me that you can use as a pretext for not helping my friend. For his sake I gladly suffer insults. Tell all the world, if you will, that you have turned me out of your house."

"It would not be much to boast of."

Pilgrim's breath came short and quick; his lips grew white, and without another word he left the room.

Petrovitsch sent after him such a look of triumph as a satisfied fox might send after the wounded and fugitive hare whose blood he had sucked, but whose life the poor creature might save as he could.

With great satisfaction he paced about his room, stroking himself down with his hands. He seemed actually so puffed up with satisfaction that he had to let out the tasseled cord of his dressing-gown. Now Petrovitsch is himself again, his every motion seemed to say; last night you behaved like an old fool and forfeited all right to revile the dish-clouts about you.

Pilgrim silently wended his way homeward, but, being in no mood for entering his room at once, passed his house and took a long walk through the fields. On returning, he was most agreeably surprised by finding his friend's little boy. That is the way, he thought, when friends heartily love one another. At the very moment I was thinking of Lenz, his heart was full of me. Perhaps he had a presentiment of my intended visit to Petrovitsch, and so sent his boy to help my petition. But the child could have done no good. The voices of men and angels would have been alike useless.

There was no end to the games Pilgrim invented, and the pictures he drew, for the child's entertainment. Little William screamed with delight at the hare and hounds made out of a handkerchief and a black necktie, and called for the same stories over and over again. Pilgrim's great story was of a Turk named Kulikali, who had an immense nose and could swallow smoke. He dressed himself up like the Turk Kulikali, and spreading a cloth on the floor, sat in the middle of it with his legs crossed, and played all manner of tricks. He was as much of a child for the time as his little godson. After dinner, which they ate down stairs with Don Bastian, William insisted on being taken, in spite of the sleet and slosh, down to the brook. That was the best fun of all. Great blocks of ice went floating by with ravens perched upon them; and when one of their rafts cracked and broke to pieces, the ravens flew up and perched upon another. It was dizzying to look down on them from the height where the two stood. The earth seemed to be in motion while the ice stood still. The child clung anxiously to Pilgrim. When that entertainment failed, Pilgrim took his godson home and made him up a bed on his well-worn sofa, which they agreed should be little Lenz's own, and he should never go away any more. "At home papa cries," the little fellow said; "and mamma too; and mamma says papa is a wicked man." Poor Pilgrim was cut to the heart at hearing of it. The snow and rain increased so much in violence, and the avalanches from the roofs of the houses and from the upland slopes were so constant, that it soon became impossible to step out of doors. The evening came, but no Lenz. The servant-maid told of her having met Petrovitsch on his way to the Morgenhalde, not far from the house. He had asked whose the child was, and on her replying it was Lenz's William, had given him a little bit of sugar,--not a whole lump, for he broke off half of it first and put it into his own mouth.

"Is it possible? can Petrovitsch really have been softened? Who can read the hearts of men?"

Petrovitsch, after giving full scope to his exultation at this double triumph over the doctor and Pilgrim, felt very tranquil in his mind. He sat at his window watching the groups of church-goers, till at last all were gone by except a single woman and a single man, who came hurrying along to take their seats before the service should begin. Petrovitsch's custom was to go to church himself; in fact, so regular was his attendance that it was reported he meant to leave a handsome sum in his will towards erecting a new building. To day, however, he stayed at home, being busy with his own thoughts. One idea in particular occupied his mind: The fellow has good friends in his time of need. Pooh! would they be quite so good if they were rich? Pilgrim's friendship perhaps is sincere; it almost looked so. He was very near letting his passion break out at one time; but he kept it down and let me say what I would, rather than injure his friend's cause.--It was all a trick likely enough,--and yet there is such a thing as friendship.

He heard the rumbling of the organ from the distant church, the singing of the congregation, and then came a silence which implied that the minister had begun his sermon. A voice seemed to be preaching to Petrovitsch as he sat with folded hands in his chair. Suddenly he rose saying half aloud: "It is very well to show men their master, but it is pleasant too to be thought well off.--No, no; that is not worth while; that is not what I mean; but to make men rub their eyes and cry: 'Thunder and lightning, who would have thought it?' there is some fun in that."

Petrovitsch had not for many years dressed himself so quickly as he did to-day. Generally he took his dressing easily and comfortably, like most things that he did, spending at least an hour over it; but to-day he was soon ready, even to the putting on of his costly fur coat which he had brought from Russia himself. The old housekeeper, who had seen him a few minutes before in dressing-gown and slippers, stared in amazement, but dared not utter a word, as she was not spoken to. With his gold-headed cane, furnished with a hard, sharp ferrule at the bottom, in case of need, Petrovitsch walked through the village and straight up the hill. No human being was in the street; none at the windows to wonder at seeing him leave his house at this unwonted hour and in this ugly weather. Bubby had to represent the whole absent humanity, and proclaimed, as well as his barking could: My master is behaving himself in a way you would not believe; I would not have believed it myself. He barked it at a raven sitting meditatively on a hedge, sagely reflecting upon the melting snow; he barked it for his own gratification as he leaped ever higher and higher through the deepening drifts, on his useless digressions to and fro; and between his barks his look at his master seemed to say: No human soul understands us two; but we know each other.

I sacrifice all my peace of mind by doing it, said Petrovitsch to himself; but if I don't do it I have no peace of mind either. I might as well secure some thanks at least. After all, he is a good, simple, honest fellow, as his father was before him.

Lenz's door was locked when the two reached the house. Bubby was already on the threshold, and Petrovitsch had his hand on the latch when--he sank to the ground, and an avalanche of snow overwhelmed him. So much for troubling yourself about other men, was his first thought and his last, for immediately consciousness failed him.

CHAPTER XXXIV
BURIED ALIVE

"Strike a light, Lenz; strike a light! If there is any danger, I must see it. What makes you stand there crying in the dark. I feel your tears on my hand. What is the matter? Let me go; I will get up myself and light a lamp."

"Be quiet, Annele," said Lenz, his teeth chattering so he could hardly speak. "Annele, I had meant to kill myself here before your eyes."

"Better kill me; I should be too glad to die."

"Did you not understand me, Annele? We are blocked up by the snow; buried alive with our child."

"If death had had to wait for you to bring it, it never would have come."

Still that hard, cutting tone; those biting, stinging words! Lenz felt his breath come hard.

"Let me get up, let me get up!" continued Annele; "I am not like you, to let my arms hang down at my side. I don't care what becomes of me; but I choose to see the danger. You would like to wait till some one came to dig you out or till the snow went away of itself; that is not my way. Defend yourself, is our family motto."

"Stay where you are; I will strike a light," answered Lenz; but hardly had he reached the next room before Annele stood beside him with the child in her arms. On attempting to go to the garret a new misfortune disclosed itself; the roof had been broken in. "The snow alone could not have done the damage," he said; "it has brought trunks of trees down with it, and that was what made such a crash."

"I don't care what made it; only let us find some help, some way of escape."

She ran hither and thither trying all the windows and doors. Not till she found that all were firmly walled up and yielded nothing under her fiercest efforts, did she admit the full extent of the catastrophe, and setting the child down upon the table, broke out into screams and tears. Lenz took the child in his arms, and with difficulty persuaded Annele to be quiet. "The hand of death is upon our house," he said; "all struggle is unavailing. Did you keep William too at home? Is he concealed anywhere here?"

"No; he went with the maid. I kept only the baby."

"Thank God! we are not all lost; one of us at least is saved. Poor little child! I sent the boy away, Annele, that he might not see his father kill himself; but now all is changed. God summons us all. Poor child, to have to perish for your parents' sins!"

"I have not sinned; I have nothing to reproach myself with."

"Good; hold to that to the last. Do you not know that you have murdered me, poisoned the very heart in my body, disgraced me in my own eyes, trodden me under foot, taken all strength from me?"

"A man who allows his strength to be taken from him deserves nothing better."

"An hour more and we may be standing before another judgment-seat. Look into your heart, Annele."

"Keep your preaching to yourself; I don't want it."

An instant afterwards her screams summoned Lenz to the kitchen, whither she had gone to light the fire, and where he found her gazing in terror at the rats and mice congregated on the hearth, while a raven flew round and round the kitchen, knocking down plates and pots in his course.

"Kill them! kill them!" shrieked Annele, and fled into the adjoining room.

The rats and mice were soon disposed of, but the raven it would have been impossible to catch without breaking every article of crockery in the kitchen. The lamp made the bird frantic, and without a light it was impossible to find him. "I might shoot the raven with my pistol which I have here, ready loaded," he said, returning to Annele in the sitting-room; "but the jar would hasten the fall of the house. The best thing I can do is to make this room safe."

He drew a heavy press into the middle of the room directly under the main beam, piled a smaller one above it, and filled in the space so tightly with clothes as to prop up the roof against a considerable pressure from without.

"We must bring all the eatables we have in here." That too he did quickly and handily, while Annele sat like one paralyzed, and could only look on in wonder.

Lenz brought his own prayer-book and Annele's, opened them both at the same place,--the preparation for death,--and laying his wife's open before her, began to read aloud. Seeing she did not follow him, he looked up presently and said: "You are right not to read; there is nothing there for us. Never were any two like us, who should have lived together in peace, each doubling the other's life; but who instead of that pulled away from each other, and are now both imprisoned at the gates of death, and must die together, since they could not live together. Hark! Do you not hear cries? I thought there was a growling sound."

"I hear nothing."

"We cannot light a fire," continued Lenz; "for there is no way for the smoke to escape, and we should be stifled. Thank God, there is the spirit-lamp that my mother bought. You help even in death, mother," he said, looking up at the picture. "Light it, Annele; only economize the spirit; we cannot tell how long we shall have to make it last."

Annele watched his movements in blank amazement. She was often tempted to ask whether this were really that Lenz who had been so incapable of helping himself. But no words came from her stiffened lips. She was like a person in a deathly trance who tries to speak and cannot.

Her first swallow of warm milk revived her. "What if the mice should come in here?" was her first question.

"I will kill them here too, and bury them in the snow to get rid of the stench. By the way, I must bury those I killed in the kitchen."

Again Annele looked at him in amazement. Was this man, so bold in the face of death, the old, sensitive, shiftless Lenz? A kind word rose to her lips, but did not get spoken.

"That plaguy raven has bitten me," said Lenz, returning with his hand bleeding. "The fellow is wild with terror at having been swept away by the force of the avalanche; there is no catching him. A whole pillar of snow has fallen down the chimney. Hark! that is ten o'clock. People are coming out of church now. We were buried just as the last bells were ringing. It was our death-knell."

"I will not die yet; I am so young! And my child! I never knew, I never imagined that I was going to my death when I condescended to live in this desert with you clockmakers."

"It is your father's fault," answered Lenz. "My parents were three times snowed up, so that for two and three days they could not go outside the house, on account of the depth of snow that lay there; but they were never buried. Your father disposed of the wood, and had it cut down over my head. This is his work."

"You have no one but yourself to blame. He wanted to give you the wood."

"That is true."

"Oh, if I and my child were but out of this place!" cried Annele, beginning her lamentations afresh.

"And do you care nothing for me?"

Without appearing to hear him she cried again, "O God, why must I die thus? What have I done?"

"What have you done? yet a little while and God himself will tell you. My words are spent in vain."

Both were silent; a secret power seemed forcing Annele to speak, but she could not.

"Good God!" began Lenz; "here we two stand at the gates of death and with what feelings towards each other! If we should be saved, it would be only to renew the old pain and torment. My parents were three times snowed up. My mother always made provision against such an event, and kept on hand a plentiful supply of salt and oil. Of the first two times I know nothing, but the last is distinct in my memory to this day. Dearly as my father and mother loved each other, I never before saw them kiss. When my father said: 'Mary, we are once more alone in the world, out of the world'; then for the first time I saw my mother kiss him. For those three days it was like living in eternity, in paradise. Morning, noon, and night my father and mother sang together out of the hymn-book, and every word they spoke was more sweet and holy than tongue can tell. I remember my mother's saying once: 'Would we might die at such a moment as this; pass out of this earthly rest into the eternal, neither one left behind to grieve for the other!' Then and only then did I hear my father speak of my uncle. 'If I were to die now,' he said, 'I should leave no enemy behind. I owe no man anything. My one grief is that my brother Peter dislikes me.'"

Lenz suddenly paused in his story. There was a scratching at the house-door, a whimpering and howling. "What is there? I must see what it is," said Lenz.

"No, no; for Heaven's sake!" cried Annele, sending a thrill through him by the touch of her hand on his shoulder. "Let it be, Lenz! It is a fox howling, or a wolf. I heard the howl of a wolf once, and it sounded just like that."

Whatever the creature was outside, it seemed to be roused to fresh exertion by the sound of voices within; the scratching and barking grew louder.

"That is no wolf; it is a dog. Hark! it is Hubby's bark. Great Heavens, it is Bubby! and where his dog is my uncle must be too. He must be buried in the snow."

"Let him lie there, if he is; it serves him right."

"Woman! are you mad? must you still spit out your poison?"

"I am full of poison up to my throat. For days and days I had nothing else to drink; it has been my only food."

Lenz went to the kitchen and returned with an axe.

"What do you mean to do?" screamed Annele, holding the child as a shield before her.

"Out of my way!" he cried, and raising the axe brought it down with all his force against the door, which fell outward. It was indeed Bubby, who now sprang in howling, but in an instant was back again scratching in the snow, and uttering short, sharp barks.

Lenz began to shovel away the snow. A piece of fur soon came to view, and laying shovel and pick aside, he set carefully to work, digging with his hands, and bringing the snow into the house in order to clear a space. When he found his uncle, the old man's consciousness was gone. All Lenz's strength was required to drag his seemingly lifeless body out of the snow. He bore him into the chamber, stripped off his clothing, put him to bed, and began rubbing him with all his might, till he at last drew a deep breath.

"Where am I?" groaned Petrovitsch; "where am I?"

"In my house, uncle."

"Who brought me here? who took off my clothes? where are my clothes? where is my fur? where is my waistcoat? it has my keys in it. So you have me at last, have you?"

"Be calm, uncle; I will find everything for you. See, here is your fur, and here is your waistcoat."

"Let me have them. Are the keys in the pocket? yes, there they are. Ha, Bubby, are you here too?"

"Yes, uncle, he saved your life."

"Ah, now I remember. We were buried by the snow. How long ago was it? was it not yesterday?"

"Scarce an hour ago," said Lenz.

"Hear you no help coming?"

"I hear nothing. Keep quiet a few minutes while I go into the other room, and get you something to drink."

"Leave me the light; bring me something warm."

"Serves me right," said Petrovitsch when he was left by himself; "serves me exactly right. What business had I to go out of my accustomed way?"

He seemed revived by the brandy Lenz brought him, and caressing his dog, who had nestled close to his master's side, said: "Let me go to sleep now. What is that noise? Is there not a raven crying?"

"Yes, one was swept down the kitchen chimney by the snow."

"Very well; let me sleep now."

CHAPTER XXXV
SMITTEN TO THE HEART

Lenz and Annele sat without in the sitting-room, neither speaking a word. The child laughed and stretched out its little hands now towards the light, and now towards its father's eyes, that were broodingly fixed upon it. "If we must die, thank God our son is saved!" said Lenz. Still Annele was silent. The monotonous ticking of the clocks was suddenly interrupted by one of the musical works beginning to play a hymn. For the first time the eyes of husband and wife met. Annele changed the child's position on her lap, and clasped her hands over its buoyant bosom.

"If you can pray," said Lenz, "you ought to be able to look into your heart and repent."

"I have nothing to repent of in my conduct towards you; whatever other sins I may have committed, I confess only to God. I have meant nothing that was not kind and honest towards you."

"And I?"

"You did right too, as far as you knew how. I am more just to you than you are to me. You would never put me in a position where I could earn anything."

"And your horrible words?"

"Pooh! words break no bones."

Lenz implored her to be kind and peaceable before his uncle. "Your uncle and the raven in the kitchen tell me we must die," she answered as in a dream.

"You are not generally superstitious; I hope, for your sake, you are not going to be so now. It was you who threw the writing and the plant to the wind, and called on the storm to visit us."

Annele made no answer. After another interval of silence Lenz arose, saying he would go on digging at the place where he had found his uncle, for if he could dig through to the mountain, he should be able to crawl out and summon help. Annele had her hand stretched out to detain him, imagining the horror of having him buried in the snow, and she and Petrovitsch too weak to dig him out. She had her hand stretched out to detain him, but passed it over her face instead, and let him go. He soon returned, however, and reported the snow to be so loose that every space filled in again as soon as cleared. There was reason to fear, also, that the snow still continued to fall. The best he could do was to shovel out again what he had been obliged to bring into the house, and push a clothes-press against the entrance, where the battered door no longer served as a protection.

His wet clothes had to be changed for his Sunday suit; it was no wedding garment he put on.

"Five years ago to-day," he murmured, "many sleighs stood before the door of the Lion inn; would that the guests were here now to dig us out!"

Petrovitsch had awaked from a short sleep, but still lay quiet in bed in the sleeping-room. He thought over with calmness all that had happened. Haste and complaints were here equally unavailing. Yesterday he had recalled his whole past life, had lived it over again in a few short moments, and here was the end. He accepted it with indifference. How to conduct himself towards those in the next room was the question that chiefly occupied him. At last he called Lenz and asked for his clothes, as he wished to get up. Lenz advised him to remain where he was, for the sitting-room was cold and his clothes wet, there being no way of lighting a fire. Petrovitsch, however, still desired to get up, and asked if there was no comfortable dressing-gown in the house.

"One of my father's," replied Lenz; "will you have that?"

"If there is no other, give me that," said Petrovitsch, angrily, while in his heart was a sorrow, almost a fear, at the thought of wearing what had been his brother's.

"You look quite like my father in it," cried Lenz; "quite like him, only a little smaller."

"I had a hard youth, or I should have been larger," said the old man, looking at himself in the glass, as he entered the room. The cry of the raven in the kitchen startled him; he imperatively ordered Lenz to kill the bird. Lenz's chief occupation, however, for the time was to keep the peace between Bubby and the cat. The dog betrayed his discomfort by continued barks and whines, till the cat was finally shut up in the kitchen, where she did them good service by silencing the raven. Petrovitsch called for more cherry-brandy, of which Lenz said there were happily three bottles left of his mother's making, at least twelve years ago; with hot water and sugar he mixed himself a nice glass of grog. "How absurd all this is!" he cried, growing talkative under its genial influence; "I have dragged my body over the whole world, only to be squeezed to death in my father's house. It serves me right; why could I not have conquered that foolish homesickness? Homesickness indeed!" he gave a laugh of derision and continued: "there is an insurance on my life, but of what use is that to me now? Do you know who has buried us here? that man of honor, the stout landlord, destroyed the forest over our heads."

"Alas! he buries his child and his child's child with us," added Lenz.

"You are neither of you fit to mention my father's name," cried Annele, passionately. "My father was unfortunate, but he was never dishonest. If you say another word against him, I will set fire to the house."

"You are mad!" cried Petrovitsch; "shall we thank him for throwing this little snow-ball at our heads? Be quiet, Annele; come, sit here by me; give me your hand. I have something to say to you, Annele; I never fancied that you yourself were quite good and true; but now I see you are. I like you for not letting any word of blame fall on your father. Few keep loyal to a ruined man. 'Oh, how I love you!' is only heard as long as we have money in our pocket. I like you for it, Annele." Annele cast a quick glance at her husband, whose eyes were fixed on the ground.

"It is well that we should spend this hour together," continued Petrovitsch; "who knows but it may be our last? Let us come to a full and free understanding with each other. Draw your chair nearer, Lenz. You looked for consolation from your wife in your misfortune. Because you were dissatisfied with yourself and could give yourself no praise, you craved it from others, instead of helping her, the proud Annele of the Lion. You are proud, Annele, you need not shake your head. A good thing pride is; I only wish Lenz had a little more of it. Your turn is coming; don't be impatient."

"Yes," cried Annele; "he deceived me, he said he had given up the security for Faller; it was false."

"I did not tell you so; I only tried to escape from your importunities."

"Your turn is coming. Now tell me one thing, on your honor, Annele," continued Petrovitsch. "Did you know when you married Lenz that your father was a ruined man?"

"Must I tell you honestly?"

"Yes."

"Well, then, I swear before God, that I knew my father was no longer rich, although I thought he had still a considerable property. I liked Lenz while we were rich, but then my mother would not hear of my marrying him. She was very ambitious for her daughters, and especially disliked the idea of one of us living with a mother-in-law."

"For yourself, then, you would have come to my mother had she been living? Pilgrim said you would not."

"If Pilgrim said so, he was right. I said many foolish things as a girl, that I might be thought well of and be praised for my saucy wit."

Lenz looked earnestly at her, and Petrovitsch went on: "Talk no more of that yet, till I ask you some questions. You both deceived each other and yourselves. You both persuaded yourselves you were marrying from pure love, when in reality each thought the other rich; and when that turned out not to be the case, mutual anger and recriminations arose between you. Say, Lenz; did you not think Annele was rich."

"I did think so; but, uncle, that is not the cause of the misery that consumes me,--of my bleeding heart and my burning brain. I thought the landlord was rich, but I did not care for his money."

"And you, Annele?"

"I did not think Lenz was rich. You may tear me in pieces between you if you will; I did not."

"You have not made a full confession yet; one thing, however, you will admit, that you are both sick with the same disease. You, Lenz, prided yourself on your good-nature, and you on your cleverness, did you not, Annele?"

"I did not pride myself on my cleverness, but I am more capable and more experienced than he, and better able to take care of myself. If he had let me have my way, and be at the head of a hotel, we should not now be in misery and waiting for death."

"And what measures did you take to persuade him to do as you liked?"

"I showed him that he was a do-little, a good-for-nothing pin-sticker. I deny nothing. I took all the life out of him; I said whatever came to my lips, and the more it pained him, the better I was pleased."

"Annele, do you believe in hell?"

"I must, for I have it before me. I am in the power of you two men; can any hell be worse? You can torment me as you will; I am a weak woman, unable to defend myself."

"A weak woman?" cried Petrovitsch, with unwonted sharpness. "A weak woman? a pretty way, to drive a man distracted with your obstinacy, to drop poison into his heart till he is on the verge of despair, and then say, 'I am a weak woman!'"

"I might tell a lie," continued Annele, "and make promises for the future; but I will not. Rather will I let myself be torn in pieces than give up one jot of my rights. All I said was true, and that I knew it was poison is also true."

"All true?" cried Lenz, pale as death. "Think of one thing you said: that my good deeds were only a cloak for my laziness, and that I ill-treated my mother. My mother! In one hour perhaps we shall stand before her; how can you meet her face to face?"

Annele was silent. Petrovitsch, too angry to speak, sat pressing his teeth against his lips, till at last he broke out: "Annele, if Lenz had throttled you when you said those words, he would have been hung, but he would have been innocent in the sight of God. You inn-keeper's daughter, used to the wretched rabble that haunts a tavern, you have a quick wit of your own, and hearing from some gallows-bird of a postilion that the way to urge a horse in a race was to put burning tinder in his ears, you laid your words like burning tinder in Lenz's ears, and drove him mad. There is my hand, Lenz; you are a beggar for kind looks and words, which is pitiful; but you have not deserved a punishment like this, to be driven mad by a devil in your house. Give me the child! you are not fit to hold an innocent child in your arms."

The little girl screamed as he snatched her from her mother. Lenz interposed: "Not so, uncle, not so. Listen to me, Annele; I have only kind words to speak. Annele, we are standing beside an open grave--"

Annele shrieked and covered her face with her hands. "You, too, are standing by your open grave," he continued.

Without uttering a word Annele sank lifeless to the ground.

CHAPTER XXXVI
VOICES FROM THE DEAD

The lamp was thrown from the table and extinguished by Annele's fall, leaving the four in total darkness. Lenz rubbed her with the brandy, which happily was just under his hand, until she presently drew a shuddering breath and placed her hand on his face. He laid her on the bed in the next chamber, and hastened to strike a fresh light.

The raven, in his flight about the kitchen, had upset and broken a great jug of oil of turpentine, which Lenz kept on hand for use in his night work, and an intolerable smell of resin filled the room the moment the door was opened. He poured brandy into the lamp. A pale blue light spread a ghastly hue over the faces of the buried party.

Petrovitsch laid the child on the bed, and finding its little feet were stone cold, called Bubby to lie upon them. Then he took Lenz by the arm and led him back into the sitting-room, leaving the chamber-door open. The cat and the raven were fighting together in the kitchen, but were left to settle the quarrel between themselves.

"Have you nothing to eat?" asked Petrovitsch; "it is five o'clock and I am half famished."

There was plenty to eat; a ham which had been thrown down from its place in the chimney, bread, and a bag of dried fruit.

Petrovitsch ate with a good appetite, and pressed Lenz to do the same; he was too intent upon what went on in the adjoining room, however, to swallow a morsel. The child talked in its sleep, an unintelligible murmur, that seemed their one connecting link with the world of nature. It chilled their hearts to hear the unconscious little thing laugh in its dreams. Annele breathed quietly. Lenz went in to take the child, but started back with a cry of horror, for he had seized Bubby instead, and the dog snapped at him. His cry awoke Annele, who, sitting up in bed, called him and Petrovitsch to her. "Thank God, I am still alive, if it be but for one hour! I pray forgiveness of all; chiefly of you, Lenz."

"Don't try to talk now," he interposed. "Will you not swallow something? I have found the coffee, but not the mill; if the child is awake I will pound it up. There is nice ham here too."

"I want nothing; let me speak. What happened? What made you scream, Lenz?"

"Nothing; I only took hold of the dog instead of the child, and he snapped at me; in my excitement he seemed a monster seeking to devour me."

"Yes, yes; this distraction," said Annele; "this distraction that I have made! O Lenz, my dream has come to pass as you described. Last night I stood before an open grave and looked down into its dark depths. Little clods of earth kept rolling into it, and I tried to hold myself back, but could not; I began falling, falling; some power drew me down. Hold me! There, there, now it is over; it is passed now. Lay your hand upon my face; so. O gracious God! that you all should have to die with me! that all this should have come upon you for my sins! I have deserved it! but you and my child! and oh, my William; my poor William! You looked at me so pitifully when you went away, and said, 'I will bring you something good when I come back, mother.' You must bring me something good in heaven. Be true and good and--"

Tears choked her voice; she grasped Lenz's hand and held it to her face. "An hour ago I had gladly died; now I long to live, to have one more chance of showing in this world that I can be true and loving. I see now what a woman I have been. Henceforth I will pray for a kind look and word. O God, save us, but for one hour, for one day! I will send for Franzl, Lenz; that was the beginning of my evil-doing."

"I really believe now that the devil is driven out," said Petrovitsch; "your thinking of Franzl, and wanting to show kindness to one whose life you have imbittered, is a sure sign. There is my hand; now all is well."

Lenz could speak no word. He hurried to the sitting-room, and bringing what was left of the brandy his uncle had mixed, put it to Annele's lips, saying: "Drink, and for every drop you swallow I would gladly give you a thousand blissful words! Drink more, drink it all!" he continued, as Annele set down the glass. "And then lie still and don't speak another word."

"I cannot drink any more; believe me, I cannot," said Annele. She lamented piteously that they all must die. When Lenz tried to soothe her by telling her that they had provisions for many days yet, and that before those were exhausted help would surely come, she broke out into fresh lamentations over her wicked life, her ingratitude and hardness of heart in turning her back upon the abundance of good things that were given her, and persisting in demanding those she could not have.

"My head seems covered with snakes. Put your hand on it; is not every hair a serpent? O Heavens! only this very day, or was it yesterday, I put on my crown of braids. Go away! I must take down my hair!"

With trembling and feverish hands she took down her hair, and as it hung about her shoulders she looked like one crazed with grief.

Lenz and Petrovitsch had great difficulty in quieting her. The old man finally persuaded his nephew to go with him into the sitting-room and leave her to herself. "Keep calm," he said, when they were alone together, "else your wife will die before help comes. I never saw such a change in any human being, and never would have believed it possible. It is more than human constitution can bear. Tell me now what sort of a letter this is which I found in your little girl's dress when I laid Bubby on her feet."

Lenz told the horrible resolution he had formed, and begged his uncle to give back the letter which contained his farewell to life. The old man, however, held it fast and read it half aloud.

Lenz's heart trembled at hearing the words which were not to have been read till he was out of the world. He tried to make out his uncle's thoughts, as far as the pale blue light would let him study the expression of his features. The old man read steadily to the end without once looking up, and then, with a short, quick glance at his nephew put the letter in his pocket.

"Give me the letter; we will burn it," said Lenz, scarcely above a whisper.

In the same low tone Petrovitsch answered: "No; I will keep it; I never half knew you till now."

Whether the words were meant favorably or otherwise it was hard to tell.

The old man rose, took his brother's file from the wall, held it firmly, and pressed his thumb into the groove worn by the dead man's steady toil of years. Perhaps he was registering there a vow to fill a father's place to Lenz, if they should be saved. He only said: "Come here; I have something to whisper in your ear. The meanest act a man can commit is to take his own life. I once knew a man whose father had killed himself. 'My father took the easiest way for himself and the hardest for us,' he said, and the son"-- here Petrovitsch drew Lenz close to him, and shouted in his ear--"cursed his father's memory."

Lenz staggered backward and almost fell to the ground at the words.

"Lenz, for Heaven's sake, Lenz, stand up!" cried Annele from the chamber. "Dear Lenz," she continued, as the two men hastened to her, "you had meant to take your own life. I know not whether you could really have done it; but that you thought of it, and meant to do it, was my fault. Oh, how your heart must have suffered! I cannot tell what sin of mine most needs your forgiveness."

"It is over now," said Petrovitsch, soothingly. It was strange that Annele's mind should be working on the same subject they had been discussing in the next room. Their tone was so low that she could not possibly have heard them. Both men did their best to soothe her.

"Is that noon or night?" asked Annele, as several clocks struck three.

"It must be night."

They rehearsed together all that had happened since the avalanche, and concluded it must be past midnight.

"O Day! if I could once, but once again, behold the sun! rise and help me, Sun!" was Annele's constant cry. "I will live, I must live for long years yet. If a single day could but undo such great misery! but it will need years. I will persevere faithfully and patiently." There was no quieting her till presently she dropped asleep.

Petrovitsch too slept, leaving to Lenz his solitary watch. He dared not sleep; he must face this threatening death, and avert it if he could. He extinguished the light to save their precious store of brandy, for they could not tell how long it might be needed. As he sat gazing into the darkness, one moment he thought it was day, the next that it must be night; now one was a comfort to him, now the other. If it was day, help was nearer; if night, the work of forcing a passage through the snow and gravel and fallen trees had been going on the longer.

At times he seemed to hear a sound without; it was only seeming. There was no sound save the raven croaking in his sleep.

CHAPTER XXXVII
A PHALANX

At noon of that same Sunday Faller started for the Morgenhalde to tell Lenz the good news about his house. It was impossible to see his way before him, so fiercely did the snow and rain beat against his face. He plodded along with his head down till he supposed his place of destination must be nearly reached, when he looked up and rubbed his eyes in wonder and consternation. Where was he? had he lost his way? where was Lenz's house? There were the pine-trees that stood by it, but the house, the house! In his excitement he lost the path and fell into a deep snow-drift, into which all his efforts to extricate himself only made him sink the deeper. He cried in vain for help; no one heard him. He had just strength left to work his way along to a tree, by whose branches he clung till a fresh avalanche from above bore the snow away from under him and left him free. By following the clearing which the avalanche had made in its descent he succeeded in reaching the valley. It was already dark, and the lights were shining from the houses as he ran through the village, crying, "Help! help!" in a tone loud enough to wake the seven sleepers. All hastened to the windows or into the street, and the report quickly spread from mouth to mouth that the house of Lenz of the Morgenhalde had been buried under the snow.

The alarm-bell which Faller hastened to ring from the church had small effect in bringing persons from beyond the village. The wind prevented the sound from reaching to any great distance, and those who heard it were deterred by the violence of the storm from obeying the summons.

Pilgrim and the engineer were the first who appeared on the square before the church. Pilgrim was struck dumb with horror at the terrible misfortune which had overtaken his friend in this night of fearful storm. The engineer displayed the greatest bravery and presence of mind. "Bring all the ladders and cords you can lay hands on," he cried; "and shovels and picks besides."

Torches flared in the wind, casting a wild light upon the pale, dishevelled women, who, with their cloaks thrown over their heads to keep out the sleet and rain, clung to their husbands and sons, and besought them not to risk their lives in this dreadful storm.

The engineer fastened one end of a long rope about his body, and, instinctively assuming the place of leader, commanded that every six men should fasten themselves together at convenient distances to afford mutual support, and prevent loss of time from having to hunt up scattering members of the party. Pilgrim tied himself to the same rope with the engineer; Don Bastian was about to do likewise, but their temporary leader advised his heading a second company of six. A quantity of dry wood was collected to light fires with, and, armed with picks, shovels, and ladders, the party began the ascent of the mountain.

Within fifty paces of the house,--they could not approach nearer,--a clearing was made in a comparatively sheltered spot, and a fire lighted. Ladders were placed against the wall of snow, which proved, however, too soft to bear a man's weight. Cries of "I am sinking! I am sulking!" were heard here and there, while the confusion and danger were increased by the impossibility of keeping the torches alight in the wind. All expedients having failed, it was pronounced useless to attempt the rescue in the night, and the party went homewards. Faller at once offered to remain behind to watch the fire,--a duty which Pilgrim would have shared, had not the engineer, seeing how the poor fellow's teeth were chattering, made him go home with him, comforting him with the assurance that, if the buried inmates were still alive, they would be able to hold out till morning.

It soon became known in the village that Petrovitsch also must be buried under the snow. He had started for the Morgenhalde in the morning, and had not since returned. Ibrahim, his companion at cards, appeared in the street at the ringing of the alarm-bell with the cards in his hand, crying out, "Where is Petrovitsch? I am waiting for Petrovitsch."

"It would be terrible," said Pilgrim to his new friend the engineer, "if Petrovitsch should have perished in attempting to offer his tardy help."

Pilgrim reproached himself bitterly for having spent the whole day in childish games, instead of going to the Morgenhalde. His mind had misgiven him all the while that things were not right with Lenz, but he had reasoned away his fears and been merry with his godson. The child lay quietly sleeping in bed, unconscious of the fate which that night might be bringing him, perhaps had already brought. Pilgrim established himself in a chair by the little fellow's side, and sat watching him till his anxious eyes closed, and he too fell asleep.

Faller, meanwhile, remained like a soldier at his post, happily not quite alone, for a workman of the village, who had once been a pioneer, stayed behind with him on the field of danger. The two held counsel together how the snow-fortress should best be taken, but no possible mode of attack did they see. Poor Faller poked the fire in wrath that he could be of so little use.

A stranger joined them at their watch-fire,--a messenger from the city who had been sent to summon Annele to her mother's death-bed.

"There she is," said Faller, in bitter irony. "Fetch her out, if you can!" After learning what had happened, the man returned as he had come, through the night and storm.

Faller managed, by means of a by-path, to mount up into what had been the forest, hoping thus to be able to reach the pine-trees by the house and bring help nearer. With his comrade's assistance he rolled several great logs down the slope towards the pines. Some rolled beyond the trees and remained upright in the snow, while one fell in the desired position, with its end resting upon one of the projecting branches.

The second man here suddenly bethought himself, that the logs they had been rolling down might break in the roof and crush all under it.

"What a fool I am!" cried poor Faller; "the greatest fool in all the world. Dear, dear Lenz, God grant I may not have been your murderer!"

Finally he crawled across the bridge which the one log had formed and succeeded in kindling by his torch several of the other logs that stood or lay near it.

"That will melt the snow," he cried, exultingly.

"Yes; and set fire to the thatched roof," returned his comrade.

Faller stood in mute despair. The two began rolling up great snowballs and throwing them into the fire, just as the day was dawning, which they succeeded in extinguishing.

It was a clear day, almost as warm as spring. The sun shone bright on the Morgenhalde, seeking the house it had so often greeted; seeking the master who on Monday morning always sat busy at work in the window, as his father and grandfather had done before him. It found neither house nor master. The sunbeams quivered and shimmered here and there as if they had lost their way. There lay the defiant snow, challenging them to do their worst. The sun sent its fiery darts against the few cowardly flakes that yielded, but the solid fortress would hold out for days.

All the villagers were on the spot, the engineer at their head. Other villages too and other parishes had sent men and help in abundance.

Faller's logs offered a firm support, and companies were organized for working systematically both from below and above. A single raven flew persistently round and round the workmen and would not be frightened away. The men perched high in the air shouted at him; he heeded not their cries, but watched them at their work as if he knew what they were about, and had something to tell them if he could but have spoken.

CHAPTER XXXVIII
A PLANT GROWS UNDER THE SNOW

Lenz sat mute and motionless, watching in the face of night and death.

Petrovitsch was the first to rouse himself. He told of a house that had once been buried in this way, and of those who came to the rescue finding the bodies of four peasants with the cards still in their hands, crushed to death at the table round which they had been sitting. The old man shuddered as he told the story, and yet he could not keep it to himself; he must tell it and relieve his mind, though it should freeze the hearer's blood. But God would save them, he added, for the sake of the innocent child. He almost railed against the Providence which could doom the child as well as themselves to destruction.

"She too is like a child again," replied Lenz. Petrovitsch shook his head and warned him not to trust to such sudden conversion. If ever they got out he must oblige Annele to sue daily and hourly for his love. Lenz disputed the matter with his uncle, who had never known what it was to be married; there was an angel in Annele, he said, that might well raise a man to a heaven on earth; the trouble had been that, in her frenzy, she had debased the good in her to the level of the evil.

Petrovitsch only shook his head; he was evidently not convinced.

Annele and the child awoke simultaneously with a cry of terror: "The roof is breaking in!" screamed Annele. "Where are you, Lenz? Keep by me; let us die together! put the child in my arms."

When she was quieted, they all went together into the sitting-room. Lenz pounded up Cousin Ernestine's coffee-beans, and they drank their coffee by the light of the ghastly blue flame. The clocks struck. Annele said she should stop counting the strokes, and asking whether it was night or day; they were already in eternity. If the last cruel step were only over!--She had hoped for some answer to relieve her fears, her certainty of death; but none came.

They sat for a long while in silence; words were useless. Lenz ventured at last to take advantage of the pleasant terms on which he and his uncle now stood, to ask why he had manifested such cruel reserve towards him.

"Because I hated the man whose dressing-gown I now am wearing; yes, hated him. He treated me cruelly in my youth, and fixed the nickname of goatherd on me. Constant pressure leaves its mark on the hard wood, why not on a human heart? The thought that my only brother had rejected and banished me was always wearing into my soul. I came home in the hope of laying down the burden of hate which I had so long carried about the world. I can truly say, I hated him to his death. Why did he die before the word of reconciliation was spoken between us? On the long journey home I rejoiced at the prospect of having a brother again, and I found none. In the bottom of my heart I did not hate him, or why should I have come home? Never again in this world shall I hear the name of brother; soon elsewhere--"

"Uncle," said Annele, "at the very moment we heard Bubby scratching at the door Lenz was telling me how his father, when he was once snowed up here, though not buried as we are, said that if he should have to die then, he should leave no enemy behind but his brother Peter, and that he would gladly be friends with him."

"So, so?" said Petrovitsch, pressing one hand to his eyes, while the other closed convulsively over that grooved handle which his brother's hand had worn.

For a while nothing was heard but the ticking of the clocks, till Lenz asked again why his uncle had refused to recognize him, during the first year after his return home, when his heart was yearning towards his father's only brother, and he had longed, whenever he met him in the street, to run to him and grasp his hand.

"I knew how you felt," replied Petrovitsch, "but I was angry with both you and your mother. I was told she petted you to death, and praised you half a dozen times a day for being the best son, and the wisest, cleverest man in all the world. That is a bad plan. Men are like birds. There are certain fly-catchers who must always have something in their crops. You are just such a bird, always crying out for a pat of the hand or a kind word."

"He is right, Annele,--is he not?" said Lenz with a bitter smile.

"Perhaps so," answered Annele.

"You need not talk!" cried Petrovitsch. "You are a bird yourself, or at least have been; and do you know what kind of a one? A bird of prey, who can go for days without food, but when he does eat, devours all he can seize hold of, innocent singing-birds or little kittens, swallowing bones, skin, hair and all."

"Alas! he is right there, too," said Annele. "I never was so happy as when I had some one to worry and tear to pieces. I was not conscious of it till our first drive together, when you asked me how I could take pleasure in exulting over Ernestine as I did. The words dwelt in my heart, and I determined to become as good as you. It seemed to me I should be much happier so. When on the way home you wanted to give old Pröbler a seat in the carriage, I could have pitched you out for being such a simpleton; but afterwards, when you gave up the idea, excusing yourself to God and your conscience for not giving a poor old fellow a lift on the road, and seeming so happy, I could gladly have kissed your hands for love of your goodness, if my pride had permitted. I resolved to be like you, yet still I kept on in my old way, putting off from day to day beginning on my new life, till the old devil took possession of me again. I first grew ashamed of my good resolutions, and finally ceased to entertain them. I was Annele of the Lion, whom all flattered; I needed not to change. You were the first person who blamed in me what others had found pretty and amusing. I was angry, fearfully angry. I resolved to show you that you were no better than the rest of the world. Finally, one idea took entire possession of me: I must be once more at the head of a public-house; then you and the world would see what talents I had. So I went on from worse to worse. Yesterday,--was it yesterday that the minister was here?--hark! uncle is asleep. That is good. I want one hour with you alone before we go into eternity. No third person can understand our two hearts after all we have been through together. Yesterday, Lenz, as I was sitting here by myself, the thought came to me, that I had never known what it was to love with my whole heart. I had been your wife for five years, and never found out till yesterday how much I loved you. If you had come home then, I should have kissed your eyes and your hands. Oh, you do not know how dearly I can love! But instead came Faller, who first frightened me, and then told how you had deceived me about the security. I became again possessed with the evil spirit that makes me do and say what he will, not what I will. But he is gone now; his power is over. I would crouch at your feet if it would serve you. Oh, if I could but see you once more; only once in the light of day! There is no seeing by this blue flame. If I could but once more see your kind, good face, your honest eyes! To die thus without seeing or being seen; it is terrible! How often I met your eyes with averted looks! Oh for one flash, one single flash of light, to show you to me!"

Petrovitsch had only feigned sleep, seeing that Annele wanted to open her heart to her husband, alone. The child was playing with Bubby. "If I could but call back the years!" continued Annele. "One day at noon you said, 'Is there anything better than the sun?' and in the evening, 'O, this good fresh air! it is pure blessing.' I laughed at your folly; yet you were right,--you were happy. Happiness came to you as naturally as the light and air. I sinned against you in all ways. When I threw down your father's file and broke it, the point pierced my heart; but I would not show that I was sorry. I threw out of the window that dear writing of your mother's and that memento of her. Nothing that was sacred to you escaped my venom. You forgive me, I know; pray God to forgive me, whether I live or die."

A musical clock began to play. Petrovitsch turned involuntarily in his chair, but appeared to drop off to sleep again. When the piece was finished, Annele cried again: "I must beg forgiveness of everything, even of the clock. I was always ridiculing it, and now I hear how beautiful it is. O God! not for myself I pray. Save us, save us all! Let me show that I can make all well again."

"All is well now," said Lenz; "even though we die. While the clock was playing the thought came to me that we have our edelweiss again. It has grown up in your good heart and in the hearts of us all? Why do you tremble so?"

"I am so cold; my feet are like ice."

"Take off your shoes and let me warm your feet. So will I bear you up in my hands my life long. Are you not better now?"

"Yes, much better; but oh, my head! every hair seems dropping blood. Hark! I hear the cock crow and the raven scream. Thank God, it is day."

They all rose, even the uncle from his pretended sleep, as if deliverance were at hand. A fearful pounding now began overhead. "We are lost," cried Petrovitsch. Again all was still. The roof of the sleeping-room had been broken in, so that the door refused to open. After the first shock Lenz thanked God that a presentiment of the coming danger had startled both wife and child from their sleep. He comforted his companions by telling them that the sleeping chamber had been lately added to the original house, and was quite independent of it. The old oaken timbers of the main building would resist every shock. Even while he spoke he thought he saw the roof giving way in the direction of the sleeping-room; but he did not express his fears, thinking he might easily be mistaken in this uncertain blue light.

Again followed a long, breathless silence, unbroken except when a distant cock-crow was answered by a bark from Bubby and a croak from the raven in the kitchen.

"This is a veritable Noah's ark," said Petrovitsch.

"Whether we are nearing life or death, we are saved from the deluge of sin," returned Lenz.

Annele laid her hand upon his face.

"If I only had a pipe of tobacco! it is a shame you don't smoke, Lenz," complained Petrovitsch. Reminded of his fire-proof safe by the thought of his row of pipes at home, he continued: "One thing I tell you; if we ever are saved, you will get no money from me: not a penny."

"We shall not need it now," replied Lenz; while Annele said, cheerfully, "Do you know who will not believe that?"

"You?"

"No; the world. Nobody will believe, though you swear it a hundred times, that one who was in death with us will not continue with us in life. The world will give us credit on your account, and make us rich if we will let it."

"You are the same old rogue as ever," said Petrovitsh, trying to scold. "I thought you were done with your jests."

"Thank God, she is not!" cried Lenz. "Keep your happy heart, Annele, if God delivers us."

Annele threw her arms about her husband's neck and hugged and kissed him. All were surprised at finding they had suddenly grown as gay as if the danger were passed, whereas it was really at its height. Neither communicated his fears to the others, but each saw how the walls trembled and the main beam seemed about to fall.

Annele and Lenz held each other in a close embrace. "So let us die and shelter our child!" cried Annele.

"Hark! there is a hollow sound without. It is our deliverers; they are coming, they are coming! they will save us!--"

CHAPTER XXXIX
SAVED

"There are two blows following close upon each other," cried Lenz. "I will make the clocks play together, as a sign to those without."

He set the two musical clocks in motion, but the dreadful confusion of sounds drove him almost frantic. Even in this hour of deadly danger a discord was intolerable to him. He stopped them suddenly. With a pang as of the severing of a heart-string he heard something in his great clock snap at the hasty check.

Again they held their breath and listened; no further sounds were heard.

"You rejoiced too soon," said Petrovitsch, his teeth chattering so that he could hardly speak. "We are nearer death than life now."

The pounding was repeated from above. "Bum, bum!" imitated the child, while Petrovitsch complained that he felt every blow of the hammer in his brain.

Lenz could not have touched the right spring in one of the clocks, for it suddenly began to play the air of the grand Hallelujah. "Hallelujah, blessed be God the Lord!" sang Lenz with the full force of his voice. Annele sang too, keeping one hand upon Lenz's shoulder, and the other upon the head of the child. "Hallelujah! Hallelujah!" cried a voice from above.

Once more that piercing cry of old rang through the house "My Pilgrim! my faithful brother!"

The chamber-door was battered down with an axe.

"Are you all alive?" cried Pilgrim,

"All; thank God!"

Pilgrim embraced Petrovitsch first, taking him for Lenz, and the old man returned the greeting with a kiss on both cheeks, after the Russian fashion.

Close upon Pilgrim came the engineer, followed by Faller, Don Bastian, and the members of the Liederkranz.

"Is my William safe?" asked Lenz.

"Yes indeed, safe in my house," answered Don Bastian.

Some of the men shovelled away the snow from the outside of the windows.

"Sun, sun! I behold you again!" cried Annele, sinking upon her knees.

The clock kept on playing the Hallelujah, the schoolmaster added his voice, and the whole Liederkranz joined in with full, firm tones. As if shaken by the mighty song, the snow-fortress in front of the house suddenly loosened and rolled down the valley.

The house stood free.

The door into the kitchen was opened, and, upon the window being lifted, the raven darted across the room above the head of the child out into the open air.

"Birdie gone!" cried the child. A second raven was waiting without, and the two now soaring high in the air, now swooping towards the ground, flew up through the valley.

The first woman who made her way to Annele was Ernestine, who, having heard of the disaster on the Morgenhalde, and also of the landlady's death, had lost no time in coming to her cousin's help. She knelt beside her. Lenz leaned upon Pilgrim's bosom.

Petrovitsch was beginning to be angry because no one paid him any attention, when happily the engineer approached him, and, with a manner at once respectful and cordial, congratulated him on his deliverance. The best fellow of the whole company, thought the old man. Pilgrim politely apologized for the embrace he had inadvertently given, and was treated to a cordial shake of the hand.

"I have found a scrap of your mother's handwriting in the snow," said Faller hoarsely; "most of the writing is washed out, but these few words are left: 'This little plant is called edelweiss. Marie Lenz.'"

"The paper is mine!" cried Annele, rising. All looked at her in astonishment. "Why, Annele!" screamed Ernestine, "what in Heaven's name have you on your head? your hair is all white!"

Annele went to the mirror, and, with a cry of anguish, clasped both hands above her head.

"An old woman! an old woman!" she moaned, and fell upon Lenz's neck. After a while she rose, sobbing, dried her tears and whispered in his ear, "That is my edelweiss that has grown for me under the snow."

CHAPTER XL
ALL IS WELL

The ravens flew across the valley and over the mountains, past a humble cottage where sat an old woman at the window, spinning coarse yarn, while big tears rolled down her withered cheeks upon the threads she spun. It was Franzl. The tidings that Lenz with his whole household had been buried in the snow had reached Knuslingen, and men from her village had gone to their rescue. Franzl would gladly have gone with them and done her part; but her poor old feet refused to bear her. Moreover, she had lent her one good pair of shoes to a poor woman who had to go to the doctor's. In the midst of her sorrow Franzl often clapped her hands to her stupid head and said to herself: Why did I not think of it yesterday, while he was here? it is too late now. I had it on my tongue's end to tell him he must make provision against being snowed up. We were thrice snowed up for days at a time, and such an accident should be provided for every winter. It is too late now. The old mistress was right in saying, as she did a hundred times: "Franzl, you are always very clever, an hour behind the time."

The ravens that now flew past her window might have told Franzl to dry her tears, for the buried family was saved. Unhappily man cannot understand the ravens, and is a long while conveying his good news across mountain and valley.

At evening a sleigh with merry jingling bells came driving up to the door. What could it want? there was no one at home but Franzl. It stopped just before her window. Who was getting out from it? was it not Pilgrim? She tried to go to meet him, but her strength failed her.

"Franzl, I have come for you," cried Pilgrim. The old woman rubbed her forehead. Was it a dream? or what was it? "Lenz and his household are saved," continued Pilgrim; "and I am sent to fetch you, most high and mighty princess Cinderella. Will you trust yourself to the Swan."

"I have no shoes," stammered out Franzl.

"For that reason I have brought you fur boots that will just fit your little foot," returned Pilgrim; "and here is the skin, I mean the sheep-skin, of the monster Petrovitsch. You must drive with me, well-beloved Franzl of

Knuslingen, Fuchsberg, and Knebringen. Your magic spinning-wheel you must leave behind, unless it chooses to hop after us on its wooden legs.

"'So gird thyself, my Gretchen,
Thou must with me to-day;
The corn is cut and garnered,
The wine is stored away.'"

Thus merrily singing, Pilgrim offered old Franzl his arm, as if to lead her to the dance. She was in a state of perfect bewilderment. Happily her sister-in-law came home at this moment, and was by no means displeased at the idea of having Franzl carried off in a sleigh. The old woman, however, turned her unceremoniously out of the room when she wanted to help her pack up her things: she could have no one by to see her stow away that mysterious shoe.

"The bed is my own; can you not pack it away in the sleigh?" she asked.

"Let Knuslingen have it to sleep upon," answered Pilgrim. "Use your pillow for a footstool and leave the rest behind. You will be cushioned like a queen."

"Must I leave my hens and my geese behind too? They are all my very own, and my gold-hammer has been sitting for six weeks."

The hen thus complimented thrust her gay crest through the bars of her coop.

The hens and geese, Pilgrim said, ran after the true princess Cinderella of their own accord, and these were free to do the same if they were so inclined; carrying them was out of the question.

Franzl recommended her beloved fowls most pressingly to the tender mercies of her sister-in-law, and charged her to send them by the first messenger that should be going her way.

The hens cackled uneasily in their coop as Franzl left the room, and the geese in the barn added their note of remonstrance when the sleigh flew by.

It was on a beautifully clear winter's night that Pilgrim and Franzl started from Knuslingen. The stars were glittering above their heads and a firmament of glittering stars was in Franzl's heart. She was obliged to seize her bag and pinch it till she felt her well-stuffed shoe in order to convince herself that the whole was not a dream.

"See, there is my potato-patch," said Franzl; "I bought it with my own money when it was nothing but a heap of stones, and in these four years the value of it has doubled. The potatoes are as white as the whitest meal."

"Let the Knuslingers enjoy your potatoes; you shall get something better," answered Pilgrim. He went on to tell of the rescue of the buried household, and how they were all living now with Petrovitsch, who was a changed man and had become one of his best friends. It was Annele's first request, he said, that Franzl should be sent for. The old woman wept aloud when she heard of Annele's white hair. She once knew a woman, she said, whose mother had a relation, a man up in Elsass, whose hair turned white in a night from fright. It was wonderful, and she was filled with compassion for Annele, who would now be the town talk. "Folks are so stupid, and yet think they must always be saying some smart thing. I will soon teach them we don't need their silly gossip."

At every house where they saw lights Franzl wanted to get out and tell what had happened. "There lives Mr. So-and-so and Mrs. Such-a-one; kind, honest people who have grieved at Lenz's fate. It is too bad they should keep on being unhappy when there is no need of it. They would be glad, too, to know that Franzl was the first person sent for. Who can tell whether there will ever be another chance to bid good-by in this world?"

Pilgrim, however, drove pitilessly past all the good peoples' houses, stopping nowhere. If a window was opened and a head thrust out to look at the sleigh, Franzl cried as loud as she could, "Good by; God bless you." It was no matter if the bells did nearly drown the words; she had had the satisfaction of sending a kindly farewell to those she might never see again.

At the farm where the bailiff's daughter lived Pilgrim had to stop. Alas! no joy is complete in this world; Katharine was not at home. Having no children of her own, she was frequently called on to assist in bringing into the world those of others, and was at that moment watching by a sick-bed. Franzl told her news twice over to the maid, to make sure of her not forgetting a word.

Her sense of content came over her afresh on re-entering the sleigh. "Now I feel better," she said. "It is like half waking up from a good night's sleep, and just being conscious of how deliciously comfortable you are, before tumbling off to sleep again. I am not asleep; though I feel as if I were already in the life everlasting."

Pilgrim came near destroying all her pleasure by an ill-timed joke.

"Franzl," he said, "you won't fare very well up there."

"Up where?"

"In the next world. You are having your paradise now. You must not expect to have it here and there too; that would be more than your share."

"Stop! stop! let me get out; I want to go home," cried Franzl. "I will have nothing to do with you! nothing on this earth shall tempt me to give up my hope of the life everlasting. Stop, or I shall jump out!"

With a greater strength than he had supposed the old woman possessed she seized hold of the reins and tried to force them from Pilgrim's hand. He had great difficulty in quieting her by protesting it was all a joke. She could not understand a man's joking about such things as that. He quoted in Greek, and obligingly translated into Black-forest German, a passage from the life of Saint Haspucias to prove that she would not after all lose the life everlasting, because a special exception was made in favor of servants, whose life in this world was hard enough at the best. Pilgrim showed a wonderful acquaintance with the heavenly arrangements, and with difficulty resisted the temptation of assuring Franzl that he was employed by St. Peter as court-painter.

Franzl was quite pacified, and fully admitted the truth of his statement about the hard life of servants. "I am so glad to be going to see my Lenz's children," she began again presently. "The boy is called William, after you, is he not? And what is the little girl's name?"

"Marie."

"O yes; for her grandmother."

"That happily reminds me of something I had quite forgotten. The children think I have gone for their grandmother, and am fetching her home in a swan. They are depending on keeping awake till we arrive. The high and mighty princess of Knuslingen, Fuchsberg, and Knebringen must let it please her grace to be called grandmother."

Franzl thought the deception very wicked; such a name was sacred, and should only be given to a blood-relation. Her only consolation was that she would soon undeceive the children; she was not born in Knuslingen for nothing. The necessity of keeping up the honor of her native town soon restored her to complete composure.

It was well that Franzl became somewhat sobered by these discussions on the way, else she would certainly have expected to see the whole population of the village drawn up by the roadside to welcome her. As it was, her first greeting was a burst of laughter from Petrovitsch, who was so convulsed by the oddity of her appearance that he had no strength to stand. Bubby, also, excited by his master's unwonted gayety, began to bark as the best substitute for laughter at his command. "Anton Striegler knew you would come to look like that some day," cried the old fellow, maliciously; "and therefore he let you be."

"And the worms will let you be for a while longer, till you are better done; you are too tough for them now," retorted Franzl, the concentrated hate of years, and indignation at being taunted with her blighted love, finding vent in the stinging answer. It silenced Bubby's bark and Petrovitsch's laughter. Both had a salutary fear of the old woman from that time forth.

Lenz was asleep, and Annele in the room with the children, who after all had not been able to keep awake. She would have thrown her arms about old Franzl's neck, if the presence of Pilgrim and Petrovitsch had not restrained her.

"See, here are our children," she said. "Give them just one kiss; it will not wake them."

She insisted on Franzl staying in the parlor while she went into the kitchen to cook her supper. Surprise at the change that had come over her former mistress kept the old woman sitting for a while in the chair where she had been placed, but she presently followed into the kitchen.

"Oh how good it is to be able to light a fire!" said Annele. Franzl looked at her in amazement, not understanding that Annele was grateful now for everything, all the thousand little blessings that the rest of us take as a matter of course.

"What do you say to my white hair?" asked Annele.

"I wish I could give you mine; there is not a white hair on my head, and never will be. My mother used to tell me that I was born into the world with a full crop of hair."

Annele said, with a smile, that her white hair was sent her as a sign that she had been in the shadow of death and must now live at peace with all the world.

"You will forgive me too, Franzl, will you not? I thought of you in that hour of death."

Franzl could only answer with her tears.

The change in Annele was indeed wonderful. The first time she heard the bells ring she took the baby in her arms, and said, as she folded its little hands together, "O child! I never thought to hear that sound again"; and when Franzl brought the first bucket of water, she exclaimed, "Oh, how clear and beautiful the water is! I thank God for giving it to us!"

Long after the memory of this time of terror had faded from the minds of her two companions in danger, the thought of it was still vivid, to Annele, making her gentle and tender, sensitive to every hasty word. Franzl could not help saying to Pilgrim sometimes, that she feared Annele would not live long, there was something so almost heavenly about her.

The burial and deliverance of Lenz's household quite cast into the shade another event, which otherwise would have given rise to much speculation and comment.

Two days after his disaster the frozen body of a man was found under the snow in a woody hollow near Knuslingen. It was poor old Pröbler. No one mourned him so deeply as Lenz. He believed now that he had heard the old man calling him, and read a lesson in the death of this poor, half-crazy discoverer that was revealed to no one else.

Annele continued to thrive in her uncle's great house, and was as fresh and blooming as ever. She and Lenz lived there till late into the summer, when their own house was ready for them. Little William sorely troubled the old man by jumping up on sofas and chairs which Bubby was allowed to tumble about on with impunity.

Petrovitsch caught a violent cold from his exposure that night, and was strongly urged by the doctor to try the baths for his cough. He steadily refused, however, resolving in his own mind that, if he must die, he would die at home; he had had enough of homesickness. He often walked with little William on the Spannreute, where well-grown larch-trees had been set out, and trenches dug to protect the house. One day he said to him reprovingly: "William, you are just like Bubby, never satisfied with the straight path. Why will you always be jumping this way and that, over a ditch or up the side of a rock? you two are fit companions for each other." "Uncle," answered little William, "a dog is not a man, nor a man a dog." These simple words so pleased the old uncle, that he begged Lenz to leave the boy behind if he ever should return to his house on the hill.

Annele was the one most desirous of going back to the Morgenhalde. Once she would have thought it a paradise upon earth to keep Petrovitsch's big house for him, in the expectation of becoming his heir; now she cared for nothing but to pass her days in quiet, happy industry among the lonely hills.

The death of her mother, which had been concealed from her for a time, did not fall upon her as a sharp and sudden blow; it counted as one of the many horrors which were crowded into that terrible night.

Petrovitsch kept little William in the house, and induced Pilgrim to make his home with them. The passersby were often entertained by the sounds that came from the big house; the neighing as of a horse, the grunting of a pig, the whistle of a nightingale, or the squeaking of little owls.

Two heads, the one of an old child, the other of a young one, were generally to be seen at the window. They were Pilgrim's and his godson's. Their great delight was trying to see which could imitate the greater number of animal sounds. Bubby joined in with a genuine bark, and Petrovitsch laughed till his laughing was cut short by his cough. For years the old man had not been out of the village. As for trying any baths, he maintained that the laughing he did at home was better than all the washing in the world.

Lenz's friends showed themselves eager to help in the rebuilding of the house on the Morgenhalde. They flocked from all sides, bringing contributions of wood and stone. But the prospect of returning to his old life gave Lenz no pleasure; he wanted to start on a new and wider field. As a man recovering from a severe illness is not satisfied with resuming the threads of his life where his illness interrupted them, so Lenz felt himself a wiser and stronger man, able to undertake larger works.

All seemed ready now for the execution of his old pet plan, and no one favored it more than Annele. Her hearty encouragement strengthened and cheered her husband. "You have always had at heart the happiness of your fellow-men. I remember your saying soon after our marriage that you rejoiced in a bright Sunday because it made thousands and thousands of persons happy. Go about among men; wherever you go, you will bring the sunlight with you. I wish I could go too and tell them all how good you are."

Accompanied by the engineer, the doctor, Pilgrim, the schoolmaster, and the weight-manufacturer, Lenz went from house to house, and from village to village, where his eloquence, his wisdom and goodness were praised by all, as well as his ready sympathy with others' needs and his quick suggestions of relief.

What in his days of prosperity he could not succeed in accomplishing was effected now as by tacit agreement; the various independent clockmakers were united in a general association.

After building afresh his old house, and bringing prosperity into those of his fellow-workmen, he now had the happiness of helping to found a new home.

He performed for Pilgrim the office which Pilgrim had once offered to perform for him in the doctor's house, and won for his friend the hand of Amanda, Pilgrim became overseer of the case-making department of the factory, and to him are due the many graceful forms of clock-cases, carved with leaves and other ornamentations, for which the wood of the new Spannreute forest, and the well-seasoned timber taken from the old house on the Morgenhalde, furnished abundant material.

In the second summer after the catastrophe on the Morgenhalde Lenz came to his uncle with the first request he had made him; it was for the means to send Faller to the baths. The doctor had recommended them as a relief for a severe bronchial affection that had been contracted on the night of the avalanche.

"There is the money for it. Tell Faller he must go to the baths for himself and me too. I am glad you do not beg on your own account. Your way of helping yourself is much better."

Great persuasions were needed to induce Faller to visit the baths. He was finally brought to consent only by Annele's earnest representations to his wife.

Annele had two friends of very different character, Faller's wife and Amanda, now Mrs. Pilgrim. Many a slip from the doctor's garden found its way up to the Morgenhalde, and was carefully planted and tended by Annele's own hand.

Faller went to the bathing establishment kept by Annele's older sister, and there fell in with an old acquaintance. The manager of the bath was the former landlord of the Lion, who had retired thither after the death of his wife. The old gentleman was as patronizing as ever, and seemed to thrive on his freedom from care. He was cheerful and even communicative. One subject, however, he never alluded to,--his past life; that would have compromised his dignity, and might have awakened awkward reminiscences between himself and Faller. He spoke handsomely of Lenz, and enjoined upon Faller to tell him that he must never allow himself to be goaded into any undertaking that he did not feel himself thoroughly fitted for. This sentence he made Faller repeat over and over again, word for word, till he knew it by heart, when the landlord put on his spectacles to see how a man actually looked who had such a sentence in his head.

His two favorite topics were the absence of justice in Brazil, and the wonder-working qualities of the springs and the whey. If some princess would only set the fashion by visiting his baths, they would become the first in importance in the world.

By telling his wish with regard to the princess, the landlord thought to show his forethought as well as the loftiness of his aspirations. Poor Faller had it impressed upon him again and again, as if he might at any moment have the disposing of a couple of dozen princesses great and small.

Faller came home apparently improved in health. Early in the spring, however, when the snow was beginning to melt, he died.

Not long afterward old Petrovitsch, too, was buried. He had made a brave struggle against death. His paroxysms of coughing had increased in violence and frequency since the autumn, and in one of them he was finally choked to death. As the doctor had conjectured, he left no property except a life-annuity which he had bought with what little money the gaming-table at Baden-Baden had spared. Thus many seeming inconsistencies in the old man's conduct were accounted for. The doctor maintained that all his dislike of other men sprang from dissatisfaction with himself.

Faller's sons were all provided for. Lenz took one into his house, and Katharine adopted the second pair of twins. She only wanted one, but the children could not bear to be parted. The little girl remained with her mother.

Franzl took delight in telling her old friend Katharine of the sort of life that was led on the Morgenhalde.

"I don't know which of us Annele spoils the most, her husband or me. The angels in heaven must rejoice to see the life they lead together. You know I am from Knuslingen, and therefore, though I mean to take no credit to myself, manage to see more than most persons. At first there lurked a fear of each other in their hearts,--a fear lest some thoughtless word might open the old wound, as flames sometimes break out afresh amid the ruins of a house that has been burned. But they gradually learned that each had always dearly loved the other, and that what had seemed unkindness and hate was only the pain of not having rightly learned to conform to each other's habits. Now Annele has given up all desire for a hotel, and Lenz has grown more of a man. The Liederkranz has become quite a different sort of society, and my Lenz is the chief member of it; all say he has the finest voice and the best managed of all the singers. There is a new society started which in some way is to help everybody. The weight-manufacturer from Knuslingen can explain it better than I can, for he is one of the members. Did you know that my Lenz's musical clock had taken the first prize at some great exhibition, and that he had received a medal from England? He told Annele that he cared for it only as it might prove to her that he was capable of accomplishing something after all; at which she cried and told him, all that was buried with their past life, and never to be recalled; that she needed no one now to bear witness to his worth; none knew it as well as she. Then Lenz looked up to his mother's picture and said, 'Mother, sing in heaven! Your children are happy.'"

Katharine listened to this glowing account with proper expressions of joy. Franzl, however, was not easily stopped when once wound up, and continued: "Do you know what we inherited from Petrovitsch? Nothing but his dog, which has to be fed on the fat of the land. I say dry bread and potatoes are good enough for him, but Lenz pets him on account of his having saved little Marie's life. Not a penny did Petrovitsch leave us. The doctor always said he had put all his money into a life-insurance company,--I think he called it,--which paid him so much a year. The handsome fortune that he scraped together from all parts of the world was lost at the gaming-table. Players are certainly the cleverest and the stupidest creatures in the world. The doctor says so, and it must be true.--Don't you mean to stay over to-morrow for the funeral of the old mayoress? She was nearly seventy-eight years old, and the last of that generation. Lenz said, when his uncle died, that he was glad he left him nothing, for he would rather make his own way in the world. He means to take William and young Faller as apprentices, and later to send them abroad."

"And do they treat you well?" asked Katharine, for the sake of saying something.

"Dear me, only too well! I don't know why it is that every one thinks life could not go on happily without me. I wish I was not quite so old; my comfort is that my grandmother lived to be eighty-three, and for aught any one can tell, it might have been ninety-three; those old people who can't read and write often make mistakes. Perhaps I shall live as long myself. I enjoy my food and my sleep. There is a blessing on all that goes on in this house. Look at the wood; has it not grown nicely? and it is all our own. As truly as that forest grows and thrives where God planted it, so truly does all good grow and thrive with us. Are they not fine young trees? we shall live to see them grow strong and tall."

Katharine could not wait for that, and as she went off with the twins, accompanied by their mother, Lenz, and Annele, Franzl called after her from the kitchen: "Katharine, you must make up your mind to stand god-mother next time."

That is the story of Lenz and Annele of the Morgenhalde; which explains why the young, white-haired mother asked her son, when he was setting off for foreign lands, to bring her home a sprig of edelweiss.

When Lenz returned from starting the two youths on their way, he found a garland of fresh flowers about his mother's picture. Eighteen years ago that day she had been buried, and Annele always kept the anniversary. They felt in their hearts, though they never said it, that her blessed memory bloomed ever fresh within them, like the flowers in the field.

Faller's widow and daughter sat down to dinner with them at noon. "If my husband had but lived to see our two sons set off on their travels together!" sighed the poor woman. Lenz tried to comfort her by telling how well the twins were doing that Katharine had adopted. One had already risen to be sergeant in the army, the other was his adopted father's assistant, and would doubtless be his heir. Faller's daughter, a tall, slender girl of fifteen, said she had promised to write to William and her brother the first of every month.

After dinner Lenz sat down to his work as usual. Eighteen years ago it had calmed a greater grief than the departure of his son occasioned him to-day. Annele sat by him with her sewing; no longer full of an unrest which she communicated to him, but rather shedding a beneficent influence around her. His work prospered better when she looked on. She spoke little, and the few words she did say showed within what a narrow circle her thoughts were now confined. "William takes six shirts with him, made from the cotton your blessed mother spun."

The places of the two apprentices were already filled; for parents the country round were anxious to have their boys learn their trade with Lenz. One of the new-comers was, to Franzl's great delight, a grandson of the weight-manufacturer of Knuslingen.

Towards evening the schoolmaster came up the hill with a great bundle of papers under his arm, labelled in large letters, "Acts of the Clockmakers' Union." He asked Lenz to go a little way into the wood with him before the other members arrived, and during their absence Annele rànged two rows of chairs about the room, for Lenz was now president of the association.